I0819577

THE HANGING BONES

Also by Elle Tesch

What Wakes the Bells

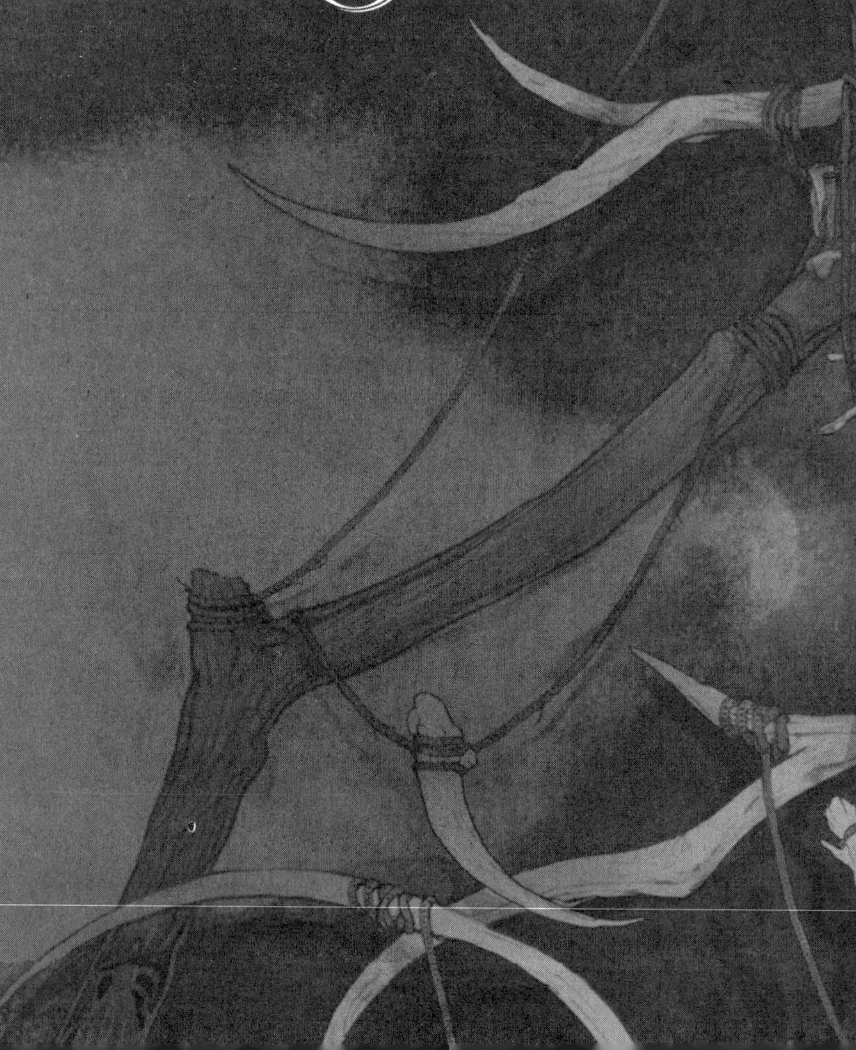

THE HANGING BONES

ELLE TESCH

FEIWEL AND FRIENDS
NEW YORK

Content warning: *This book contains rape (mentioned), sexual assault, nonconsensual touching, blood/gore/violence, animal death, and self-harm for ritual purposes.*

A Feiwel and Friends Book
An imprint of Macmillan Publishing Group, LLC
120 Broadway, New York, NY 10271 • fiercereads.com

EU representative: Macmillan Publishers Ireland Ltd, 1st Floor, The Liffey Trust Centre, 117–126 Sheriff Street Upper, Dublin 1, D01 YC43

Library of Congress Cataloging-in-Publication Data is available.

First edition, 2026
Book design by Meg Sayre
Feiwel and Friends logo designed by Filomena Tuosto
Printed in the United States of America

ISBN 978-1-250-37974-0
10 9 8 7 6 5 4 3 2 1

For Dad

Thanks for constantly indulging
my love of horror films–
the weirder, the better.

Chapter One

THIRTEEN NIGHTS UNTIL THE SCAVENGE MOON

When the deer lifts her head, one large brown eye lands squarely in my rifle's sight.

I settle my elbows deeper into the damp moss cloaking the fallen tree. A gnarled root digs into my stomach, a stone into my thigh as my knee shifts. My gloves, folded inside my coat pocket, barely cushion my hip bone. Slow and careful, I unlock the gun's bolt and trigger, a shell ready in the chamber. The dull scrape and click is a shout in the thick quiet of Wielinde Forest.

The doe stiffens. Her ears twitch in every direction as her wide gaze flickers. Thirty paces separate us. Thirty paces between her, alone in the middle of the grassy clearing, and me, hidden in the sagging shadows of a fir—and I'm aware of every inch in my evenly beating heart.

Dried needles crunch to my left. A soft huff spills into the silence.

"Rudi, stay," I murmur. The alpine pointer lying by my side lowers her head. She may appear unassuming, but pressed against me, the dog's body is a taut string, her tension coiling within. Beneath that dark-brown-and-white-speckled coat, a vital need to run, to hunt, is ready to snap.

My bare hand slides over chilled metal. I breathe in through my nose and let it out gently from my mouth. A haze partially obscures my sight in the early morning, but I trust my aim. My finger wraps around the trigger.

Crack.

Golden leaves spray as the doe darts into the trees, unharmed and leaving behind only a frantic path in the underbrush.

"*Stefan*," I groan. The rifle lowers in my now-limp hands, my forehead falling to my outstretched arm. I glance over my shoulder with a pout.

My uncle merely drops the halves of the stick he broke with a teasing smile. The foxhounds at his feet, Petra and Milo, snatch one together and race into the clearing. "Katrin, you know I didn't bring the cart today. How exactly were you planning on getting that home?"

"By yelling for you to help me," I grumble. I adjust to sit atop the log, rifle cradled in the crook of my arm. My knees and elbows are wet from the moss, and I quickly brush needles from my trousers. One click of my tongue sets Rudi loose. With a delighted bark, she bounds after the foxhounds, tail wagging. "Obviously."

Stefan steps near and cleans more needles off my heavy tweed coat. Reluctantly, I tip my head back to meet his warm brown and too-tired eyes. He left Prauen Castle before I did, and his nose and cheeks are ruddy with the dawn's bite.

"We take only what we need from this Forest, and there was no reason to take her life."

"I'm sorry," I say in a tone that shows just how unapologetic I am; the sting of losing a perfect shot still burns in my throat. "Were we not out here for the last three days hunting deer? Because we need to feed all those snobs arriving?"

Descending upon Prauen Castle, more like. Vultures, the lot of them, draped in slippery silks and fine lace. All week long, the pair of carriages bearing the Wagner family crest have navigated the treacherous mountain pass to the nearest train station four hours away, only to return full of the baron's loathsome friends—soon to be a dozen in all. A duchess, counts, the reigning royals of textiles and shipbuilding and lumber, even a prince. Each left the comforts of the crowded cities and country estates they call home to pile into Prauen's courtyard and whine about the unforgiving autumn temperatures.

Of course, not even a blizzard would keep them away. Not when they received a highly coveted invitation to the Breimar Hunt. Doesn't matter that they scoff at the ancient lore behind it and the Forest. None of them will pass up the opportunity to boast about experiencing the event firsthand.

"Someone is in a mood today," Stefan remarks, correctly reading my dark glare.

I respond by throwing a pine cone at him.

He laughs gruffly. "Yes, you're right. We were indeed hunting deer just yesterday. However, your aunt has kindly informed me that she's up to her ears in venison, and I will be sleeping outside with the shadow gaunts if I bring so much as one more hoof back."

I snort. Maybe I should have taken a shot at that doe.

Instead, a deft flick of my finger locks my rifle anew, preventing it from firing by mistake—a precautionary measure never forgotten after I almost lost a toe at age twelve. I shoulder the weapon's comforting weight and lean to the side to better adjust its position, propping myself up with a hand.

"Come on," Stefan says, hefting his own rifle and turning to head north. He whistles for Petra and Milo. "Lots of ground to cover today. I want to check the traps out by the lake."

"Carolina won't let you bring home a hoof, but a rabbit is fine?"

"I learned long ago not to argue with your aunt," he calls back.

Eyes rolling, I move to follow . . . and freeze. A sudden prickling sensation overwhelms my hand on the log—something is touching me, *crawling* on me. Warily, I glance down, hardly moving my head.

A swath of wiry moss, densely curled and as vivid green as fresh clovers, trails over the nail of my smallest finger. Tendrils resembling the legs of a spider wave about before pulling its bulk forward. As I watch, it engulfs my entire pinkie, pinning it in place on the bark with deceptive strength and surprising speed.

The tightness flees my body on an exhale. "Easy there, little monster," I say, fondness softening my voice. My free hand slips into my pocket and pulls out a tooth. A pointed incisor, likely from a fox and yellowed with age. Balanced between two fingertips, I offer it to the moss mite.

It falters in its effort to drink my skin dry, now clinging to three of my fingers. Those tentative green tendrils reach out. They seem to taste the tooth before relinquishing me, snatching the gift within itself like a spoiled child takes a sweet. I shake out my hand as the moss mite skitters beneath the log, quicker than I've ever seen one move.

Moss mites are stalwart creatures. If I had peeled it off, it would have tailed me for hours for another chance to wither my fingers. Instead, that tooth will sate the mite for a few days before it seeks to reclaim what we removed from the Forest again. I always carry a pouch of teeth for such incidents, but those offerings work best on the smaller Forest Folk. When faced with a larger being like a stream barrow, a molar is no better than a crumb. Only bones will do.

A sharp whistle brings Rudi to my side. I give her a quick scratch behind her silky ears and set off after my uncle, stuffing my hands in my pockets.

It was still fully dark when I left the room I share with my cousin Alma, but sunrise is fast approaching. After living in these mountains for seventeen years, I know them well enough to declare this my favorite time to roam Wielinde Forest. A moment teetering on that thin edge before the sun clambers over the peaks and pierces the deep valley woods, where my uncle and I serve as gamekeepers.

Although Stefan and I trudge through fallen leaves stained crimson, gold, and umber, snapping beneath our feet as finches sing in the trees, there's an unsettling quiet that hangs overhead. It smothers everything to the point of suffocation. A cold, damp mist haunts the air, drenching the moss-and-lichen-dressed trunks, the ferns and shrubs, with a permanent slickness. And in every direction the trees tower like dark sentinels, scratching at one another in their closeness. So close, it's easy for your gaze to slip past a bough spirit as she stands there watching you.

It's a wild and fickle place that will swallow you whole without a second thought, and I love it without remorse.

Stefan stops to check the first snare we encounter along the trapline and gestures for me to continue on. I nod, sending Rudi ahead. Soon, the sounds of Stefan shifting the brush are devoured by distance, and the world shrinks to nothing but me, my dog, and my steady breathing.

The next stretch of the well-trod game trail is undisturbed except for the sudden eruption of several grouse near a stream. I still, spotting fresh tracks in the soft mud of the bank. I hurry forward. My heart falls, though, before I even crouch to examine them. They're deer tracks, but far too small and nothing extraordinary.

They don't belong to the Breimar Stag.

Every few years, in the weeks before the full moon that falls on the last days of the tenth month—the Scavenge Moon—an uncanny magic awakens across Wielinde Forest. A thinning in the veil that separates this realm from another entirely unknown, allowing a beast called the Breimar Stag to step through the trees. I've seen only glimpses of him, passing through the wood or spotted on the far side of the lake. A massive creature, with antlers larger than the width of my arm span, legs as tall as my shoulder, his coat a restless snow white. And eyes glowing the burnt ochre of a dying coal.

So he appeared three years ago, and four before that—and every few since for the last four hundred years. It is a Prauen Castle tradition, this Hunt for the mythical Stag. The beast continues to live despite the few lucky bullets and crossbow bolts that have found their targets—but nothing can stop him returning to offer his prize.

A single wish, granted to the person who slays him. To kill the Breimar Stag is to earn the death of another person of their choosing. And if they do not catch him, the Stag will take one of the hunters back through the veil instead.

No matter what, the Hunt always ends with a life snuffed out.

As gamekeepers, it's my and Stefan's job to discover the first traces of his return. Even though the Breimar Stag arrived in

Wielinde with the setting of the last full moon, and the invitations were sent to guests months prior, the Hunt cannot begin until the Stag is seen. Only then does he release the magic the hunters will bind themselves to. Like a candle waiting in the dark to be lit. Less than two weeks remain until the Scavenge Moon rises, but the Stag always reveals himself before then. There's still time.

I rise, surprised by the disappointment that ladens my limbs. I bet Alma I'd be the first to locate the Stag this year, and while the stakes are high for me—she'll cut off a foot of the unruly chestnut brown hair that took me *years* to grow out if I lose—I don't actually want to find him.

Bet or no, I prefer that the Stag never show at all.

The whole Hunt feels wrong. To point at someone and declare their life over, that's not something anyone should get to decide. No one life is worth more than another. It's why I hate all these nobles coming up here for the fun of it. They dismiss a real threat as a toothless, provincial ghost story, yet even the *idea* of removing a business rival or the sibling blocking them from an inheritance makes them accept the baron's invitation the moment it lands on their gilded doorsteps.

At least I draw comfort from knowing that the Stag will never be taken down by any of these pompous twits. The way they tumbled out of their carriages, already half soused—I have my work cut out for me. This will be the first Breimar Hunt in which I'll be leading one of the hunting parties. Split between Stefan and me, six of those fops will be under my care in the Forest and I'll be amazed if they can even hold their rifles steady with the amount of liquor they'll imbibe to fend off the cold. We haven't even seen the Stag yet and I'm already annoyed by what I'll be dealing with. And at the end, when one of them is taken against their will from this mortal plane by the Stag, they'll be too drunk to notice or care.

Rudi jolts me from my dark thoughts, racing past to chase a lone grouse. I hop over the small stream after her.

Before I reach the next set of traps, though, a flash of red catches my eye. I find a large puddle among the lush green ferns, drying to a dark crimson on the golden leaves below. I dig a hand through the litter on the ground. Where are the footprints of whatever left the blood?

I lift my chin, but there's nothing overhead except the brightening sky through the branches and a single magpie taking flight. Confusion settles over me like a cape. Perhaps a hawk dropped a fresh kill?

I glance back down at the stain. No. That's far too much blood for anything a raptor would carry.

"Rudi, come here, girl," I call. Maybe she can track the source of the blood. It's still wet, and recent. Whatever left it is injured badly. I need to make sure it's dead and not suffering.

"Rudi?" I call again, looking around. The alpine pointer stands ten paces back, motionless. "Rudi, *come*."

But then I register her stance. Tense, her body slung low and quivering. But she's not pointing toward a kill—she's afraid. Her hackles rise, her lips hitching to reveal teeth as her rumbled growl reaches my ears.

"Rudi?" My voice sounds flat, no longer confident. "What is it?"

Her answering bark is vicious, making me jump. My bewilderment leaches away, replaced by dread.

I survey the woods with a new vigilance. It strings between my ribs and makes it difficult to breathe. When I spot the second patch of blood farther ahead, a small whimper escapes my throat, but I forge on, readying my rifle.

This streak of blood is much the same. Slightly larger and in the middle of a blackberry thicket. None of the thorny branches are broken or disturbed. No prints lead in or out of the bush to place the blood there.

I round the bend and my heart leaps into my throat.

A great brown bear lies on its side on the trail. More red stains the earth around it as I creep forward. Still no footprints. It's as though the body was simply dropped from the sky. I feel slightly dizzy as I approach, stopping a step away from its massive front paw.

The animal was . . . slaughtered. I don't know how else to describe it. The only other word that crosses my mind as I stare down at the dead bear in gape-mouthed horror is *wrong, wrong, wrong.*

It's been torn apart. Plump from its preparations for hibernation, the bear's side is ravaged, split in three separate places, as if something cut itself free from the inside with little care for how it did so. This was not a kill made to take home and skin, nor done to feed a pack of wolves. This was pointless. Senseless.

I try to avoid looking too closely at what the fatally deep cuts reveal as I bend over the bear's shoulder. My fingers burrow between thick, coarse hair to the skin.

Still warm.

I scramble away with a gasp, wrenching my gun back into my grip. A barbed cold spills down my spine. *Wrong, wrong, wrong.*

This must have *just* happened. What's worse is I can't begin to guess what could have done something this mindlessly cruel to the biggest predator in Wielinde Forest. And I'm out here alone.

"Stefan!" I bellow. My voice cracks on the last syllable, but the panicked shout still crashes through the quiet. Several birds take flight from their roosts. They cover the sky, casting faint shadows over me as I stumble back. "*Stefan!*"

It only takes a minute for my uncle's presence to be heard, but it feels like an entire lifetime wasted standing near the bear's corpse. When he rounds the bend, the teasing lightness that warmed his face before is gone. His complexion turns wan when he spots me, rushing forward.

"What is it? Are you hurt?" he demands, seizing me by the shoulders. He's curt, firm, trying to turn me to either side, inspecting for injuries. "What happened?"

"Look," I whisper. My arm lifts to point behind me.

His thick, dark brows lower as he sees the bear at last. "Stay here," he commands.

I don't listen. I try calling once more for Rudi, but she senses the danger and stays put with a steady stream of whimpers. Petra and Milo flank her, heads thrown back as they bay wildly. I hurry to join my uncle.

"What could have done this?" I ask.

He shakes his head, kneeling beside the bear to inspect its gutted stomach. Stefan is as speechless as I am, and for the gamekeeper of these woods for over two decades to be struck silent, that does not lend me any measure of comfort.

Suddenly, a huff comes from the bear's throat. Pained and thready and *impossible*. I shriek.

It's dead.

It. Is. *Dead.*

Nothing can survive this kind of injury. It hasn't breathed once and yet its eye just opened.

I don't think. Don't hesitate. I unsheathe the knife strapped at the top of my thigh and jam it into its throat.

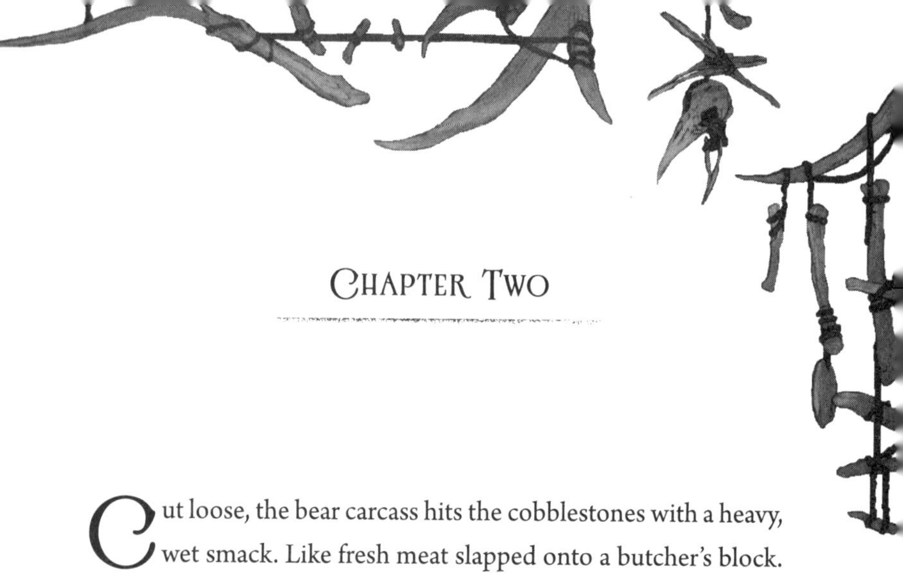

Chapter Two

Cut loose, the bear carcass hits the cobblestones with a heavy, wet smack. Like fresh meat slapped onto a butcher's block. My mouth turns as dry as cotton. In a way, I suppose the ground outside my uncle's workshop in the lower courtyard serves the same purpose for this poor beast.

While Stefan watched over its body, a more than willing Rudi and I ran back to Prauen Castle for help. The handcart we use can carry a few hunted deer, not a massive, winter-ready bear—it required two extra sets of hands and a pair of horses to bind it with rope and drag it back. Ravaged though the bear may be, there's enough unscathed fur to find a use for once it's skinned. The organs and bones will be given back to Wielinde.

But first Stefan wants to take a closer look and determine what could tear open its flank like shears through parchment. And I'm right by his side, leaning in to examine it with a dwindling number of guesses.

My nose wrinkles against the strange scent that lingers. I hadn't noticed before, too alarmed by the grisly discovery and Rudi's refusal to come near—and she still doesn't want to, hiding inside Stefan's workshop with the foxhounds—but now it's all I smell. Instead of the musky, metallic odor I expect, something sharper overpowers it. It reminds me of how the air tastes when a heavy storm looms above the mountain peaks.

We try not to waste anything from the Forest, but this meat . . . I don't even trust it as food for the dogs.

"What do you reckon, Stefan?" Elena asks. The castle's groundskeeper, olive-skinned and almost as tall as Stefan, crosses her arms over her ample chest. While the stable hand who helped us guides the two horses back to the stables, Elena stays. A leery curiosity brings her a step closer. "One of the meaner Forest Folk?"

I shake my head. "They wouldn't do this. Not where anyone could see, at least," I add darkly, and she concedes the point with a wince. Whatever the moss mites, bough spirits, mushroom goblins, and stream barrows do where no one watches is not for us to know, and they keep it that way. Which suits us fine.

"I'm not sure what did this," Stefan says slowly, scratching the greying stubble along his jaw. He prods the beast's thick neck. Above the rustle of his coat and clinking buckles, the hollow clack of several bone chimes rings through the courtyard. "But something is wrong with this bear."

"Yeah, I don't know if you noticed, but it's been shredded."

He brushes aside my sarcastic comment as though wafting away smoke. "No, no. Something else. I've never seen anything like this before—like it burst from the inside out. But I just can't . . ."

Disgust rumbles low in his throat and he reaches into his pocket, pulling out his spectacles. I don't miss the flash of irritation that pinches his eyes as he sets the wire frames atop his nose. It makes me smile, despite everything. Stefan finally deigned to get the glasses half a year ago yet still avoids wearing them unless absolutely necessary. He hates that he even needs them. I think they make him appear rather distinguished.

When his touch shifts to the underside of the bear's jaw and the mark made by my knife, I look away. A shiver trips down my spine. The memory of its dark, glassy eye, that pitiful groan, squeezes my stomach in a tight fist. That bear shouldn't have been alive. Every piece of its insides was exposed to the elements, the red of its life drained over the soil. Nothing should have survived that, yet it tried.

I straighten and lift my gaze, stealing a deep breath in through my nose and letting the crisp morning steady me.

When the sun rises, it glazes first the westernmost peaks before dripping over each crag and treetop. It doesn't truly gleam until it kisses the tallest turret of Prauen Castle and the golden spire atop its slate roof.

As the ancestral seat of the Wagner barony, Prauen Castle has perched high on the Spindal Ridge for the last four hundred years. A proud and austere bastion, completely at odds with the rugged valley it surveys. Large blocks of creamy limestone carry its elegant walls and towers upward while thick swathes of scarlet ivy chase after. Six rows of twinned arched windows catch the watery sunlight in their glass panes. From where I stand, I don't see much beyond the castle's main structure.

Although this particular courtyard is the domain of the castle's workers, it is no less a place of beauty. My eyes trace the graceful arches of the colonnade crossing every doorway from the kitchen passage to the armory, over sharp crenelations above the forge, and delicately edged gables leading to the stables. Along the friezes chiseled with vines and fir boughs before dropping to Stefan's workshop.

And the young man watching from its darkened doorway.

I jolt when I notice him. He leans against the frame, arms and ankles crossed as he observes the bear with naked interest. His presence and easy comfort at being here isn't what surprises me, though. It's that I don't know who he is.

My mind vaguely conjures an image of him from when Rudi and I rushed into the courtyard earlier, standing near where he is now, a heavy traveling bag slung over his shoulder. I think he tried to speak to me, but I was too distracted to give him a second glance. Now I feel like I've forgotten something crucial.

"Katrin."

I shake my head. From the sharpness edging Stefan's tone, I realize that wasn't the first time he called me. "Hmm?"

He follows the line of my previous gaze and spots the boy himself. Unlike me, however, confusion does not cloud his brow. Rather, warm delight replaces his brooding mien. "Ah, you must be Elias."

"I am. And you're Stefan." The boy—Elias—pushes gracefully off the frame and grasps my uncle's outstretched hand. His voice is deep, smooth. A soft accent files down his vowels. "Pleased to meet you."

"Right," Elena says. "Forgot to mention—he arrived after you both left this morning."

"I meant to come yesterday, but a landslide wiped out one of the roads." He grimaces, exhaustion showing on his face. "Arrived so late I spent the night in Steigert with an old friend instead."

Spent it drinking too, I think, judging by his wince as he leaves the shade of the colonnade.

Stefan nods knowingly, despite not bothering to travel farther than that same village himself in over a decade. "Glad you made it in one piece, then."

"Me too. Although, it looks like I missed out on some excitement." He casts a pleasant smile in my direction, the first he's acknowledged me. It makes my skin prickle. With so many new faces appearing in the fabric of the castle, many of whom I would rather tear out thread by silken thread, this stranger's presence feels no different than scissors ready to ruin.

"Not sure *excitement* is the right word for this."

Elena snorts, side-eyeing the ravaged bear.

"But you've come right on time," my uncle continues. "The Hunt will likely start any day now, and we'll—"

"I don't mean to be rude," I say, sounding exactly that, "but *who* are you?"

"This is Elias," Stefan answers. When I only shrug, he pulls me aside to the stone well at the courtyard's center. "He's our new gamekeeper. To replace Otto."

My stomach drops. Thoughts fly through my head faster than I can pin them down. "And you didn't think I should know about that?"

Otto, a man ten years my senior and newly married to one of Prauen's maids, abruptly announced their intention to leave a little over three weeks ago. He said it was because his wife missed her family in the south, but I still have a dark suspicion the true reason is named Baron August Ludwig Wagner III.

Given how close Otto's departure was to the start of the Hunt, and mindful of what Elias—an *outsider*—needs to learn about Wielinde and the ways of the Forest Folk, I wasn't expecting my uncle to hire a replacement yet. I'm not upset he did; a third gamekeeper is greatly needed. Part of me is rejoicing that I'll now be dealing with four hunting nobles instead of the six I was dreading.

But Stefan never said a word. Not once in the last few weeks, and I don't understand how. Feeling too hot, I unbutton my coat. Densely embroidered leaves and owls itch against my fingers as I wrench my dark green vest straight.

"I sent out a job notice after Otto left. Elias responded. He was a gamekeeper at a small estate before." Stefan's brow creases once more, this time in distress. "Did I really not tell you?"

"I'm apparently the last to know, so yes," I say with a forced calm.

"I'm—" An agitated hand runs through his silvering mane of dark brown hair. He looks more tired than ever. "Damn, I'm sorry, Katrin. This *Hunt*—the baron has asked me to do a hundred things and I keep forgetting. I left myself notes—"

"Left notes—*Stefan!*" I groan, understanding at once what happened. *Again.* My fist flies into his upper arm. "Stop. Trying. To do. Everything. By yourself. You know you can't. You *never* can."

If there's one trait my uncle and mother share, it's a fatal stubbornness.

He will refuse to see clearly, lose an entire fingernail from trying to move a cabinet all by himself, or squander a night's sleep to bookkeeping rather than ask for help.

She will try to make it as a stage actress, move from city to city to avoid paying a landlord, or become another man's mistress rather than remember she has a daughter.

Two sides of the same coin, but only one of them is truly my parent, and I glare at him while folding my arms.

He scrubs a hand down his weary face. "Yes, I know. I know. I'm sorry."

"Here I thought my workload hadn't changed because Otto did nothing, and instead you're doing it all. No wonder you've looked so ragged." It's a terrible pattern with him, quietly taking on too much to properly function. If it's happened once, it's happened a dozen times, but this must have been bad for him to have forgotten to tell me something so important.

Unable to stay mad at him, I ask, "Is he any good, at least? Elias?"

"From what I hear, he might give you a run for your money on being the best shot out here."

"Then send him home. I have a reputation to protect."

With a chuckle, Stefan returns us to the others, one comforting hand on my shoulder. Resuming his examination of the bear, he drops to one knee with a groan and carefully pokes about the chest cavity.

"Hi," Elias says kindly. He extends his hand to me over the animal. "I'd have introduced myself earlier, but you were in a bit of a hurry."

His grasp is firm but not unpleasant. I mumble an awkward greeting, grateful he doesn't draw attention to my ignorance of him. I'm still a little flustered by his suddenly being here, but it doesn't set warning bells ringing anymore.

I observe Elias closely as he turns to ask Stefan questions. When the sun touches his neatly trimmed hair, the gilded color slips from gold to white. His height places him between my uncle and me, and his strong frame is broad in the chest. Piercing green eyes don't miss a single detail as they roam over the bear. His nose is a little large for his face, but it suits the chiseled quality his cheeks and jaw hold. Alma will think him handsome. I don't see what qualifies for that, but I've heard enough about *jawlines you could cut yourself on* to know where she'll stand.

My attraction to him simply does not exist. Nor does it to anyone else, for that matter. It's a fact about myself as irrefutable as stating it snows in winter and lichen nyxes can fly. Romance, attraction—it's never ignited within me the way Alma describes it from the romance novels she steals from Aunt Carolina. I even enjoy reading them after her, but I've never turned the last page and wanted what the heroines found. And I don't think I ever will. Family is family, friends are friends, and that's all the love my heart needs to feel full.

"Well, I'll be damned."

Stefan's hushed exclamation knocks me out of my cluttered mind.

"What?" I shuffle closer. Elena mirrors me on the other side. My boot nudges the rough pads of the bear's hind paw, and I quickly toe it back.

"Look." Stefan carefully peels away the remaining shreds of flesh to fully expose the inside cavity. "What's missing?"

I'm far from squeamish. This isn't the first bloody kill I've stumbled upon in Wielinde, but this bear isn't like those picked-over remains left in tree hollows and under bushes. I peer inside with wariness tightening my muscles.

"What do you mean, what's missing? It's a dead animal." Elias crouches. As he does, a small medallion swings loose from his coat collar on a leather thong. An emblem etches over the silver, but I can't make it out. "Heart, lungs, stomach—anything missing could have been taken by a scavenger, if not by what killed it."

A sudden wind breathes cold through the courtyard, shaking the bone chimes over every doorway. I watch the one I made above Stefan's workshop rattle. The delicate bones of a mallard, strung in five lines. They are the talismans we use to protect us and the castle from the Forest Folk. We don't take from Wielinde without a reason, and we always give back what we don't need. Bones hang from every tree within half a mile of Prauen; the innards we find no purpose for are buried in their roots. The game we hunt returned to restore a fragile balance the Folk govern.

The answer hits me then as sure as the chill that curls into the space at my neck and flattens the flames in the wall lanterns.

"Ribs," I whisper. "The ribs are missing."

A beast this size should possess a solid rib cage. Impossible to miss, even if the bones had broken in such a vicious attack. Instead, there's nothing but a gaping wound, the slimy organs left entirely unprotected.

Elena harrumphs, but her face blanches. "What do you mean, *missing*?"

"They're not there."

Stefan shucks off his coat and rolls up the sleeves of his thick woolen sweater. Before I can wonder, he slots his hand inside and roots around. That sharp storm scent increases with each wet squelch. Elias watches with razor-sharp focus, his own hands ice-still on his knees.

A loud bark snaps through the air, and I jump. Rudi stands braced in the open doorway of the workshop. I try to call her to me, but she only lies down on the threshold, another warning snarl fading to a pathetic whine.

When Stefan withdraws, red slicks his hand. He shakes it off to the side with two swift flicks before accepting Elena's soil-smudged rag. "Its rib cage is gone."

"On both sides?" I ask, brow lowering.

A nod. "The spine too." He runs his clean hand over the area in question. Applies pressure, only for it to sink in farther than is natural.

Guided by an intrusive hunch, I wrap both hands around the nearest hind leg and lift. In any normal circumstance, the limb would bend along the knee and hip joint.

Instead, it sags. The foot dangles at an angle only possible if it was broken.

Or if there were no bones at all.

The leg slips from my grasp, flopping to the ground with a muffled thump. I step back, barely resisting the urge to hide with Rudi.

Elias strokes the bear's pelt, voice soft. "How did no one notice?"

Now that I know what to look for, I don't understand how we *didn't*. There is a slightly . . . flattened quality to it. How its head lies, the way its body puddles a little at the edges. Bile creeps up my throat.

"Because it's easy to miss with an animal this bulked up with fat." Stefan tries to give the now-red rag back to Elena but thinks better of it. "And we weren't checking for bones when we roped it up."

I shake my head. The corners of my vision blur as my mind races.

Though a gifted tooth or a femur on a branch may sate them, there is no mistaking the Forest Folk for anything less than dangerous. Bough spirits can lure you into their heart trees with a song, and the caress of a mushroom goblin at night will turn your fingers black with rot. Cautionary tales I grew up with, but never in any of them was there mention of something that can pull the entire skeleton from a beast.

"There's an explanation somewhere," Stefan says, reading my thoughts. Except he's spent more time in Wielinde than anyone I know. If he still doesn't have an answer, it turns my stomach into a gnawing pit of nerves.

"Stefan, it was alive." I wait until my uncle meets my wide eyes, his obscured by a glare on his glasses. "It had no bones and it was still *alive*."

The corner of his mouth screws up. He knows what I'm not saying. This isn't the standard fare of Forest Folk. It's not a pile of rocks stuffed inside one of our traps or a bird left in its nest with wings torn by teeth. This was merciless, deliberate, and unknown. And with the Hunt about to start at any moment . . .

"Do we tell the baron?"

My uncle stares at me while he thinks. Elias and Elena have been seemingly forgotten, the pair of us focused on each other.

It should be a simple question to answer. When the previous baron was still alive, Stefan wouldn't have hesitated like this. Now there are more facets to this flawed situation to consider for everyone involved.

So, of course, he says exactly what I expect. "I'll speak with him, but he won't call off the Hunt. Not when the Stag is already here. It's too late for that."

"Yes, but if he saw what happened—"

"Katrin, *we* don't even know what happened. This could have been some new entity or kids from the village pulling a prank."

"But—"

"He won't stop four hundred years of a fucked-up tradition just for a dead bear." He looks directly at Elias and me. "Just . . . be vigilant, both of you. Look out for each other. Whatever did this, it's still out there."

The wind takes a turn for the worse, silencing my argument. It shoves through the courtyard with a scream. Extinguishes multiple lanterns, knocks the empty bucket off the well's lip with a loud splash, and forces Elena to slap a hand over her flat-brimmed hat to keep it in place.

When the mallard bone chimes come free of their hook and crash to the ground in a heap, setting Rudi off into a barking frenzy, it's difficult not to see it as an omen.

Chapter Three

When my aunt sets a steaming bowl of mushroom soup before me, I'm too famished to let it cool. It scalds my tongue, but after spending hours breaking down the boneless bear, this kind of comfort is just what I need.

Without warning, Carolina upends a massive ceramic bowl beside me. A boulder of dough plops onto the long wooden counter. A startled choke splits my throat, and I drop my spoon to cover my mouth.

"I need you to help your cousin make the bread for tonight," she says, distracted.

I swallow with difficulty. "Wait, what?"

"You heard me." She readjusts the scarf holding her black locs away from her face, her rich brown skin aglow from the heat of the kitchen.

"Yes, but why do you need me?"

"Because," says a familiar voice behind me. My heart stutters again when a dozen flat pans slam down next to me. "We are now short three pairs of hands, and you've got one we can use."

"Three?"

Alma separates the pans, spreading them out on the counter. "Hurry up and eat. We've an hour to get these loaves into the oven."

"Ugh. Fine."

I eat another spoonful of soup without tasting it. Unable to think past what she said, I glance around the kitchen.

The cavernous space my aunt commandeers is overly warm compared to the drafty rooms Stefan and I claim. A perfect square, supported by white plaster columns and oak beams, blackened by soot and warped by steam. Counters run along two walls and down the middle while a long black stove with ovens enough to roast a dozen whole geese takes up the back. Several apron-clad people hurry about, stirring sauces, chopping vegetables, and seasoning haunches of meat, but it's immediately obvious where the gaps lie.

"Where are the Lohens?" I ask. My grip tightens on my spoon in anticipation of an answer I already fear.

"Quit. Left last night." Carolina moves to the other side of the counter and begins cutting onions. There's a deftness to her knife that shouts of frustration.

"Left—like, they *left*? Prauen?"

"Well, they certainly aren't coming back." Someone beside a pot bubbling over shouts for Carolina. With an almost regretful look at her half-cut onion, she slams down the knife. I watch her go, a frown deepening on my forehead.

The Lohen family have worked at Prauen Castle in the kitchen since before my mother dumped me as an infant in my aunt's and uncle's arms. Like Carolina and Stefan, the elder Lohens met here when they were younger, and their daughter, Brigitte, grew up with Alma and me.

"They're still living in Steigert," Alma assures me softly, tossing flour across the countertop. She pulls a small chunk from the larger dough, expertly rolling and shaping it. The white powder soon coats her hands, dusting them to a color closer to her father's complexion than her mother's. "But they couldn't stay here anymore."

I lose my appetite entirely. Carefully, I lay down my spoon. "It's because of *him*, isn't it?"

She scoffs. Without looking up, she scores an *x* into the soft bread with a knife. "Of course it is. I heard talk there was a"—she drops the dough on the first tray with a loud smack—"bun in the oven, if you know what I mean."

Red flashes across my vision. My fingers flex before curling in my lap. "Fucking *bastard*."

Alma, ever receptive to my moods, tears a fresh knob of dough away and swaps out my abandoned bowl for it. "Take it out on that, please."

I stand so fast my chair scrapes loudly across the darkened ceramic tiles.

The dough doesn't need more kneading, and I worry the bread will come out hard and chewy, but damn it feels good. It takes little effort to imagine this yeasty blob as his face. Goodness knows I've wanted to give Baron August Wagner a black eye more times than I can count.

After a few minutes of pummeling, though, a gentle arm wraps around my shoulders and the fight collapses within me. Alma's sugared scent fills my nose. Knuckles still in the dough, I lean my head against hers. Her thick, dark curls tickle my cheek.

"I was furious, too, when I heard last night," she murmurs. "Pa tried to convince them to stay, but I don't think they feel safe anymore. And if Brigitte really is . . . *you know*, I can't blame them."

"That makes twelve people gone in the last six months. And he's only been baron for seven." I straighten and twist to face Alma. Her skirts and bodice, prettily stitched with cornflowers, have several floury handprints on them. "How much longer is this going to go on?"

I'm taller than my cousin by a few inches, but the softness in her gaze makes me feel smaller. "Until there's no one left for him to step on, I guess."

Despite myself, a devious grin lifts my mouth. "My previous suggestion still stands."

Alma rolls her eyes. "And I told you, it has to *look* like an accident."

"But it doesn't have to be in the hedge maze," I insist. "I'm fine with us just pushing him out a tower window. Ply him with enough beer and he might do it himself."

She huffs, a smile flickering as she turns to finish my battered dough. "You want us to meet the gallows so bad."

"That implies we'll be caught. And I run faster than Felix."

"I don't!" she says with an indignant gasp.

Alma may be my cousin, but she's as good as my sister. With only eight months separating us, we've spent countless sleepless nights giggling in whatever bed the other sneaked into, and long days helping each other with chores so we can be together. There isn't a corner in this castle we haven't huddled in to simply talk. We know each other inside and out. And for all our terrible jokes of murdering August and outrunning his personal guard, the look she gives tells me her anger is mine, her fear a mirror.

This castle is our family. Even if no blood connects us, every person who works within Prauen's walls is considered an aunt, an uncle, or a cousin. Elena taught me about my monthly bleedings as much as Carolina did. Klaus, the guard captain, taught me in secret how to shoot and convinced Stefan to take me into Wielinde when I was twelve. My own mother can't even be bothered to write a birthday letter while the stable hands risk Carolina's wrath to bake me a too-sweet cake.

This is the only family that matters to me.

And it's splintering apart beneath the selfish wickedness of one stupid baron.

"I don't blame the Lohens for leaving," Alma says, "but Greta—"

"I'll miss her stories," we finish together.

Greta Lohen is—or was—Prauen's authority on Wielinde and its inhabitants. She is a direct descendant of those who lived in this valley long before the first Wagner baron arrived to declare the land his. Her stories of the Forest Folk have been passed down for generations, rooted in deep history and experience. She knows every tale and legend, and she told them well.

"No one made me more scared of the dark than her."

"You're *still* scared of the dark," I say with a snicker.

"I'll have you know that candle is for efficiency's sake."

"Mm-hmm." I move my second, less-abused loaf to the pan. Beside Alma's perfect ones, mine just looks sad and lumpy. I hope August is served it.

"For when I wake up in the middle of the night. So I don't trip."

"Right, of course."

"Shut up." But she says it with a smile and a hip bump. "So, that new gamekeeper . . ."

"Yes?" She changed the topic so abruptly, her words spilling fast, that I brace for impact. "What about him?"

Alma blushes. "He's handsome and I think you should introduce me."

I throw my head back. "I *knew* it! The moment I saw him, I knew you'd find him attractive."

"Those shoulders. So broad. And so strong."

"Careful, your knees are going to buckle if you swoon any harder."

She sighs, suddenly so wistful and earnest I want to fold her into my pocket and protect her forever. To let her stay safe in her dreams of love. It gives her an optimism so many women in this castle have lost in the last year.

"I'll think about it," I say, injecting false reluctance into my voice.

Alma gives a small squeal, then lunges for me. "You're the best," she says when she lets go. "You can officiate our wedding."

"*Down*, girl."

"Katrin," comes from behind me then, and Aunt Carolina appears. Before I can protest, she deposits a sagging basket of potatoes into my arms. "Would you please put those in the larder, dear? Reiner pulled out far too many, and if I don't take them away, he'll peel them all and leave us with nothing for winter."

I shift the basket to sit on my hip. "Sure."

The hall off the kitchen is blessedly cool in comparison. This passage exits to the courtyard, and with the doors left open, the wind wails ominously between the stone walls as I walk. My own cry is far shriller when I crash into someone.

"Elias!" I exclaim. We both kneel, returning scattered potatoes to the basket I dropped. Because of *course* it's him and his shoulders. "Where did you come from?"

"Sorry," he groans. He collects three potatoes in each hand. "I've been trying to find the kitchen for the last hour and I keep getting lost."

"Perseverance pays off. You found it at last," I say, unable to help laughing at how flustered he sounds. I deposit the last two escapees, but before I can grab the basket, Elias takes it and stands.

"Good. I was worried someone would find me passed out in a stairwell soon. Haven't eaten since last night, and even then it was more ale than food."

"Well, my aunt will have you rolling down the stairs once she's fed you."

The light in the passage is dim. Only a few lanterns flicker overhead, and the glow from the courtyard behind me angles softly across his face. Although we just met this morning, he's quickly growing on me, and might actually be worth setting in Alma's path. The impulse to be friendlier makes the next words fly out.

"Do you want a tour of the castle?"

His expression relaxes. He hefts the basket higher, the wicker catching on the knit of his sweater. "You have time?"

"Not now, no. And we can't have you collapsing from hunger in the middle of the ballroom." We share a smile, warmer than anything we've exchanged so far. "But later, when the feast is in full swing. No one will bother us then."

"I'll take that offer," he says, a noticeable brightness in his tone. He gestures to the potatoes. "But what about these?"

"Oh, here, I'll take them. They need to go to the larder."

"No, no." He steps out of reach. "Consider this the beginning of my tour."

I point to the darkened stairs a few paces behind him. "Just go down to the bottom and drop them in the corner with the rest."

He leaves without complaint, and I wait until he vanishes from view before I turn on my heel.

And nearly collide with the sole person I would rather sacrifice myself to the shadow gaunts than spend time with.

I attempt to step back, but hands wrap around my upper arms, pivoting my spine against the wall. Hot air grazes the skin bared below my collarbones. Sapphire velvet and a silken waistcoat against the backs of my fingers. I wince, bruises threatening to emerge beneath the unforgiving grip of Baron August Wagner.

"Get. Your hands. Off." The careful words spit through gritted teeth.

"Now, just a minute, Katrin," he drawls in a smooth voice. Too close. *Too close.* I wrinkle my nose against the stench of garlic on his breath. "You've been avoiding me lately. And it got me thinking."

"Did it hurt?" The response slips out before I can consider it. I immediately bite my tongue. I'm reacting like a cornered animal.

"The answer came to me, last night, and now you're forcing me to switch tactics."

"Am I."

"Because you're a tough little nut. Gentle doesn't seem to work on you, and I have a feeling that you . . ." He breaks off meaningfully before leaning closer to hiss in my ear. "Like it rough."

Wiser than I was a moment ago, I only think the retort, *Let me go and my fist will show you rough.* But the words still sit as heavy as bullets in my mouth, and I long to shoot them at him.

I turn my head away, refusing to give him the satisfaction of seeing what burns in my eyes. This close to the kitchen, the doors thrown wide and several people within earshot, I'm certain he won't dare try anything with me. But there's still a drop of doubt in the bucket of my confidence. Just enough to cause it to tip.

His hold loosens, but his touch only slides to my wrists. I remain motionless, staring at the distant glare of the courtyard. Inside, everything is liquid burning in a pot. Blackened and sticking to the sides, leaving me feeling ashamed. Which makes no sense. I know how to fend for myself; Stefan taught me well. Every weak spot is within reach. I can shove him away if his hands drift too far. I can bite, kick. There's a knife at my thigh, for goodness' sake.

But however much I want to ram my knee between his legs, a tendril of fear always snares my limbs whenever August looks at me with his thoughts written so plainly across his face.

I feel his gaze boring into my temple even now. A smugness likely pulls at those full lips, tightens his expression over sculpted features framed by sleek black hair that swings just above his shoulders. Even I can admit he's handsome, and it's all a trap. So lovely on the outside while inside is nothing but cobwebs and an ugly, rotten heart. August isn't muscled or broad, but he's a full head taller, and he abuses every single inch by leaning over me so I have to shift.

Anger flares within me. My heart thunders in my chest, and I wonder if he feels it vibrating through my too-warm skin.

This is what he does—what he's *always* done. Pushes his way into the space of others without consent to take and take and take. Everyone and everything beneath his station is nothing but a toy to him, and I've never hated anyone more.

But what makes me angriest is that *I* am in this situation at all. And I don't know how to get out of it without bringing hell down upon me. I can punch dough and joke about him tumbling out a window, but when it truly comes down to it, faced with his arrogance, I can't do anything at all. It's humiliating.

"Nothing to say?" August bends to the side, forcing himself into my line of sight. He laughs, the sound slippery. "Help me, Katrin.

Will a little *fun* crack that shell of yours? I told you, I can make you realize what you're missing."

Pain shoots through my jaw from clenching it so tight. I made the mistake of gently rejecting one of the young new guards in August's vicinity. A year ago, he heard me explain how I'm not interested in people that way and took it as a *challenge*. The bastard heard a declaration that means a lot to me when people understand it and decided it was a vulnerability. That all I need to want to kiss someone—to be *fixed*—is the right person *forcing* it on me.

"Wouldn't your little wife prefer all these attentions?" I say.

Annoyance flickers across his face, making my gaze focus on him for the briefest moment. "You know my *little* wife is in a delicate state. Mustn't upset her."

I nearly laugh. By delicate, he means pregnant with their first child. A state the entire castle knows August finds necessary but inconvenient and disgusting. *A man has needs, after all.* The rounder her belly grows, the more the baroness becomes the only woman in this castle earning herself any peace.

August pulls back, and I blink against the returned brightness of the courtyard. For the first time, I notice the hulking figure looming a few paces behind August.

I'd be more surprised if Felix wasn't here. Taller than anyone else in the castle and thick with muscle that must make him impervious to the cold, Felix is a stretched, second shadow to August.

Five years ago and not yet baron, August was stabbed in the dark streets of the capital. To my dismay, the desperate man, sore at losing all his money in a card game, didn't aim a little higher and to the right. August was left with little more than a thin scar on his belly. It put the fear of mortality into him, though, and Felix was hired. Now he accompanies August everywhere like a red-haired mountain of a chaperone.

Felix's presence is my resignation rather than hope. He's here to keep anyone from hurting August, not the other way around. Even now his hand hovers over a knife at his belt, just in case *I* do something. But there's little risk of that.

The first staff to leave Prauen six months ago did not do so willingly. Frank, August's former valet, spoke up when he learned who cornered his granddaughter, Mari, in a broom closet. He summoned the meager authorities from Steigert, prepared to have the baron arrested. Instead, it was August's word—and coin-heavy palm—against his. Mari was easy to frame for theft; a valuable necklace slipped inside her sock drawer spoke louder than she ever could. A day later, the mace that vanished from a suit of armor shattered Frank's shinbone.

August's orders, carried out by an indifferent Felix.

Monstrous acts repeated until it became clear there could be no justice. Jobs in these mountains are hard to come by, and for many it's simpler to stay quiet or leave rather than face Felix's violence. Whatever keeps them and their loved ones safe.

I hate Felix. I hate his silence, his bought obedience. Almost as much as I hate the man making my skin crawl with every finger stroke of my wrist.

I can't do this anymore.

Sharply, I wrench myself back. With the wall against my shoulders, I can't move much. One arm comes free, but August's fingers tighten on the other. It's difficult to keep my breathing even. The foulness infesting his bones seems to turn them to steel. I brace for his retaliation, dreading where that other hand will go next.

"What have I told you, Felix?" His clammy touch slowly slips around my neck, then digs into my nape. "Feisty."

"August, if you don't let me go this instant—" My voice rises against my will, a mortifying shake breaking the last word.

"If Katrin says let her go, perhaps you should."

A relieved sob nearly erupts from my throat at Elias's return. I look to him as he crests the larder stairs, his gait wary and brows raised in confusion.

Startled, the baron releases me, leaving pinpricks of ice in his wake. I sidle closer to Elias.

"You're new." August scrutinizes him, eyes narrowing as he tries and fails to place Elias. I hold my breath. His flat tone is unreadable—I don't know how he'll react toward the interruption.

"Come on, Felix," he says after a moment. "Let's leave her to work."

When Elias stepped from the shadows, my heart slowed. Safety was within reach; I could free myself of this situation.

It gives a sick squeeze now when Alma appears from the kitchen, wiping her hands on her apron.

"Katrin, are you okay? I thought I—Oh."

She stills as she takes in the scene. Hesitation pinches her mouth shut. I can almost read her thoughts, hear her search for the best way to help without making it worse.

I need her to leave. Frozen where I am, I'm more fearful for her than I am of him. My eyes widen, begging her to understand what I scream in my head.

Get out. Just leave.

I can handle myself to an extent, but Alma . . . She needs someone to stand between her and the monsters of this world.

And this monster I've kept away from her for seven months.

"Alma," drawls August. "My, haven't you grown up."

His gaze sweeps up and down her body slowly. Lingering a touch too long on her full chest, her soft hips. She always smells of sugar. Stefan jokes she turned sweet from all the desserts she bakes, but I would smother her in salt if it would erase that look from August's eye, as if he's going to lick his lips in anticipation.

"Alma, I think I hear Aunt Carolina calling you," I say, keeping my voice level. "You should go back. Elias and I will be a minute."

She nods and takes one tentative step backward, then whirls to disappear entirely. I breathe again.

Unfazed, August gives me a last smirk before chucking me under the chin with his cold fingers and leaving. I stay where I am until both his and Felix's silhouettes vanish.

"Katrin?"

Elias's soft question nearly breaks me. I don't want to dredge up answers for him right now.

"Excuse me."

Before I can cry or scream, I push past him into the kitchen.

Chapter Four

An enormous, wearied sigh comes from the floor between Alma and me. Eyebrow arched, I look down at Rudi. "What do *you* have to be bothered about?"

"She's impatient too. When did—" Alma breaks off with a gasp. "Is that him?" She stares down the corridor to our left at the man who came into view.

Half a glance tells me she's completely lost it. "That's Klaus." Indeed, the guard captain, grey-haired, pale-skinned, and dressed in his dark green uniform, lifts a hand in greeting before vanishing through a door.

She slumps against the banister, hands fussing with her navy-blue tweed skirts, quickly changed into after she finished helping with dinner. All to impress Elias. Trying to hide my grin, I lean down to scratch Rudi's long ears. The alpine pointer takes advantage of my affection and rolls to expose her spotted belly.

The thick carpet underfoot is as lavish as the rest of Prauen's foyer, cutting a long, ruby-red path across the wood herringbone floors. A dark timber skeleton of columns, paneling, and beams flicker as the chandeliers catch the gold leaf in each intricately carved design. Ahead, behind the Great Hall's heavy doors, lies a feast in full swing; behind us, at the bottom of twin staircases, squats the castle's stone entrance. To either side, minor hallways lead to other parts of Prauen, and Alma watches all four directions like a hawk.

"Is that—oh, no, that's a woman."

I stand, narrowing my eyes. "Are you going to be weird when he gets here?"

"No." She adjusts her jacket. It's her favorite, red and embroidered with white edelweiss flowers and sprigs of ivy. "I just want to meet him. You have no interest, right?" But even as she says it, doubt creeps over her face.

Alma knows how I feel about relationships. She was the first person I talked myself through with, and not once has she thought less of me for it. Nor has she assumed to know what I want with every new person met. It makes me love her all the more.

After August fled earlier, I hid with Alma in a corner of the kitchen with sauces. She *was* okay, thankfully, and more upset that she didn't even meet Elias when he came to eat. So when she heard I offered him a tour, feral bramble sprites couldn't keep her away. And I wouldn't stop her either.

I nod in response to her question. "But I know how you . . ."

"Flirt?"

"If that's what you want to call it. Just remember, Elias works with Stefan and me, and we would like him to stay. Be nice."

False offense molds her expression, and she presses a hand to her chest. "I'm always nice. Although"—she peers at the grandfather clock on the landing—"he's quite late, isn't he?"

He is. I won't admit it out loud, but I'm beginning to worry. I told Elias to meet here at half past seven. Figured the castle entrance was easy enough to find. But just then, the clock chimes to declare it's quarter to eight.

"Is *that* him?" she asks.

"No," I answer without looking, but Rudi's head shoots up, and she scrambles to her feet. Her nose points toward the rightmost hallway, body stock-still. I follow her gaze and straighten. "Oh, wait, yes, it is."

Alma releases a giddy squeal.

"I'm sorry," Elias calls as he hurries toward us. "Sorry. I know I'm late."

I move to intercept him, Alma and Rudi at my heels.

Like the last time I saw him, he's slightly flustered. He apologizes again without offering much of an explanation, and I put the pieces together.

"You got lost again."

His shoulders sag. "*Yes.*"

"Really wondering if we should put a leash on you or something."

"Hi," Alma chirps from my shoulder. She thrusts out her hand, a pretty flush in her cheeks and her brown eyes sparkling.

Startled, Elias takes her hand and gives it a light squeeze. "Hello." Redness floods *his* face now.

I stifle a sigh, fighting back another smile. "Elias, this is my cousin Alma."

"A pleasure," she says sweetly.

I shake my head. "Alma works in the kitchen and has a particularly unique insight into the history of Prauen Castle that may be of benefit to you."

She points to a dark alcove shielding the marble sculpture of a former baroness. "That's where Regina the stable hand cornered Anna the lady's maid and made her confess her feelings. They're married now."

Elias blinks, his expression shifting in small increments as he works out how to properly react. All it does is make me like him a little more.

"As I said," I say, linking arms with Alma and dragging her forward, "*may* be of benefit."

The next two hours pass quickly. Alma and I guide Elias around the castle, distributing the little tidbits of knowledge we've obtained over the years. Secret passages, doors with locks that stick, rooms to avoid if you don't want to be roped into extra work, the best cracks for eavesdropping on conversations. Alma dares him to attempt the hedge maze, but it's too dark to bother.

Tour nearly complete, we stroll down a corridor that leads us past the Great Hall. The last of the baron's invited hunting party arrived this afternoon, and the raucous noise of all thirteen carousing spills beneath the doors before we reach them. I wince when something smashes, followed by drunken laughter. I hope that was just a plate and not one of the stained-glass windows.

Someone hisses Alma's name, and we turn back to the stairwell that leads up to the staff quarters.

"Oh, I forgot. I'll be a moment." Alma squeezes my arm and hurries to greet the older woman awkwardly beckoning to her, arms full of used linen. Rudi must think Alma is playing. She rushes after her with a bark and nips at her ankle, making Alma yelp.

Their departure leaves Elias and me on our own. It surprises me how much I suddenly don't *want* to be alone with him. Distracted before by Alma, I didn't realize how heavy the specter of August would hang between us. The bruises from his unwelcome grip twinge, and I know, at some point, we have to discuss what Elias saw.

I open my mouth to clear the air, but one of the doors to the Great Hall explodes open. Two finely dressed women trip out, arms slung around a broad man I recognize as the third son of some southern duke. His grand declaration that they go explore the gardens is met with sloppy enthusiasm. Their dissonant laughter fades as they stagger toward the foyer as one.

Elias jerks a thumb toward them. "Did you not want to join the feast?"

"Hell no," I blurt. When he frowns, I add, "Whenever it's Hunt season, there's one every night. Practically a plague. I don't bother unless I have to."

"Seen one, seen them all?"

I shrug. "Something like that." Not that I ever feel welcome when I do attend.

As one of the more *diplomatic* traditions started by the first Wagner baron, a number of staff may join the feasts once finished with their daily duties—at a separate table in the back of the Hall, of course. With August now hosting the Breimar Hunt, I wouldn't be surprised to find that table moved up to the gallery where the musicians hide. Sharing a meal with people who look down their noses at my clothes marked from a day in the woods only adds bitterness to the food anyway.

"Besides," I say, "I can eat and drink the same meal in the kitchen without someone three cups in trying to prove to everyone how well they can sing."

He laughs and faces a tall tapestry. The fabric depicts the Wagner family crest on a background that age and dust have faded to grey. The crest bears a four-square shield of green and black with an acorn at its heart, outlined by juniper boughs and supported on either side by rearing stags. Only one is *the* Stag, though, stitched in luminous golden thread compared to the other's drab brown.

I expect him to ask a question about it, like he's already done for almost every wall hanging we've passed so far, but instead what I dreaded most comes at last.

"Are you okay?" he asks softly. "With . . . earlier?"

"I'm fine." It's more a bark than an assurance. "Sorry I . . . ran off on you like that." My concern had been focused on Alma, but my shaking hands stirred those sauces a little harder than was needed. It was that or throw glasses against a wall.

"Don't apologize," he says quickly. "I just wasn't sure what was going on, if I'd done something wrong."

It tugs on my heartstrings, the sincerity that gentles his features. How could he know what was going on? From his vantage point in the dim shadows, it may have even seemed a consensual embrace. He might not have recognized the anger in my tense stance, the hatred brewing in my gaze. The fear in my voice.

"You didn't."

I still don't believe August would have tried anything truly untoward. In such an open hallway, so close to the kitchen, I do think I was safe. However flimsy that word is when applied to the young baron. The previous baron had kept him somewhat in check, and those boundaries are no longer fixed. They've shifted like growing mold. Ever since his father left him to his own devices by dying, August has pushed and pushed. Tested the limits of what he can get away with—without facing consequences.

"Thank you for coming when you did, though." It's honest but harder to come off my tongue than I expected.

"Of course." Staring at the threadbare tapestry, I hear him fidget, swallow, and I brace for the rest. "Can I ask who that was?"

I give him a surprised look. "That was your employer."

"What?" His jaw drops before he seems to remember himself. "*That* was the baron? He can't be doing . . . doing that?"

"Look." I face him properly, annoyance flaring. How nice it must be, to live an existence where you can deny what you saw because it's nothing you ever need to worry about. "Get one thing straight about working here: Stay beneath that man's attention at all times."

"Oh, I'm not—"

"Doesn't matter what you're not. Because he doesn't care about anything but his own damn needs." As if on cue, a tide of laughter rises from inside the Hall, and I extract his tones from the din with little difficulty. My hands curl into fists. "Whether you're attracted to men or women or both"—or none at all—"the baron sees everyone as prey. He has cornered almost every single young woman and a few men in this castle like a cruel cat after a mouse. And if you're not careful, he takes what he wants."

My heart splinters all over again remembering the Lohens and what he did to Brigitte, if the rumors are true. My plan of pitching him out a window looks more and more enticing, consequences be damned. He never sees any.

Even when his father was alive, the elder baron hid his son's sordid deeds. Ensured his proclivities for younger women were satisfied *elsewhere*. Kept them to the shadows and offered payment for silence. Gave Felix a little bonus on the side to make sure that silence *stayed* permanent. The old man was a fool to think marrying August to that meek little woman would be enough to tether his wanton ways. It changed nothing. All it resulted in was an heir on the way and a man free to do whatever he fucking wanted.

August became baron seven months ago, and the lack of oversight has left too many victims among those working for his ungrateful ass. A family breaking apart, piece by piece, and I have no idea how to stop it. I can barely protect myself.

"Hey!" Alma appears at my side. "I have to help Anna with something quick, so go on without me. I'll catch up with you after."

"Unbelievable," I say lightly, rolling my eyes as she leaves. I whistle for Rudi. Her nails skitter on the floorboards when she stops to sniff a suit of armor.

"What?" Elias asks, letting me steer us back to the castle's entryway.

"Alma begged to come along because she thinks you're cute." I can barely say it with a straight face. She didn't exactly make a secret of her opinions either. Deliberate grazes of his arms, bold remarks and compliments, laughing a touch too hard at his jokes. As a self-described hopeless romantic, Alma has never been subtle with her crushes.

"Oh." I'm rewarded by his cheeks flushing a violent pink.

"She's harmless. But wonderful." I shoulder open the castle's doors and step out into the crisp night. "So hurt her feelings and you will be dealing with me."

Elias gulps. "Noted."

"And before you ask, no, I do not also think you're cute."

"I—I wasn't going to . . . I don't think." He looks to the side as we descend the stone steps to the upper-tier courtyard. Awkwardness practically curls off him as he mumbles something under his breath. To my delight, it sounds a little like he also thinks Alma is cute.

He's desperate for a change of topic, and I've had enough fun to grant it, my grin as wide as a fox's.

"I'll introduce you to the gate guards. It's best to be on their good side if you ever come back drunk from the village pub at three in the morning. Friesen was left in the snow all night last winter because he said Wesley's wife had horse teeth."

"Also noted."

We walk past marble statues of antlered beasts glittering with fledgling frost to reach the second, wider set of stairs leading to the circled drive. The tipsy women from earlier cackle as one of them tumbles to the gravel. They appear to have lost their male companion; I can only assume he's enjoying the gardens as promised.

Prauen's main gate emerges from the bottom of the gentle slope in crenelated bricks of a rusted stone. Fifteen feet thick and two stories high, the wall houses the heavy portcullis and living quarters for eight guards.

Wesley's lanky frame is easy to spot as we near, and I raise my hand. It drops when I realize they and the two figures with them aren't looking in my direction. They stand directly beneath the spiked gate, staring into the trees that stretch beyond the road.

"What's the matter?" I call, stepping into the warm glow of the lanterns hung from the gateway's arch. Rudi runs to nudge Wesley with her nose, and Elias trails behind me as I draw level with the trio. "Is it that owl again?"

"Klaus found its nest and moved it deeper in," Hestia, the second guard on duty tonight, says in her eastern burr. She doesn't avert her eyes from the darkness. "Haven't been pelted by a rock in days."

"I swear I heard something," the petite, golden-skinned woman next to her says. I pay the fear in her voice no mind. I recognize her as a maid who arrived with one of the guests yesterday; she's just not used to the Forest at night. Wind whispering between the branches and fallen leaves, boughs creaking and breaking without warning, the low calls of animals and Forest Folk unseen but watching.

Wesley scoffs. "Wielinde is always making some noise, especially at night."

"You're not *listening*." The one-handed grip on her lapels looks tight enough to tear the wool. Perhaps she went for a walk while her mistress was occupied with dinner. She turns to me and Elias, expression imploring. "Out there. I heard a *voice*."

"Bough spirit," Hestia says dismissively. "They get tetchy during autumn, with all the changes to their heart trees."

I'm eager to add my own agreement when the wind twists sharply through the pines. Opposite the guardhouse and bordering the lone road out of Prauen, animal bones hang heavy from their lower boughs. They clack together like the first rolling pebbles of an avalanche. But beneath that unnerving sound, there's something more. Something I've never heard Wielinde speak before.

"Wait." Elias holds up a hand. "I—I think I hear it."

"Not you too." Hestia grumbles something about newcomers and their abject uselessness before pulling her uniform's coat closer around her stout frame.

There. There it is again. Like a gasp for air.

"No," I say slowly. "I heard it as well."

Not a voice, but a sound, stifled and mournful. The hair on the back of my neck rises. I leave the shelter of the gate, replacing the glare of the firelight at my back with silvered darkness. The

Scavenge Moon is still two weeks off, and the moon is but a thin sliver. I blink twice, straining to hear—*there*!

I squint down the road. Shadows and barely visible light play tricks on me, making the entire Forest seem to be moving if I stare too long in one spot. But then, on the side where the ground slopes away from stone, a flash of white.

Ignoring Wesley's protests, I creep forward. Rudi tries to run ahead, but a high whistle returns her to my side. Her tail stands erect and her ears are pinned back. When she stops completely, a ferocious growl ripping free, my stomach gives a sickening lurch.

My breath catches in my throat. The white lying on the side of the road . . .

A human hand, the body it belongs to still as ice.

Chapter Five

My feet slip on a patch of leaves, the rot beneath turning the drive slick. I barely steady myself in time.

"Elias." My voice is a thready whisper, ready to split.

"Here."

I jump to find him already behind me. A glass lantern sways in his grasp. He's taken Rudi's place at my side, the pointer still halfway up the drive and snarling like her life depends on it. It forces my mind back to that bear, and a deeper fear of what lies ahead sinks its fangs in. A dread that eats at my bones.

Whoever lies at the road's edge, they're not wearing a jacket. Elias holds the light higher, and it catches the satin sheen of a white shirt, a dark waistcoat unbuttoned. The hand I first spotted is limp. It rests in a pool of blood, fingers curled up toward the night sky. The size of it, the body—it must be a man.

I stumble forward with my heart stuck in my throat. Softly, I call, "Hello? Are you—?" I swallow, clear my throat. "Are you all right?" A jolt stutters through me when that horrible, promised-storm scent assaults my nose again.

My grip finds Elias's arm as the man's profile sharpens. One we last saw blundering out of the Great Hall on the arms of two women.

Emil. I think that's his name. The spare to the spare of a duke, who not half an hour ago was healthy and whole. Now he lies still in the fallen leaves, slowly staining them a deeper crimson.

But where's the blood coming from?

Flat on his back, Emil's vacant eyes stare at the rattling underside of a towering fir. At first glance, it looks as though he was cast aside—like a doll tossed by a petulant child. But all that keeps him from skidding down the slope is a large boulder, and beyond it snakes a muddy and uneven furrow across the Forest floor. Although the lantern throws patchy shadows between the boughs, the trail of blood through leaves is plain.

Whatever happened to Emil, it took place elsewhere. He crawled here in this state before finally dying. Not even moments ago, if that was his distress we heard.

Carefully, afraid to disturb the scene, I tread to his other side.

"Oh, *fuck*."

I whirl and vomit at the foot of a pine. All the banquet delicacies pilfered from the kitchen, spattered and wasted. I wave for Elias to stay back, my other hand pressing into the rough bark as I heave. Retch until there's nothing left but burning bile and spittle, and then I wish for a little more because I don't want to look again.

But there's no avoiding it. A bat screeches deeper among the trees, and I count the answering chirps while dragging in deep, slow breaths. Once somewhat composed, I straighten and return to the sight I fear is already irrevocably burned into my mind.

A bloody *hole*, the size of both my fists together and perfectly round, has been punched through Emil's left ear. Brown hair, flesh, and—I gag anew—bone. Gone. When Elias joins me, the blackness of it does not lessen in the light. His skull is simply . . . empty.

And I can't fathom how.

Especially when a single finger, half coated in blood, twitches.

Emil blinks watery eyes. A weak plea tumbles from his chapped lips. Rudi's yelps take on a frenzied pitch.

"Fuck," Elias exhales, staggering back and nearly slipping as I did. "*He's not dead.*"

I concur, speechless. Every sensible thought is stuck behind a door locked by confusion and horror. My knees sink to the ground in a stilted motion. Avoiding the pool of blood, I gather Emil's hand into mine. It spasms in my grip before tightening a fraction. His pulse flutters against my smallest finger.

Wrong, wrong, wrong.

By all accounts, this man should be *dead*. Lifeless as the creatures that once owned the bones swaying above my head. His brain is gone, yet he still moves, still tries to speak. It's the same as that wretched bear, and not one bit of it sits right.

My hold on him readjusts. I don't know why—there's nothing anyone can do for him. He's another guest I find loathsome, and I doubt getting to know him would change that. But not even he deserves to go through *this* alone.

"Katrin, what's going on?"

"No!" My head snaps up at the sound of Alma's voice. The vehemence in mine stops her in her tracks. Elias moves to block as much of Emil as he can. "Don't . . . don't come any closer. Stay there, please." I swallow hard.

"I-is someone hurt?"

"Go get help," I say, seizing the direction her question gives my mind. My thoughts still jimmy at the lock, but this—this is something I can grasp. "Go inside and find someone. Stefan, Klaus, *anyone.* Magnus!" I yell, remembering the castle's doctor. "Get Magnus. Quickly!"

Alma's shadowed figure nods. She grabs Rudi's collar and yanks the still-growling dog along with her.

Elias crouches before me. He sets down the lantern, and wax leaks from the candle as it adjusts to the slope of the drive. Its light reflects in his wide, distant eyes, drains the warmth from his skin.

"Do you have your knife?" he asks, voice gravelly.

When I stare uncomprehending at him, he repeats, "A knife, Katrin," sharper than before. "I didn't bring mine tonight."

Oh. I glance down at Emil's strained face and nod, reaching for the blade still sheathed at my thigh. We can't do much for him, and maybe he'll die on his own, but we can at least offer him the same mercy as the bear. I could use a rock, or my hands to break his neck, but what good will those be with a hole in his head already? The knife is easiest.

Elias takes it gingerly. He sets the cold tip along the uninjured side of Emil's head but must realize what I also did. The blade shifts to his throat yet hesitates still.

"The heart," I whisper.

A shaky inhale. He pierces the satin like sliding into water. The knife finds its mark. Emil releases a small, breathless squeak, mouth twisting. His eyes flutter shut a moment later.

"Whatever attacked that bear . . ." Elias's expression hardens as he withdraws the weapon. He cleans it with a clump of moss. "It did this, too, didn't it?"

I gently lay Emil's hand over his broad chest before taking my knife back and rising to my feet, feeling rickety. "Whoever, whatever—I don't know."

A flurry of footfalls erupts from the castle, heralding my uncle's arrival. He pauses at the top of the drive to exchange words with Wesley and Hestia before catching sight of us. Alma appears, and I groan as she hurries after him.

"Who is it?" Stefan calls. "Who's hurt—"

He breaks off when Elias steps aside. His heel accidentally nudges Emil, rocking his head toward my uncle's feet so that his ghastly wound is visible to all.

Alma shrieks. Her hands fly to cover her mouth. She gapes at Emil, visibly trembling in her horror. I move to comfort her, remembering too late the blood on my hands. My cousin whimpers and retreats a step, tears pouring down her cheeks.

"Here, here," Elias soothes. He offers his palms to show they're clean. "It's okay. You're okay. Come with me." Once she nods, he steers her off to the side with an arm about her waist.

Ever calm and clinical in the face of gore, Stefan squats and snatches up the lantern. From this angle, I see directly inside. I avert my gaze to not gag again.

I've seen animals killed. Of course, I have. It's part of my job. But like the bear, this was butchery for the sake of it. And this, a human—this is different.

Calculated too, a little voice at the back of my mind supplies. Why else would it take his brain and no more? The bear's bones and nothing else?

"Is Magnus coming?" I ask, trying to focus.

"As fast as he can. Went to fetch his bag first. That *smell,*" Stefan muses. His knee cracks as he stands.

"Same as the bear," I confirm.

"And you found him like this?" His attention fixes on me. I raise a hand to brush aside wisps of hair blowing into my face, again forgetting the red stains.

I nod. "He . . . he was still alive."

Stefan stills midway through lifting the lantern to the trees around us. "That's not possible."

My bark of laughter is choked, wet sounding. "And yet, same as the bear," I reiterate, feeling close to tears myself.

"This is not good." He breathes in deep and lets it out as a slow exhale through his mouth. I barely stifle another burst of laughter. What is *wrong* with me?

A bear without bones; a man without a mind. Whatever wants these things, it's not of this world, but the Forest. And it is proving to be a very dangerous threat.

Stefan's thoughts align with mine. "No one goes into Wielinde Forest alone. *No one.*" Said solely for my benefit, and I don't have the energy to be offended. "Not until whatever spirit or beast responsible is caught or migrates out. An animal is one thing, but when it starts preying on humans, and this close to Prauen . . ."

He doesn't need to finish that sentence.

All who live at the castle and in the village at the end of this road have done so in harmony with Wielinde. So long as we respect it and follow the few rules remembered through countless generations, the Folk leave us be. We take no life from the Forest without reason, what isn't used we return, and we claim only the spaces set with stone. It's a delicate balance we all obey. Stefan and I know ways to appease them, with teeth and small bones, how to get around their individual quirks, but even we aren't impervious if they're upset.

In the heart of the Forest, we live at their mercy, no matter what.

But never have they crossed the border of trees and bones to take what isn't *theirs*.

I don't understand the change now. Did we misplace a set of bones somewhere in the castle? Throw off the balance by mistake because we haven't emptied one bucket of entrails?

"All right, what's-s-s all the fuss now?"

My muscles stiffen, the command to flee ringing in my head. Even slurred by drink, that voice belongs to just one despicable person. Sure enough, the baron swaggers down the drive, stalked by his sober shadow, Felix. August holds his liquor better than most people I know, but he literally still clutches a cup from the feast, and it sets my teeth grinding.

Stefan turns as if to pass August, flinging an arm out to stop the other man. Felix's knuckles snap menacingly. "We have a serious problem, sir."

"So serious," he imitates, chuckling. I try to give him the benefit of the doubt. He hasn't looked down yet. I don't even think he's noticed me.

"Someone was murdered," Stefan hisses in his ear. He steps back, gesturing to Emil's body.

August tips his eyes, then his head follows. He blinks hard, imprinting the image of his dead friend onto the back of his eyelids. I expect him to rage, to throw a fit, to fret—hell, to sic Felix on my uncle.

Instead, he offers a small "I wondered where he'd gone."

"I believe this was the work of what we discussed earlier," Stefan says firmly. "Whatever attacked the bear probably did this, too, and for it to have happened this close, you need to order extra precautions. No guests outside without one of us gamekeepers—"

"My guests will do whatever the fuck they want," he cuts in. His dismissive wave sloshes wine onto the ground, mixing with the blood. "I don't care. My venison is getting cold. Just deal with it."

He stumbles a little as he pivots on his heel. Felix reaches out to steady him and is shoved away when he blocks August's view of something he finds far more interesting than a dead guest. My heart freezes in my chest.

Elias and Alma stand close together on the other side of the road. He talks quietly enough that I can't hear, but whatever he says seems to keep her calm. Elias draped his coat over her shoulders at some point. Those broad shoulders she likes so much mean the coat swamps her, but that doesn't make a difference.

It's just as August was outside the kitchen. The way his eyes wander over her figure, taking in the visible curves beneath her bodice, the flare of her skirts. Except this time, he does lick his lips.

My pulse restarts, fast enough to send a wave of dizziness through me. I want to button up that coat, stand in front of her, punch him in the stomach, claw at his eyes, unsheathe my knife. Heat sears through my chest. No option ends well, and digging my nails into my palms isn't enough.

"Baron Wagner." Stefan's voice hardens. If he noticed how the man just ogled his daughter, he gives no indication. "We cannot just 'deal with it.' We don't even know *what* we're dealing with. Nothing has ever killed this close to the castle before."

"Well, if you're s-s-s-so worried, offer yourself up as bait, then," he sneers. "One less person I have to pay to feed up here."

The simmering within me boils over with a scream of rage.

"That's it?" I splutter.

"Katrin," Stefan admonishes.

"No," I snap, brushing him away. "His friend was murdered, anyone at *his* castle could be in danger, and that's all he has to say?"

Salt rubbed in a wound, the baron flashes me a syrupy grin and *winks.*

"You really don't care, do you?" I stride around Emil, not stopping until I *feel* the heat of his drink-soaked breath on my face as he laughs.

Felix's hulking shape looms closer. "That's enough—"

"Felix. Fuck *off* for a minute," I snarl over August's shoulder. "He's not worth you."

My frustration wears fangs, but I'm surprised to learn the words bite too. For once, the hulking man heeds someone other than August. I wish it was because he's finally reading an awful situation correctly, but I know it's that he doesn't think I'm a threat. His narrowed eyes don't leave me, though, and his hands are ready to injure.

August peers down his nose at me, the ugliness inside oozing through his curled lip. It feels good to take up *his* space for once, however ill-advised it may be.

"Just deal with it—like it's spilled wine." My voice is deadly calm. "Do you care about anyone but yourself? Have you *ever*?"

"Who else would matter, dear Katrin?" he drawls.

"Your friends, family, the people who work for you? Would you seriously not consider their safety because it doesn't kiss you back or let you fondle them?"

"Katrin," Stefan warns sharply.

"I could be persuaded in the former," August says in a dark, quiet voice, all traces of drunkenness gone. "And in my experience with the latter, others can be too."

To my sickening horror, his gaze flicks back to Alma. Lingers. *Devours.*

I fight to hold my ground. To not bare my teeth at him like Rudi would. The world narrows down to a pinprick, nothing existing but the monstrous desire that sinks into the set of his mouth, the shine in his eyes.

"*Katrin.*" Stefan grabs my arm and yanks me back. Yet I can't look away from August. Something deep in the woods releases a chilling howl then, and I imagine it came from him.

With a clarity that nearly makes me vomit again, I know—*I know*—he's found a new target. A new young woman to abuse in the lonely shadows.

That cloying smile returns. "Have a good night, Katrin. And Stefan? Since you *work* for me, do your job and"—his gaze drops to my face—"deal with it."

With one last leer in Alma's direction, he saunters back to his precious feast and wine and venison and *selfishness*. I expel a scream behind clenched teeth.

"Take a walk!" Stefan snaps, pointing to the castle.

I tear free of his grip. "I'm fine here, thanks."

"Do *not* argue with me. Of all the reckless, foolish, irresponsible—"

"Keep going. There are a few more adjectives you can tack on there."

"Go. *Now.*"

I shy away from the growl that enters his voice. Even caught in the throes of my own anger, I know when to concede. I won't give him the satisfaction and storm off, though. I'll take my time, dragging my feet in a slow and measured retreat. I glance at Alma as I go, still standing close to Elias. She looks wan and distressed, and I desperately hope she didn't notice August's newfound intentions.

Wesley and Hestia wait beneath the gate, but I push past them and their questions. Rudi appears in the dark courtyard and falls into step without command. In the distance, the castle doors open and Magnus emerges, his cane leading the way down the stairs. He's too late—Emil is beyond his help now.

I jam my sticky hands into my pockets. My conversation with Elias earlier swirls to the forefront, and I laugh coldly. Everything I said about being okay—lies. I am *not* fine. I haven't been *fine* since that pitiful excuse for a man inherited his title.

And now he wants my cousin. My sister. Because he can.

Fear sits heavy in my stomach, but it's nothing compared to my fury. There's too much of it curdling inside me, and I don't know where to put it. I can't just rip it out and toss it aside like a bramble sprite from Rudi's fur. This emotion has roots deeper than any can see, coiling around every bone and tracing each vein, infiltrating my body so it's all I breathe and think.

Trapped in my thoughts, I don't realize where my feet carry me until I reach a dead end at the garden terraces. In the distance, the faint moonlight polishes the lake to glass, the peaks pearly grey. I should have told Stefan that Emil may have been snatched from this clifftop, but I'm too pissed to care. And if the beast wants to take me, too, it would make my life so much easier.

Turning my back on Wielinde, I sink to the cool ground, spine pressed to the stone railing. The hedge maze lurks before me as a towering wall. Rudi collapses beside me, panting but quiet. My fingers claw into her fur.

For all my anger, I don't know how to fix this. I don't know how to make it all stop. The loss of my family, of personal space, and dignity. Will more people die before August sees beyond himself? How long will he toy with Alma before moving in to claim her like he did Brigitte? A tear drips from my jaw.

My blurry gaze roams the border of the maze before settling on the luminous marble sculpture of the Breimar Stag in front of one entrance.

A rusted lock in my mind springs open, letting a dazzling light cut through the gloom.

Could it really be that simple? Chilled fingers swipe away my tears. My vision sharpens on the statue. In my heart, I know the only option we have to stop a man like August is to kill him. But there's only one way to murder without facing a single consequence. To show that I am a threat after all.

This year, I'll enter the Hunt. I'll find the Stag myself, and I'll claim the death of August Wagner for my prize.

We never take a life from Wielinde Forest without reason, and there is no better reason than this.

Chapter Six

NINE NIGHTS UNTIL THE SCAVENGE MOON

Rudi's growls curl deep in her throat. A constant rumble that hitches each time she breathes in.

I tighten my grip on the stick she tugs, foot digging deeper into the pebbled ground. "For heaven's sake, do you want me to throw it or not?"

She quiets and releases the hunk of wood. I quickly plant my other foot to avoid falling backward. While I huff tendrils of hair out of my face, Rudi sits, tail wagging. A forgery of patience.

"Silly girl." I hurl the stick into the lake. Frigid drops spray my face as she launches into the water. I don't usually let her swim this late in the year, when the weather turns fickle and grey, but the sun hangs in a cloudless sky today, sparkling on the surface—enough to keep the reed hobs confined to darker depths. I chuck a few small teeth in beyond the shallows though, just in case.

The lake reflects almost solid gold. Along the length of the shore, larches stand watch more than any other tree, resplendently dressed in needles blazing a bold yellow. They tower over other conifers like they no longer have something to prove, their true colors revealed.

A sharp, trilling whistle pierces the still air, and I spin to face the trees behind me. The unnatural mix of wren and snow sparrow calls stops me from reaching for my rifle. I swear the Forest echoes my response back, the bough spirits feeding on the song. Elias and

I agreed on the signal when we left Prauen this morning, so we don't shoot the other by mistake while checking traps.

Emil was found outside the castle's gate four nights ago. After two unexplainable deaths on the same day, there have thankfully been no more incidents since. But that hasn't stopped a strained mood from engulfing the castle. A shaken Alma returning to the kitchen with Elias's coat still about her shoulders was all it took for the news to spread. Soon, everyone knew what happened and wondered what may still lurk in those bone-laden trees, testing its boundaries.

A few days of inactivity isn't enough to assume the culprit has left the valley, and we are no closer to knowing *what* it is or how to defend against any future attacks.

Anger, a constant simmer in my veins lately, flares red-hot again. Greta was our authority on the magic of Wielinde, and her entire family left days ago because of the baron. Because he *preyed* on their daughter. An entire wealth of important knowledge in the castle, lost overnight.

Rudi paddles back to shore and drops the stick at my feet. I cringe as she shakes, water flying everywhere. She barks when I take too long to pick up the stick. I feed all my fury into the next throw.

Stefan won't let Elias and me leave Prauen without the other, but August still couldn't care less. Until it impacts him, the threat is apparently not worth acknowledging. I've seen several nobles go for walks beyond the castle walls without so much as a hairpin for protection. I want to scream at them all. Between them believing the Forest Folk as just some tale told to keep children inside at night, and the Breimar Hunt as merely a little game, I question if they even know what happened. Did any of them notice that Emil no longer drinks beside them at dinner? Do they even care?

I readjust the satchel slung across my body. Three dead hares lie stacked inside, stiff from a night in snares. They have no worries anymore, no fears. I wish I could say the same, but my priorities changed after Emil's death.

Too much of my day revolves around knowing August's whereabouts. I now spend enough time in the kitchen that Aunt Carolina threatens to give me a job. But I'm there to make sure Alma isn't alone, to invent tasks that will take her away when his honeyed voice whisks down the hall. At night, I check the bolt to our bedroom door twice before going to sleep.

She hasn't said it, but I know Alma is baffled by my behavior, yet I haven't the heart to explain. There's no sense worrying her if nothing comes of it.

And I intend to make sure that nothing does.

Four nights have passed and I remain certain about what I need to do. What I *must* do to protect my family. I've barely slept, going over it again and again in my mind, looking for a single reason that would keep me from entering the Hunt.

I can't.

No one uninvited has entered the Breimar Hunt. I assumed it was some ironclad rule, that you must receive an invitation to bind yourself to the Stag's magic. But last night, watching the play of Alma's candle on the ceiling, I realized the truth hiding in the Hunt's history.

The Stag appeared in Wielinde Forest long before the first stone of Prauen Castle was laid. The people who lived in this valley before the Wagners, they had the secrets of the Hunt and its magic forced out of them by the first baron. Like all things in the Forest, the Breimar Stag arrived to maintain an unspoken balance, and they participated to honor the beast. He sought a life, and they gave one, willingly.

It was that first usurping Wagner who turned the Hunt into a petty rich person's game. No one else can afford to waste weeks drinking their weight in ale before brandishing a gun to eliminate a rival without blood spilled—but there's no rule that can stop someone from entering. In the Stag's eyes, a life is a life, no matter how fancy their clothes or large their homes.

The only doubt that tugs at a loose thread in my conviction is how to enter quietly. August cannot know. He's not a complete fool. I think half the reason why he antagonizes me is because he knows I hate him. He'll piece together my motives quickly, and by then it'll be too late to touch me. The binding of the Hunt puts protections on all participants until the Scavenge Moon sets to prevent them from taking any deaths for themselves.

But that doesn't mean August won't go after my family instead.

If he finds out I entered the Hunt alongside him, there's no telling what he'll do to make me regret that choice. Especially to Alma. The thought alone puts me in a cold sweat. Not to mention he could fire Carolina and Stefan, set Felix on them in the night, or frame them for theft and have them thrown in jail. And if he discovers me and I *don't* kill the Stag, the Lohens won't be the only family leaving Prauen in the dark for their safety.

Never mind that by entering the Hunt, I'll be on equal footing with the nobles, bound to the same magic. No matter what, one hunter will die.

They're all possible consequences of my decision that make me want to curl up beneath my bed and never leave, but I won't let them happen. I refuse. I *will* have my death.

I'm not a fool for thinking I can win, either. Only Stefan is a better sharpshooter than me in these mountains, and by the slimmest margin. And unlike the nobles, I won't be drinking or messing around while in these woods I know like the back of my hand. They don't stand a chance against me.

Now if the Stag would just show himself so the binding magic can be released. There's still been no sign of him. Elias and I are out here looking for him as much as we are for the mysterious Forest spirit with a penchant for stealing body parts. This is the latest in the moon cycle the Breimar Stag has ever eluded us. It gnaws at my already tenuous confidence.

Another mixed birdcall and the crunch of Elias's footsteps carries over the water lapping the rocky shore. We agreed to meet at the lake after we each checked a trapline. The balance between staying together while helping Elias learn the lay of the Forest and keeping a horde of snobs fed is a fine one, but hungry nobles trump an overabundance of caution—we'll suffer the brunt of their distress otherwise.

Elias appears in fits and starts, broken by the trunks and branches, before he emerges farther down the shore. Rudi splashes toward him and instantly captures his attention. I whistle through my teeth, startling them both. He offers a funny little wave and picks his way to my side. A grouse wing hangs out the side of his game satchel.

"Any trouble?" I ask.

"Not too bad. Had a run-in with a lichen nyx, but I left a tooth like you suggested and it flew off." He pats the spot over his heart where he tucked the small bag of teeth I gave him yesterday, looking oddly pleased with himself.

"Told you."

"Saw a heart tree too." Elias throws Rudi's stick, but she appears to be done, her panting loud in the cold quiet. It lands with a pitiful splash, abandoned. "But thankfully it looked to be occupied."

"Count your lucky stars it was," I say with a laugh, readjusting both my rifle and bag. "Come on. We'll check one more trapline, then head back."

We walk through the trees in silence. The sun cuts between the branches in thick shafts, illuminating the motes floating in the air and burnishing our trail of moss. It also makes the shadows beyond darker.

At the first stream crossing, my boot leaves a deep imprint in the mud as I hold out an arm for Elias to stop.

"What's—?"

I whirl, shoving a finger against his lips hard enough to reveal white teeth. Barely louder than the babble of water, I whisper, "Walk along the bank, that way. Don't touch the water."

He lowers my hand from his mouth and leans around me.

This stream, one of many that stem from the mountain slopes, is easy enough to cross. The banks are a few feet apart, the bed inches below the surface. Red elderberry and dogwood shrubs dot either side. Nothing out of the ordinary at first glance, but you need to know what you're looking for.

At its center, the water traces an invisible barrier. Ripples ricochet outward, twisting around a contour of tranquility on the surface. In the exact same shape as a person lying face down in the water.

Elias breathes over my shoulder, intrigue in his voice. "*Stream barrow.*"

"And teeth will not help with this one," I say, nudging him to follow Rudi.

Minutes later, we cross upstream using a fallen tree. It may not be deep water, but I've seen stream barrows drown men in less.

Elias takes the lead, talking quietly to Rudi as she trots at his side. My fingers worry at the end of my messy braid. A frown creases my brow as I watch him. I've encountered many a stream barrow in my life, but usually their outline is more childlike. That one was as tall as an adult. And come to think of it, the moss mite from the other day, I've never seen one move that fast before. But that's not what bothers me the most.

I stop and blurt out, "How did you know?"

He glances over his shoulder and does a double take when he realizes I'm no longer behind him. "Know what?"

"The stream barrow. How'd you know what it was? I haven't told you about them yet." He opens his mouth to answer, but another thing he said earlier pokes at me. "And the heart tree you saw—I never showed you one of those."

He shrugs and shoves his hands in his pockets. "Is it a secret?"

"No, it's just . . ." In my confusion, I struggle to find the right words without coming off as accusatory. I don't even know what I'd be accusing him of. "For a stranger, you've taken everything in stride remarkably well, like you've been in Wielinde before."

"First time."

"To the village?"

"The other night was also my first."

"Then how do you not only accept the Forest Folk, but you're *excited* to see them?" The nobles who come for the Hunt don't even believe in their existence, yet he does as easily as breathing. "No one does that unless they spend most of their life here, and I know you haven't. Not with that accent."

Elias offers a light laugh, void of teasing or belittling. "Not everyone the Wagners forced out of Wielinde moved south."

My jaw drops. "You mean—?"

"My family has roots in this Forest as deep as any tree."

He reaches beneath his coat collar and pulls out the silver medallion that hangs from his neck. The same one I saw when we first met. I step closer without asking, pinching the metal warmed from his skin between my fingers. Etched roughly on its surface is a pair of antlers crossed by a bare branch—the same symbol Greta wears at her wrist.

"My mother put me to bed with tales of mushroom goblins and shadow gaunts." Elias tucks the medallion away. "She died last year, so when I saw the posting to work here . . . it felt a little like coming home. Wielinde has my respect, not my fear."

A splutter sticks in my throat. "A little fear is healthy. Keeps you on your toes."

He snorts.

"Did your mother by chance tell you a story about a Folk who steals body parts?" I hate the hopeful note that lifts the end of the question.

"Afraid not. Whatever did that, I'm as in the dark as you are." Suddenly, his gaze locks on something over my shoulder, eyes widening, and that vital fear seeps into my muscles. "What exactly are we looking for, to find the Stag?"

My head tips to the side, surprised by the change in topic. "He leaves markings. Obvious ones."

"So, like that?" He points behind me with a single finger.

It's as though my very soul knows right where to look. I don't hesitate once I turn. My foot slips into a grassy burrow, but I barely notice. I push myself back up and press on. Not stopping until I touch the jagged scratch in the boulder and convince myself it's real.

A set of four lines gouged deep into the stone, dripping gold like sap from a tree. A coppery scent floods my senses like an old penny placed on my tongue. Rudi tries to lick the longest rivulet, and I tap her nose away. I know as it hardens, the gold will retreat into itself and pack the marks like gilded plaster. Then nothing green will grow within a hand's width until the next Scavenge Moon. Old scratches like these are all over the Forest, hidden beneath layers of moss and lichen and mushrooms. Hundreds of years' worth.

"If Alma asks," I murmur, heart racing, "I saw it first." Bet or no, she is *not* cutting my hair.

"We'll discuss that later, because I think I see another up ahead."

Elias and I rush through the trees, failing in the thrill of our discovery to keep our steps quiet. Rudi races ahead with wolfish grace. With every crush of undergrowth, each new set of markings spotted, a small knot of anxiety I hadn't noticed unravels in my chest. The Breimar Stag has never had a hand in my own fate before and I feel like I can breathe again.

The golden trail leads us to a wide, rocky ravine. I nearly twist an ankle when I skid down the steep slope, my hand pressing a moss-slick cobble to regain my balance. Rudi circles back, tail wagging as she waits for me to stand upright again. Elias lands with a curse.

A great river must have once carved it from the bedrock, but now the ravine is fed only by rain and snowmelt. All that remains is a narrow ribbon of stagnant water and a handful of pools twitching with insects.

"This way." I hurry northward. My boots keep slipping on the rocks, forcing my gaze to the ground. I divert around a larger pool and—

Between one step and the next, the air thins and *presses* down. A compression that makes me clutch at my throat for fear of suffocation. I stop, fighting not to double over while blackness pulses at the edges of my vision. Elias gasps when he comes to my side in concern, and I know he feels it too.

Rudi clatters over the rocks, shifting my harried focus. She races ten paces ahead of us and freezes, nose pointing to something around the bend. Then, the strangest thing, she lowers herself to the ground with a soft huff. It takes everything within me not to follow suit. I reach out and squeeze Elias's arm, keeping him still while using him to stay steady as *he* steps gracefully into view.

Antlers larger than the width of my arm span, legs as tall as my shoulder. Eyes glowing the burnt ochre of a dying coal. An ethereal golden glow clings to his frame, exuding an impossible sense of power.

The Breimar Stag.

This is the closest I've ever come to him; I can think of nothing but to be in awe. His ghostly aura sparkles as tears well in my eyes.

Regal and sure—and ignoring us entirely—he dips down to drink. One of his many antler points scrapes an old log, leaving behind a weeping line of gold. Every movement ripples muscles beneath a coat that can't stay a solid color in the dappled sunlight.

A snow-white on the surface, but ever restless. Silver, gold, palest blue—each individual hair shifts. When his head lifts, it's a sharp and deliberate move to look directly at me. Through me. Under the flesh and between my bones to my very core. One blazing eye catches a ray of sunlight, setting it on fire.

I choose to see it as a sign.

After everything I've considered and worried about for myself, for Alma, for everyone I love, finding the Stag like this—it's a vindication. Staring him in the eye, the intelligence that flames in that golden gaze, he sees all of me. This beast that passes through the veil of the Forest from an unearthly realm knows *me*.

His chin raises the smallest bit, as if in challenge. A competitor meeting a worthy opponent at last. I wonder if he knows what he can give me. How the death of a single man taken with him can change my entire life.

The Stag extinguishes our connection by shutting his eyes. The gesture reads as acceptance, an acknowledgment that more is required of him now that he's been found.

All at once, something is undone, set into motion. A tremor slithers through the ground, magic spreading outward from the Stag and nearly bringing me to my knees. It stretches unseen beneath us, tugged thinner and thinner, the world feeling heavier with every hard-won breath until . . . everything stills. The air loosens like a taut string snapping. I no longer feel like I'm being smothered. His white aura fades beneath his coat, vanishing altogether.

With all the confidence of a predator, he turns away and gallops across the cobbles, vanishing around the bend and out of sight.

Elias and I both exhale at the same time.

Let the Hunt begin.

Chapter Seven

EIGHT NIGHTS UNTIL THE SCAVENGE MOON

Dawn breaks over a scene of chaos. Prauen's lower courtyard is a mess of whinnying horses and shouting. With every clop of hooves that spills through the doorway of my uncle's workshop, a string pulls tighter around my stomach.

"Knives," Stefan says brusquely. Not only is he on edge for the first true day of the Hunt, but I accidentally spilled his coffee too—an expensive luxury Carolina orders specially for him, despite my insistence he skim off the baron's stash. I'm quick to oblige and pass the two sheathed hunting knives across the stained table.

In exchange, he slides several boxes of rifle shells toward me. "Make sure you've got enough on you."

I nod, unable to trust my voice. Before slinging his rucksack over his shoulder, he pauses to give me a once-over, beginning from my tightly braided hair and ending with my hands, busy oiling the bolt removed from my rifle. He exhales roughly through his nose.

"It's a bolt, Katrin, not a bar of soap. You need to be able to grab it." Then he leaves me alone in the soft light of the overhead lantern. Petra and Milo scramble up from the lumpy cushion they share in the corner and hurry after him.

I glance down at the part with a curse. He's right: It's lubricated enough that it slips through the cloth, landing on the tabletop with a clatter. Shaking my head, I drop heavily on the nearest wobbly chair. Rudi rises from her place by the smoldering hearth to sit beside me, head on my lap. She alone senses my tangled nerves. I stroke her head, dragging a finger up her snout and between her eyes, hoping it will calm me as it does her.

There's no avoiding my decision to enter the Hunt now. I think I've figured out how I'll do it without anyone knowing, but it'll be risky. All the confidence built up in my chest over the last few days has turned to mush. The string around my stomach constricts tight enough to tie a neat bow.

Outside, the sky is lightening. The tumult in the courtyard grows even louder as the saddled horses are led through the archway that leads to the main gate. I need to go. Time ticks forward, and it's not waiting for me to steady myself.

"Get a grip," I whisper, scraping my chair closer to the table and reassembling the bolt piece.

When I lay the completed rifle down, a knock sounds at the open door.

"Morning," Alma calls, far too happily for this time of day, stepping inside with a large, covered basket. Rudi trots to greet her with a wagging tail.

Elias is close on my cousin's heels, and ready to go from the looks of it. I suspect Alma's sunniness is mainly due to her spending time alone with him. Her crush hasn't diminished one bit, especially after he shielded her from the grisly sight of Emil's body. The best part—Elias doesn't seem to mind. Her smile as he steps aside to let her pass turns his cheeks pink. It loosens some of the tightness inside me. No, he doesn't mind at all.

"Morning," I reply, pleased to find my voice level.

"Where's Pa?" She heaves the basket onto the table. The wicker creaks as she releases the handle.

"Out front already. I was about to join him."

"Well, not without this, you're not." She yanks open a cabinet and grabs three saddlebags, stuffing them with the food unveiled in the basket. Dried meats, flasks of elderflower juice, cheese, and my favorite grained brown bread. She waves something wrapped in cloth before placing it in the bag for Elias. "Made this without raisins, just for you."

His blush deepens, and my heart lifts. This is what Alma deserves. Not August's disgusting notice, but a kind boy who gets flustered by a bun made specially for him. It's a temporary reprieve from my uneasiness of what's to come.

"And for you . . ." Alma tosses a piece of meat to Rudi, who snatches it without so much as a blink. The begging wretch.

"Nervous about today?"

"What?" I jolt, looking to Elias. Heat creeps up my chest.

He frowns but takes my reaction in stride. "Your uncle told me this is the first time you're taking a hunting group out by yourself, and you look kind of . . . pale."

Alma snorts; she constantly teases me about how pallid I am. Even after a summer that kept me outside every day, all I have to show for it are more freckles that have already faded.

"Oh," I say with a too-loud laugh. My attention diverts to loading my rifle. With each shell slotted inside the chamber, I pretend it's my anxiety leaving my fingers. "Right. No, I'm not nervous about that. Excited, actually."

Last time the Stag came, I was fourteen and forced to tag along with either Stefan's or Otto's group. This is the first Hunt we're able to split the nobles into three groups, each led by a gamekeeper. We'll move faster and be able to watch out for wildlife and Folk with fewer bodies to supervise. It won't lessen the noise about to be made in Wielinde, though, if the whining I've heard the last few days is anything to go by. I swear it's half the reason the Stag is left unharmed most seasons—he hears everyone coming from a mile away.

This will be my first time leading a hunting party, and I intend to abandon it the moment I see the Stag's tracks. I only wish the thought didn't make my stomach feel this rancid.

"You sure you're okay?" Elias nudges softly. Alma glances up from her packing, expression curious. I don't like that he notices my tension. Stefan didn't, Alma hasn't, so why does this near stranger sense what I'm certain I've masked so well?

"Yes." I plant my palms on the table and rise, straight-backed. "Just tired. That's all."

"All right," he says, finally removing his piercing gaze. A black mare rearing in protest snags it instead. Her large hooves land with solid metallic thuds.

Like Rudi, these northern draft horses are bred for the rugged terrain of Wielinde. They stand a hand shorter than the thoroughbreds favored by those living beyond these mountains, but twice as proud and heavily muscled. I don't envy the stable hands who'll have to groom their thick coats later. Bramble sprites tend to hitch a ride in their long manes and tails, making the horses irritable and bitey until the thorny little imps are removed.

"Here we go." Alma passes a packed bag to Elias, and two to me.

"Make sure that gets to Pa. You know how cranky he is when he's hungry. Worse than any whinging noble."

I snort, knowing exactly what she means. She's just like him in that respect.

Rucksack and rifle in place on my back, I face the doorway. The tightness in my gut worsens, my heart flying into my throat. No sense putting it off any longer.

"I want the black mare," I declare. I need some of her spirit to rub off on me.

The bones we hang from the trees act as the shoreline between the natural and the artificial. To one side stands Wielinde. On the other, Prauen Castle and its winding trail of cobbles to the village of Steigert. A gruesome border of femurs, hip bones, and gaping skulls.

Only one place blurs that boundary between *theirs* and *ours* beyond recognition. If Wielinde is the sea, and Prauen an island, Atlin Bower is the tip of a peninsula. A spit shrinking in size from a rising tide of saplings.

I secure my horse's lead to a low branch and move to Elias's side on the edge of the clearing. Rudi and Petra settle themselves among the four horses—one for each hunting party and August's white gelding—content with their giant friends. Milo tries to entice the roan into playing with him, but a stamped hoof startles him into submission. The nobles, now eleven in total, stand in a crescent moon formation facing the center of the Bower. Behind them lurks Felix, who stands on the shaded path back to the main road. If the trees were thinner, less crowded, I could see the castle's towering spires from here.

So close to the safety of home, yet this location could not feel more isolated or wild.

A copse of red maples rings Atlin Bower, and there are few creatures slender enough to slip into the narrow spaces between their lichen-crusted trunks. The trees grapple for one another across the clearing. Bare branches tangle overhead, casting shadows to create an unshakable twilight. From every gap hangs a polished white bone. No wind blows, yet they sway from lengths of sturdy twine, clacking like the chatter of teeth in winter. Garnet-red leaves carpet the grass, concealing treacherous roots and crackling without remorse.

I breathe in the sweet scent of rot that undercuts everything else, relishing the marrow-deep reverence the Bower always fills me with. It's as though its significance waits in the motes sparkling in the air. Each year, these maples curl a little closer, their crowns higher, roots digging deeper. I think Elena tried to clear the Bower, but there's just too many leaves, catching the nobles ankle-deep in red. Already I hear grumblings about chilled feet and stones in boots.

Positioned before them all are Stefan and the baron.

August appears unchanged. A man wearing power, and comfortable in how it fits over his shoulders. The loss of his friend did not make a single impression, and it tightens my hand around the hilt of the knife at my thigh. That now-familiar anger bubbles nearer to the surface, boiling away some of my nerves.

His life is mine to play with, and I wish he knew that.

Stefan brushes dry leaves and growths of moss off the remains of a large, unnamed tree in the heart of the clearing. A stump really, but a monolith in truth. Ravaged by time and the cruel elements, its bark was stripped long ago to leave behind smooth, petrified wood. I know from playing here as a child that when you climb atop it, there exists a hole that must lead to the bottom of the world. We would drop items down it only to never hear them land. It's no wonder this place is thought to be where the Breimar Stag steps through each time.

"Is that the Binding Alder?" Elias asks in my ear.

I nod, but August's loud voice prevents further explanation.

"Welcome, friends," he yells to silence the others. His arms fling wide, almost smacking my uncle. "To the one hundred and second Breimar Hunt."

Hands lift in applause. The pattering sound is muffled by their gloves, sounding like the hollow gesture it is. Breaches in the wall of honoring the Stag and the Forest, patched with disrespect. It's all just a lark to them. Being invited grants them prestige and mystery among their wealthy friends back home, and any glimmer of hope to advance their already gilded stations in life is enough for them. They don't care nor understand that they're entering a contract only fulfilled when someone dies. They never do.

"As you are all new to this legendary event as *my* esteemed guests," August continues, "there are a few rules."

A groan rises above the click of bones, and a few of the nobles begin careless side conversations. My mouth tastes sour. I eye the shrewish woman who produces a nail file from her pocket and works on her left hand, fervently hoping she won't be in my group.

"I know, I know." August waves his hands to stem the dissent. A vein pulses in his temple, and I can tell he's annoyed by the clear lack of deference to him. This is his first Hunt as host, his first time inviting the people he wants, yet his late father commanded far more respect from his guests. He hides it well behind that sickening charm, though. His smile—lovely, white, and straight—is his greatest deception. A beautiful flower with poison in its pollen. "But who are we to turn up our noses at tradition when tradition demands order to function?"

Elias bumps my shoulder to whisper, "Considering this lot hasn't caught so much as a mouse, order is the least of their problems for this Hunt."

"They catch colds pretty easy, though," I reply, watching one lanky, glassy-eyed man blow his nose into a handkerchief with a deafening honk.

Our shared snorts echo between the trees. Stefan shoots us a severe look, and I quickly school my expression to one of indifference.

"Gamekeeper!" August calls. "The blade, if you will."

Stefan moves toward the Binding Alder, reaching with hands sheathed in leather gloves. Of all the objects fed to it, only one item refuses to be lost to the depths of the pale wood. Although knowing nothing will happen, I hold my breath as he grasps the polished bone hilt that protrudes from the top of the stump. Despite the moss that seals it in place, the blade now pulls free in a smooth motion. The silver metal glints bright and razor-edged in the dimness. Balancing it across both palms, Stefan carefully offers the knife to August. There's no significance to the gesture—the Wagners just enjoy the pageantry they forced upon the event centuries ago.

August picks it up in one fist. His wrist turns so the light races along the sharp length, reflects upon his smug face. The steel is no longer than the hunting knife I wear and looks no more useful, but the two weapons could not be more different. A knife as old as the Hunt itself, and just as steeped in magic.

"It is here, my friends," he says softly, for now he has the attention he craves. Even the birdsong and skitter of creatures have fallen silent. "That order shall be drawn forth from chaos."

As he holds the knife aloft, his jacket shifts to reveal his personal dagger strapped to his belt. A gaudy thing of gold that I doubt is used for anything other than spearing sausage at the banquet table, yet the binding knife is still the more impressive weapon. It draws every gaze like the eyes of a shadow gaunt in the dark.

"Allow me to demonstrate."

August shoves his jacket sleeve up. The heavy velvet bunches too tight, unable to move farther, once he exposes a few inches of his forearm. For what comes next, I'm impressed he doesn't hesitate, and immediately bite the thought in half.

Quick as the snap of a bone, the blade slices over the skin of his wrist. A thin cut as long as my thumb emerges. Blood wells, spilling in a single ruby tear.

"So begins my binding to the Forest I stand within," he says in an uncharacteristically humble voice.

He turns to the Alder and sets the knife on its surface, gentle, as though atop an altar. Several drops of blood spatter the leaves before he drags a finger over the wound. A long, slow movement smears it across the wood's side.

"To the pursuit of the Stag through its depths."

The blood sizzles, turns molten. It flares bright crimson.

"To the power that wakes beneath every root and above every bough."

It spreads of its own accord, defying nature to form a slender horizontal line in the desiccated wood. A mirror to his self-inflicted wound.

"Until the moon herself releases me from this bond."

August's blood sinks into the wood. A black strike remains, dry and binding as ink. An agreement between him and Wielinde. Fixed in mountain stone and impossible to dissolve until the Scavenge Moon sets.

He closes his eyes and shivers as though something unpleasant just poured into his body. When he opens them, triumph shines in his cold gaze. The cut on his wrist no longer bleeds. Instead, it gleams from within, a scar as golden as the markings left by the Stag, to blaze until the end.

Then he beckons the first person forward.

"Shit," Elias breathes. "That's all it takes?"

I nod, my voice untrustworthy once more. That's *all* it takes. From the way the blood courses through my veins, I want to move. Run. Snatch that knife from August's hand and repeat what he did. It requires every ounce of patience I have to listen to the small voice in my head. I'll only get one chance to do this right.

The second person to join the Hunt accepts the knife, but cynicism weighs the young, petite countess's shoulders. After a few false starts, she removes her glove and presses the knife—still wet with August's blood, I notice with disgust—to her light brown skin. She cut her palm, the fool. That'll only cause her pain. Her panicked expression declares she realizes the mistake, too, but her hand barely shakes as she smears her blood across the wood.

After the injury turns gold, the ritual complete, she looks at it in annoyance. "What was that supposed to do?" she complains. "You made me smear blood all over some dirty log like a heathen, and for what?"

I groan under my breath. When Elias glances askance at me, I gesture with my chin. "This happens every time." The same disdain always rears its ugly head this way, but what inevitably comes next isn't easy to watch. They think all this beneath them when they cannot grasp the scope of what this binding is. Until . . .

"Oh, Ilse," August simpers. "It's quite simple."

In a smooth motion, he pulls a revolver from inside his coat, presses it to Ilse's temple, and squeezes the trigger.

Several people scream. The much older man I know to be her husband bellows in fury, held back by the sudden appearance of Felix. The shot reverberates through the Bower. The hanging bones above all shiver.

Smoke issues from the gun as August lowers it.

The countess is still standing. Barely. She doubles over, shrieking and clutching the bullet wound. No blood leaks between her fingers, though.

August holsters the pistol and rolls his eyes. "Enough with the theatrics, Countess." He looks to his audience and mocks in a deeper voice, "Women."

The few startled guffaws are drowned out by the rushing in my ears.

A moment later, Ilse pulls herself upright and slowly lowers her hand. Black soot marks her temple, but the skin is whole. There's an obvious dent, a thumbprint pressed deep into her skull, yet even that quickly smooths itself out as the binding magic proves its value. She shakes her head, as if to knock out the bells that surely ring, and nearly falls over. August bends to collect the spent bullet from the leaves. Between thumb and forefinger, he unveils a crushed ball. As if it had encountered an impenetrable wall of steel rather than a fragile skull.

A palpable change sweeps through the nobles. A monumental shift in their beliefs that they should have possessed from the very start.

"The binding protects us," August says, reveling in how everyone clings to his speech. "While the Hunt is ongoing, no permanent harm may come to a hunter by any but the Forest. We enter this game to claim the life of a rival, an enemy, who may well be among us now, but the Hunt keeps us honest. No bullets in the back to pretend you won or make your desired death look like an accident. Not without putting in the work. Right, Lotte?" he adds with a wink.

The pale, blond woman who was cleaning her nails earlier has the grace to blush. She casts a malicious grin at the man with dark brown skin behind her, the owner of the only textiles company in the entire kingdom who can still outbid hers on lucrative contracts. "No hard feelings, Schultz. It's only business."

He smirks, refusing to look at her. "I'll tell your wife the same thing when I attend your wake."

A titter sweeps through the group. They turn to snickers as Ilse, wan and a little unsteady on her legs, returns to her husband's side. He tries to reach for his young bride, and she rips her arm away, snapping at him with a thunderous expression. I can guess what name she would give the Breimar Stag.

Emboldened by what they witnessed of the countess, the rest of the nobles now line up swiftly. They move forward to claim the knife and their share of invincibility the moment the next is done, boasting about who they'll kill and placing wagers on others.

A woman, forearm freshly golden, passes by Elias and me. To her companion, she says in an undertone, "That party trick the baron pulled? Wagner tradition. My mother was a guest of August's father years ago, and apparently someone new is always shot or stabbed."

As the pair walk away, I overhear the other remark how dark the demonstration is. But this is a Hunt to indirectly kill another human. The whole thing is dark.

The moment the thought enters my mind, though, the reminder that I am ready to fit into that storyline this year hits me with a visceral lurch. With each person done signing their blood, my heart ramps up a little faster. A high-pitched ringing starts in my ears. I'm terrified of what I'm about to do while also desperate to do it.

Finally, Felix is the last to complete the ritual. This surprises me. I didn't expect the guard to join. While in the Hunt, August is invincible to the other hunters, so I'm not sure if he's participating because he wants to or because August ordered it.

"Right." The baron holds the knife and hands it lazily behind him for Stefan to take. "Now that that's done, let's get on with it. Felix, with me. You, boy." He snaps his fingers at Elias as though speaking to Rudi. "Bring me my horse."

"*Boy?*" Elias says incredulously under his breath. He turns to fetch the white gelding and the roan horse he's claimed for his hunting party and calls for Petra. Without a dog of his own, Stefan insisted one of the foxhounds accompany his group. "I'm bigger than he is."

"He knows just how to make you smaller if you're not careful,"

I mutter. My gaze is fixed on Stefan, my insides a riot of nerves that thrash harder with his every movement.

As August and the others begin down the shadowed path that takes them into the heart of Wielinde, my uncle carefully wipes the knife clear of blood with a tattered but clean handkerchief. He turns to sheathe it in the Alder.

Where it will seal itself in place until the Stag returns next season.

"Stefan, *wait*—"

I lurch forward, voice catching at the end of my frantic cry. He freezes at the sudden crash of leaves. Only ten paces separate us, but now that I have to cross it, he feels so much farther. As if every step I take pulls the ground out from under me, tugging all my aims out of reach.

"Wait."

"Katrin, what's the matter?" He looks at me, brow creased. "We need to go."

I glance at the departing group. Elias's eyes narrow as he looks back over his shoulder from between the two horses, but he continues onto the path, vanishing into the gloom beyond the maples.

"Can I put the knife back?" The words stumble over one another, fighting to get out at the same time. Inside, I flinch.

Whenever I thought of how I would do this, the scenarios unfolded a dozen different ways. In my head, Stefan fought me, forced me not to do this, helped me, lectured me. In reality, my uncle almost disappoints me.

"Don't see why not." And drops the knife into my waiting hand.

My bare fingers snap shut around the hilt. It's heavier than I assumed. Like the marrow of the bone is cement rather than hollow. And cold, so cold I almost hiss through my teeth.

There's no going back now. With it in my grasp, only two options lie before me. I either bind myself to the magic and put myself at the Hunt's mercy, or I return the knife and hope the baron can be stopped some other way. And I'm not sure which I'll regret more.

I don't realize Stefan wants to leave until he comes up from behind, leading his dappled grey horse. "While we're young, please."

"Sorry," I say cheerily. I force a laugh into my voice, a smile onto my face, a casual shrug. "Just . . . wanting to savor the moment. First real Breimar Hunt and all that."

I can't even believe what I'm saying, but again, he doesn't do what I expect.

Stefan nods sympathetically. "I was the same at your age, for my first Hunt. Buzzing with more nerves than a summer hive. But I survived it, and so will you." He gently ruffles my hair. "Don't be too long, okay? I'll wait with your group at the fork until you come."

It takes about five minutes of walking until the wandering path branches into three—I'll only need two for this.

"Thank you," I whisper.

As he and his horse disappear through the trees, a corrosive guilt settles in the distance between us. *What the hell am I thinking?* Only nobles are despicable enough to do this. Without morals and values, thinking only of themselves and what they can gain through such nefarious means. How can I even consider lowering myself to their level for something so wicked? The Hunt beneath the Wagners' guidance is a warped version of what it once was. My grip on the knife loosens, arm twitching to extend.

But it always comes back to my reason for this. And it's a *damn* good one compared to their company profits and lines of succession. I'm not doing this just for myself. It's never been for me alone. Alma needs this, too, but so does Stefan, Carolina, the Lohens, and every other person who has suffered at the hands of *that* man.

My decision is made for me as I undo the first button of my coat. Keeping a firm grip on the knife, I pull my right arm free of its sleeve. I push my thick sweater up past my elbow and bare my pale skin to the murky light. The mark needs to be somewhere I won't accidentally reveal it, and this, too, I've thought through.

With a deep breath that stoppers my throat, I bring the knife down over the crook of my elbow. I don't even feel the cut. Too many other sensations spark through me. I don't mean to drop the knife, but I'm shaking as I drag two fingers through the warm blood. I smear it across the Alder where none of this season's hunters did. I'm not one of them.

"So begins my binding to the Forest I stand within," I say in a rush. "To the pursuit of the Stag through its depths. To the power that wakes beneath every root and above every bough. Until the moon herself releases me from this bond."

A torrent of something thorny and glacial and entirely awful streams into every limb. I close my eyes against the invasion, inhale sharply. I hate how this feels, as though something is coating my bones and replacing them with something that can't be broken but also isn't mine. A gruesome feeling that refuses to let go.

As abrupt as it started, the awful needling is ripped from my body. A weed wrenched up from the soil.

I open my eyes, and all I see is the golden scar. Tentative, I probe it with first one finger, then three. It's sensitive, overly warm, and proof.

It's done.

I quickly yank down my sleeve. The dark blue weave of the knit conceals the glow, and relief soothes my aching muscles. Delving beneath the leaves, I retrieve the knife and slam it home in the Alder. The moss crawls around the base of the hilt like a hundred tiny mites come to life.

I did it.

Chapter Eight

The nobles have dressed more appropriately. Gone are the thin silks and flimsy satins they arrived in. Each of the four in my hunting party wears heavier wool, tweed, and velvet, trimmed in the finest sable and mink money can buy. Leather gloves so new they creak. Boots with solid, unworn soles. They're warm against the chill and walking well enough.

Beyond that, the rest is exactly as annoying as I feared.

A flask taps my cheek *again*, and I smack it away. The metallic noise makes Sybil's ears flatten. I rub the black mare's neck before looking up at the lanky man teetering in the saddle. "For the last time," I say, each word uttered like a lash, "I do not want to share your liquor."

My refusal is no hardship for Jannik. Clutching the saddle horn, he tips back and drains the rest of the bitter drink. It's a miracle he doesn't *keep* tipping back. Whoever planted the idea in the viscount's head that alcohol would alleviate his cold is dead to me. He stopped walking in a straight line over an hour ago and I had no choice but to help him onto Sybil's back and unload his gun. His ruddy cheeks and nose are almost the same color as his auburn hair.

Alcohol is the last thing I need right now, but oh, do I want it.

Four nobles are more trouble than a dozen precocious toddlers.

Even with Rudi circling us, I need multiple sets of eyes. Not to watch for signs of the Forest Folk or the Breimar Stag, but to make sure none of them do anything stupid. Just because they can't harm one another doesn't mean they won't fall into a ravine and break their necks.

"Why does this tree look like this?"

I glance over Sybil's mane in the direction of Lotte's voice. The blond textiles magnate has stepped off the narrow game trail and stands staring at a dogwood tree.

"No," I blurt. "Shit, get back."

Releasing Sybil's lead, I duck under her head and leap over a holly bush to yank Lotte away. Shrill protests are inevitable, but I don't care. Neither does Rudi. She sits beside the horse and adds her howls to the din. The tall woman weighs more than me, but I'm stronger. I don't release Lotte's rich, pink velvet sleeve until I force her back onto the path behind a curious Ilse and Gerwin.

"*Never* go near heart trees. Am I clear? Quiet, Rudi," I snap at my dog.

Lotte sneers down at me, her sharp features made fox-like. "It's just a tree—"

I step closer. "*Am I clear?*"

"Take it easy, little girl." She straightens the shiny white fur around her collar. "Fine. I won't go near the creepy tree again."

"Or any of them," I insist, hackles raising at the "little" comment. She can't be more than ten years older than me. "If it has a face, assume it's prettier than you and ignore it."

She scoffs and forces herself between the other two, ending the conversation.

Eyes closed, two fingers massaging the space between my brows, I allow myself a moment of pretend solitude.

Three hours. *Three hours*, and we've maybe traveled a couple of miles north through Wielinde. Seen nothing of the Stag. Not even a mark. And with all the noise this group makes, it'd be a miracle if he was even within ten miles of us. And knowing I may have to go through another week of this—I might cry.

Respite over, I return through the holly to fetch Sybil. Left unattended, she wandered off-trail to graze, bringing along an oblivious Jannik singing drunkenly under his breath. Before I guide her back, I pause to examine the face in the dogwood.

When a bough spirit takes a person to wed, it's often a drag to the altar. Once she lures you in, there are no vows spoken, no rings exchanged—you simply become one inside her heart tree. The fine ridges in the grey bark of this tree curve and protrude to form a woman's face. Except—I lean closer, frowning. Most of the visages I find pressed into the wood from the inside boast miserable expressions. It's rare to find a bride or groom who went willingly, but I've never seen *this* before.

The round face taken by the dogwood is frozen in utter anguish.

When the branches above rustle, I gasp and quickly pull Sybil away. Even when occupied, bough spirits are no less aggressive when it comes to protecting their spouse. Best to keep a distance.

I lead the horse and Rudi past the others and expect them to follow. Lotte watches me with a murderous expression, but Ilse is too busy drinking primly from her own flask. Black powder still dusts the countess's temple and dark hair where August shot her. Even if the bullet didn't harm her, she felt it as brutally as though it had. I suspect she encouraged Jannik to drink for his head cold, but I think she does it to settle her lingering edginess.

And to escape Gerwin's incessant monologuing.

"Pearl inlaid. Sailed as far west as you can go to get these beauties done. Cost a king's ransom, but it was worth it. See how it shines? I polish them twice a day. With special oil too."

My teeth grind, jaw clicking. If I hear one more word about those stupid revolvers—I tug my woolen hat farther over my ears.

The two women and Jannik carry rifles, pristine and probably used for little more than trips to country estates. They aren't like mine, handled daily for survival, but will cause the same damage. Gerwin wears two silver revolvers at either hip like some kind of outlaw, good for nothing but close range. And after the demonstration the shipbuilding mogul gave Ilse earlier, I cannot imagine he'll hit a single thing anyway, even with nine bullets shot in a row.

My arm gives a sudden twinge, and I wince. I barely resist clamping my free hand over the golden scar hidden under my sleeve, annoyed that it hasn't stopped itching.

I still can't believe I did it. That it *worked*. The same magic that prevents Gerwin from using Jannik as target practice now stops me from strangling Lotte. And brings me one step closer to killing a baron without losing anyone I love in the crossfire.

As relieved as I am that I cleared the first hurdle to protecting Alma, a rumbling cloud of dread still hovers over me, waiting to strike. In this Forest, I am one of the nobles' peers. If this Hunt does end without that Stag caught, if I *fail*, I have just as much chance as the others to lose my life to the Stag's will. The heat beneath my coat turns clammy. The Breimar Stag needs one death, however that must happen.

The sole difference between me and the four at my back is I'm the only one trying to take this seriously. The only one who knows the full risks that come with this temporary gift of invincibility.

A quarter of an hour later, I halt to help Ilse up from where her foot tangled in a root. Ten minutes after that, it's stopping Gerwin from shooting a wood pigeon. Three aggravating minutes more for him to understand it's to protect the species after an unusual late spring freeze killed half the nests, not some conspiracy against his precious guns.

Finally, we reach the Hand. It's an unoriginal name for the crooked and ancient beech. Five thick trunks sprout from the enormous main stem, each resembling a finger extending from an open palm. At this time of day, the sunlight angles through the boughs just right, creating shafts of golden mist. The patches of moss and ladders of creamy fungus engulfing the bark glitter with dew. Stefan and Elias agreed to all meet here for a lunch break. It's also as far north as we'll go today.

Ignoring the grumbles about getting their coats dirty, I order everyone to sit in the cradle of the beech's clutch. Jannik tumbles out of the saddle as I secure Sybil. There are no signs of the other parties, although I'm not sure I'm ready to see their leaders yet. I worry the truth and guilt of what I did will be written all over my face in a language only they can read. It was hard enough keeping a straight face in front of Stefan when I met him at the trail fork, minutes after I completed the binding ritual.

"Why is it so damn cold here?" Gerwin tugs the fox fur draped artfully around his shoulders closer at his throat. I cast my eyes skyward with a harsh breath—one that barely silvers the air—before turning back to the group. Gerwin shivers visibly, and I remember then his invitation traveled the farthest. His tawny complexion is indicative of a sun far more pressing and fiercer than the one I know in these mountains.

Now that they've stopped moving, the two women look just as affected by the autumn chill. Ilse has her hands jammed into her armpits and glowers at her feet while Lotte's knees bounce furiously. Jannik—I think he might have fallen asleep against the tree.

Against my will, the sight melts something inside me.

"All right, wait here for the others to come. I'll see about some wood for a fire and—"

"You can't leave us!" Lotte insists, her voice pitching into a screech. Jannik snorts in his sleep, but the others look behind me in dawning terror. "What *is* that thing?"

I whirl, wrenching my rifle up and clicking off the safety catch. I point it between the trees, my feet digging in and gaze darting to every flicker of movement. When I spot it roosting in the branches overhead, I lower my gun and reach for my pocket instead.

First a heart tree, and now a lichen nyx. "Should I be concerned that you're proving to be a magnet for Forest Folk?" I ask dryly. Lotte does not recognize my sarcastic tone.

"What are you doing? Kill it," she demands. "*Kill it!*"

The nyx is a great owl. Or the vague shape of one, at least. I slowly approach from below, keeping my eyes on it as I pull free a small tooth. The owl is composed of large flakes of pale green, lilac, and brown, held together by sheer willpower. As its head tips to watch me, I can see straight through to the other side in several places. No organs, no bones, only air. The nyx flaps gaping wings in warning, a ghostly scream following.

"Here you go." I stretch my arm up in offering.

After a moment under its shrewd stare, the nyx snatches my gift in a soft beak that still pinches my skin. The tooth vanishes, and the nyx shrinks. The spaces between the lichen compress until a whole and peeling owl small enough to fit in my palm remains.

I brush off my hands and whistle for Rudi. "I'll be back with firewood."

"Wait!" Ilse this time. "What about, about—bears?"

"Don't worry," I assure them over my shoulder. "You're all loud enough to keep every animal of consequence away."

There isn't a lot of dry wood to be found in the fall. Most of it is slick with moss or caked in wet leaves, and it rains often, but you simply need to know where to look. I walk until I can't hear whining voices, and then I walk a little farther. Until the silence of the Forest soothes my aching heart. I scratch idly at my golden scar.

Under a spruce I find success. Dense and low to the ground, the prickly branches leave little space for moisture to reach, but on a bed of dry needles lies a few viable sticks. I duck beneath three more such trees before I have an armful of acceptable firewood.

"You want it?" I tease Rudi with a stick so green I doubt it will burn until next summer. "I know you do." The pointer's claws skitter over soil and leaves in false starts as I pretend to throw it. Her dark eyes lock on her favorite toy. Taking pity, I hurl the stick as far as I can, and she takes off like a shot.

My smile collapses as I turn around. A pine cone crunches beneath my foot. Every stick clatters to the ground.

"Hello, Katrin."

August.

Chapter Nine

The baron stands too near, too close. How, I don't know. I didn't hear him sneak up on me. My mind trips over itself, scrambling to figure out how to protect myself, what I did wrong to land in this situation.

I give myself a mental shake. It hardly matters. The predator is undiscerning, and he has me cornered. All that's left is to put up a defense and hope with every fiber of my body that I don't get eaten.

I take a quick sidestep, another backward.

"August," I greet, struggling to keep my voice steady, to stop my hand from straying to my knife hilt, the strap of my rifle. My startled heart races like a terrified rabbit in my chest, making me dizzy. "I guess this means my uncle and the rest of your group found mine all right?"

"I don't care about the others," he says smoothly, mirroring my movement. I avoid meeting his gaze. Whatever lurks in it, I'd rather not add its effect to the slimy sensation crawling through me and instead look to the trees behind him. The thick bear fur wrapped over his shoulders shines like an oil slick in the sun.

"You should." Another step back, easily matched.

"I care more about the secrets *you* keep, Katrin."

Thoughts collide, but nothing holds firm to help me out of this situation. In the castle halls is one thing—any number of people are within shouting distance if I'm brave enough. But I've never encountered him in Wielinde. *Alone.* There's no one to hear me scream except the bough spirits and nyxes, and that knowledge magnifies every noxious feeling tenfold.

"I don't have secrets," I answer slowly, barely paying attention to what I'm saying. *Think, think, think.* My thumb grazes the sheath of my knife.

In my mind, a scale teeters from side to side.

August's presence means Stefan is somewhere nearby. That's good. The scale tips to the right. Except I deliberately walked a distance from the Hand and my group, far enough that I can't hear them. Bad. Tilt to the left. But the Forest is quiet, and sound carries if the trees pick it up just right. Stefan would hear my scream. Back to the right. Only I don't know how close Stefan is, and there's no guarantee he would find me in time.

The last weight added breaks the scale.

"Felix with you?" A desperate stalling measure. I disgust myself, to be honest. Even if he was lurking behind a tree, August's guard wouldn't do a thing to help. He *never* has.

"The Hunt has put Felix temporarily out of a job, I'm afraid." A soft, slippery laugh. He takes another step closer. "Who can even touch me now?"

My spine slams into a stiff trunk. My rifle slips off my shoulder and drops to the ground. A pair of leaves clinging to their branch with slipping fingers let go, fluttering into my periphery.

It's a minuscule distraction August abuses. He steals the space between us. Presses too close, crowding me against the tree.

August raises a bare hand, and I hate myself for flinching. He merely strokes a knuckle down my cheek. "Always so soft. You continue to make me wonder where else you're soft." His green eyes rove over my face, along the freckles of my cheekbones, the line of my jaw, the column of my neck.

I gasp when his grip suddenly seizes my throat. My hands fly up to pull at his fingers, but I only succeed in scratching my skin. August applies the tiniest amount of force, his thumb pushing against my windpipe enough to make me freeze, hands moving to hold his wrist instead.

"Soft here," he whispers. The hard bark catches on my hat and pulls it away from my forehead a fraction. "Any others are more secrets I'll find one day, but they're not the ones I'm most interested in today."

"What are you talking about?" I manage to say, my tongue feeling too thick in my mouth.

August leans in close to my ear so all I smell is the heavy cologne he dabbed on his neck. "What were you doing in Atlin Bower all by yourself, little Katrin?"

Panic swells hot within me. Both hands *shove* his chest. "Get off me."

He staggers back on one foot, his hand freeing my throat, but the other boot stays firmly planted, letting him easily trespass on my space again. A knee slips between my legs. His answering smile shows too many teeth. A rush of icy horror douses the heat. The faint haze under my nose thickens, comes faster, betraying me.

"Well," he says around another laugh, this one low and dangerous. "We are hiding something, aren't we."

"I'm *not*." But it's a pitch too high to be convincing.

As small and ineffective as that push was, it was the first time I ever physically fought back against August. It should empower me, bolster my spine. I never did that before because his constant, hulking shadow was a threat of worse retaliation. But it doesn't matter that Felix isn't here now—all August has to do is say one word to him later. They don't know I'm also under the Hunt's protection, but one attempt to hurt me as a reminder that I can't do the same to my harasser will expose my secret to the cold, unforgiving air.

Fuck.

I feel so stupid. Of course August noticed. He's part of Stefan's hunting party—they all waited at the fork for me to join them after the binding ritual. My only advantage is that he doesn't know what I did, or that he's the cause for it.

"I'm not hiding anything," I snap. "And I wasn't doing anything in the Bower that you need to know, so let me go. Please." The last added through gritted teeth.

"You're so easy to read," he says with a leer. His gaze narrows on mine, knee shifting higher up my thigh. I wince but force myself not to let it show. "Always thinking so hard how to get away from what I'll have in the end."

I shrink back farther against the tree. "And how many times do I have to say no? I have nothing to give you. Ever."

The moment they leave my lips, I regret my words. If I thought his smile before was unsettling, his mouth now thaws, melting into its full wicked curve. But more chilling is what next falls from his black tongue.

"There's a pretty little maid in the kitchen. I think you know her well, but I would like to know her *very* well."

I stiffen. My bones turn to icicles, fragile and cracking beneath my weight.

"See?" His tongue darts across his lips, hand folding over my waist. "So *easy* to read."

Fingers slide around my back, slip under the hem of my jacket, my sweater. My skin immediately crawls and I draw up straighter, as if I can pull away from his searching touch. "Please stop, August."

"Another soft place," he says quietly, staring at my mouth while grazing the skin beside my spine. "Do you think I don't notice you dragging your little cousin away, every time you spot me? It's a source of great amusement."

"Why can't you just find someone willing?" It's almost a pathetic whimper.

"And then you hide *yourself*, because I think, deep down, you're scared of what I can show a girl like you. That I'll finally give you what you've been missing."

My voice rises. "I've told you I don't want anything from you—"

"But really, you or Alma, it doesn't matter to me."

And that's what terrifies me the most about this man: He doesn't care. We're just toys to break and discard on the floor for someone else to clean up, quickly replaced by the next shiny thing.

"So what else are you trying to hide from me, Katrin? What did you do all by yourself in the Bower?"

"*Nothing.*" I shove him again with the force of my yell. This time he pitches back several steps, his cool touch gone from my skin and his heavy presence off my body. I pivot away from the tree, putting space between us. I pant like I just ran for my life. "Back. Off."

Rudi chooses that moment to return with her prized stick. A treasure dropped and forgotten once she sees me under threat.

Her lips pull back from her teeth as she growls. Hackles raised, she slinks lower to the ground. Her warm brown eyes glow a reflective green as she dips her head into a line of deep shadow.

"Rudi, down." I step closer to her as I issue the command. She's only going to make things worse if she doesn't listen, but I don't know how to dispel the tension in my body to tell her I'm okay.

"Fine," August says, almost to himself. He isn't watching either of us, his attention lazy on the trees. "Fine."

He flips back the edge of his coat, draws out his pistol, and aims it at Rudi.

"*Whoa!*" I yell. My hands wrench up, and I almost trip over a root to block his line of sight, but he turns the gun on me. His eyes are chips of jade behind the muzzle of the gun. My stomach drops. "What are you *doing*?"

"Tell me what you were doing alone in the Bower." Satisfied that I won't move again, he swivels his arm back to Rudi. The silver glints in his unwavering grip. He won't hesitate to shoot her, and unlike me, there's no binding magic that can protect her.

"Leave my dog alone!"

This is insane. I *feel* insane. I don't know what answer he wants to hear that will stop this madness. To lie or tell the truth. What will keep us both safe. Only two paces separate the pistol and Rudi's nose; not even Gerwin could miss that close.

"I was just adjusting my horse's saddle. It was nothing." Hands raised by my head now, I creep toward him. Leaves crunch with every tentative shuffle of my feet. "I promise. Please, it was *nothing*."

"I don't believe you."

The solid click of the gun cocking jams my heart into my throat.

It breaks something in me. Sense and caution all flee my head. Something else takes over my body, my mind, crimson with anger and fear. I snatch my knife into my grip without so much as blinking. My steps are surer now, the crackles underfoot the snaps of a blazing fire. His attention is still on Rudi.

"What the *hell* is going on here?"

I nearly burst into tears at Elias's voice.

An almost imperceptible change comes over August. The smallest quiver in his outstretched arm, flickers of light over the gun barrel. It takes him a full five heartbeats to lower the weapon, disarm it, and return it to its holster. His expression when he faces Elias behind him is saccharine.

"I see nothing the matter."

"Right," Elias says, soft yet firm. "Because I just came to help Katrin with the firewood, and I didn't think I'd need my gun for that."

His gaze lifts over August's shoulder to meet mine. The green of his eyes is a calming light through fresh spring leaves, warm and welcome after a harsh winter. He silently asks the only question possible: *Do you want me here?*

I answer with a tiny nod, trying to punch down the tide of emotions that surges up within me. What floats on top, eating into the edges of my tremulous relief, is embarrassment. This is the second time Elias has rescued me from a situation I shouldn't even be in. No one should. My hands shake so badly that I accidentally tear my trousers before my knife slides home without August noticing it. I retrieve my rifle from where it fell at the base of the tree, and my grip on that is stronger.

"Rudi, come," I say, voice hoarse. I pin my gaze to the moss mite scurrying up the tree beside Elias as I stride in front of August.

"Run along to your little savior, Katrin," August whispers as I pass him. "Maybe once I'm done with your cousin, I'll let him have my scraps."

Red returns as a haze across my vision. I stop in my tracks. There's no thinking it through, no dwelling on the consequences—only action. Visceral, hot, and furious.

I hook my rifle around the back of his knee and *yank*.

Time slows to a honeyed crawl. For one glorious moment, August hangs suspended, his arms flailing, legs tipping above his head. Leaves cast upward by the skid of his boots fly in a graceful dance. If I had any skill with a paintbrush, I would capture the scene in oils and display it above my mantel. Instead, the memory will have to suffice, because time always catches up to reality.

A large pine cone splinters under his heavy fall. It's a beautiful sound, reminiscent of ice cracking beneath too much weight. Promising violence and destruction in the quiet that follows as I level my gun at him.

At the lump of coal he calls a heart.

Better yet is the alarm plain on August's face. It's evident his pretty features rarely shape the expression, making him appear comically grotesque. He lies flat on his back, mouth agape, hair mussed and full of leaf litter. His chest lifts faster than usual, in time with mine. Wide eyes move from Rudi baring her teeth at my side and up to the determined set of my jaw.

Power surges through me with every rapid heartbeat. Now he knows, now he understands how it feels to be on the other side. And it feels good. Like I've been slowly drowning and this is my first gasp of air at the surface.

"Fuck!" Elias exclaims. He hurries over and grabs my shoulder, dragging me back. Our scuffling releases the sweet scent of rot from beneath the dry leaves.

He's stopped from saying more to me by the chuckle that slips from August's mouth. It's watery, a little stunned.

"Put that away." Elias clamps a hand on my forearm, lowering my rifle. A tightly reined-in tremor rocks his voice. My insides are a riot. Too many emotions and functions running too fast and hot to think clearly beyond what is right in front of me.

August laughs louder, and my brow lowers. He sits up and brushes dirt from his hands. I almost ask what's so funny, but the new menacing note in his laughter keeps the question on my tongue. A thread of panic stretches taut along my spine.

"Who knew you had it in you, Katrin?" He pulls a leaf from his hair and crumbles it inside his fist. His voice takes on a strange lilt, like explaining something simple to a child. "I wonder what Felix will make of this, hmm? Shall I tell him what happened, how you pulled a gun on me while I was just minding my own business?"

Oh no. *Oh no.*

Elias steps slightly in front of me. "If you want to run to your little bodyguard and cry that a young woman knocked you on your ass in half a second, be my guest. I wouldn't want to be too loud about it, but that's just me."

Suspicion hardens August's gaze. His mouth snapping shut marks the exact moment his read on the situation alters.

It doesn't matter that all he has is the pistol and gaudy knife tucked inside his jacket, or that Elias is fully armed, hand resting on the barrel of his rifle. August is protected by the Hunt; Elias isn't. But just one of them is cornered now. His only options for when he returns to the rest of the party looking so disheveled and filthy is to confess what I did or lie that he tripped. And he's too proud to admit to either in front of friends he's trying to impress.

"Thought so," Elias mumbles. Louder, he says to me, "Come on."

He seizes my arm, fingers wrapping around the golden scar beneath my sleeve—I barely refrain from hissing—and pulls me deeper into the woods. Elias yells for Rudi to follow, and I'm surprised she listens.

August watches me go with a lingering glower full of dark foreboding.

Once we're out of sight, I wrench free while still walking. The itch in my arm is worse than ever. I scratch at it, but the tweed and my sweater are too thick for the gesture to do more than rub.

"Fucking asshole," Elias says after we've put more distance between August and us. "I'm going to talk to Stefan about him."

"No," I snap. My heart is still beating too fast. "Don't bother."

"Why the hell not?" he demands, whirling on me. His expression is a thundercloud. "I know I haven't been here long and don't understand everything that goes on, but I'm pretty sure I shouldn't have found the pair of you in a messed-up situation like that *twice*."

"You're right, you *don't* know." He reels back from the coarseness of my tone. "And saying something will only make things worse. Do not get my uncle involved."

Stefan has no idea that August tries to take advantage of me. Alma never told him or Carolina after I spilled my secrets to her last spring. And it needs to stay that way. My uncle will fight battles for me and Alma and *lose*, just like Frank did for Mari, and I can't let him. The whole point of me entering this damn Hunt is so he won't ever have to. Elias too. He's wrapped up in this now whether he likes it or not. August may not tell the others what I just did to him out of pride, but we still embarrassed him. Nothing can stop August from sending Felix with a hammer as retaliation later except our silence now.

Elias looks like he wants to punch a tree. "Please tell me you hear how messed up that is?" It's almost a plea.

"You think I don't?" I stop walking, and it's a mistake. Everything catches up to me. The adrenaline that helped me stand earlier fades, leaving behind wearied and unreliable limbs. "Elias, I hate *all* of this, but complaining about it won't help. For all our sakes, let it go."

"Katrin." His voice softens in disbelief. "I heard what he said about Alma."

"I have a plan." I don't mean to say it, but that constant simmer of anger is all that's left, desperate for some outlet. And it's too late to take it back.

His eyes narrow. "What kind of plan?"

I grip my rifle tighter. "Just . . . trust me." That awful guilt swarms me again.

Standing still, Elias calls, "What was he talking about, you in the Bower?"

"Nothing. A misunderstanding."

"And the scratching?"

My hand drops immediately. I didn't realize I was still itching the scar, the gesture so absentminded.

He jabs his finger at me. "I swear, if this plan ends with you dead at the base of a tree—"

"Drop it, Elias. I know what I'm doing." Without waiting to see if he'll follow, I trudge back toward the Hand, Rudi at my side.

Chapter Ten

A hundred pairs of empty eyes stare down, pinning me. I glance up and meet the snarling gaze of a wolf mounted directly above the cavernous fireplace. The warm light kisses its silver fur, glazing its teeth gold and burning ominously in its glass eyes.

I return to my supper, disturbed as I ever am to sit in the Great Hall. To ignore the wolf is to also avoid the stares of moose, bears, cougars, deer, and boars, and that's simply not possible when every inch of stone wall is claimed by one stuffed head or another. Heavy antlers throw spidery shadows over the dusky windows and thick wooden beams. Open mouths become hungry monsters of darkness on paneling and the mosaic floor.

None of these beasts came from Wielinde, of course. The Forest wouldn't allow us to hoard such frivolous trophies. No, these are hundreds of years' worth of dusty gifts and cobwebbed prizes won from hunting trips elsewhere in the world, and it always feels like a crime to sit here.

Tonight in particular is uniquely unbearable. I can't tell what's worse: the anxiety that's twisting my stomach or the unending noise in the Hall that may as well be nails on glass to my senses.

After the first day of the Breimar Hunt, the atmosphere in the Hall always seems off. Like an apple polished a little too brightly before a knife quarters it. Banquets are held every night until the last guest leaves Prauen, and I attend a small number of those. But the festivities after everyone has spent hours in the damp, cold Forest—it turns them into people with too much to prove.

The nobles are louder, their laughter more brassy and easier to unleash. They eat far more than they should with mouths open as wide as the creatures overhead; drink just enough wine to always stay a sip ahead of their tablemates. So quick to dance to the lively music strummed by the trio of hired musicians, and just as quick to break into fisticuffs.

These aristocrats and industry titans just spent an entire day in the wilds of Wielinde Forest. They're true outdoors people now. Don't they deserve this loss of their inhibitions?

I scoff into my stew. Seated a few empty chairs away from me, Klaus gives me a puzzled look before his attention returns to his book and food. I can usually tolerate feasts—even enjoy them. In the past, Alma and I loved sequestering ourselves in a back corner to watch the others behave like fools. Without fail, someone always stands too close to one of the four immense hearths, a spark catching on their trailing hem or sloppily arranged fur. This year, it looks as though Schultz will take the honor—that silk scarf dangles precariously off his arm as he regales his tablemates with a bawdy tale.

Before, Alma and I took turns sneaking under the nobles' tables and carefully stealing goblets of drink from unsuspecting diners. This year I sit alone in stilted silence at the end of the long, solitary table set for staff with red wine I poured myself. Rudi completes the portrait of isolation, lying beside my chair with a meaty bone between her paws.

I changed my mind, I think, dragging my spoon through my

stew. What's worse right now is the leaden concern that accompanies wondering where the hell my cousin is.

After returning from today's Hunt, I put away all my gear and came straight here. There was no one whose company I wanted more than Alma's after the day I had. We agreed we would both attend tonight, and Alma isn't one to forget things like that. So where is she? I keep casting furtive glances at each door, hoping she'll appear with that cheerful smile.

The stew is thick and savory with cubes of rabbit that peel apart when touched. Everything I could want after a long, chilled day in the woods—and I can barely stomach more than a few mouthfuls. The heat from the flames at my back is all at once too hot.

I might have come straight here, but not everyone else did.

A loud uproar of laughter and shouting draws my gaze. In the floor space separating the tables, Gerwin and Ilse's husband roll up their sleeves, knees dipping into boxing stances.

While everyone else's attention is on the two drunken fighters, cold instinct sets my sights beyond them. To another wolf that stares at me. Only this one has not yet been mounted to the wall.

August lolls at the head of the table. He slouches comfortably in the corner of his great scrolled chair, one leg flung over the opposite cushioned arm. One hand clutches a cup carved from an elk antler while the other lightly holds his wife's. The mousy-haired baroness sits rigid in her smaller seat. With her belly gently round by their first child and her timid expression appalled by the display before her, there's little I can give her but a fleeting glance.

Her presence at his side doesn't mean anything. A formality, really. Her existence didn't stop August from cornering me today, from attacking Brigitte weeks before—from threatening to have his way with Alma soon.

My concern grows claws, scratching at the inside of my ribs. I glance at the empty doorway again before looking back to August.

When Elias and I returned to the Hand long after August did, he had just finished telling a story about how a boar had burst out of the bush and bowled him over. How lucky he'd been to escape with only a few smears of dirt on his coat. And the responses had been: "Oh, how brave." "You must have been terrified."

He saved face publicly, but I still can't believe he'll ignore what I did to him. Despite the entire length of the Hall separating us, the flickering candlelight and flames gilding his eyes, I *know* he watches my every move. My heart wouldn't be beating so erratically otherwise. Something calculating lurks in his mind and it makes me sick to my stomach to consider the possibilities. To him, Alma and I are peaches to pluck from a tree, devour, and toss aside the pits. And today he learned that under my soft pink skin lies a tough, sour bite.

"Katrin, there you are."

Her sugary scent fills my nose before she slips into the chair beside me. Relief softens my rib cage as I turn to Alma. The bubbly demeanor I expect does not greet me. Instead, a deep frown creases her brow.

"Where have you been?" I ask.

"With Elias. Talking."

I groan. It's instantly obvious that she already knows what happened today. "As much as I like him for you, can he keep *some* stories for me to tell?"

Alma pivots so her knees press into my thigh. "Were you even going to tell me this story?"

"What?" I push away my bowl to fully face her, my right elbow propped on the table. "Why would you ask something like that? Of course I would."

She shrugs and snatches a piece of sliced bread from the table. I nudge my knife toward her for the butter. "Elias told me what he saw, but I think there's quite a bit still missing from your side."

"There's not much more to tell," I say slowly. Alma is an open book I know backward and forward, yet she's upset about something I can't get a read on. "August was harassing me, and he threatened Rudi."

"With a *gun*."

"Yes, but nothing happened," I say, even as that confident click of the pistol echoes in my head. "We're fine."

"Don't lie to me. And that's not even what I'm talking about." She takes her time scraping butter off the block. Methodical and exact. My skin feels every pass of the knife, prickling with trepidation.

Then, quietly: "What's this secret plan of yours, Katrin?"

Frost burrows through my veins. *Damn it, Elias.* Did he reenact the entire scene for her too? I shouldn't have said that to him. I knew it would come back to bite me. To stall for an answer, I seize my cup and tip too much wine into my mouth, red dripping down my chin. The aftertaste carries notes of charred guilt.

"That was nothing." I wipe away the spill lines with my napkin. "I just said that to get him off my back. I didn't want him getting involved with August."

"I see. Your sleeve is glowing."

"No." I clamp a hand over my right arm without thinking. The sleeve is pulled down to my wrist despite the stuffiness of the room, but the knit is still thick enough to hide the scar's light. "No, you can't see . . ."

My voice trails off as I realize the glaring mistake my panic just made.

Alma slams down the butter-coated knife. "I knew it. Elias mentioned you kept scratching your arm and I just *knew* it. You *idiot*," she adds with biting venom.

"Keep your voice down!"

We both know no one can hear our hissed exchange above the raucous noise at the other end of the room, but heat still flushes her cheeks as she glances back at Klaus.

Certain nobody is listening to us, she admonishes me with the half-dressed bread, waving it in my face. "After Emil d-died and you started acting all weird, I knew you were up to something. You were being clingy with me, and then with August—" Her eyes close as if she also just realized something monumental. "You entered for him."

I snort, and almost tell her the truth—that it's for her, actually. Instead, I say, "What choice do we have?"

No sense keeping that to myself anymore. If I hoped the admission would make me feel better, I'm disappointed. The loss of it leaves the inside of my chest bare, scraped down to the bone.

"Holy—" Alma drops the bread onto the tablecloth and buries her face in her hands. "You hate the Hunt. You *hate* it, what it's become. And now you've thrown yourself at the Stag's mercy with all of them, for *him*—"

When she lifts her head, her brown-eyed stare is worse than any of the ones mounted on the walls. A piece of my soul crumbles beneath its weight. "Katrin, what have you done?"

Suddenly, I am too aware of the room. The sounds, the lights, the smells—it all swamps me, fills me to bursting. I can't be here anymore. It's just—I can't do this right now.

The candlesticks rattle as I push away from the table. Startled, Rudi scrabbles to her feet, bone gnawed clean. My chair screeches over the mosaic floor, but no one notices amid the cheering as the first punch lands.

I wrench open the closest side door, Rudi on my heels.

The narrow hallway I stagger into is dim, most of the sconces extinguished for the evening. It's cooler, too, less stuffy. Each inhalation clears my head a bit more.

Alma bursts through the door as I reach the branch in the passage. "Katrin, wait."

Rudi looks back, tail wagging and hopeful. Her ears droop when I dash right, heading for the peace and solitude of my quarters . . . only to remember that I share the room with Alma. *Fuck.*

There is no escape from her—now that she knows about the Hunt, she won't rest until she gets answers. *What have you done?* With four little words, she asked me for a defense I don't have the strength to give tonight. Especially since I hoped to never explain myself at all. I entered for her, but there's so much more to it than that. She was the last playing card added to a stack about to collapse.

"Katrin, you cannot run from me forever!" Alma cries as I switch directions. "I know you're not *that* dumb."

"No," I say under my breath, moving faster, the thick carpet eating my hard steps, "but I can pretend."

I bolt down the first set of stairs that appear. With any luck, I'll lose Alma, and she'll give up and go to bed so I can sneak in later.

My hands slam flat against a wooden door, narrowly missing the stained glass set within it, and push into a bitter night.

The wide stone slabs of the balcony are slick with dew. I steady myself on a column as I veer to the north. Huddled one floor below it, this exposed passage traces the edges of the Great Hall, its outer walls lined not in animal heads but ornate twinned arches. A sweeping view of Wielinde peeks around each ivy-strangled pillar. Thick clouds shroud the moon, drawing the trees and mountains in ink. The only light comes from the few flames guttering beyond the windows I pass.

I almost reach the corner when a flicker of movement on the ground forces me to a skidding halt. An awkward hop is the only way to avoid stepping on the dark shape.

Despite the shadows, my eyes have adjusted enough to know that whatever lies at my feet is nothing good. I shiver. I pat my trousers, wondering if I still have—aha! From my pocket, I pull out the small matchbook I used earlier to kindle the fire at the Hand. With everything else on my mind, I forgot to return it to my bag after.

Before I strike the first match, a high-pitched screech emanates from the floor. The pained sound squeezes my heart. Dread unfurls in my gut as I slowly crouch.

The small flame ignites between my trembling fingers. It illuminates a feathered body, the glossy red puddle steadily growing beneath it.

I drop the match with a gasp, then fumble to light another, nearly breaking the thin stick. The sulfurous smell I expect is masked by that of a now-all-too-familiar brewing storm.

An eagle. Lying flat on its back, wings spread wide. Its dark chest cracked open, and both its lungs gone.

The match burning down to my fingers knocks me from my horrified stupor. I hiss and drop it. Another flame sparks at the same time I hear Alma call my name. Farther away, Rudi's bark fractures the night, the aggressive note echoing into the blackened mountains.

It happened again. First the bear, then Emil, and now this raptor. A golden eagle still clinging impossibly to life. Its wings twitch as it releases a low keen, and my vision blurs. I drop the third match, prepared to snap its neck, but with a final wheeze, the eagle succumbs on its own.

A loud exhale rolls into the quiet. Not the final breath of a slain bird, but of something else. My head whips up.

Something big.

Straight ahead, the balcony takes a sharp turn to the left, where it wraps around the rear of Prauen. Before I leapt over the eagle, I was only a few paces away from the corner. And from behind it now comes a great, silvery plume of air.

Not at the ground, not at my height. But from near the ceiling.

"Who's there?" I demand. I lurch to my feet and retreat a step. My hand drops to my knife.

"Why is your dog being so weird? She refuses to step outside." Alma comes up beside me, panting. She stretches her arm out for support from the wall; her flat shoes are ill-suited to the slippery floor. "And why did you run? You're—*Mmph!*"

I press my hand tight over her mouth. "Shhh!"

We stand before a window. The warm light behind the diamond panes shines on half her face, painting her a motley of indigo shadow and gold radiance. Her eyes sparkle wide above my smallest finger.

With a meaningful tilt of my head, I gesture toward the end of the passage. She doesn't understand until I repeat the motion twice more. My hand muffles the frightened sound that emerges from Alma's throat.

Another plume of hot air billows down from the ceiling. A low, rattling whistle accompanies the breath.

With a third corpse missing body parts at our feet, I know we've finally found the culprit. And I don't think anything would stop it from turning on us next, but I'm not going down without a fight.

Once I receive assurance that she'll keep silent, I drop my hand from Alma's mouth. My knife lifts in my fist. I readjust my grip, the hilt feeling sticky against my palm. My heart thunders in my chest. It vibrates through my veins and makes me feel like a match ready to ignite.

I take one large, careful step, then pause.

Another exhalation ahead.

Two more steps and a lunge into the next corridor—

To find it empty.

Chapter Eleven

I push forward. Slowly at first, then picking up speed. The soles of my boots slap the stone as I rush toward the next corner. A biting western wind whips through the arches and blows the wisps of hair out of my face.

Someone must be here. There has to be, otherwise it makes no sense. Whoever butchered that bird, they were breathing—they stood *right there*. They can't have just disappeared. There's nowhere for them to go. All that stands on the other side of the railing is a cliffside and a treacherous fall straight down to merciless rocks.

So where the hell did they go?

I grasp the stone corner, relying on its support and my own momentum to curve me around without slipping, knife still in my grip. My pulse thrashes through me.

Only one figure waits around the bend, smoke expelling from his mouth. And it's the last person I expected to find.

Shock reverberates through my bones, locking me in place. "Elias?"

Elbows propped against the stone railing, Elias faces Wielinde with a pensive set to his mouth. A lantern balanced beside him limns his sharpened profile and pale hair in quivering gold. It's enough light by which to see him jump. He stuffs his hands behind his back and spins to flash me a strained smile.

"Katrin," he says. Surprise equal to mine braids through his voice, but one of those strands strikes me as guilty. My eyes narrow.

Alma crashes into my back with a breathless *oof*.

"Oh, hello," she says slowly. "Fancy seeing you here."

"What *are* you doing here?" It rings with unbridled rudeness, and I can't find it in me to care.

He looks between us both. I didn't imagine it before—there's an evasive quality to his movements as he straightens, readjusts his hidden hands. The uneasiness already scratching along my spine sharpens, digging into my skin like talons.

Someone was there, and so is Elias.

"We were chasing a—*Ow?*"

I shut Alma up with an elbow to the ribs. I have a question I need him to answer first.

"What are you hiding?" I demand. Despite the cold, my cheeks feel scorched. My fingers tighten on my knife, holding it a little higher. The firelight must catch on the silver blade; his gaze follows its slight motions. He swallows hard.

"Show me. Now."

His shoulders slump with a heavy exhale. "I should never have started, but bad habit now, I guess." Both hands emerge from behind his back.

The wonders never cease. Elias reveals not smears of blood nor torn-out feathers, but a wooden pipe—still lit—and a pouch that I assume contains tobacco.

"I . . . I don't understand," I say, stepping closer.

"I don't smoke often. Not unless I've had a rough day." The weighted look he levels in my direction makes me suppress a flinch. If there are any words to easily describe what he interrupted in the woods earlier, one would certainly be *rough*. "The butler at the last estate where I worked started me on it. But the smell irritated my mother so much, I had to sneak around to do it."

"You're hiding to smoke?" Alma asks, incredulous.

"Like I said, bad habit." He turns sheepish. "Haven't been able to kick it."

"No, it's not that. I don't care if you do it, but you can just join my father."

Stefan has his pipe every night in the kitchen. Feet up by the fire, Carolina in the chair beside him with recipes to organize, a sweet and grassy haze between them as they talk. It's become a ritual for them, like they can't sleep unless they do it.

"Never mind that," I say dismissively. Elias's vices, the truths spilled to Alma at dinner, my desperate need to avoid facing them—it all feels trivial in comparison. I close the distance between Elias and me. "Did you see anyone?"

He leans back a fraction. "What do you mean?"

I bite back a growl of frustration, barely resisting the urge to grab him by the lapels. "Just now, did you see anything? Did *anyone* run by you in the last two minutes?"

"No." His brows dip farther as I deflate, feeling like a decadent treat dangled before me was ripped away. "No one besides you two. Which, by the way, you still haven't answered my question of why *you're* here."

"Chasing a ghost, apparently," Alma supplies in her usual cheerful tone. I hear where it splinters.

Elias and I immediately get nowhere. He asks questions, I talk over him with answers, he tries to rationalize it, I shoot him down. Round and round until Alma quietly snags his wrist and leads him to the golden eagle, putting sense to everything.

I drop to one knee with Elias's lantern rattling in my grip. The light falls over the congealing blood, the ruffled feathers, the cruel beak. Inside its cracked-open chest, though, everything glistens in that macabre way that screams *wrong, wrong, wrong*.

"And it's missing its lungs?" he asks, lips screwing to one side as he mulls over the scene. He bends down to poke the dead eagle with the end of his pipe but pulls back when he realizes it needs to go in his mouth again.

I nod. Alma sniffles.

"I swear I didn't see anyone go by. I was only outside a few minutes before you found me, and if you think someone was there—"

"There was," Alma and I both insist in the same sharp tone.

She hasn't released Elias's wrist, I notice. Nor has he tried to free himself. They're close enough that their elbows brush whenever one of them moves. However inappropriate it is to feel, a tiny kernel of warmth bursts in my heart.

"Okay, okay. I believe you," he assures us. "But . . . whoever did this, they can't have gone inside. If neither of us saw them, then they still have to be outside."

I jump to my feet. The lantern swings my shadow across every surface. "Where would they have gone, Elias? That's a fifty-foot drop on the other side of the railing."

He shrugs, looking as helpless as I feel. "Maybe they rappelled down."

"Elias, this isn't a person."

I know the moment the statement passes my lips that it's true. Deep in my gut I know I'm right. Alma called it a ghost, but I think it's more than that. Something corporeal and dangerous and far from human. To disappear like that unseen, to be breathing from such a height with that much curling heat—not a someone, but a something. A monster.

"You didn't see it," I say, staring across Wielinde without really perceiving its silhouettes. "Those exhalations, they were practically coming from the ceiling."

"Meaning it was *tall*." Alma shudders.

"People can be tall," Elias says weakly.

"At nine feet?"

"*Nine?* I thought you were exaggerating."

"Things that big don't just vanish into thin air," I interject smoothly. "And whatever it's doing . . ." My gaze drops to the eagle, spread wide like an offering. "It's attacking with intention. Precision."

None of us speak what we must all be thinking. It's killed three times, and with each death it draws closer to Prauen. First in the Forest, then out on the drive, and now here, beneath the very heart of the castle itself. Whatever it is, no number of bones hung from trees is keeping this being away from what it wants.

A tiny little voice at the back of my head whispers a terrible thought. I try to ignore it, to shake it free, but each denial plants another root that won't break.

Perhaps this beast isn't of these woods. Maybe all the rules passed down for generations, the rules that the Forest Folk adhere to, the ones we know, respect, and obey for our own protection—maybe they don't apply anymore because this monster exists outside of them.

"But why the body parts?" I ask, my tone distant. "What is it doing with them? The lungs of a bird, the skeleton of a bear—I don't get it."

"Maybe it's building a body?" Alma chuckles nervously at her dark joke but stops immediately when I release an enormous gasp.

"What?" she asks in breathless terror. She clutches Elias tighter with both hands now. "What is it? Is it back?"

I step toward her, firmly grab both sides of her warm face, and press a kiss to her forehead. Pulling back while still holding her bemused expression, I can't help the grin that shapes my own. "Alma, you're a *genius*."

"Wait, what?" She calls after me in a panicked tone as I hurry back toward the castle door. "Katrin, what the hell? What did I say?"

I only gesture for them to follow, lifting the lantern like they're moths in search of a flame.

It's as though some vital piece of me has been painfully askew. A dislocated shoulder, popped back into the joint correctly with the slightest pressure applied in the right spot. Everything works how it should now, the solution so obvious I don't know why I didn't try to fix the injury sooner.

The heady warmth of Prauen embraces me as I step inside. Rudi scrambles up from where she lay whimpering and gives an anxious bark. She falls into step beside me after I give her a quick, comforting scratch. We retreat to the stairs I used to escape Alma, only now I take them an additional flight down.

Maybe it's building a body.

I hear the hurried footsteps behind me, the questions called, but I ignore them all. A buzzing in my ears, in my veins, keeps my focus solely on what lies before me. Around corners, through timber arches, along passageways lit only by the lantern in my hand. The small flame throws writhing shadows deep as the night itself.

My feet don't stop until I reach the library nestled in the belly of Prauen, and even then, the pause is infinitesimal. The pair of oak doors open together beneath my palms. The wood is heavy, requiring considerable force; the hinges protest with deafening creaks.

It's not a grand room, the library. If anything, the sheer number of shelves and books within make it quite cramped. A high ceiling that seems to suffocate, windows too shrouded to welcome light, the dying fire at the far end too hot. Rudi immediately moves to lie on the thick rug before the latter. The baroness must have been in earlier. She often hides here—I question if August even knows he has a library. The aisle down the middle of the room is divided by a long table, the chairs tucked in and the few candelabras on its bare surface cold. I pluck one candlestick free, using the lantern to light its wick and, in turn, the rest.

"Katrin?" Alma's raised voice approaches the library doors, but her muffled steps walk her and Elias past it, farther down the hall.

"In here," I call. Candles now ablaze, their light infuses the dust-laden air with gold. I snap my lantern shut and carry it between the first set of shelves.

I'm halfway through searching the second shelf when Alma and Elias finally arrive.

"Will you please explain what was so important for you to rush off like that?" Alma's breathlessness undermines her frustration. She scratches at her ribs, like she can undo the apparent stitch in her side by force. "I hate running."

"That was barely a jog." I round the shelf cap and slip down the next. The lantern light bobs as I examine the gilt lettering on the spines, many leather-bound or velvet cloaked.

"What are you looking for?" Elias asks, stepping in beside me.

"I've seen it before. Heard it," I mutter. Down the third line of shelves, swerving around Elias's solid figure.

"For goodness' sake," Alma huffs. She hops up to sit on the table, not seeming to care that her skirts bunch high enough to show her white stockings almost to her knee. Her arms cross in an excellent imitation of her mother. "Use your words—seen what?"

"Patience," I snap back.

Broad sections of books covering agricultural practices, horticulture, animal husbandry, an entire shelf devoted to the castle's finances going back at least seventy years. None of these are what I'm looking for.

Except, I don't exactly know *what* I'm looking for, and that's the problem. In my mind, I picture it leather-bound, soft and limp. Maybe green, but just as easily brown.

Greasy tension gathers along my spine as I move down the next set of shelves. What Alma said, about building a body, I *know* I've seen such a phrase before. Heard it. It's an itch in my brain that I can't reach, and I want to scream because I feel so damn close to something important.

My foot catches briefly on the leg of a chair before I subject new shelves, new books, to my surveying gaze. From left to right, top to bottom, then turning behind me to find—"Aha!"

I set the lantern on the window ledge. All that's visible in the geometric panes is my hazy reflection, and I quickly look away from it. I start hauling out books. One by one, a swift glance at their covers—*Folklore of Wielinde, Prauen and Its Forest, The Mysteries Lurking: A Study of Wielinde*—before they're dropped to the floor with thunderous slaps.

"Yikes!" Elias leaps out of the way just in time to avoid his toes being crushed. From the fire, Rudi gives a startled woof but doesn't leave her post. "Watch it."

Smack. "No," I mumble. *Smack.* "No." *Smack.* "Nope." *Smack.* "No—wait." A gasp of triumph. "There you are."

I shoulder by Elias and slam my discovery down on the table. Alma jumps, as do the candelabras, but she recovers her annoyance with me with little effort. The chair in my way is bumped aside, pushing the rest into a crooked line. I was almost right: The slender book is loose and buttery soft with age and fingerprints, but the leather is a carmine red. It bears no title, only a symbol embossed in flaking gold.

A pair of antlers crossed by a bare branch.

Even upside down, Elias, seated on the other side of the table now, recognizes the emblem. His hand floats to the medallion hidden under his shirt and his chair squeaks as he leans closer. "Is that what I think it is?"

I don't answer. My attention is reserved for this book, the memory of a page, a storyteller's voice guiding my hand to undo the leather tie holding it closed. The first section reveals painstakingly drawn illustrations of the Forest Folk, numbered and describing their unique physical features. My cousin turns toward the book, indulging me. Her shoulder brushes mine.

"Don't worry," she adds in an aside to Elias. "At some point, she'll realize other people exist in this world besides her and explain what the hell she's up to. Because the questions today are *stacking up*." The last is said louder than necessary, the exasperation in its meaning clear.

As I frantically flip through the pages, tearing a few by mistake, a small part of my brain releases the single-minded focus I have. I at least owe Alma this.

"What you said earlier, about it building a body—"

"I meant that as a joke," she insists, almost defensive.

"I think you're right."

Her mouth shuts with an audible click of her teeth.

"And I know . . . I *know* I've seen something about it before."

Distracted, I roll up my sleeves past my elbows between pages turned. I forget why that's a bad idea until a new golden light spills across the black ink.

A scowl darkens Elias's face. "Is *that* what I think it is?"

Fuck.

At this point, I'm questioning how I managed to survive this long in life. Clearly, I lack the necessary self-preservation to keep the single most important secret I possess to myself. Not even half a day has passed since I entered the Hunt and already I inadvertently revealed it twice.

"I told you she did it," Alma replies, a veneer of smugness slipping through her irritation with me. "The second you said she was scratching—"

"If you don't mind," I interrupt, pinning them both with a severe stare. "I would really like to not talk about it right now."

Suddenly self-conscious, I fumble with my sleeves. No longer shielded beneath the thick knit, I'm surprised by how radiant the binding scar appears in the dim library. For the first time, I notice the wound is alive. Like slowly swirling honey beneath the thinnest layer of skin. It makes me feel tainted. Like I desecrated the Forest in a way I can never atone for.

It's not just for me, I remind myself. *I'm not doing this just for me.*

"I don't know if I should hug you or stuff you in one of my ovens," Alma grumbles once I douse the golden glow.

The fretful twist of hands in her skirts tells me one of those is an empty threat, but all I can reply is a weary, "Yeah."

"*Oh,*" she gasps, scaring me. Her finger taps a particularly gruesome image of a stone nymph crushing someone in the blackness of a cave. "I remember this book—it was Greta's! I hated whenever she brought it out because it always scared me." She gestures for me to keep going with it, open curiosity in her gaze now.

More a journal than a book, the pages are whisper thin. Flimsy and on the verge of turning transparent as the light passes through each.

I still don't know precisely what I'm looking for, but I do know this is the right book. It's old, a collection of encounters and observations of all the Forest Folk started long before Prauen was built and handed down through Greta's family. She would often pull it out in the evenings to add her own recordings and to teach us younger children about the Forest. It's her voice I hear in my head now.

"The first account of moss mites, the people lost to bough spirits, when the mushroom goblins migrated into the valley . . ."

The itch in my mind becomes stronger, the foggy image in my brain getting closer to clarity.

As I near the end, my fingers slow. They're dying to turn the pages faster, practically shaking to know what's next. It's here, it has to be—

The back cover folds itself shut once the last weight of paper lifts.

"I don't understand." Soft as an inhalation. For the second time tonight, I turned a corner with the expectation of seeing one thing, only to be left disappointed and with more questions than before. Wrong and lost still. "I swore it was in here."

Alma glances hopefully at the shelves I never searched. "Maybe you grabbed the wrong book. There could be others." She slides to her feet.

"Don't bother." I pull out a chair and collapse onto it. "It was a shot in the dark to begin with."

Elias holds out a hand. "Can I see?"

"Knock yourself out." I nudge the book toward him and lower my head to the table, using my forearms as a buffer.

What a waste of time, what a stupid day. With how drained I suddenly feel, I bet I could fall asleep to the gentle sound of Elias fanning through pages. At least in my dreams I can pretend everything is fine. No problems to face there.

It takes me a moment to notice Elias stopped perusing the book. Nor do I lift my head until he says, "You may have been onto something here, Katrin."

Frowning, I take back the book, waiting on a page just before the middle. The cover is so limp the book stays open on its own. I lightly drag my finger down the center seam.

Along the torn edges where a page has been ripped out.

"It's gone." I sit up straight, parsing through the entire volume again.

Elias nods. "In two places, as far as I can tell. Looks like it was done a while ago too. The edges have softened."

I gnaw on my lip. Discontent sits like a rock in my gut as I look closer at the blatant vandalism. "But who would do such a thing? Why take pages out?"

“Are you sure those missing pages are even the ones you want?” Alma asks with clear hesitation.

“Yes.” I snap the book shut in one hand, a plan brewing. “And without them, I know of only one way we’re going to find out what they said.”

She leans back against the table’s edge. “Am I going to like this idea?”

“I think it’s time we return Greta’s book to her.”

Chapter Twelve

SEVEN NIGHTS UNTIL THE SCAVENGE MOON

I cast a dark glare at the sky for the fifth time, as if that will make the rain too scared to fall from the heavy, iron-bellied clouds that blanket the Forest. A single drop lands on the slope of my nose anyway.

Disgruntled, I look back over my shoulder. "Hurry up."

"I told you." Alma shoots me a warning look that *would* stop the rain. She clutches Elias's arm as she walks with a slight limp. "I have a blister."

Lifting my coat collar higher, I pivot to face them, striding backward along the cobbled road—alone, since I left Rudi at home. She gets too high-strung in the bustle of Steigert and is a menace when leashed, so it's best for everyone if she doesn't come. "It's like you've never left the castle in your life."

"Well—" She searches in the trees for something scathing to say and lands on: "Well, this is what happens when you have to walk an hour at the crack of dawn."

"Oh please," I scoff. My heel hits an upraised stone in the road, and I barely keep my balance. "No one forced you to come."

Despite my impatience to reach the village nestled at the lower slope of the mountain, her cutting expression only makes me laugh. Elias looks between us in bemused silence.

When we first set out from Prauen this morning, he easily matched my pace, but Alma . . . a nature-loving person she is not.

And she made it swiftly clear that she had ulterior motives in accompanying us. Clear to me, at least. Elias played right into her hands with soft concern and chivalry.

Alma doesn't have a blister—and we both know it. She brushed off Elias's insistence that she return to the castle with a brave face. I note with amusement that her supposed limp has changed feet three times.

But Elias remains ignorant of it, delighted to help Alma, and so I'm willing to let this mind-numbing pace continue. For now. I'd rather her be with us than somewhere for August to find, anyway.

I turn to walk forward again, and dodge to the side to avoid bumping into Olga and Wilhelm. The older married couple pause their conversation to return my smile as they pass me, heading to work—in the castle's kitchen for her, the laundry for him. Alma stalls us further by chatting with Olga about some new piece of gossip. I already heard the latest drama from the stable boys, and toe at more lifted stones rather than listen, flinching as another raindrop lands on my forehead.

The road winding between Prauen and the village of Steigert is not well maintained. Pines, cedars, and hemlocks ornamented with bones lean over the road, leaving a narrow, jagged strip of stormy sky. Over the years, their roots have tunneled beneath our feet in defiance, popping individual stones up like mole hills. Moss threads between each crack, making them slick and soft. Every summer, workers smash the cobbles back down, try to cut away at the roots. But the trees grow quickly, and once the snow and ice settle in for the winter, it becomes pointless to keep the road in reasonable condition. Those making the journey to Prauen every day find it easier to walk rather than risk a wagon or carriage wheel unless necessary.

As we continue downhill, the rain falls harder. The dark spots that form on the stones fade slower.

"How much longer?" whines Alma.

I bite my tongue, patience wearing thin. If we had gone at the pace I initially set, we would already be at Greta's and getting the answers we desperately need. Her book sits inside my coat pocket, red leather poking out the top, and I lay a protective hand over its shape.

Still, a quick glance at the bordering trees tells me we're almost there. Their boughs are growing heavier beneath the weight of bones. From the scattered few on each tree to bleached bones hung *everywhere* the tallest ladders can reach.

Minutes later, we round a bend. The threads of moss underfoot blend to soil, the stones smoother and more reliable as the pale stone gate leading into Steigert looms before us. I don't visit the village more than a few times each month, but the guard seated inside the gatehouse nods an unsuspecting greeting as we approach. He waves us beneath the portcullis before tipping his hat back down over his eyes.

Founded by those who were ousted from the mountain valley, Steigert is far from being described as a large village. It's laughable even, when held against the great cities of the world, but those places can burn down for all I care. To me, Steigert pervades a coziness through every street that makes it feel far more important.

On either side of the road, the buildings stand close. Milky-white bricks and textured stucco, dark and cracked timber framing every line, door, and mullioned window; gabled roofs stretching tall. The narrow streets strung between are dim, but warm light from the opening shops beats back the gloom. In the spring and summer, the window boxes and planters burst with color. Now they look wilted and dull. Browning petals clinging to stems for no other reason than they have nothing better to do.

Although still early, the village is awake and loud. Not even ten feet past the gate, my nose nearly loses me inside the sugary depths of a bakery. The butcher shouts about the meat cuts she has as we walk by. A grocer accidentally upends a barrel of crisp fall apples in front of his stoop. Behind a window, a seamstress's elbow hits the glass each time she adjusts the lay of a skirt on a mannequin.

We reach the main square, a large space pinned in place by a fountain in the middle and surrounded by brittle and bare shrubs and trees. Opposite us, a clock tower announces half past seven with a sharp clang of its bell. I curse. Elias and I need to be back at Prauen by eleven to take the next hunting party into Wielinde. We're running out of time.

I stop a young delivery boy who carries a stack of parcels as tall as him to ask for directions. The little cad wouldn't talk until I slipped a coin in his pocket, but soon I beckon Elias and Alma across the square.

In the shadows of an alleyway, we climb a set of cracked stairs in single file. First me, then Alma, followed by Elias. A wreath of juniper branches tied with holly berries and animal teeth hangs from the door. I try to swallow my nerves, fisting my hands to avoid adjusting my jacket hem or tucking my hair behind my ears. As many times as I've been to Steigert, I've never visited Greta. I only hope that after everything that happened at Prauen, she won't take unkindly to us showing up on her doorstep.

Without looking to the others for encouragement, I raise my

gloved hand and knock. The sound is muffled. Weak. The rain falls in earnest now, pinging off drainpipes and dripping from eaves.

After a minute, I fear I didn't knock hard enough. Or worse, no one is even home. I remove one glove to try again when a clatter sounds from inside. There's the clack of three separate bolts thrown back before the door swings inward, my hand still hovering.

"You're not the milk delivery," Greta says with a dry tone. The older woman looks me up and down slowly, entirely unsurprised to see me, then leans against the doorframe to scrutinize Alma and Elias. Her mouth purses. Finally, she steps back, opening the door farther as she walks away. "Come in then. And take off your shoes."

No concern over why we're bothering her so early, no questions about our sudden appearance a week after she and her family abruptly quit their jobs. Greta takes our arrival in stride, almost as though she was expecting us. Then again, she always was impossible to fluster.

The three of us cram into the foyer, trying to remove our shoes without falling into one another. Elias takes Alma's coat and hangs both of theirs on the wall rack. Stairs lead up to what I assume are the bedrooms. As I'm jostled further by Elias closing the door, I trip over a suitcase at the foot of them. I stay upright by catching myself on the banister and Alma grabbing a fistful of my coat.

"Careful now," Greta says on her way to the kitchen. I notice the high-pitched whistle of a kettle the second before it stops. "Upend that case and I'm making you refold everything in it."

The Lohens' home is well lived in. I step into the sitting room, almost overwhelmed by the number of cushions, blankets, and rugs, the plants in clay pots. A tiny kitchen hides through another doorway. All I can see is a table for three jammed in the corner. A large oil painting of a lichen nyx hangs above the fireplace. But the entire place is warm and smells wonderful. Like freshly baked gingerbread and fir needles.

I pause, unsure of where I can sit. Alma perches daintily on the sofa covered by a well-worn quilt. With a shrug, Elias sits beside her. Close enough that Alma tips toward him as his weight sinks into the cushion. Feeling weird for still standing, I quickly cross to the other side of the battered coffee table and sit in the rocking chair. But first, I shrug off my coat and hang it by the tall, metal fire screen.

Above the banging in the kitchen, I hear creaking overhead—someone is upstairs.

"Are you traveling somewhere?" I ask when Greta bustles into the room with a tray of mismatched cups and a chipped teapot. She doesn't answer as she sets down the tray on the table, but when she looks at me over her wire-framed glasses, I fear I've overstepped.

"Not me," she finally says. "Brigitte." This time, a bite of something dark steals into her casual demeanor. I look at her properly for the first time since entering her home.

A week has passed since I last saw Greta in Prauen's kitchen, her sleeves rolled up and her hands coated with flour as she formed perfectly round dumplings. Silver lightens her coarse black hair at the temples; lines frame her mouth and the corners of her brown eyes. She's the same height as me, but round about the middle, her edges soft. A week gone, yet she looks far older. Weighed down by too many worries. She sits in her armchair like it's the first rest she's had in ages.

More floorboards groan upstairs, and I know with absolute certainty who it is now.

Alma realizes too. She perks up as she accepts her tea from Greta, glancing sidelong at the stairs. "Can we see her? Say hello?"

"I would like her to, but she doesn't want to see anyone."

"Oh." She struggles to hide her crestfallen expression behind her cup. Brigitte was her constant companion in the kitchen. Although five years separate them, Alma views her as a sisterly figure, someone she can look up to while also relying on her for help. That she wouldn't even come see Alma speaks volumes.

I share my cousin's dismay. The Lohens left Prauen because of August and his boundless depravity. There's still no confirmation from the people closest to her if he really got Brigitte pregnant, but it doesn't matter. The damage is done. And now the Lohens are hiding, having left without saying goodbye, a ready suitcase in the foyer—there's an inexcusable air of shame lingering in this home.

My anger—*my* constant companion as of late—boils hotter. The fading itch of my binding scar sears beneath my shirtsleeve, and I start rocking the chair with one foot. August needs to be punished. To die. And only *I* have a chance to do that without involving others. For Alma, for Brigitte, for everyone else that bastard has hurt.

"Now, I suspect you have something to tell me." Greta lifts her cup to her lips, swallowing the still-steaming tea without so much as a wince. "Otherwise, you wouldn't be here without warning."

I clutch my tea with both hands, like the heat will lend me the strength I need to survive whatever answers we're about to receive. "More like something to *ask* you," I say slowly.

"That's a shame," she replies, voice light. "I was hoping to talk about Elias here."

He chokes on his tea. "Why? How do you know who I am?"

She tuts. "Come now. I may not work in the castle anymore, but I still have friends, and word does travel quickly when it wants to. Handsome new gamekeeper arriving the day after I quit? That's of interest to me, and the girls know I love a good story." She glances meaningfully at Elias and Alma, the shrinking distance between them, before sharing a knowing look with me.

I fight back a smile. Focus. We're here for a story, not gossip.

"Then maybe you heard." I swallow, my mouth suddenly dry. "About what's been happening at the castle?"

"I heard one of the baron's little friends died on the driveway."

"It was *horrible.*" Alma says it so fast, looking immediately ill.

Elias notices and shifts even closer to her, before adding, "Katrin and I found the body."

"His head was . . . empty." I shudder.

Greta laughs, shifting forward to refill her cup. "If you're referring to Emil, that's hardly surprising. The whole lot of them are brainless."

"No, we mean literally." I take a delicate sip. "His brain was *gone.*"

She freezes. I rock my chair a little harder.

"And he . . . wasn't the only one," Elias says. He hasn't known Greta for more than a handful of minutes, but if he picks up on the subtle shift of temperature in the room, he doesn't show it.

"Tell me," she demands quietly.

"A bear with no bones," I say. "And a bird missing—"

"Lungs."

Then Greta—sturdy, unflappable Greta—drops her cup.

Chapter Thirteen

The cup hits the edge of the table and shatters. Alma releases a ragged gasp. Large pieces of ceramic fly beneath Greta's armchair. What little tea remains sprays outward. It flecks my boot, Alma's skirts, drips from the table to the rug. Overhead, the creaking pauses.

"Greta," Alma exclaims. She begins to rise, likely to clean up the mess, but Elias puts his hand on her arm. He stands instead and disappears into the kitchen.

"Are you all right?" she asks. "Did it cut you?"

Greta waves away the question and fixes her attention on me. Steel gleams in her gaze, cold and impossibly sharp. "What order did it happen in?"

"Order? I—I don't understand," I stutter, still alarmed by her reaction. Quickly, I put aside my tea. I've known this woman my entire life. Seen her burn herself on hot pots, slice her thumb with a knife, twist an ankle after slipping on a spill—and she never gave away more than a wince. Greta does not make clumsy gestures. She doesn't get *rattled*.

But she knew the eagle was missing lungs. Proof that pieces to this strange macabre puzzle are already in her head, and vindication sparks in my gut. I was right to bring us here. The book still hiding in my coat pocket sings like a bough spirit melody only I can hear.

"The *deaths,* Katrin." Greta pushes herself to the edge of her seat. I can't tell if insistence or irritation tightens her voice. "What order were the deaths in?"

Elias reemerges from the kitchen with a dishcloth and sets to clearing the mess. His eyes don't focus on the task, though—he's simply staring hard at a single point on the floor. He's listening as intently as Alma, who pulls her knees up to her chest and wedges herself into the corner of the sofa, as though fearful of the conversation about to unfold.

"The bear and bones the day after you left. Then Emil that night, and the eagle with the lungs yesterday."

She leans back. Her slippered foot shifts to let Elias collect a broken shard from under her chair. Quietly, almost to herself, she says, "Tongue, eyes, flesh, and heart."

"What?" Alma croaks. "What does that mean?"

Her eyes widen, and for a moment she looks like the child she once was. When the chores for the day were done and we gleefully ignored Carolina's order to go to bed because Greta promised us a story. I remember Greta preferred to sit with the kitchen fire at her back. With us at her feet, the eerie shadows always crept over her face and lent her tales a haunting aura.

Elias stands, the broken pieces of ceramic clinking inside the wet cloth. On his way back to the kitchen, he asks, "Does this mean you know what's doing this, then?" He doesn't sound troubled, nor relieved. More that he's unsure, bracing for an answer he doesn't want to hear.

Greta gestures between Alma and me like a disappointed

schoolteacher. “The pair of you should know. I told you the story once.”

Alma bristles. “No offense, Greta, but I blocked out a lot of your stories. It’s been nine years since you first told us about shadow gaunts, and I still can’t sleep without a candle lit.”

Her voice fades toward the end of her confession, and I know she’s embarrassed to have admitted that. Allowing me to tease her about it is one thing—she can’t hide it when our beds are feet apart—but it’s become a point of pride to deny the impression Greta’s stories made on her. It’s an irrational fear to believe others will think less of her for losing sleep over the ghost stories that govern our lives at Prauen. And it doesn’t change her very valid fear of the creatures that dwell in the darkest corners of Wielinde’s caves and burrows, that they will enter the castle and steal away every pleasant dream she’ll ever have.

When Greta turns her severe gaze on me, I cover my heart with my hand. “I wouldn’t be asking if I could remember. We tried to figure it out on our own, but—”

I tip out of the rocking chair and dig in the pocket of my coat for the book. The soft leather is warm from its proximity to the fire. When I pass it to her, she looks blankly at the gold symbol on the cover before taking it with a nod of thanks. Laying it flat on her lap, she sets a protective hand over it, and I realize she must have forgotten it in their haste to flee the castle.

“There are pages missing,” I add, almost daring her to contradict me.

Her laugh is harsh. “*You’re* the reason for that.”

“Me?” I drop back into the chair, toes rocking it again. “I didn’t do that—”

"No, you didn't tear them out yourself, but *I* had to. To protect you from your own reckless idiocy."

Alma snorts. "This I have to hear."

"You don't remember?" Greta's stern gaze watches me above the lenses of her spectacles.

Despite my mind conjuring only fog, childish remorse claws at me beneath her scrutiny. I shrug with a sheepish grin. "I blocked it out too?"

"The day after I told the story, you and Brigitte tried to summon it—"

"Wait, summon what?"

"—like it was all some kind of joke," she continues, distaste rasping her tone. "Although how you managed to convince *my* daughter five years your senior to try such a witless, *foolish* thing, I'll never know."

"Where was I?" Alma demands.

"You wanted no part of it. Too scared."

"Sounds about right," I snap, but fondness laces the edges.

"Sounds like common sense, actually," Alma snipes back with a smirk.

Greta cuts over us as Elias leans against the kitchen's doorframe. "Sounds like someone who *listened*. I had no choice but to rip out those pages afterward. There's a reason I only ever told you girls that story once."

"Fine, but go back. To what you said before." I lean forward, stilling my chair. "Summon *what*?"

Greta sighs. Her eyes flicker to Elias, who now crosses his arms and waits with as much blatant interest as the rest of us. "It's not a tale I enjoy telling."

I readjust the needlepoint pillow at my back and settle in. The wood squeaks each time my heel lifts off the floor, a pulse in time to my growing anticipation. Alma wriggles farther into the sofa, putting distance between herself and Greta's dark story as it falls from her lips.

"Since the first sapling plunged its roots deep into this mountain valley, there dwelled alongside the bough spirits and moss mites a terrible, sovereign beast. Assured of its power, it lorded over every riverbed, tree, and creature. But as with all things, and with all rulers, their tightly held reigns must come to an end—and this beast was no exception."

I close my eyes, falling into the easy cadence of Greta's voice. One made to share grim tales with bramble-sharp honesty.

"The beast, once whole, hearty, and hale, was cast out. Stripped of its name, its face, its entire being, the beast became a monster.

"Where the Breimar Stag bides his time in secret realms, so, too, does this monster wait. It will not come through the veil to Wielinde until it is called, but you will know of its arrival from the victims left in its wake. For when it does come, it is but a spirit. A wisp of wind and mist. A ghost with no body of its own, yet it takes from the Forest that banished it to give itself form. First in bone, second in mind."

Alma whimpers. "I didn't want to be right." I open my eyes as she drops her chin to her knees.

"Third of breath and fourth of voice. Sight comes fifth, flesh comes sixth. Then, last in heart. A monster made, the—" Greta cuts herself off, tearing free of her story, and presses her lips thinly around something she clearly doesn't want to say. Finally, she bites out, "*It* in name."

Aside from the crackling fire and the rain pounding against the window, my creaking chair is the only disruption. I chew my lip. Greta does not seem to have more to tell, yet the tale feels incomplete. Any hope I had for an epiphany or a swell of memory from hearing what she did share is dashed.

Alma surprises me by breaking the silence. "Does it not have a name?"

The lines of Greta's face soften a touch. "Everything worth knowing of has a name."

"Of course." Alma picks at a loose thread in the pattern embroidered at her skirts' hem. "So, what is this one called?"

"I do not say it." Her response is instant. "To name it thrice is to summon it, and nothing good can come of saying its name once, let alone three times." Her gaze turns distant, lost somewhere no one else can follow. "It's why this story is rarely told. Better left to rot in the minds of those who turn senile and forgetful if you ask me, and I wish I'd left it there myself."

"Could you write its name down?" I try to dampen my longing for the answer. After finding all three of its victims, I want to know every detail Greta has to offer on this monster.

Her stare sharpens on me, closing the miles between her thoughts and this room with a single blink. When it narrows, I push. "That wouldn't count as a summoning—it was already written in your book before."

With a tired sigh that signals a victory, Greta turns in her seat to speak to Elias. "There's a pen and ink in the top drawer of the hutch."

Hearing the unspoken order, Elias stumbles back inside the kitchen. The drag of the drawer opening, followed by the clatter of what sounds like cutlery, floats through the doorway before he reemerges. He sets the steel nib pen and blackened inkwell on the table and sits beside Alma again.

Greta's movements as she unstoppers the ink, dips the pen, and flips to the back of her journal are deft and sure. Her hand loses all confidence in the space between her hovering pen and the page. She stills, gazing down at the blank paper as though she can set it ablaze. When a fat drop of ink spatters the white, she begins to write.

The letters appear in short, decisive scratches. So small I have to lean forward to better make them out upside down.

T-H-E

K-R-A-U-V-E-L

Elias stiffens as she forms the last letter. Without realizing it, I sound them out under my breath. "The Kr—"

"*Not in this house,*" Greta thunders without raising the volume of her voice. I shrink back into the rocking chair, heat flooding my cheeks. "I don't care what you do outside of it, but if you ever want to be welcomed beneath this roof again, you will not utter that name."

"But if it's already here," I say haltingly, already fortifying myself to receive a scathing response, "surely saying it won't do anything."

"Perhaps not. Or perhaps you will call it straight to you and mark yourself as its next victim. Whichever it is, I will not have that tested in my home."

She collects more ink and scratches out the name. Without waiting for the page to dry, she slams the book shut.

"Did you know about this . . . monster?" I ask Elias.

He clears his throat. "Why would I?"

"You told me you grew up with the stories of Wielinde and the Forest Folk." In an aside, I tell Greta, "He's like you. Same ancestors."

She tosses the pen onto the table. "I saw his medallion." In explanation to his questioning look, Greta rolls back her sleeve to show the same branch-and-antler symbol tattooed clumsily on her left wrist. The distress clouding his brow evaporates and relief lowers his shoulders.

"Did you lie to me about not knowing what it was?" I ask. The internal reminder that I had been told this story before and forgot everything important about it helps file down the accusation in my voice.

Alma shoots me a chiding look, and I know Elias also told her of his upbringing before now. "*Or* did your mother never share that story with you?"

"No," he insists, raising one hand to calm us both. "My mother never told me this. I mean, not really. Not on purpose." Almost apologetic, he says, "I *have* heard the name before. One of the older stewards at the estate said it once when I was little, so I asked my mother, and she made me swear to never say it again unless I wanted to have my skin turned inside out. I didn't think she meant that literally, though." He pales at the realization.

I believe him. Although it makes little difference whether I learned of this Krauvel from him days ago or from Greta now—how do you stop a ghost that wears the bones of another beast?

"My mother called it a king." Greta's words roll over the well-worn grooves of her storyteller's voice, lulling the three of us into silence. "My great-grandmother called it the only one of its kind; my grandfather—a creature reviled and feared.

"All three of these are true. Wearied of its long, iron-fisted rule over Wielinde, the Forest Folk rebelled. Over the passing of several full moons, they toiled in stone and moss and wood to unpick a seam that separated our realm from those unknown. Before the rip could close, they lured the monster there and exiled it beyond the veil. Torn from its body yet never forgetting its beloved home. Each time it journeys back, it is with the intent to stay. To reclaim its place among the Forest Folk and regain its full power."

"But . . . what is its full power?" Elias asks softly.

Each of the Forest Folk has its own well of magic to turn on those it likes. The shadow gaunts tamper with our dreams, the bough spirits prey on loneliness, the stream barrows feed on oxygen from drowning lungs, the Breimar Stag claims a life whether caught or not. It's for them that we string our trees with bones, to keep the tenuous balance of give-and-take from the Forest as even as possible. But for the king of Wielinde—what could the Krauvel possibly be capable of?

"To bend the Forest Folk to its will." Greta's simple deliverance, her expression, are grave. They make my blood run cold. "To protect us or to turn them against us, I do not know."

I glance at the artwork above the fireplace. Herman, Greta's husband, painted it as an anniversary gift for her years ago. The lichen nyx resembling a broken raven is rendered unnaturally large, its proportions all off. Suddenly, I'm reminded of the stream barrow Elias and I encountered that was too big. Of a moss mite that devoured a hand too fast, a heart tree screaming in silent agony.

Quietly, I ask, "Do the Forest Folk act . . . different when it's back?"

When I tear my eyes away from the painting, I think Greta can see my memories in their blue depths. She nods and it could almost be mistaken for pity.

"It takes without giving back. The balance is knocked askew by its very existence."

"Oh," is all I can think to say.

"You see why I prefer not to tell its story, why I wish to never speak its name. To acknowledge it is to strengthen it. To grant it passage to kill. And the bones we hang—they're not enough to shield us from it. Not enough to shield us from *any* of them if the monster resumes its throne."

My rocking increases, the squeaks growing louder. It serves as a distraction to both soothe my horror and grate on my nerves.

"I-it's already crossed onto the castle grounds," Elias says.

Greta hums, as if this was expected. Meanwhile, the repeat of that knowledge only makes the knot in my stomach more complicated.

Alma shifts to sit cross-legged, adjusting the fall of her skirts over her knees. "Has it ever come back before?"

Another nod. "Quite a few times, and by mistake as often as on purpose. The last was before my lifetime, but if what you say is true, the deaths you've encountered in the last week . . . well." She shakes her head. "The monster has been summoned once more."

"Okay, but . . ." I look around the room at the other two, floundering to find the words. "If the monster only returns with the intent to stay, and it's back *again*, that means it can be stopped, right?"

"The only reason it comes back is because it has not yet finished building a body that will allow it to stay. Each time, the monster has been denied the final form it so desperately needs."

How? I mouth, my voice suddenly gone. As much as I wanted every detail about the Krauvel, this is the only information we truly require. The real reason we came here this morning, whether we'll admit it or not.

"It's quite simple: refuse the monster its prey." Her dry smile practically mocks her response. "If you remove its quarry from its sight, the monster will disappear back through the veil."

"How do you stop something you can't even catch from killing?" Elias looks at me, Alma following suit with true alarm, and I know what they're remembering. Breaths of air too near the ceiling, vanishing into thin air without three people glimpsing it.

"Its only wish is to hunt. *That* is simple. You merely need to be in the right place at the right time."

In other words, luck.

"What does it even look like?" I ask. It already has a set of bones and a few loose organs, but a body those do not make.

"I don't know." Greta takes my half-full cup of tea and tops it up fresh but keeps it for herself. "It's different every time."

"What does that mean?" Elias asks.

"Exactly what I said. Once it was the bones of a fox, the next time a deer. A rabbit with stolen organs that don't fit smaller confines. I told you." She takes a long sip. "It only wishes to hunt. The monster has no preference for its appearance or functionality, just sheer determination to return home."

My cousin groans and buries her face in her hands.

"You have four more chances to find and stop it from hunting. All it needs is a tongue, eyes, skin, and a heart to complete its regeneration. It will rule all of Wielinde Forest if it is not stopped, and there will be no protection for us anymore. No teeth, no bones, nor buried organs will save us."

I cup my binding scar. The Stag and a monster. Both are now life-and-death to find, and I don't know which I have less time to hunt for.

Chapter Fourteen

Only the span of the courtyard separates us from Stefan's workshop, and still I would rather stay sheltered at the mouth of the long archway. The rain that started so gently this morning is now a torrential downpour. Each drop pounds against every surface, causing it to be nearly impossible to hear myself think.

A glance at Alma and Elias makes me bark a laugh. We rushed up the road from Steigert yet look as though we swam home instead. Even with her hood, Alma's curls are plastered to her cheeks and sodden shoulders, her pout *miserable*. Elias's light hair has darkened to grey, and his face is ruddy with exertion. I doubt I look any better, but all I care about is the damp cold seeping into my bones, questioning if I'll ever know warmth again.

Whatever preparations we expected to find for today's Hunt, they are nonexistent. Through the sheets of rain, I spot Elena seated on the covered steps to her greenhouse, surrounded by clay pots and eating a piece of toast. A few stable hands peer out while leaning on pitchforks and brooms, no horses in sight.

In unspoken agreement, the three of us race across the courtyard. Alma shrieks, raising her arms over her head like that will keep her any drier. Our boots splash through the deep puddles atop the cobbles.

I enter the workshop last, and I'm surprised to find Stefan's voice already twining between the exposed rafters, threatening to drown out the rain itself.

"Get to the kitchen," he orders. My foot instinctively retreats a step before I realize the command is for Alma. He points a finger toward the door, but it might as well be a dagger for how sharp his words are. "All morning you've been missing. No note, empty beds, dog waiting here, and your mother worried *sick*."

The dog in question rises from the sleeping pile formed by Petra and Milo in the corner to greet me. I scratch under Rudi's chin.

"But, Pa, we found out—"

"No excuses. Go. *Now*," he adds in an ominous undertone, slamming the tin of linseed oil in his other hand down onto the table. I flinch. The brief look he scorches Elias and me with declares he'll deal with us next.

Alma glares at him, holding firm. A vein pulses in his temple. One of them has to break first. Finally, Alma releases a frustrated growl and storms outside. Her feet are angry slaps against the flooding stone that quickly fade.

Victorious, Stefan turns on me and Elias. His tone still bears that low note of fury as he asks through gritted teeth, "And I assume you were with her?"

To his credit, Elias only backs up a step. His spine remains rigid, his face cool as the rainwater dripping from his jaw. He nods.

"Did you not think for one second how it would look with all these strange deaths happening around the castle?"

My lips, open to explain where we were, seal shut. Every part of me that's wet feels as though it has frozen solid.

"Yes, just as I expected." Stefan looks at us as though we're an expensive new rifle that jammed on the first pull of the trigger. A disappointment that hardens my body further. "You didn't think of that."

"But that's why we were gone," I insist. "We didn't mean to scare anyone, but we learned—"

"You wait." He cuts me off with a single finger. "I know you were the ringleader for this, but I don't want to hear any lies." Stefan instead digs into Elias's steady demeanor, as though sensing a weak spot to exploit. "What was so important for my newest hire to vanish at dawn and avoid helping prepare for the Hunt?"

Elias glances at me for guidance, the first crack in his stoicism.

Annoyance crackles under my skin at my uncle. This is supposed to be my conversation to lead. Just because I lied in the past to protect myself and Alma, he thinks I won't give him the whole truth now when that is exactly why I came straight here in a storm.

I cut over Elias's hesitant response with honed precision. "Elias, go get changed. I'll talk to my uncle."

Grateful for the escape, Elias nods and flees.

Rudi bumps my thigh with her head, and I dig my fingers into her warm fur. "We went to see Greta."

"To Steigert?" His hand twists the tin of linseed oil. With an hour until we're supposed to set out, he must have just finished treating his gun stock. The gesture is idle, but his gaze bores a hole into me. "Whatever for?"

"Another animal showed up dead last night. An eagle. Missing lungs."

His wrath melts slightly, loosening his muscles. But white knuckles still appear around the tin. "And?"

"And she knows what's been killing for these body parts."

He sighs. "Do I need to sit down for this?"

I set the example, taking the chair opposite him at the worktable. The rancid scent of the oil lingers between us as I tell Stefan everything we learned. Measured and calm, despite battling involuntary shivers. A heaviness separate from the sodden weight of my jacket sits on my shoulders as I repeat every word of Greta's story, the memory of her voice alive with the terrible omen of knowing how close the Krauvel could be in the trees beyond these walls. By the time I reach the end, a puddle has formed on the floor beneath me.

"She basically threatened to exsanguinate me if I said it out loud, but this is its name." I write *The Krauvel* on a piece of scrap parchment and push it across the table.

Stefan turns it right side up and squints hard enough to wrinkle his forehead. When he lifts the paper close to his face, I understand. I glance around the room and spot the gleam against glass. Two exasperated steps and I snatch up his hateful spectacles. "Here, you stubborn old man."

Almost reluctant, he takes them and hooks them around his ears. Instantly his expression relaxes. "Call me old again and *I'll* exsanguinate you."

"This is *serious*, Stefan."

"So am I. *Oh.*" His mouth forms a comprehending circle as he reads the monster's name. He notices my surprise. "I remember this story from when *I* was a boy—Greta's grandfather told us, only once. Your mother was a nuisance for weeks after, pulling the bones out of her chicken at dinner and pretending to wear them, asking if she could take my tongue."

I resist rolling my eyes. What little I know of my mother comes from Stefan, and the harmful drama she thrives on clearly started young, her little brother the most reliable victim.

"The *body parts.*" He shakes his head and lightly pounds the table. "I should have remembered."

"I didn't either, if that helps."

He meets my gaze with a humor I know well sparkling in his eyes. "For a story they don't like to tell, Greta and her family are pretty useless at not sharing it."

My low laugh drags over sandpaper. "Right? Maybe they all summon it while sleep talking because no one else seems to remember its name but them."

"It would explain a lot." Stefan nods, his expression shifting to one of grim determination. Petra pads over to him, but before he can stroke her, the foxhound collapses with a tired huff beneath the table. I wish I could join her. "Sounds like it's up to us to turn this monster back. Hunt it down, separate it from its prey, and cast it out again."

Still both so simple and the most complicated thing for us to do. Where to even begin?

"And I need to talk to the baron. Tell him what you figured out."

I splutter, earning me a pointed look from my uncle. No amount of rainwater can dilute the derision in my tone. "You think he's going to care? His own friend died for this monster and he didn't even bat an eye."

"We're in the middle of the Breimar Hunt. I'm not delusional enough to think he'll pause it to let us try to track this thing down, but with so many people in the woods every day bound to the Hunt and vulnerable to *only* the Forest and its beasts, we can't keep this a secret. It's too dangerous not to. August needs to at least know what we're up against and that we gamekeepers will be looking for more than just the Stag."

"It won't make a difference." Whether August cares or not, the Krauvel must be stopped if we're to defend against the Forest Folk. Or defend the Forest Folk. Not even Greta was sure if the Krauvel would bend them to its will or guard them close. Only that the bones, the balance of protection we take heed of, will be as good as matchsticks in this rain.

"Maybe. But in the meantime, you and Elias need to keep an eye out while with your hunting parties." He looks to the window. The courtyard holds a thin mirror of water now, the gutters too clogged with leaves to drain it quickly enough. "If this rain keeps up, though, we won't be out long today. Or at all, and the baron *will* have to pause the Hunt." With a dark chuckle, he adds, "And with how they all hunt, one of them is going to die at the full moon anyway."

The chill in my bones deepens as my right arm simultaneously twinges.

"There's, uh . . . one more thing I need to tell you." I fumble with the buttons of my coat. It takes a few attempts to undo the first one at my throat, my fingers still so cold.

Finally, I peel off the wet garment and roll my shoulders. Thankfully, my sweater is only damp there and around my collar, but it still leaves me with an overwhelming clammy sensation as I shut the door and stand with my back to the window. Rudi steps onto my discarded coat, turns on the spot three times, and lies down in a tight ball of fur.

When we were leaving Greta's home, I pretended something had fallen out of my pocket in the sitting room and told Elias and

Alma to wait outside for me. Shrewd as ever, Greta saw through the ruse when I returned but let me ask my question as she cleaned up our cups.

"Do you regret leaving Prauen?"

"No." Her answer was a gunshot. Noticing the hurt on my face, she straightened with the laden tray and added, "Don't misunderstand me, Katrin. I miss you all, I miss the work—there's not much of that in Steigert right now, so I'm not sure how we'll fare this winter—but keeping my family safe is something I will *never* regret." The last she directed to the ceiling, to her daughter pacing again overhead.

I glanced at the suitcase by the door. "Is it true then, that she's—?"

Greta bustled past me to the kitchen, and I followed. "Yes."

Our worst suspicions, confirmed. It left me with a hollowness that made it hard to breathe. Knowing exactly who was responsible for her violation, how far he was truly willing to go now without repercussion, just made it worse. "What will she do? Where is she going to go?"

"Brigitte doesn't want to be a mother, so she won't be." She placed the tray down a touch too hard, the lid of the teapot rattling. But her grip on my elbow, steering me to the front door, was gentle. "Tomorrow I'm taking her to get the medical care and rest she needs. She's going to be all right, and that's all she would want you to know."

Hand on the doorknob, she looked me dead in the eye, leaving no room for misinterpretation as she said, "I would do *anything* to protect my daughter. Never forget that."

As painful as it had been to hear, that conversation with Greta cleared up my dilemma. Time *is* ticking out on the two magical beasts stalking Wielinde. The Stag to hunt down and a monster to thwart, but only one feels like it's slipping through my grasp.

Under Stefan's curious gaze, I roll up my sleeve.

While the rain pelted my face and steadily soaked me through, I decided which of the two needed to be my priority. The Krauvel is an unprecedented danger in my lifetime, there is no denying that. The clack of bone chimes outside serves as a rhythmic reminder for what could happen if it's left unchecked.

But I tied my life to the Breimar Stag. Too much is at stake with that.

Stefan can joke about the nobles dying. We both know they entered the Hunt for purely selfish reasons without understanding the consequence that awaits one of them once the Scavenge Moon sets. I didn't, though. Greta removed her family from this castle for the right reasons, and I'm doing the same now. For Alma, for myself, for everyone else who crosses paths with August and has their peace spat upon.

I committed to this because I also would do anything to protect my cousin, and *know* I can find the Stag. I can take him down, claim August's death, and keep my life my own.

Remove a monster born before turning to the monster made.

The Krauvel still has four body parts to find and has been stopped every time before, but the Hunt has a definite timeline. A window of opportunity I cannot miss, and my gun won't miss either once I see those ember eyes. I just can't do this alone like I thought yesterday when I set that knife to my skin.

The itch ceased overnight, but the golden glow of my scar

remains as bright and molten as ever. In the dim room, its glow bathes the rafters as gently as candlelight.

"Daughter mine," Stefan breathes. He shuffles to stand in front of me and seizes my arm with a too-hot grip. Turns it to either side. His eyes narrow, not to see it better but to keep some emotion I can't read beneath the surface. "You little fool."

"Please don't be upset," I beg, horrified by how my voice immediately trembles.

He blinks. "Upset? I don't know that I would call it that."

"I just want . . . *need*"—I close my eyes to say that word with such force—"you to not think less of me for this."

"I'm sure you're about to give me a *very* good reason for this, but I won't pretend to understand. This feels . . ." Stefan meets my stare, and I can't pull out the threads of his tone that would tell me exactly what he feels. His hold tightens, his fingers flaring. "Years of us teaching you about the Forest Folk, their history. Watching you shape your own opinions about the nobles and how they've twisted this damn Hunt—watching you stick to them so firmly."

"I still do," I say. "Stefan, nothing has changed. I'm still the same as I was."

"Then why would you do something so stupid?"

His voice is softer than I deserve, and I don't know why that's the thought my mind latches on to. To my dismay, tears start to burn in the corners of my eyes. Stefan's face wavers in my vision.

"August." A tear breaks free, but I don't dare wipe it away.

Stefan's teeth click together, almost indistinguishable from the rain pounding outside. "What?" he breathes.

"I entered to kill August."

He lets me go and stumbles backward, bumping into the edge of the table. In horror, he looks at my golden scar as if seeing it in an entirely different light. Like approaching a wild animal, he pulls my sleeve back down, extinguishing the glow.

"'Please don't be upset,' she asks me," he says, disbelief in his voice. "*Katrin.*"

"Are you upset that I entered the Hunt at all, or that I didn't tell you before I did it?"

"*Both.* But that doesn't help anything now." He runs his hand through his hair, leaving his fingers clawed against his scalp. Then he yanks me into a fierce hug. I squeeze him back. Tight enough that he might be able to take me in like a heart tree, encasing me in bark where I can't be hurt by anything. A watery laugh escapes when Rudi comes and paws at his leg, evidently feeling left out.

Into my wet hair, Stefan says, "Your reason for this better be very, *very* good."

"I'm just so—" I break off to swallow, suddenly unable to breathe through the lump in my throat. "I'm so tired of him constantly hurting us. He's caused so much damage since he became the baron, and I could think of no other way to stand up to him. Him threatening to hurt my *actual* family was the last straw."

Slowly, he asks, "What does that mean?" His heart beats beneath my ear.

The sobs break from my throat now. No point sugarcoating it anymore. Into his shoulder, I whisper, "He finally noticed Alma."

Stefan stiffens. When he tries to pull away, I fist my hands into his shirt. A patch of the white linen has darkened to grey.

"No! No, you can't do anything to him." I selfishly force him to return to hugging me again. It feels like it's keeping us both in one piece right now. "He's protected by the Hunt. If you confront him, he'll just hurt you. I can't live with that."

His hand shifts to cradle my head. "Now I'm upset you didn't trust me enough to tell me," he murmurs. "We could have figured something out to protect Alma together, not you going rogue like this."

"My mind was made up and you would have talked me out of it."

"You and I both know I couldn't."

We laugh, but mine is garbled against his shirt. I turn my head to the side to rest my cheek on him, staring sightlessly across the room. "But you know that I can do this, right? That *I* can get the Stag and end this. Protect us all from him."

"I think that's what scares me the most." His arms around me readjust, and I feel the catch in his breath. "Is his murder really something you want on your conscience?"

"August is a monster." My conviction rings clear as a bell. "Not even his own wife will weep over his death."

Finally, he releases me, but only enough to grab my shoulders and peer into my eyes. His are filled with that same determination from before, and gratitude bursts within me.

"Who else knows about this?" he asks.

"Elias and Alma. I haven't actually talked to them about it, but they both saw my scar and figured out enough."

He nods. "Okay, this is what's going to happen. You are going to hunt for the Stag. We'll all look for this monster, but you need to focus on the Stag." His fingers dig into my shoulders, hard enough to feel through the thick knit. "First chance you see of that beast, you go after him. Whatever it takes."

"What about my hunting party?" I ask dryly, certain I'll be told to make sure they're all right first. It doesn't matter that abandoning them was already my plan.

"*Fuck them.*" Acid drips from his voice, fire in his gaze. A startled laugh spills from my throat. He shakes me back to seriousness. "I don't care about them. If it would help, I would box them all into a cave and let the stone nymphs feast, but there's a one-in-fourteen chance the Stag will choose you at the end—I'm not making those odds worse."

"August suspects something. He doesn't know," I quickly add as he pales. My heart swells and breaks all in one beat. "But he noticed I was alone in the Bower and was making comments, threats. There were . . . guns involved."

"*Fuck.*"

I still haven't seen August since dinner last night, but the memory of how his eyes bore into me across the hall reminds me how careful I need to be until my bullet is lodged between that Stag's ribs. It's a mark on the mental list that convinced me to tell Stefan. I cannot do this alone, and my uncle's reaction, his instant thinking of how to make this work for me, proves going to him was the right thing to do.

"I'll keep that bastard away from you, best I can." He straightens my sweater, rubbing the wrinkles down my arms. "Maybe this bone monster being back is a good thing for us."

"What? How?"

"Because if the three of us are spending extra time looking for it, it's that much more for you to hunt for the Stag uninterrupted. This season, that Stag is going down, even if I have to herd him to you myself." He punctuates this loving statement by planting a firm kiss on my forehead.

"Thank you," I whisper.

"Now go dry off and get ready. Until I hear thunder, we are going out in that Forest. If those delicate nobles want to join us, that's up to them. I couldn't care less if they think a little moisture will melt them."

He pushes me toward the door. Panic grips me anew as my hand finds the doorknob, Rudi trotting to my side. "Please don't tell Carolina about what I did. She's the only one of us who doesn't know, and I don't need her to worry too."

"Oh, no," he says, tipping an imaginary hat, "that wrath is all yours to face when you're ready."

Chapter Fifteen

SIX NIGHTS UNTIL THE SCAVENGE MOON

When the low rumble of thunder knocks me loose from my dreams, I wake with a curse on my lips.

Before my eyes open, I know the poor weather that started yesterday hasn't improved. Despite Alma's candle burning through its last pinch of wick, it's too dark in the room. From their banished corners, I half expect the shadows to blink glowing eyes against the green wallpaper. More telling are the endless waves of rain that batter the windows. Wind screams through the cracks in our door, and I hear the violent rustle of the Forest.

With a groan, I flip onto my back and rub my face. A bleary glance at the bed beside mine shows Alma already gone. As usual, she did little more than tug up the blanket and throw her second pillow on top. The sleeve of her nightgown dangles over the side.

No doubt Rudi followed her down for breakfast as well—that dog has no sense of loyalty when food is on the line.

I throw back the covers and sit at the edge of the stuffed mattress as a blinding flash of lightning blazes through the window. Thunder rolls in the distance several seconds later. Impatience settles into my bones. Until this storm clears, I'm stuck inside, and not by choice.

Stefan has one immutable rule in Wielinde: If the sky talks, stay where you can't hear it. Which is a ridiculous thing for anyone to say when I can *hear* it from my bed, but it's a rule worth heeding.

This valley is volatile when nature lashes out. There's the typical risks of flash floods, mudslides, and trees being struck, but also the spawning of spark imps. Not all Forest Folk have a permanent presence, and the tiny insects live long enough to slip beneath your clothes and shock you unconscious if you can't pull out a tooth first.

While others trudge down the tower stairs to their daily tasks, I scramble to get dressed in the gloom. I shiver as I strip off my nightgown. The damp chill seeps through the glass and embeds itself in the stone of the castle, making me opt for warmth with thick trousers and heavy wool. We'll have to light the narrow hearth in our room tonight so it burns through to dawn, the first indication that the seasons truly are taking a turn for the worse.

I blow out Alma's candle and enter Prauen's kitchen ten minutes later. The steamed space is a flurry of activity, but it smells of cinnamon and bacon fat, and those long ago became synonymous with comfort for me. Rudi trots to my side. I crouch to greet her but recoil from how wet her mouth is as she licks my face. She definitely just ate.

Alma and Stefan sit side by side at the long counter. The former's presence is an expected sight; the latter's is the final pin to my shrinking bubble of optimism. Stefan being here, eating so languidly, means there's zero chance anyone is going outside today.

He looks up from his strudel as I pull out the chair across from him. He chews slowly, his eyes following me as he reaches for his precious cup of coffee. Before I can utter so much as a word, Carolina sweeps in to kiss my temple, setting a fresh pastry in front of me. At a glance, the sugar-dusted strudel is stuffed with apples, walnuts, and quark cheese—my absolute favorite.

"Good morning, Katrin. Dreary one that it is." She smooths down my wild hair, then tuts when she realizes she has flour on her hand. I wave her off with a laugh. My aunt rounds the counter to plant a kiss on Stefan's head before tapping Alma's shoulder. "Hurry up, dear. We need everyone helping this morning—no one can make it up the mountain with this rain."

She bustles away to tend the ovens, and Alma mutters around her buttered toast, "I still need ten minutes to wake up. She can wait."

"Don't talk to your mother that way." But there's no heat in Stefan's admonishment.

"Can't talk to her when she's not here, can I?"

He closes his eyes, seeking out patience. It's enough to make me smirk. Until another strike of lightning glazes every window set high in the walls.

"I suppose there's no point asking."

"No one is going out in this storm." Stefan levels a calm stare at me, but a tension strings through his shoulders that resembles what I feel running down my spine. When my mouth opens, he adds, apologetic and firm, "No exceptions."

I take a large bite of strudel. My favorite, warm and flaky and gooey, and I can't taste a thing.

Weeks ago, I would have prayed for this kind of inclement weather. No babysitting any nobles, the Stag left undisturbed, a day to myself to do whatever I wanted. I'd have woken up this morning in giddy delight.

Now this storm costs too much. Time, opportunity, desperate ambition, and possibly some poor animal's organ.

I swallow, and my stomach grumbles in protest.

The Breimar Stag roams Wielinde with the inevitable promise of death tailing him. So maddeningly close to me and my rifle's aim, yet he might as well be on the far shore of an ocean. And somewhere, *anywhere*—hiding in a tree or burrow, beneath a rock or the lake's surface—the Krauvel hunts with single-minded purpose.

Less than a week to catch the Stag.

Four chances to stop the Krauvel from stealing the body parts it needs.

My heart sinks. If I shoot my gun at the sky, will that make it clear faster? Because I'm willing to try anything at this point. Anything to unclasp this choker beaded with dread and panic from my throat.

Stefan notices my fretful expression. "This storm will pass," he says softly. "They always do."

Alma suddenly perks up. Her chair squeaks as her back straightens, mouth working furiously to chew her bite. I glance over my shoulder, ready to tease.

It's generous to say Elias looks as though he just tumbled out of bed. His hair is a disheveled mess, the circles beneath his eyes resembling bruises. He shuffles to the seat beside mine and collapses into it with a half-hearted pat for Rudi.

"Good morning," Alma says cheerily, all tiredness gone. Elias actually winces. "How did you sleep?"

"Barely," he grouses. "I'm a light sleeper." As if to goad him, lightning reflects off the pots hanging from the ceiling.

"I know the feeling," Carolina sings. She passes behind us to hand Elias his breakfast and he releases a nearly sinful sound as the fresh-baked smell hits him. Sweet cherry with almonds, by the look of it.

"I have cotton you can use for your ears," Alma says, tone earnest. "For tonight, if you want. If it keeps storming. So you can sleep."

Elias looks up from his food and smiles. It brightens his entire being and I swear Alma melts a little. "That would be helpful, thank you."

Stefan looks between them with what I can only describe as mildly curdled horror. The sight makes me choke on my glass of water. After Alma's last crush fizzled in no small part due to Stefan's interference, Carolina all but threatened him with divorce if he meddled again in their daughter's romantic endeavors. He tried to comfort himself by saying at least he wouldn't have to worry about boys with me, and I scared him with an enigmatic, *Well, you never know*.

"Great!" Alma says. "Wonderful. I'll give it to you later."

I meet her gaze and make an imperceptible version of the gesture I use when Rudi gets too excited. The *down girl* is implied by my lifting eyebrow. Her cheeks flush, and she returns to her breakfast with a sheepish smile.

"We should speak to the baron today." Stefan draws my attention back to the situation at hand with a graceless thump.

Elias swallows his mouthful. "About the monster?"

He nods grimly. "I need to see what kind of support he can give once this storm passes, if we can pull some of the stable hands or guards to join us. Maybe the threat of someone losing their tongue will sway him."

"Only if you imply the monster is after him," I mutter darkly. "His black heart will fit perfectly."

But I eat faster. If I sit here too long, Carolina will recruit me, and I don't have the patience to watch water boil today.

The woman draped languorously across August's lap is not his wife.

While Stefan explains about the Krauvel, I watch the pair with thinly veiled disgust. August picks at his bacon and she nibbles his earlobe.

I told him to find a willing woman for once, and it appears he has. And Rowena Gluck, heir to her father's newspaper empire, has never been averse to scandal. The rosy silk robe that barely covers her pale skin is trimmed in delicate lace. Jewels wink at her ears, throat, and fingers, and her onyx curls are tangles.

I'm grateful we didn't enter August's private quarters to find him with another reluctant maid, and that his bedroom is hidden behind closed doors, but this scene is revolting no matter what.

"Ooh, a *monster*," Rowena croons against August's unshaven cheek, boldly looking at the three of us standing in the middle of the room. "What a front-page story that would be."

"Remember, Row," he says smugly, "it's off the record. Just like this." He pinches her bottom, making her squeal.

Stefan continues speaking with a straight face, his tone level. He's a better person than I—I want to throw up.

I wipe my expression blank when August's attention lands on me, though. Wherever his gaze slithers, needles jab into my skin like fangs. I feel it even as I turn to look beyond Felix's hulking silhouette in front of the windows.

Through the dripping glass, the Forest is a bleak and miserable wash of color. A hazy blue in the mountain stone not shielded by the iron-grey tufts of cloud. Muted green and brown in the trees that thrash; any hope for spots of red and gold were obliterated earlier by the wind. The pines sway with drunken balance, and any one of them will soon tip too far to recover and crash to the ground.

"So you can see—" Stefan stops the moment a blinding bolt of lightning blazes through the sky, followed immediately by thunder that rattles the windowpanes and rolls through the stone beneath our feet. He waits for it to peter out before continuing. "You can see the dilemma we're facing."

August heaves a sigh. "My eggs are getting cold, Stefan."

"*I'm* getting cold," Rowena complains, wriggling closer to him. Her fingers part his robe farther to stroke the bristly hair on his chest.

"I'll fix that soon." His oily, suggestive tone turns icy as he glares at my uncle. "Out with it. What do you want?"

My eyes narrow. August plays with his fork, pushing the tines so that the end of the utensil lifts and falls against the tablecloth with a thud. Unbothered by the knowledge that a very dangerous monster skulks in the trees at his doorstep. I expected no different but strangely hoped he might prove me wrong, just once.

"While it would be best for the Breimar Hunt activities to be suspended until we can find the monster—"

"Did my gamekeeper really suggest such a thing?" His sweet smile drips with venom as Rowena snickers. "Why, Stefan, if you're not up to the task anymore—"

"Why don't you let him finish his sentence?" I snap. It strikes across the room, jagged as the lightning that sparks outside.

Stefan's look could wither Wielinde's mightiest oak. He hisses my name through his teeth, but I'm too incensed to feel shame for my outburst. Besides, that was nothing. True disrespect would have been ending it with the string of increasingly vile names that clamor in my head.

"I can't help but notice, Katrin," August drawls, unperturbed. His hand sketches idle circles in the silk on Rowena's back and it's so easy to picture them as talons. "You don't have your dog with you today. I do hope nothing is wrong."

The terrible memory of a gun cocking tears my thoughts asunder. Turns them all white as though a storm rages through me.

I can't hurt him, I can't hurt him, I can't hurt him. My golden scar thrums in time to the reminder. My fingers curl into fists, but that's all I do. All I *can* do.

Movement still flickers in every corner of my vision.

Felix takes a menacing step closer, somehow making himself even bigger. Stefan tenses. August's grin shrinks to a malevolent curve. But it's Elias, reaching around Stefan to graze my wrist, who makes my hands relax.

"While it is preferred to pause the Hunt for the safety of your guests," Stefan continues as though he was never interrupted, with all the solemnity of a soldier entering the front lines, "I'm requesting support. If any staff can be spared to help in the search for this monster, it would be highly expedient. The sooner this monster is stopped, the sooner we can focus solely on the Hunt."

August chews the inside of his cheek. Nurses the answer before letting it go with the air of a man denying a child an extra serving of dessert. "No."

I told you so, screams through every vein of my body.

Again, I expected no better than this reliable indifference. Why it should burn to hear out loud is beyond me. If his friend's brain being wrenched from his head wasn't enough to sway him, nothing will.

"But, sir," Stefan tries again, and frustration finally leaks through his patience. I look to him and notice Elias's disapproval as he watches August. "This monster is a danger to everyone at Prauen, yourself included. The binding won't protect you from it."

"I don't pay you to run around and hunt down monsters—oh, trust me, Katrin, I believe in *this* monster," he says drily to my scoff, and it's a rare moment of hearing him sound insulted.

Funny enough, I do believe him. He grew up very differently from those of us who were told stories in the kitchen, but his childhood was framed by Wielinde and its trees too. For all that he participates in this twisted iteration of the Hunt, he respects it in a way his guests never will. I've packed his saddlebags before, and even though he would probably rather die than ever pull them out, I know he keeps a small bag of teeth in there.

He readjusts Rowena on his thigh. "I grew up with the same tales you did, from a governess I was very glad to see the back of once I was allowed to fire her. She told me of it once, the Kratel, Krauvel, Kraven." He laughs at the pun, as does Rowena a beat late. "Or whatever its name is."

Elias turns away from the right name with a sharp inhale through his nose. I wince.

"As I was saying, Stefan, I pay you, your niece, and this boy here to manage my game, and lead my guests for the Breimar Hunt. I pay you—handsomely, I might add—to help them have a good time."

Once more, his eyes slip to me, and despite Rowena now lifting his hand and kissing his binding scar with swollen lips, his last words are full of innuendo for me alone. I clasp my hands behind my back hard enough for the delicate bones to shift.

"Yet you come here and beg me to pull my hardworking staff from their jobs to help you do something I *don't* pay them for?" He settles farther into his chair, Rowena slipping from her perch. "If you can't do *your* job, you're more than welcome to resign."

After a shocked moment, Stefan's shoulders slump. However he thought his conversation might go, I know this was not it. This is a slap in the face to my uncle. It stirs my anger hotter, that August would threaten another of my family members so easily and without a care.

Fuck, I need this storm to stop. I *need* to be out there more than ever.

"I understand, sir," Stefan says.

"I can find a replacement for you like *that*." August snaps his fingers.

Louder, his words more serrated, Stefan repeats, "I understand."

"Good. Make no mistake: While you're with my guests, there will be no talk of this Krauvcl. No dividing your attention to look for it either." His wandering fingers wrap around several of Rowena's curls and tug hard enough to expose her throat. He places a wet kiss there. Judging from the breathy noise that escapes her, it appears she doesn't mind, but my skin crawls. "My guests travel all this way under highly coveted invitations, and I won't be made the laughingstock of this hunting season by my staff's incompetence."

Stefan clears his throat. "If I could just remind you that there's been three deaths already, the last almost inside the castle itself, and my only concern is for the safety of—"

"Tell you what." His mouth slowly works its way up to Rowena's jaw, but his gaze is on me. This time I force myself to meet it head-on. What lurks beneath belongs in a dark and forgotten corner. "Until the weather breaks, you can have all the time that you like to hunt this Krauvel."

Another strike of lighting hits too close outside. I feel its power as sharply as I do the cruel smile that unfurls across August's face at our silent reactions. He knows damn well that no one is going out in this storm, and if past autumns are anything to go by, it could take days to pass.

"Beyond that, your duties to me and my guests come first. I don't care what you do in your spare time, but your focus will be the Breimar Stag, regardless of what you think. As you said, it's never succeeded in staying, and I don't see why this time will be any different."

He loads his fork with a bite of egg, then prepares a second to put in Rowena's waiting mouth. End of discussion, apparently.

"Stefan, stay a moment, would you? I'd like to discuss the grouse numbers for next year."

I know a dismissal when I hear one. Before Stefan can say anything more, I snatch Elias by the sleeve and haul him toward the door. We leave the way we came in, feeling no better about the current situation.

A man willing to name the Krauvel three times was never going to help us.

Chapter Sixteen

THREE NIGHTS UNTIL THE SCAVENGE MOON

As unpredictable as the storms in Wielinde can be, one thing always holds true after the first of the season. Wind, rain, and violence beat the valley until it bruises, and in their wake drags the true northern cold. A relentless chill that will only worsen as winter nears. Frost now glitters on every surface, and each step fractures the moss.

I endured three days of going stir crazy inside Prauen. Three days of watching in despair as more clouds sank low enough to snag on trees. Of rain persistent enough to knock roof shingles loose, leak through windowpanes, and flood the castle's lowest levels. My knee *still* hurts from slipping on the stone cellar steps while carrying up bushels of onions and potatoes so they wouldn't rot.

Three whole fucking days wasted.

And as Stefan, Elias, and I approach the Pinch, it's with a sickening clench in my gut that I fully grasp how much of a difference that time may have wrought in Wielinde.

Pebbles skitter over the precipitous bank as I peer down at the Forest's most prominent river. These are the headwaters to a vast system that flows into the sea five days south of here as the crow flies, and the Pinch is its narrowest point. A deep stone gorge carved by water, now swollen with leaves, branches, and mangled tree trunks. And jammed against it all are the remains of a footbridge that stood here for the last fifty years.

Stefan grabs a fistful of my coat and eases me back from the edge. He says something, but it's garbled beneath the roaring water.

"What?" I yell.

"The bridge is gone, but I don't need you joining it."

It's too early in the morning to argue. Eyes still sweeping over the devastation below, I rub away tired grit, as though that will clear the debris and return the crossing to its former place.

When Elias says more that I can't catch, Stefan waves for us to follow him back into the trees until I can hear my footsteps again.

"Looks like we're stuck on this side for now." My uncle gives a shudder and rubs his gloved hands together. "We fan out and head north. Elias, you take along the riverbank, see if the next crossing is still intact. Katrin, through the ruins—and check the traps while you're there. I'll head for the mountain slope."

"Works for me," Elias says around a yawn.

"Any sign of the monster *or* the Stag, you call." He pats the horn at his belt. While mine and Stefan's are smooth, curled sheep horns, Elias's is a longer cow horn rimmed with silver. I readjust my horn's strap so it doesn't tangle with my gun. Stefan and I rarely need them for our usual excursions, so I hate wearing one—too bulky.

"Use the blowing-out call, three long notes. Understood?"

He waits until we nod before saying, "Meet back here in *two hours*."

Not a request, but a command. Stefan woke Elias and me up barely half an hour ago after he learned the storm finally broke overnight. It had been pitch-black out when we left, but with another hunting party preparing for us to lead them later in the morning, time is a precious commodity.

We separate, branching off through the underbrush.

Although the ground is hardened, everything above it is heavy with moisture. Every branch sparkles like crystal in the dim morning light. Each brush of a pine bough shakes icy drops free, and I tug my hood over my woolen hat and hair to keep water from slinking beneath my collar. Stubborn mushrooms spring from every crevice in the earth and climb exposed bark. The air smells rich of decay and life and I *revel* in it.

I'm just taken aback by how lonely I feel.

As much as it pains me, I left Rudi behind with Alma and the two foxhounds. Rudi is well trained, an excellent tracker, but the very essence of the Krauvel makes her more nervous than any other predator might. She refuses to go near its kills. Even if her barking is a reliable indicator of the Krauvel, it takes away every element of surprise we so desperately need to be able to find the monster and take its next prey from it. There are only so many chances left.

And I don't want Rudi becoming its next victim either.

Finally, I clear the dense growth and stumble onto a game trail. Some deer passed through not long ago, and the worn grass holds the frozen impression of a hoof and a fresh pile of scat. I move faster, quieter. My gaze roves over every tree, fern, and rock sliver as though my life depends on it. *Might actually depend on it,* I silently correct with a shiver. My grip on my rifle's strap tightens.

I'm not even certain what I'm meant to look for. The Breimar Stag is easy: Any dripping mark of gold will tell me what direction to head in. To track the Krauvel, though . . . I feel lost in the place I know like the back of my hand. The deer prints I step beside are perfectly preserved, but I've never seen *bone* tracks. I'm not sure if I would recognize them in the mud and fallen leaves. The monster vanished from that balcony with eagle lungs as though it stole wings as well—should I be looking in the trees? And even if I did know what to search for, unless it came through here in the last few hours, the rain likely washed away all traces.

Frustrated, I kick at a large fern rather than step around its drooping fronds. It doesn't make me feel any better. Nor do the chitters from a watching squirrel—that creature is too small to be mocking anyone.

The trail threads through two large rocky outcroppings before it slopes into a wide, grassy meadow. Between several green knolls lie overgrown rooms of stone rubble. Spaces wait for doors, crumbled hearths sit cold, and collapsed frames of timber rot beneath layers of lichen and moss. Foundations that represent the remains of Greta's and Elias's ancestors' time in Wielinde.

These ruins never fail to chill me to the bone. Whenever I cross into the unnerving silence of this place, it's difficult not to imagine a horde of ghosts trailing my every step. Even now I sense eyes on the back of my neck. That's not what makes me stop midstep, though.

Smeared in a shaky streak across the ruins of a low wall—blood. Wet and shiny and bright red.

I clutch my rifle in front of me. Carefully, I remove the safety latch. In the dead quiet, I strain to hear signs of a wounded animal or worse, but there's *nothing*.

With a steadying swallow, I creep forward. My vision fades to black and white, the only color of importance to me now red instead of gold. Except the flashes of red I see next only reveal an unfortunate nuisance.

Mushroom goblins, capped with scarlet and white-spotted, their bodies a rotting cream, chase after me. No more than a few inches tall, yet the sight of them in the grass makes my blood freeze. They spring gracefully from the ground in delicate growths, a dozen in all. Up through the frozen soil and back beneath nearly as quick, trying to emerge in a perfect circle around me. I widen my strides. If they ensnare just one foot, there's no escape. Those goblins will have it and the rest of me for a meal that will sate them all winter long.

Frantic, I throw down one, two—*four* teeth before they halt. Before molars and canines become more interesting than me.

Four, when only one was ever needed to throw them off a scent. Another of the Forest Folk acting strange beneath the fugue of the Krauvel's presence. How much worse will they get in the coming days, weeks? If we fail to stop the Krauvel, what then? My fingers fold tighter around my gun, but not before I tear off the glove of my trigger hand with my teeth.

The meadow's largest knoll comes into view. In the spring, larkspur and poppies wave from its peak, alive with buzzing bees. Now they are dead and brittle, as slumped as the wood that once supported the door dug from the earth. The sensation of being watched unfurls further as I tip my body low to peer inside the dark and derelict space.

"*Psst!*" I hiss. I cluck my tongue, trying to provoke a reaction while fervently hoping nothing will.

It's the small mark of blood at the threshold that decides for me. I drag in a deep, steadying breath.

The opening is too low to walk through, and with the propped timber blocking part of it, I'm forced to crook into an odd contortionist angle. Not once do I lower my rifle. A few hard blinks bring the space into a sharper light.

Inside, I can't stand up straight. My neck sits at an awkward slant if I don't bend my knees. Water drips somewhere out of sight despite the dry packed ground. This was once a larder for storing meats and grains. Now it holds only small animal bones from the time a fox claimed it as a den. I turn slowly on the spot. Much of the earthen walls are cracked, and from the roof hang stringy roots, cobwebs, and—I bolt for escape.

A flock of five shadow gaunts roost upside down. Larger than the bats they resemble and made of restless, inky shadows. I know they're asleep—no luminous eyes light the gloom like beacons at sea—and I want them to stay that way. Whatever behavioral change sours in them, I have no interest in discovering it.

I freeze in the dusty shaft of daylight before the door.

It wasn't dripping water I heard, not at all. I was wrong. My heart leaps into my throat, my pulse frenzied as I drop to one knee.

Outside, above the opening, red runs in thick rivulets. It splashes against the wood and stains the grass.

I smell it. Rich and iron. My insides are a skittering riot of hot and cold. I don't know what to do.

Wrong, wrong, wrong. The litany repeats inside my head over and over as blood continues to pour. *I don't know what to do.*

I scream when a large, hairy mass falls at the threshold. Lands with a bone-cracking thump. Dark and four-legged and dead.

My hand clamps over my mouth. Shifts to cover my nose when my breaths are still too loud. Behind me, a harsh screech sounds, wings rustle. Fool. I'm trapped inside a burrow with waking shadow gaunts at my back and . . . and—whatever just killed that. And I just threw away my chance to stay hidden.

Overhead, a low snarling splits the air before rolling into a sinister howl. Whatever threatens me, its weight shaking loose showers of soil from the ceiling, its sound *rattles.* Clacks and wheezes, as though held together by string.

Clarity pierces my fear with deadly aim. The Krauvel. It's here; it's outside. I can try to stop it. Maybe I already did with my scream. The monster's prey is there and now it's not.

Suddenly emboldened, my bones gilded with bravery, I lunge through the opening with a nearly feral yell.

My rifle rips up in one fluid motion as I whirl to face the monster atop the knoll and aim at . . . nothing. There's nothing there. Pebbles crunch beneath my shuffling feet, my gold courage melting to reveal pyrite stupidity.

"Where the fuck did you go?" I shriek in a ragged whisper.

Without taking my eyes off the nearby trees, I fumble for my horn and bring it to my lips. After a few spluttered noises, I finally make the long and mournful calls I need for help.

What answers is the mad twitter of dozens of woodlarks that burst from the meadow. An explosion of leaves, grass, and shadows of brown-and-white feathers.

I don't think.

The fire of my gun is deafening. It makes my ears feel like they're stuffed with cotton, muffling the world for several seconds. The recoil barely registers against my shoulder.

One small bird flops at my feet. I never miss, frightened or not. But the shame that rises in me as I stare at its body is a devouring beast. I lower my gun, the fear that governed me fading. This woodlark isn't a worthwhile meal, its feathers too few to utilize well. It's not something I needed to take from the Forest.

Uncertain, I collect the woodlark and tie its feet to my belt loop. I'll deal with it later. Bury it beneath a tree. For now, I turn to the creature whose blood washed the burrow's entrance. Bile crawls up my throat as I gaze down at the corpse.

A wolf. What's left of one, rather. Its lower jaw and throat were torn clean away. Blood still leaks from the ghastly wound, pooling on the hard ground and staining its fur. Missing from among all that gore I can barely digest is a tongue and larynx. A howl stolen for another predator.

I didn't come between the Krauvel and its prey at all—how laughable to think I could.

When its paws twitch, impossibly alive like the others before, I brush all hesitancy away. My knife finds its swift mark in its heart.

"Katrin!"

Stefan's voice reaches me, coming from deep in the trees to the west.

I stand, wiping my blade clean. Never mind the horn call—he was probably still close enough to have heard the gunshot. The crash of underbrush grows louder, but so does the restlessness sinking into my muscles. I don't want to be found standing here with a dead bird at my hip and a dead wolf at my feet. A damning picture of fear and failure. Of a uselessness I don't want acknowledged.

"Katrin?" My uncle emerges in the meadow, searching wildly in every direction before spotting me climbing the knoll. He trips over a ruined foundation in his hurry but manages to keep his footing. "Oh thank heavens. I heard the shot and thought the worst—"

To some, finding the mutilated wolf might very well *be* the worst. The sight certainly holds its weight where Stefan is concerned. Visibly paler, he swears then asks, "Are you all right?"

"It was here." I reach the top of the knoll and crouch.

"Tell me if you're all right."

"It did it right above me, right here, and I couldn't get to it. Couldn't stop it." My voice is surprisingly calm, but it rises quickly in volume. "And that monster fucking vanished again!"

"*Katrin*," he snaps. He steps over the wolf and looks up into my face, reaches for my still-gloved hand in the grass above the door. "Are you okay?"

My gaze drops to his, and I nod. "I'm fine. Just . . ."

"Shaken."

"Very." My voice cracks.

"Fine but shaken is good. Come down from there." He holds out his arms like I'm a little girl who climbed too high on the garden wall and can't jump down on her own. It nearly makes me cry.

I swing my leg around to sit on the edge. Doing so brushes aside a dried cluster of dead poppies, revealing a single footprint. It's several imprints close together, but as one they form five scrawny clawed toes and a bony heel.

Stefan's bruising grip on my waist lifts me down, and I step past him to shove aside more grass. I disregard his questions until I find another footprint in the soil before the hearth of a ruined cottage.

"It's heading for the river," I whisper.

"What?" Stefan asks, upset at being ignored.

"The river," I say, a thrill surging within me. "It's heading to the river."

I take off after the Krauvel's trail.

Branches smack me in the face. I trip on an uplifted root once, slip on moss twice. Elias hollers as I pass within twenty feet of him heading to the ruins. Soon, the roar of the river replaces the shouts at my back, growing louder with each bough I battle back.

The river comes up sooner than expected, and I throw myself backward just in time, landing in a holly thicket. A chunk of grass torn up by my skidding boot slips over the edge, falling silently into the raging water below. Breath sawing in and out of my lungs, I prowl along the bank.

Footprints. They have to be here somewhere. Where did it go?

When I do find one, crisp in stiff clovers, a bitter shock spills through me. Upstream of the Pinch, the river is much wider, the eddies looser but no less violent. No one in their right mind would try to cross here under their own power.

But the Krauvel stole its mind.

It didn't run along the length of the river, cut off from the rest of Wielinde like we are. No, its tracks face the gorge. As though it jumped clear across to the other side.

Chapter Seventeen

Hours after the Krauvel slipped through my fingers, I find myself beneath Wielinde's trees for a second time. It turned into a beautiful day—the sun shines bright and distant in a crystalline sky while thrushes serenade overhead. The ideal weather after a days-long deluge, yet my attitude now could not be more different from when I first set out in the morning dark.

I feel as though brambles might erupt through my skin at the slightest provocation. When the tap of a woodpecker causes my horse to shy away in alarm from how fast I grab my rifle, I tell my mind to accept that it's spiraling. That I'm overreacting. But it refuses to listen.

Sybil, the black mare more patient than I deserve, nudges my shoulder with her nose as we walk. Her hooves land softly against the ground. On my other side trots Rudi—after what I experienced today, I couldn't stand to leave behind her warm, comforting presence again. If the Krauvel wants her, it'll have to take us both.

Ahead of our trio saunters my small hunting party. The four nobles are wasps buzzing about my sensitive nerves, endlessly griping about the most useless things.

"No," Lotte says, too loud to ignore. "Preferring theater over opera simply reveals you as an uncultured *swine*."

Gerwin releases a dramatic gasp. "How dare—calling me a

swine when *you're* the one auditioning for the role!" The pair have argued back and forth on the topic for the last ten minutes, zealously enough that I slowed my step to put some distance between us.

"Jannik." Ilse appears almost afraid to engage the viscount, but she seems far more amiable to him than I've seen her be with her elder husband. "Did you see Milos Freiteg's performance in *The Man the Sea Despised*? I thought he was—"

"Nobody asked *your* opinion," sneers Lotte, before rounding on Gerwin anew. "You call *The Doll's Demise* a good show, yet it pales in comparison to the worst rendition of *Scarmenita*."

"Apologies for not wishing to be sung at for three hours."

I wrap Sybil's lead around two fingers tight enough to cut off circulation. This is so unfair. The moment the thought surfaces, I try not to nurse it, but the imbalance is obvious. They can blather on about such pointless, irrelevant things while I have to watch the Forest as though a single shadow will be our downfall.

I should be using this dedicated time to hunt for signs of the Breimar Stag. After Stefan took the woodlark I mistakenly shot to bury, I promised him I would. Slashes of gold in the rocks and bark should be my only priority and instead smears of bloody red lie atop my vision everywhere I look. I hear howls where there are none, rattling bones in empty spaces. The wrongness of eagles without lungs and wolves without jaws has spread to infest every root in Wielinde—it makes me sick to my stomach.

And the dissonance of their bickering worsens it all.

"Well, Sybil?" I ask, scratching her chin. "Shall we discuss the merits of oats compared to barley? Or should I yell at Rudi about her choice of meats?"

The mare tosses her head with a peeved wicker.

The trees around us gradually shift from heavy pines to slender birches. Overhead, the canopy thins. Weak, watery sunlight douses my face as the grasses grow thicker and a carpet of golden leaves unfurls. When the world suddenly feels too large, too daunting, the nobles subtly slow to let me take the lead without pausing their argument.

Crowded along the base of the mountain slope, the peeling birches play tricks with my unreliable sight. The dark knots and scratches in their white bark look like hateful eyes at first glimpse. I know a bough spirit keeps one of these as her heart tree, but at least I'm not worried about her. As long as the nobles stay with me, she won't claim any of them for a spouse. They don't like an audience to their marriages.

Still, as we pass through the thin ivory trees, each rippling in and out of sight behind their fellows, my heart skips a beat with every sideways glance. They resemble bones walking. Once more, I try to reassure my mind that it's overreacting, but that bird has flown the nest.

For the first time in my life, I am truly fearful of Wielinde Forest.

In the wolf's brutal death, the Krauvel claimed its fourth body part. All that remains are eyes, skin, and a heart. Already a grave situation before we heard the story repeated from Greta's lips, and now the chances to stop it are dwindling.

With it weighing so heavily on me despite needing to find the Stag, something feels fundamentally changed in Wielinde. The air tastes different—crisper, sharper. Like a struck match might burn blue instead of gold. The trees lean closer in my peripheral, the roots lifting higher to pin me down and cage me.

Unsettling and *wrong*.

All we have to do is come between the Krauvel and its prey before it can steal its next organ, yet it feels fruitless. I want to shout at Greta for making it seem simple. I didn't see the monster earlier, didn't hear it until it was too late. How did any of them stop such a phantom in the past?

Behind me, above the squabbling, a loud crack splits the air. Too high-strung to perceive it as anything other than an approaching threat, I spin, primed to shoot.

Lined up in my rifle's sight, the four nobles freeze. In Lotte's case, even jumping back with a small yelp. The tall woman regrets her reaction instantly from how her expression sours. The two halves of a broken stick briefly lever upward as Gerwin lifts his boot from it.

I quickly lower my gun and straighten. Heat blazes into my cheeks. "Sorry," I mutter grumpily, as though they pried the apology from me by force. "Startled me."

"Startled *you*?" Lotte repeats, outraged. I bristle, expecting her to call me a swine too. "How shit are you at your job that a little twig scares you?"

"You almost killed us," Ilse says with a haughty cross of her arms. The impression is dimmed by her struggle to hold the position with such a heavy coat and gloves.

My teeth click together, and anxiety sharpens my voice to whip out, "You were shot point-blank in the head a week ago. If I had shot you—which I didn't—you'd be fine."

Nerves sparking alongside blood running too hot, I turn around and snatch at Sybil's fallen lead. But the horse keeps dropping her head to graze and I keep missing it. Rudi starts to bark at the nobles, her body rigid and her nose pointing directly at them. "*Quiet*, Rudi." Hardly need a tracking dog to tell me where the pests are in this Forest.

Finally, I grab hold of Sybil. Grass hangs out the side of her mouth.

"Rudi," I snap as she continues to bark. "Enough."

"Look at them," Lotte says coyly behind me while someone snickers. "They always say dogs take after their owners and all I see are two yapping bitches."

That's it. Thorns burst through my skin at last, weeping blood and venom in equal measure. I drop the horse's lead again and turn.

"Do you *ever* shut up?" I stalk a few paces closer to the blond woman. "Even for a minute, or will the earth swallow you whole if you don't annoy it into submission with your incessant whining?"

After a beat, she says, slow and indignant, "Why you sniveling little wretch."

I point at her. "You flaunt how you'll kill your business rival right in front of him. You make no secret of how much you'd rather your husband be dead after marrying him for his money." My finger moves off Ilse to Gerwin. "You, you probably want to kill whoever has revolvers more expensive than yours. And you—" I narrow my eyes on Jannik, realizing I don't know what he wants the Stag for. "You're all terrible people! You don't even believe in the magic of the Stag yet want it for the most selfish reasons."

Gerwin blusters like a bull moose, laying a protective hand over one shiny revolver at his hip. "What did you just say to us?"

"Exactly what you heard," I snap. "You don't understand or respect any part of this Forest. You have no idea what lies in these trees, what dangers I'm trying to watch out for, yet you expect me to find you the Stag when I couldn't even track a fucking pigeon with the way you cockheads carry on."

"How dare you—"

"Easily. I dare *very* easily." I shake with the regret I won't actually feel until later when the consequences of this outburst come down on my head. Although in this moment, I don't think I will bear an ounce of regret. I'm so done with this.

"I will not—"

"*Rudi, what?*" I bellow at my dog, who stands off to the side, still barking, still pointing. Not at the nobles, but to the trees and path behind. What is so important? I follow the line of her nose to the last of the pines still growing nearby.

All my barbed anger and anxiety drain out of me. I can't believe it. In the rough brown bark, dripping like too much paint on a brush, is a set of three gleaming golden slashes.

And deeper in the trees, dappled by shadow and its own ghostly radiance, is the Breimar Stag. His antlers snag on a low-hanging bough, then sever it without faltering in step as he walks away from me. Unhurried and unbothered that he is my salvation.

Cool instinct takes over. My rifle returns to my grip, the safety clicked off. Rudi, satisfied that I now understand, silences herself and lies low to the ground in anticipation. Cautiously, I step to the side to see around the oblivious hunters. I don't have a clear shot. I must get closer and hope he won't spook if the others notice.

"Wait!" Jannik shouts. I nearly burst into a sprint before I realize he hasn't turned around. His eyes light up, riveted to a spot in the birches *behind me*. "I see it, I see it!"

Deeply confused, I glance over my shoulder to where he points.

Nothing is there. No monsters, certainly no Stag. Just birch trees and their spindly shadows.

"No, it's mine!" Ilse yells.

"Back off, Countess," snarls Lotte.

"Not if I get it first," Gerwin declares.

They become reed hobs after they taste blood in the water. All pompous outrage flees, chased out by a frenzy of sheer stupidity. They're a clumsy clatter of furs and leather and gleaming metal—I don't know who acts first.

I barely duck in time before the first bullet fires into the trees.

"*Whoa-whoa-whoa!*" I scream. My hands cover my head as I flatten myself across the leaves. Blindly grasping, I seize Rudi's collar and drag her to my side, throwing my arm around her body. Sybil bolts with a high-pitched whinny.

Bullets whistle through the air overhead, one after another. Bang after deafening bang. An endless explosion of sound that ricochets between the tree trunks and against the mountain. Rockslides have started with less. I don't know how many rounds they have loaded, how fast they *can* reload—they just keep coming.

"Stop! Fucking stop!"

Splinters of birch bark spray everywhere. An entire bough snaps and crashes down. Shadows blitz over the ground as every nesting bird takes flight in fear. Time seems to hang still until only one person remains firing. Gerwin, a revolver in each hand, aiming like he's trying to shoot down flies. He can hardly keep his balance with the small shocks of recoil, but that doesn't deter him.

Then, finally, peace. Only the clicks of empty weapons.

I slowly drop my hand from my head, the other still holding Rudi's quivering body. A leaf clings to my hair and scratches the space beneath my jaw. Awareness trickles into my shock like the first cracks in a dam before the entire structure collapses.

My breaths come hard and fast, pushing through my nose. Blood pumps through my veins so fiery I feel dizzy as I lurch to my feet.

“What the fuck is *wrong* with you?” I shout. I storm over to Gerwin and wrench one revolver from his slack grip. The barrel is blistering hot against my bare palm, and I quickly switch to holding the pearl-inlaid grip. He drops the other, losing it beneath the leaves. Smoke lingers in the air from their complete leave of sanity.

I round on the other three, Rudi stuck to my side like tree sap. “Are you trying to bring the mountain down on us?” They back away, but I keep equal distance with them, prowling closer.

Without looking, I know the Breimar Stag is gone. I still do it anyway. The sight of the Forest void of movement is a punch to my stomach. I can almost feel the weight of sand slipping through an hourglass on top of me. The closest I’ve come to saving my family since this Hunt began, and these idiots just cost me everything.

Lotte retreats a step while Jannik continues to stare over my shoulder at whatever ghost they shot at. Ilse shuffles to the right, toward Gerwin. At least she wears the appropriate amount of fear. She understands that, between us, I’m the only one still with a loaded gun. And I am *furious*.

“Sure, *now* you all shut up. Now, suddenly, you have no words to explain the absolute madness that just unfolded. You could have killed me, and for what?” I gesture behind me with Gerwin’s revolver. “*Nothing.*”

It doesn’t matter that I’m protected by the same binding magic as they are. They don’t know that, and the fact remains that Rudi,

Sybil, or any other living being in this Forest could have been harmed. All I picture is Stefan or Elias coming to meet us and being riddled with bullet holes, and it makes me want to shame them into oblivion. For something other than their own self-interest to get through their thick skulls.

"It wasn't nothing." Gerwin stands where I left him, his hands curled around guns no longer in his grip.

"Did it have antlers?"

A shake of the head.

"Exactly, *nothing*. Nothing that you would be allowed to shoot at in this Forest."

"I saw something move, though," Lotte says quietly, but a touch of arrogance is creeping back in. Assured by something she seems to think I don't know. "Something big."

"Oh, did you?" I say, as though speaking to a child. "Did the shadows scare you? Maybe a little ghost?"

No, I definitely won't feel a shred of regret for my behavior later. In the sunlight cutting through the birches, these snobs have unleashed something in me. The tight rein I kept on my frustrations and worries these last few days slipped from my fist and was given its head to run.

"I saw it too," Ilse insists.

"Why don't we go see, then?" I wave the empty revolver for her to move. "Go on. Be my guest. Prove me wrong."

The petite woman readjusts the lay of her fur-trimmed coat against her stomach. "Jannik is already doing that."

"What?" I turn around, not realizing the viscount had sneaked away.

Jannik walks with purpose, stepping into the swath of birches where he first claimed to have spotted something. The top layer of yellow leaves crunches beneath his feet, a slow marker of his progress. His auburn hair burnishes bronze in the sun.

"Don't you hear it?" he calls back. There's an almost dreamy quality to his voice. "I can *hear* it. It's so beautiful."

His hands graze the chunks shot out of the trunks. Soon, the trees obstruct my view of Jannik. Vertical lines that dissect him into ever-changing pieces.

Beautiful? What is he talking about? There's no sound out here aside from the birds still squawking overhead and the rustle of the wind. The only thing he might hear is . . . I gasp.

"Wait! Jannik, stop—"

His scream is a guttural cry. I raise Gerwin's revolver, but the chamber is still empty, and the small bullets would do little anyway. I throw it aside and race toward the trees, fumbling for my rifle.

Maybe they did see something after all, because I see her now too.

Like an optical illusion breaking apart when tilted on its side, the bough spirit slips from her heart tree. Peels herself away like the bark that tears beneath my touch as I spring through the tightly knit maze of birches. Panic jams in my throat as she seizes Jannik.

Taller than his lanky frame and far spindlier, her strength is deceptive. Sticklike fingers that should snap under my boot wrap around Jannik's shining hair and tug him off his feet. Twigs form her own brittle hair, a few valiant leaves still holding on. Roots slither up her wooden legs as she nears her heart tree.

As time runs out for me to save him.

But how? I've never seen a bough spirit *take* someone before. They don't do it with witnesses—ever. And I can throw every tooth I carry at her, but it would be as useful as an aphid. I try to raise my gun and aim, but I can't get a good shot. She's in perfect view, impossible to not see, and I can't get a clear sight line.

Jannik continues to scream. His voice cracks in a different place on each cry for help. The bough spirit is unmoved by his distress; her groom answered her song, and she'll have him one way or another. She drags him kicking across the fallen leaves, his shoulder slamming into her sisters.

She steps inside her heart tree, melding seamlessly with its bark. With that crackle of wood comes the understanding that I'm too late.

It happens so fast. Jannik there one moment, gone the next. Both slender hands grip him tight and pull him inside. Devour him whole, sliding him beneath the papery bark and silencing his screams.

A husband claimed by his bough spirit.

I stay rooted among the birches, unsure of what to do. My heart pounds, breathing erratic as my rifle slips between my fingers. It clacks against the hilt of my knife before swinging to rest behind me.

This is bad. This is so, so bad.

I want to cry. I should cry and instead, drowned in shock, release a sharp burst of laughter. I try to stifle it, to stop it from veering out of control and into something I *can't* stop. It takes several minutes to get ahold of myself.

The Forest is too quiet now. I don't like it. It's oppressive, suffocating.

I swallow hard and gingerly approach the heart tree. In this sea of birches, it isn't difficult to find. Its white bark is brighter, the black markings starker, the twitching branches proud in how they reach for the sky.

All that remains of Jannik is his face, encased in wood. His closed eyes, protruding nose and chin, whittled beneath bark. A birch-borne scream that will stay frozen as time and moss grow over it.

Chapter Eighteen

The click of the carriage clock on the mantel is a death knell. Each tick brings me closer to something I don't want to face. I don't feel the heat of the flames in the grate. As I stare at my hands, filthy with dirt and my nails full of bark, I question if this awful sensation sitting on my chest will ever go away.

I was entirely wrong. The regret I was so certain would not touch me—it is one misled thought away from sinking me beneath the floor of August's study.

Stefan paces before the fire. Hands tucked behind his back, he doesn't look at me, but I know he believes me. Over every other voice, he trusts me beyond a shadow of a doubt. It might be all that's keeping me on solid ground.

After I tracked down Sybil, her lead snagged on a branch farther up the path, the quiet horror of what my hunting party witnessed finally shattered. I didn't stand a chance. Even before we met up with the other groups, their nearly incoherent and hysterical wails were the first heard. Stefan and Elias were the only people willing to listen to my side. Not that I expected that to play out any differently—it would have been more prudent to throw myself into the lake.

Now my uncle and I both wait for the baron as instructed, and it's hard not to see this as the last moment before an execution. A small reprieve before I rise from my chair and greet my ending.

A tragedy occurred today. Unfortunate falls into ravines, animal attacks, a wrong step in water hiding a stream barrow—participants in the Breimar Hunt have died before without the Stag's intervention, but it's rare. The last was seventy years ago and now Jannik is as good as dead. A coffin of wood and a grave covered in bark. When I was supposed to keep him safe.

The setting sun peeks around the window frame, suddenly blinding me. I shift my upholstered chair to the right. Shafts of deep orange light spear through the large windows at the back of the study, turning the top of August's formidable desk glossy. Its surface is clear of clutter except for a miniature bronze sculpture of the Breimar Stag, an elephant tusk, and the skull of a panther. Heavy, faded tapestries of Forest scenes hang over dark paneling that gently curve with the tower's walls. Tall shelves bow beneath generations of identical leather-bound books I'm certain August hasn't added to since assuming the title of baron.

Voices clamor in the distance, growing nearer. Stefan's boot snags on the edge of the rug as he stills. We both stare at the door.

"Brace yourself," he murmurs, and I nod without looking at him.

That shrill tone may sound indistinct through the heavy wood, but I know who it belongs to. The vicious words it shaped from the birch grove all the way back to the castle still ring in my memory.

Monster. Murdered. Her fault.

The door bangs open, admitting a wall of shouting, and my stomach drops with clammy dread.

August strides in, still wearing his fox overcoat. The dying sunlight turns the reddish fur a bloody hue. Beneath pinched brows lies a dark glower, a muscle ticking in his jaw, and knowing what that means for his mood digs my fingers into the chair's damask.

The three remaining members of my hunting party collide with one another as they all try to enter at the same time.

"*Her!* It's all her fault!" Lotte shrieks the moment she spots me. "*She's* the reason poor Jannik is dead!"

"I am not," I spit before I can help myself. Stefan tilts his head slightly with a warning. I know, I know—I can't let her get to me. I need to stay calm.

"She lured him into the trees!"

My jaw drops. Her audacity turns my blood to sludge as she follows August to his desk and fixes him with doe eyes. What does she hope to gain from lying?

"She deliberately lured him in and set that . . . that—that *monster* on him!"

"That is *not* true, and you know it!" The door shuts softly behind me, and I twist to look at the other two. "Tell him. Tell him what happened."

Gerwin and Ilse, however, studiously avoid meeting my eye. They stand together in front of a tapestry as though they would rather blend in with its stitches. Evidently, they have no qualms with Lotte speaking falsehoods on their behalf.

I scream internally. *Useless.*

Stefan comes up from behind and places a warm hand on my shoulder. Whether to offer support or comfort, or to keep me in my seat, I'm not sure which I prefer. I force my limbs to relax, though.

August sighs and removes his fur coat. It falls to the floor as he folds himself into his seat. "Go on then, Katrin. Let's hear what you have to say."

His dirty, boot-clad feet land on the desk's surface. A picture of indifference were it not for how the sun limns him in fiery light from behind. It makes him appear a vengeful saint, sent to settle petty squabbles. I don't like the sharp gleam in his eyes. August has his own thoughts, and no matter what Lotte or I say in this room, I know he's already made up his mind. The silent appearance of Felix in my periphery speaks volumes about the severity of this situation.

That awful regret weighs my ankles down even more.

Another of August's guests died, but this time there were witnesses of importance. Someone has to face the consequences, and there *will* be consequences.

That doesn't stop me from telling the truth.

"I didn't *set* the bough spirit on him," I say, glaring daggers at Lotte. "Nobody can do that. I stood right in front of you—after you nearly murdered *me* and half the Forest, I'll add—while Jannik went into those trees on his own. He heard her song. That bough spirit lured him in and I . . . I don't know why she did."

Except, as my voice trails off, I realize I do know. It's for the same reason that mushroom goblins now need half a jaw of teeth for distraction, why stream barrows are twice their size, why other heart trees wear faces of agony.

Bough spirits don't behave how that birch did. The longer I sit with the memory of her actions, the more gravely concerning they become. Every record of bough spirits claiming their spouses is shared either secondhand or from someone who watched from a great distance. They are fiercely protective and private beings, never wedding where others can see. Their song is their greatest weapon. A melody only their chosen love hears, used to separate and lure their spouse before pulling them into their heart tree.

I've walked through Wielinde countless times and seen them standing guard near their heart trees, but only one sang to me. A larch tried to claim me for her own last year. If Rudi hadn't nipped my hand hard enough to draw blood, she might even have succeeded. I stuff my ears with cotton whenever I venture near now, but her song still haunts my dreams. Unspeakably lonely and plaintive, yet just as beautiful.

This birch wanted Jannik, and I doubt an axe could have stopped her. There's only one possible explanation for such a change in behavior, and it just gained a fourth body part this morning.

"She's a *liar*!" Lotte's lower lip begins to tremble, her voice shaking. But not a single tear forms.

"That's enough, Lotte." August's voice is firm and surprisingly cold. His level gaze on me is as unwelcome as ever, but there's something new in it that lends me unfathomable hope. I sit a little straighter when the corner of his mouth crooks.

He believes me.

Like when we told him about the Krauvel, he believes my account of the bough spirit. It's as he said: He grew up on the same stories of the Forest Folk as the rest of us. He knows bough spirits don't act like that.

Of course, I'm getting ahead of myself, letting that small bite of hope sustain me. This is August. A devil of a man who thinks only of himself and his desires. The small degree of connection between us was as valuable as a pine cone in convincing him of the looming danger of the Krauvel. All that matters in his mind is the Hunt and his guests' perception of him.

What matters to me is still being allowed in these woods to finish that Hunt for him. That means not being fired or having Felix shatter my kneecaps.

"But, Augey," Lotte wails, her coat slipping off one shoulder. Her eyes are still dry despite her best efforts to pretend-cry. "I don't trust her. I don't feel safe with her anymore. None of us do, right?" She directs this to Ilse and Gerwin.

The pair's continued silence folds my hand into a fist. I can't be the only one to see through Lotte's ridiculous performance. She and the others are not friends. They don't pop by one another's homes for tea and scones. The only gifts they exchange are strategic, meant to either unsettle or show off how much better they are. I don't even think Lotte liked Jannik, yet she cries crocodile tears over August's desk. So why? What is she angling for in all this drama?

In that moment, she drops her gaze to me and answers my silent question with a catty smile.

Stefan's grip on my shoulder tightens, and it's now solely to keep me seated. Helpful, since my leaden regret is filed thinner.

I should have picked out her motives the second she began her despairing wails at August on the way back to Prauen, and I feel stupid for not preparing myself for this too. The woman unafraid to tell her business rival she wants him dead is seeking retribution for what I said in the Forest. I dared insult her to her face. She wants my job taken from me but doesn't actually care what will happen to me, only that something does.

The birch should have done us all a favor and taken her instead.

"Yeah, well, I don't feel safe with any of you either," I snarl. This woman is making me see red as bright as the sky now burns. "Loons, the lot of you. Firing off guns without a care in the world for who or what you'll hit."

Lotte glares at me, her jaw working as she mulls over her next words. An imperiousness tips her chin up. "I demand to be reassigned to a new hunting party."

I laugh. "Fine by me."

"I can rearrange the groups," Stefan says, eager to latch on to what he clearly believes to be sufficient punishment for what happened today. I couldn't agree more. "Switch a few people out—"

"That won't be necessary," August interrupts, smooth as rancid oil. He examines his hand, then digs in his desk drawer for a letter opener. The dull tip slides beneath the nail of his middle finger.

"But, *Augey,* I told you I don't want—"

His voice quietly cuts over hers, but to me it's as loud as a bell ringing a warning. "I'll go in Katrin's group."

I sink deep into my chair, unable to take my eyes off his. A yawning pit opens in my stomach. Hungry and greedy, it swallows down every scrap of hope and comfort I have left. In my anger at Lotte, I forgot for a moment who I was dealing with.

And from the smirk that curls one corner of his mouth, August knows exactly what he's doing. Tormentors always know which levers to pull to gain the reaction they want.

"Sir," Stefan begins slowly. His grip on me is ironclad, and I suspect it's more for him now. "I don't think that's a good idea."

"Do you doubt Katrin's ability as a gamekeeper and guide?" Shrewd, conniving bastard.

"No, of course not," he replies, defiant enough to make my chest swell with love for him. "I would trust Katrin with my life out there.

But I just wonder if . . . if you might feel more . . . more comfortable with . . . if—"

But whatever Stefan wonders, it never materializes. He doesn't know what to say to make August change his mind. Lying is not one of Stefan's strengths, and he truly believes I'm good at what we both do. The ironic truth is that August will be just as safe with me as he would be with my uncle.

Whether he knows it or not, this is the worst punishment August could deal. Despite his comments and pressure, he still doesn't know I joined the Hunt—this is solely to toy with me. To push me closer to the edge. But worse than that, August is aware of me in a way the other nobles aren't. Most couldn't care less for me until I inconvenience them or can serve their whims. Lotte wishes for me to suffer in obscurity. But August knows keeping me close is the best way to get under my skin.

An overwhelming wave of grief washes over me, and it takes everything I have not to let it show. No matter how much I try to reassure myself otherwise, I can't shake off the thought that I've already lost the Hunt and failed Alma. That my only chance to catch the Breimar Stag was today, and now it will never come again. Because if I do spot the gold markings again, there's no way in hell I'll be able to slip away from August's unwanted attention to track it alone.

I only entered this Hunt because August would never find out and use it against me or my family, and now I fear I'll be forced to fight him in the end anyway.

The pit in my stomach yawns wider, this time devouring all but sickening disquiet. The mantel clock ticks louder. Time is running out on all fronts. To take down the Stag, to stop the Krauvel, to keep Prauen my home and feel any measure of safety in it. Tick, tick, tick. August has us all cornered now.

"Ilse, Gerwin?" he calls lightly. "Do you have any concerns with me and Felix rounding out your party?"

"We'd be delighted," Gerwin responds with so saccharine a tone I wouldn't be surprised if I turned around to find him on his knees. "An honor."

August drops his feet to the rug, leaving a smear of mud across the desk's polished surface. Pocketing the letter opener, he slaps down his hands and stands. "It's settled then. Tomorrow, I join Katrin's hunting party. And she won't let me down—will you?"

I lower my gaze to the floor, where it feels safest to burn a hole. "No," I grumble when I realize he's expecting an answer.

"Good." Braced on the tips of his fingers, he leans over the desk, eating away the separation. "We're going to have a *wonderful* time."

Lotte looks between August and me in disbelief. She doesn't realize she got what she wanted: Something terrible definitely happened to me. "That's it? August, she's the reason Jannik is dead and you're just letting her—"

"Oh, my sweet, silly Lotte." He draws a silky finger down her cheek, stifling her words. Nausea rises in my throat. "You and I both know you have no love for Jannik. Just think, one less competitor to come between you and Schultz."

A wicked smile curves up her face at the bloody prospect of growing her textiles empire, and August leans in closer. She's almost the same height as him. I hear every disgusting word he speaks in her ear to make her grin fade.

"You know what that ruthless streak of yours does to me. What it makes me want to do to you. I know, you have a wife," he says, quickly cutting her off. "But I can show you what you're missing out on. What she can't give you."

Rage simmers inside my bones on Lotte's behalf. The variation of what he said about fixing me for being my most authentic self makes my lips press tighter just to keep the sick down. I can hate Lotte as a person and still think she deserves to be treated with basic decency.

Somewhat paler, she turns and leaves the room, tailed by the other two. August moves to follow, gesturing for Felix to meet him in the hall. In the doorway, though, he pauses, hand wrapped around the handle with a light touch.

"Before I forget, you should bring that daughter of yours along one day, Stefan. What's her name—Alma? Perhaps she might be a chip off the old block out there."

Then he shuts the door without another word, abandoning Stefan and me to the panicked silence he just spread like poison.

Chapter Nineteen

TWO NIGHTS UNTIL THE SCAVENGE MOON

"Katrin Liesl Regner. I have a bone to pick with you."

My sullen mood flinches, both from the intrusion into my morose thoughts and my ugly middle name. Sharing a name with my mother is not a point of pride. Alma only uses it when she's furious, and her expression as she appears around Sybil's head confirms that.

I return my attention to the saddlebags I packed with supplies for today's hunting excursion. The courtyard holds the customary tangle of shrill shouts, too-loud laughter, and the impatience of horses as everyone prepares to move out. August's silky voice rises above it all. I jam a box of shells in harder than necessary. The usual thread of irritation that tugs me through the motions in anticipation of the company I'll keep has been snipped. Now I feel bound and gagged with a thick rope of unease.

"No. Don't ignore me." Alma readjusts the basket in the crook of her elbow and thrusts out a wrapped package of what I assume is my lunch. "What is *wrong* with you lately?"

"I don't know what you mean."

Alma rolls her eyes. "Oh, spare me. You keep hiding things from me."

"I told you, I didn't take your copy of *The Bane of Love*."

"I'm going to pretend that you're taking *any* of this seriously," she snaps. "It's not my life on the line here."

The bitter taste of shame fills my mouth. I offer an apologetic grimace, still focused on my task. "I've never been more serious in my life."

"Then why are you shutting me out?" She moves to the other side of the mare, looking across the saddle at me, so I can't turn away from her. I don't look up.

"Elias had to tell me about your run-in with the m-monster." She lowers her voice, glancing behind her at the well to ensure no one is in earshot. But even hushed, her tone is as sharp as a butcher's knife. "Then I hear from Ma that a bough spirit snatched one of your nobles right in front of you, landing you and Pa in a private discussion with the baron. So imagine my surprise when I try to wait up for you, only to learn you came in after I fell asleep and left before I woke up."

That was on purpose. I needed space to think after leaving August's study. Except there isn't enough space in all of Wielinde to prepare myself for what I'm to face today.

Alma's next words, softened to a dull point, break me.

"Did I do something wrong?"

"No." With a deep breath, I lift my gaze to hers, reading the hurt in her warm brown eyes. "Alma, you could never do anything wrong. How can you think that?"

"Then why am I hearing everything from people who aren't you? You're practically my sister," she insists. "If you have a day like yesterday and don't tell me, what else am I supposed to think?"

A new, squirmy sensation floods my gut, and I'm too disgusted with myself to hold her stare. It crushes my heart that I made her feel this way. The saddle girth is already as tight as it needs to be, yet I fiddle with it anyway.

"I didn't want to worry you." It's weak, I know.

And of course, Alma picks up on it right away.

"Liar. It's not just about yesterday." The wicker of her basket squeaks as she sets it down, then leans against Sybil's side. "You still haven't told me why you . . . The Hunt. I know who for," she says, cutting me off with a slap against the saddle. Sybil's ears flick back. "But not *why*. Why you suddenly decided to join something we both hate? And honestly, Katrin, I'm beginning to think that if I hadn't been with you, you'd have kept Emil's and the eagle's deaths from me too. That scares me."

My hands freeze at last, and to my horror, tears sparkle across my vision. The writhing within me turns to solid ice. How can so many secrets be the way to protect someone? Everything I'm doing is for her, but having it thrown so directly into my face makes me feel like I belong on the bottom of Lotte's shoe.

But the sight of Elias leaving the courtyard through the long archway, Petra and his hunting party on his heels, stops the words behind my teeth. Before he vanishes into shadow, he casts a lingering look at Alma. It's full to the brim of wonder and tenderness. Not dark want, not a desire to stake a claim—only goodness.

I can't tell her she's the reason I need August dead.

I love her too much to taint the way she sees the world, how she moves through it. She doesn't deserve to live in the same fear I do, that a man might lurk around a corner, ready to do something I don't want no matter how many times I say no. She doesn't deserve to be another trophy hung on the wall, just so August can brag he once hunted her down. I want to kill August so that the only men she encounters respect and love her without question.

If that means letting a handful of secrets rot inside me, then so be it.

"You *are* my sister," I say, meeting her gaze head-on. The sun cuts through the clouds then, glazing the chilled courtyard in a soft gold. It brings out the strands of red in her dark curls and accentuates the earnest gleam in her eye that I never want to see diminished. "Can you trust me, that I'm doing all of this for a good reason?"

Her stare narrows. One cheek hollows as she pulls it between her teeth, mouth pursing. My chest feels tight, and I realize I stopped breathing in wait of her response. Finally: "Will I hear this reason eventually?"

I nod. Quick and fast, injecting as much honesty and apology into it as I can.

With a deep, beleaguered sigh, her shoulders relax. She strokes Sybil's neck. "Fine. But you better not keep anything more from me *or* do anything stupid," she accuses tartly, flinging a finger at me.

My smile is as weak as the sunlight but a hundred times warmer. "Deal."

"I *mean* it. If that Stag takes you because you didn't win, I'm cutting a hole in the veil myself to get answers from you."

"It won't come to that." I say it to reassure myself as much as her. Yesterday can't be the last time I see the Breimar Stag. I refuse to wallow in that particular fear any longer.

"It better not. That's my whole point. Honestly."

Alma collects her basket, handing me another package and a few bottles of juice across the saddle. The gesture is brusque, but relief brightens her expression now. I stuff the items into the saddlebag, glad we smoothed things over.

Glad, until she says, "Isn't that woman supposed to be in your group? Why is she leaving with Pa?" Suspicion needles her voice. I follow her glare, stones tumbling in my belly.

Stefan heads toward the archway next, and behind him, arm in arm with Rowena, walks Lotte. Deep in conversation yet capable of scowling over her shoulder at me at the same time. I can only imagine the vitriol she's spilling to the newspaper princess.

"Lotte didn't feel 'safe' with me after what happened with the bough spirit—"

"Which is *not* your fault," Alma interjects.

"No, but she also had it out for me. So August volunteered himself and Felix to switch hunting parties."

"What?"

The horse shies away, her hooves clinking against the cobbles as she dances back. I seize the reins and bring her to settle. "Easy, easy. *Easy.*" The third I direct with a sidelong glare at Alma.

"And Pa let him?" she demands. She hurries around Sybil to my side.

"What else was he supposed to do?" I look at her, my eyebrows raised. "I'm just as capable as him or Elias to guide, and *he* still doesn't know I'm after him. As much as we like to pretend otherwise, August is in charge. He could have fired me or set Felix on me, so . . ." I give a half-hearted shrug. "It could be worse."

"But—how are you going to get the Stag from under him?"

I swallow hard. "Still figuring that out."

As one, we look to the column nearest the archway Stefan's group vanishes through. Observe the man leaning against it and overlooking the courtyard like a god from on high. Arms crossed, he's already watching us. My first instinct is to move Sybil to block Alma from his view.

"Ooh, if I get that man alone, I'm going to—"

"Do absolutely nothing," I hiss. She recoils slightly from the dark vehemence honing my voice, but I don't file it down. A razored edge is needed to ensure she stays away from August. "I mean it, Alma. You keep clear of him. He's not worth a second of your time. He doesn't deserve it."

She steps back from the horse, raising her hands in surrender. "Okay, okay. Just, please be safe. You owe me a really good reason, remember?"

My heart softens. "I'll see you later. And watch Rudi for me."

The thought of leaving her behind again feels like misplacing a limb, but like the first time, it's to keep her from the clutches of another monster. August threatened to shoot her to make me tell him my secrets—I'll never forget that, nor will I give him the chance to repeat it.

"Rudi will be safe with us," Alma says, lighthearted once more. "Between Ma and me, she'll get so many kitchen scraps that she won't be able to move."

"I need my poor hunting dog to outrun bears, not become one ready for hibernation, thank you very much."

With that, I sling my rifle across my back, gather Sybil's lead, and cluck my tongue for her to move toward where Ilse, Gerwin, Felix, and August now wait. The original spineless pair eye me with trepidation that draws my posture up straighter.

Lotte didn't get to where she is business-wise by letting perceived slights go unpunished, and I've no doubt she told her lies about what happened enough times to believe them herself. If Ilse and Gerwin convinced themselves I'll set stone nymphs on them, then sure, I happily gave Jannik away as a groom. Some fearful quiet and deference from my group is exactly what I crave.

My shoulders slump when I meet August's leer. Where the sun made Alma shine, it only highlights his darkest spaces. The shadows of his cheeks and beneath his brows, the darkness of his clothes, the maw behind his smile.

He mutters something to Felix, who scowls and walks away to fetch August's white gelding. No longer needed as a bodyguard while the Hunt's binding protects them both, it appears the brutish man has been reduced to a porter. It would make me laugh if August didn't push off the column and stroll across the cobbles to meet me.

Hands tucked into the pockets of his tweed coat, he is the picture of a prowling wolf. Graceful and unhurried on the outside; lethal beneath the surface, ready to strike the moment a weakness is sensed. I refuse to show him any. My bones are encased in steel and Wielinde will not like them hanging from its trees.

He strides around, stopping behind me. I bite my tongue as his touch lands on the small of my back. Even through my coat, the points of his fingers are ice. Still, I hold my ground—taking a step forward will only encourage him to vex me further.

"This is going to be such fun," he says, breath warm on my cheek.

"Just let me do my job," I reply, staring ahead.

"I wouldn't dream of interfering with that." He leans in closer on the pretense of inspecting Sybil's saddle. "Do a good job and I might be inclined to give you a bonus."

"Let's go," I say through gritted teeth, nudging Sybil on.

August breathes a soft laugh before his presence recedes from my body. "Whatever you say, Katrin *dear*."

As we walk out of Prauen's grounds and into the trees, the endearment repeats in my head, and I can't hear it as anything other than the animal we shoot.

Chapter Twenty

With impressive calm, I dissuade myself from cutting off Sybil's entire tail when she swats me in the face again. I don't even flinch when the black mare reels her head around and clicks her square teeth together menacingly. My discarded coat lies on the ground after she last tried to nip me and letting her have it served as a short-lived distraction.

"If you would just *hold still*—" I say through gritted teeth. I seize the mare's tail anew and quickly comb through it with my bare fingers, hunting for the bramble sprite near the root. The coarse dark hairs make it nearly impossible to find the little monster.

So it finds me instead.

"Ow!" I rip my left hand back and shake it hard. But the tiny Forest Folk has sunk its thorns in deep, clinging to the skin between thumb and forefinger, sharp as a wasp sting. I don't even bother with a tooth offering—its venom will spread the longer it stays hooked in me. Instead, I pinch its segmented body and wrench it free.

Where moss mites are nibbling spiders, bramble sprites are hornets of pure malice. I watch in annoyed fascination as the silent ball of black-and-brown thorns, barely larger than a coin and just as round, thrashes between my fingers, attempting to dig its barbs into whatever it can reach.

I toss it into the trees to wreak havoc elsewhere and give Sybil a comforting pat on the rump. "There, better?"

She nudges her head against my hip, as though apologizing for her previous behavior. Not that I can blame her. I frown at the twin needle punctures on my hand where the sprite stung me. Two beads of blood glisten, and beneath the swollen skin prickles the venom that will leave it feeling cold and numb for a bit.

I drape my coat across her saddle and jam my gloves back on, like that will hide the truth. That it usually takes several stinging sprites to have any effect on myself or the horses, and just the one hurt worse than half a dozen. The Krauvel's growing influence is apparent once more, forcing itself inside my worries and stoking them higher.

Irritation claims its rightful place alongside them as I reach for Sybil's lead, only to find it already in the hands of the last person I want near me.

"I said to go on without me," I snap at August. The moment Sybil started lashing out from the sprite, kicking her hooves and throwing back her head, I instructed the rest of my hunting party to carry on down the path. With a tall, overhanging cliff on one side, pocked by clumps of wet moss, I had faith they wouldn't get lost or go too far.

The baron smiles indulgently down at me and wraps the lead around his hand. "Always so combative, Katrin."

As he clicks his tongue for Sybil to move, my feet stay rooted. Suspicion drags taloned fingers up my spine. I wouldn't be surprised to find red welts on my back when I undress before bed tonight for how much the sensation has touched me since we left Prauen. I told August to let me do my job, and so far, he has.

And I'm still waiting for the other leaf to fall.

I stomp my feet a few times and cast a silent curse into the treetops. With the hope Sybil has one more bramble sprite hidden away so she can bite August, I force myself to follow.

"You're supposed to listen to your hunting guide when they give you an order," I say, unable to help myself.

"Perhaps I didn't wish for you to be alone." He glances back, then shifts Sybil over so there's room on the path between him and the rock wall to walk. I slip around to the other side of the horse instead. "Apparently there's a frightful monster in these woods."

I laugh once, dry and bitter. "Don't act like you care now. And I can handle myself just fine." As if to prove my point, I reach under and snatch Sybil's lead back. I pull her closer to me rather than use her to pin August against the rock. Her hooves fall in steady, hollow thumps against the needle-strewn ground.

"Yes, Stefan told me of your little *run-in* with the not-to-be-named beast yesterday." August's fingers hook into Sybil's halter. She releases a startled huff as he moves to block her head and look at me fully. I stare him down, grip tightening on the rope.

"Then you know it has a fourth body part now," I say. "An increasing danger, yet still you have your gamekeepers out with permission to only look for the Breimar Stag."

"You think I don't care, but you've merely proven me right. It found *you*, Katrin dear. Not the other way around." He drags his free hand over Sybil's silky nose—not even she can get away from his unwanted touch. "It's only a matter of time before the monster is stopped. Just like it's been every time before."

"And how many more people will die before then?" Emil was the Krauvel's second victim; Jannik its victim indirectly. I flex my stung hand, failing to abate the numb, tingling sensation that rules it. The Forest Folk are behaving more and more abnormally, so a third dead guest is only a matter of time. But to him, that's just an exciting story, adding color to their memorable visit. So long as the Hunt proceeds and his guests can crow his praises in their rich little circles, what does it matter?

I shake my head with disgust and try to leave before I say something more. His hold on Sybil's halter strengthens, and she can't toss her head free.

"Let her go," I say sharply.

August ignores me. "Speaking of run-ins with monsters—Lotte wanted your head yesterday."

"And I'm sure it was very difficult for you to say no to her."

"Some might even say you owe me now."

I take his hand and remove it forcibly from the horse. "I don't owe you anything."

"I'm not asking much," he says, a deviousness tipping gravel into his voice. He lets me walk past him, but a few long-legged strides have him reappearing on my other side. "Just one little burning question answered. I think that's fair exchange."

"Fine." I stare resolutely ahead. A flash of white breaks through the trees—it must be August's horse, still managed by Felix. I walk a little faster. One question is an easy enough price to pay if it makes him go back to leaving me alone out here.

"The answer I want"—he leans over my shoulder despite us walking side by side—"is what you were doing in the Bower."

A guilty pulse draws my awareness to my golden scar as my heart speeds up. Instinct wraps itself around my throat. The fight-or-flight choice blazes bright before me, and I seize the closest of the two without pausing to consider them.

"Fuck *off*, August." It comes out loud enough to make my ears ring. To reverberate against the stone behind me and carry through the trees like birdsong. It's neither clever nor sly, but I mean it with every ounce of marrow in my bones. The numbness in my hand burns hot, raging throughout my entire body, and it feels like a cleansing.

He laughs, but his expression is anything but light. "What did you say to me?"

I whirl to face him. "Why do you care about what I did? Why do you *ever* care about what I do?"

It should add another ton to my already heavy worries that he still suspects I'm up to something, but I don't care. It's clear that unless I tell him in plain terms, my secret is safely mine. He'll never figure out my only dream is to see his bones hung from a tree. And I'm so tired of waiting for that to come to fruition.

"You are a grown man with a *wife*," I say, lifting an accusing finger, "and a *child* on the way, yet you have more room in that skull for a teenager who just wants to live in peace and do her job than anything else. I don't want to *be* in your head. And I don't understand how you can't see how twisted that is!"

August crosses his arms but says nothing. His face is stony as I rail against him. Such impassiveness only makes me continue, hoping he'll listen to me just *once*.

"This Forest is both in danger and becoming more dangerous in one. It is turning itself upside down with creatures disturbed by a slipping balance that you don't seem to think needs fixing. Because somehow, *I'm* more important to you. *Stop it.* Just leave me and my family alone and actually do something *useful*."

My chest heaves after I finish, head spinning. I said similar things to him before, but always lesser. Spoken in a tone to put him off while making him think it was his idea, leaving me unscathed but oh so very small and insignificant. Never have I said such words tempered with the heat that has simmered beneath the surface for days.

It's not just cleansing—it's a baptism of my own self and worth.

"Are you quite finished?" he asks with unreadable quiet.

My triumph sizzles out beneath the smallest flicker of movement at his mouth. When he lunges, there's nowhere to run. He snares my arm and pushes me against the mare. "Careful, Katrin. That all sounds remarkably ungrateful for someone who had their precious job saved by my uselessness."

Whatever retort builds on my tongue is swallowed by the slipping pressure at my elbow.

Exhaustion and poor planning on my part left me without a single clean sweater. This morning, my choices had been to shake the wrinkles from one of the dirty pullovers or cardigans dropped on the floor, or pull a blouse and embroidered bodice from my dresser. The white linen shirt was too thin to muffle the glow of my binding scar, so I bound my elbow with one of Alma's handkerchiefs.

With my jacket still slung over the saddle, August's grip—hard and unyielding as ever—pushes easily against the knot. A knot I thought I tied tight enough with one hand and teeth . . . until it unravels.

Just like the secret he so desperately wants to pry from me is about to do.

"August!" The yell spills distantly through the trees. "August, where are you?"

We both freeze. He turns toward the sound, but I watch him, the only danger I have space to worry over.

The same frantic voice calls again, and I recognize it as Gerwin. "Come quick! Bring that gamekeeper girl too."

With a grumble deep in his throat and not even a final glance, August releases me in a half-hearted shove. He stalks off. "Come along."

A shrill, grating gasp climbs up my throat, stripping a measure of steel from my frame. My makeshift bandage slips to my wrist, half undone. I yank it out from my sleeve and throw my jacket back on. I don't breathe again until I've done up every button. Too close. That was *too close.*

I guide Sybil along the rock wall as it curves in and out. Around a deep bend waits my entire hunting party, and the cause of Gerwin's alarm makes itself known right away. A loud rustle arises from the greenery to my right.

"Oh no, oh no, oh no," Ilse murmurs, her soft voice steadily pitching higher until I doubt even Rudi could hear it. Her retreat stalls when she bumps into Felix with a squeak, then darts to hide behind his hulking form. The armed guard gestures brusquely for August to do the same, but the baron merely stares into the shaking foliage.

I shoulder past him, snagging Gerwin's wrist and stilling his scramble for his pistols. I no longer trust him with a weapon, never mind a loaded one.

"Just stay quiet," I instruct. My attention fixes between the pines, watching the hazy shape moving behind the thicket of devil's club.

"But—but it could be—it might be—"

"It's not."

But it clearly doesn't soothe—he and Ilse are reliving yesterday. So am I. Despite being fairly certain I know what's lurking just out of sight, the memory battles its way to the forefront of my mind. The bough spirit. Another Forest Folk lashing out. *The Krauvel.* My pulse pounds in my ears.

A dull crack. The clusters of bright red berries tremble again. Shadowed and tall—it moves closer. I can't make out its edges, where it starts, where it ends. Slow, careful, I let go of Gerwin and reach for my gun. However sure I am, a pea-size amount of hesitation puts caution in charge. I creep into the dense grass.

The solid weight of my rifle is a balm. It slows my heart rate, cools the blood in my head. But still buzzing from our earlier exchange, I must fight the instinct to turn my gun on August when he joins me.

"What is it?" he asks. I'm somewhat disappointed by his steady voice, no hint of the fear the others harbor.

The bush shakes with its strongest shiver yet. A few berries tumble free. Muscles coiling tighter, I release the safety on my rifle.

The creature steps into view, ears flicking and unbothered.

I expel a long breath. I lower my rifle and laugh gently, glad I was right.

A silverback doe. Her coat is a stormy grey dappled with white, a coloring that will keep her hidden when she and her herd climb into the mountains for the winter months. We don't hunt them until they come back down in the spring and summer, and from the fading spots along her spine, she's barely older than a year. She's not to be harmed today.

August seems to disagree. He steps deeper into the grass in front of me and fits his rifle to his shoulder.

My brows furrow. "What are you doing?"

"Hunting."

"Just leave her be, August," I murmur. "It's not her time yet."

"I say when it's her time." He pulls back the bolt to load his shot, and the doe lifts her head. "She's mine, after all, isn't she?"

I bristle. "That doesn't mean it's the right thing to do."

"My guests were invited for a hunting trip. It starts by actually killing something."

"Then find something *else*," I say, approaching him. "She's too young to be hunted."

"There's an easy way to stop me, Katrin." He peers down the sight, adjusts his grip with tiny movements. "Answer my question. Tell me what I want to know."

It's a gossamer-thin strand added to a mountain to finally set off a landslide.

August's finger wraps around the trigger of his gun, but *my* bullet fires.

A sharp bang splinters the quiet of Wielinde. The recoil slams against my shoulder, but I don't feel it after so many years.

The shot whistles past August's ear and wedges into the trunk above the doe's head.

She flees before I lower my gun, disappearing into the bushes with a frantic crackle.

Slack-jawed, shoulders still drawn up to his ears, August looks back at me. Murder waits in his gaze, and I don't *care*. Wielinde Forest is on the cusp of something completely unknown, and all he has the decency to care for are his own wants. He proves it time and time again.

What *I* want is the Breimar Stag in my sights, and then nothing else will matter to me.

The butchery smells stale, every breath tasting of copper. Often, a large animal will hang from the thick ceiling beams in some state of dressing. Hide stripped, meat broken down, then its bones boiled clean to return to the Forest. But we've not brought a deer home in over a week, and the small square room is empty.

"Where *are* you two?" I mutter, feeling suddenly adrift.

I lean against the doorframe and pinch the bridge of my nose, trying to figure out where Stefan and Elias could be. I know they're back; Klaus told me as much when my hunting party passed through the gate earlier. But I've searched my uncle's workshop, their rooms, looked in the kitchen next door, and they might as well still be in the woods for all the success I've had.

Fucking August. I glance at the bare beams again. If he had his way, a silverback would be suspended there. Killed months out of season and unforgivably young. I couldn't let him have that doe, but more importantly, he needed a reminder of who he continues to antagonize. He needed to be humbled.

The Scavenge Moon is only a few days away. My chances to find the Breimar Stag and leave the Hunt unscathed are dwindling. Stefan and Elias will think it foolish I scared that doe away from August, but I realize I don't care about stepping lightly around him anymore. I'm a girl with nothing left to lose and a hundred things to prove.

Now if I could just find them to *tell* them what happened. As I decide to check Stefan's workshop again, a familiar bark tears through the hallway. Warm delight surges in my chest as Rudi barrels toward me.

"How's my girl?" I exclaim. Her entire body wriggles in time with her tail, and I crouch to give her a good rub. "Miss me?"

Her only response is heavy panting and repeatedly shoving herself closer into the space between my legs. I barely keep my footing.

"Oh, you're back!" Alma appears from the kitchen but balks when she spots the open butchery door. Her gaze immediately flies to the opposite wall. She hates the messy work that takes place in there.

"Have you seen Stefan or Elias?" I ask, rising to shut the door behind me.

"You haven't seen Elias either?" She frowns. "Pa ate dinner a while ago, but I was just on my way to see if you or Elias were back."

I readjust the roll of my sleeves at my elbow. I've not had a chance to retie the handkerchief, and the thicker, bunched fabric works as a makeshift replacement to conceal my binding scar. "That's strange. The guards said he came home first."

"Well, you can come find him with me now," she says brightly.

Alma and I head into the courtyard, Rudi sticking tight to my side.

"You better not have brought back any big game, because Ma's going to end you if you did." Said in a singsong and delivered with the sweetest smile I've ever seen.

"Only if you tattle," I respond in kind. Tone flattening, I say, "I'm the only reason we returned empty-handed, actually."

"Oh?" If curiosity was a living thing, it dwells in her voice.

She steps inside Stefan's workshop, calling Elias's name, but we both knew silence would answer before she even knocked. The windows are dark, the fire cold. No one is there. Just as it was when I first looked.

"Do I have to guess, or will you at least tell me this?" She emerges with my jacket, which I left on the worktable with the rest of my things. I catch it when she tosses it to me and drape it over my shoulders.

I flush. "It's pretty simple. I needed to beat August."

She stops in her tracks beside the well, confusion evident in the slant of her brows and the tilt of her head. Then she lets out what must be an involuntary hoot of laughter. Her hand quickly stifles it. "Simple *and* stupid. You literally told me he wasn't worth the time."

"Yes, well, he wasn't listening to me," I grumble. He never does.

"How did he take it?"

"How do you *think*?"

Not well at all, but thankfully that worked in my favor. His choice of outrage had been sullen quiet. A grown man brooding like a petulant child. August inserted himself between Ilse and Gerwin for the rest of the trip, like cutting me from their vapid conversations was punishment. Instead, it was the most at home in the Forest I'd been for weeks.

"Felt good, though."

"Well, I'm glad it was worth it for you," Alma says with another reluctant chuckle. She turns to keep walking but pauses to collect something from the base of the well—a ball. It belongs to Rudi, and I'm impressed she spotted it in the shadows. The sooty stitching holding the well-loved boar bladder together was once white.

"Did Stefan say if he had any plans when you saw him at dinner?" I ask, trying to think of where I haven't looked yet that would make sense. "Maybe Elias is with him."

Alma tosses the ball ahead of us into the passage leading to the gates. Rudi takes off with an excited yelp, claws scrabbling against the cobbles before she gets her paws under her.

"He mentioned something about the gardens earlier. That the hawks were circling again."

I grimace. "Does he think the foxes are back?"

Last spring, we had some trouble with a family of foxes that made their burrow in the hedge maze. Poor Elena kept finding their half-eaten meals of rats and rabbits in the flower beds, and every day a pair of hawks soared above, waiting to steal the rest. It was a few months before the kits were old enough for us to oust them all.

Alma intercepts Rudi's return and takes the ball with a sharp tug. She winces from the slobber that coats her hand but hurls the toy again. "I don't know, but he may have looped Elias in to go check."

The gate comes into view and our boots crunch against the main drive. Twilight sits heavy atop the castle, the waxing moon hung in a sky a salted violet that darkens with each upward glance. The shadows thrown across the main courtyard are dense as honey. They turn the ivy leaves to charcoal, the moss between stone to ink, and force the few lanterns lit to work hard to matter. Together, we hurry up the curved stairs to the upper tier of the courtyard. This time I throw the ball.

It smacks into something to the side of the staircase leading up to Prauen's doors and bounces pathetically back to land at my feet.

Something . . . large. Shrouded in darkness but the faintest gleam of the lanterns traces the edges of the moving figure.

Rudi stops behind us and barks.

Whines.

Growls.

Chapter Twenty-One

Slowly, I reach for Alma. She's already behind me, clutching my empty coat sleeve. Sharp tugs pull off the jacket before she tries to yank my arm, but I don't move. Can't move. I've entirely forgotten how.

I blink hard, unsure if I wish for my eyes to better adjust to the gloom or to erase the scene altogether. A ghastly shape unfurls from the clotted shadows. Higher, higher. More and more unnatural. Stretching until the warm firelight glances off dull white bone.

Wrong, wrong, wrong.

The Krauvel rises in all its clacking glory. What holds its clattering bones together without flesh or muscle, I don't know. I can't tell in the dark. But whether it be rotten magic or sheer will, the monster's head cricks to the side, as if considering what to do with us.

At its full height, a brown bear stands nearly eight feet, but the Krauvel hasn't arranged its bones in the same way—it's much taller. A sloping skull baring sharp teeth teeters on a long spine. Large hooping ribs crowd and cross one another to build a narrow chest. Legs crooked the wrong way resemble the hind legs of a deer, and mighty claws tip too-long, humanlike arms.

A monster thieved from nightmares.

We stare at each other across the courtyard. Those dark eye sockets pierce deeper than any other gaze I've been pinned under.

Its posture shifts, curls in a defensive gesture. My focus falters, flicks down to the ground, and I notice the body crumpled at its feet.

My heart ceases beating, my chest falling cold.

"Pa?" Alma whispers, voice torn at the edges.

Stefan lies face down, limbs sprawled every which way. His mouth gapes open, his eyes closed. I can't tell any more beyond that, but I would recognize his profile anywhere. The shadows conceal the answers to every question that races through my mind. Is he hurt, bleeding? Unconscious? Does he still have his eyes?

Is he still alive?

The only certainty is that an organ-snatching monster hovers above him with a proprietary stance. And it can't have him.

My pulse starts anew, fast enough to make me dizzy. Haltingly, I graze the top of my thigh, but I know my knife isn't there. I stupidly left it in the workshop with the rest of my things.

Think, think, think. This stalemate of surprise won't last forever. The Krauvel continues to observe us in silence. Alma still tries to hold me back while desperately begging Rudi to hush. Whatever this pause is, it's an untouched layer of frost on a well-trod path. Someone's foot has to crush it first.

With sickening fear for my uncle and a burgeoning hope in mind, I don't wait any longer to bring my boot down.

All three of us—monster and human—burst into motion as one.

The Krauvel launches. Its bones rattle violently as they collide with the castle wall, clinging to the white stone between the second-floor windows like some grotesque beetle. A freakish growl splits the air in an unsettling combination of a wolf snarl and the echoing void in its ribs.

I turn my back on it to run for the gates, but Alma surprises me. She picks up the dog's ball and whips it at the monster. Her unleashed yell teems with a rage I've never heard from her.

But the Krauvel is too fast. It crawls higher up the wall, claws tearing strands of ivy loose. The ball flies into a window below it. Glass shatters with a deafening smash, shards rain down on the cobbles.

"Alma," I say, in near disbelief. "Go see if Stefan is all right."

"What are you going to do?" she demands. Her voice is small but burns with ferocity. To harm Emil was one thing, but the Krauvel came for her father—that is unacceptable.

"I'm going to make sure it's stopped," I yell over my shoulder.

This won't be a repeat of the wolf. Stumbling upon the Krauvel and Stefan like that cannot be for nothing. I was too late to come between it and the wolf, but my uncle . . . he didn't look touched yet. Eyes are next and his were closed. In the shadows, they looked unharmed. And with a nearly feverish hope that they still are, I have to make sure. I must chase away the monster and ensure it leaves for good without the pieces it needs to stay.

Tail between her legs, Rudi runs ahead of me toward the gate. I jump the last four steps of the courtyard, landing hard in the gravel on one knee. An uneven skittering sound whips my head around in the same movement that pitches me upright. The Krauvel scales the roof, moonlight glinting over its stolen bones. I sprint, terrified I'll lose sight of it too soon. A slate tile comes loose a beat before a growl ripples through the deepening twilight. It careers to the ground, cracks in half.

"Katrin?" Wesley calls, leaving their post from beneath the portcullis. "That you?"

"Weapon!" I shout as I near. My voice breaks like another roof tile. "Give me a weapon!"

Hestia emerges from within the guardhouse. Her question is mangled by a yelp, and she lurches back as Rudi blitzes past her inside.

"What's all the racket? Castle coming apart at the seams or—"

"*Get me a damn weapon, Wesley!*" I bellow.

They startle when I run straight up to them, barely stopping in time. A crossbow sits cradled in their arms. If I had breath to spare, I would groan. I hate crossbows—so tedious to load. A glance back stifles my protest. The Krauvel heaves itself over the roof peak, vanishing into the gardens on the other side.

"Give me that." I snatch the weapon from their slack grip, then grab the few bolts I spot in a quiver at their hip. I don't know what good these will be, but better than nothing.

Wesley saw the impossible bone monster. The color in their face flees with the incoherent syllables that escape their mouth, but I'm already running.

My footsteps ring out as I tear through the passage that mirrors the one Alma and I took moments ago. Instead of another courtyard, I emerge in a verdant world bathed in silver moonlight and accented by light thrown from the castle windows.

Prauen's gardens are a battleground of shadow. Delicate plants too big to move into Elena's greenhouse are bundled in burlap. Their shapeless silhouettes face off against topiary shrubs, which change from swans and hares to devils in the dark. Directly ahead stands an entrance to the hedge maze, a black and foreboding mouth.

I tuck the three bolts I grabbed into my back pocket and drop the nose of the bow. Bracing it in the gravel with a foot while peering into every corner, I haul the string into place. It groans as both hands pull it taut. *Where is it?*

I lift the bow level in my arms, grateful it's at least light, and load the first bolt. My heart is a wild beast caged, thrashing against the bars.

A screeching cloud of birds erupts from the maze. I whirl, nearly shooting on instinct. They are a fluid blot of ink against the dark purple sky, frightened from their nests.

"Fuck," I whimper.

Of all the places I wish to hunt a monster in, the maze is near the bottom of my list. But I tighten my hold on the crossbow anyway. This may be my last chance to banish the once king of Wielinde. After losing my first opportunity in the ruins, I can't cower from this.

These hornbeam hedges were first planted when August's grandmother was a small girl. Elena spends the last month of every summer trimming the walls neat and even, the hedges' height twice that of mine. In the autumn, leaves that never drop turn as gold as spring daffodils.

They swallow me now as I step between them.

A trio of lanterns waits at the end of the long passage for any wandering guests. I take one and hold it out, propping the crossbow on that same arm.

Offered limited options, I walk to the right.

The warm flickering light doesn't reach far, and darkness unspools in an unfathomable line before me. No moonlight spills over the hedge tops either, leaving me with the feeling of being devoured. I pause after every step, straining to hear. Listening for gravel shifting, leaves rustling, the rattle of bones.

At the next branch in the path, I turn left. Move deeper into the maze and away from the castle.

As children, Alma and I chased each other between these hedges almost every day. We memorized each corner and route like it would be our only job at Prauen. Which paths led to lichen-crusted statues, bubbling fountains, alcoves with stone benches to sit upon, and which took us to dead ends.

That map so painstakingly learned by heart is illegible to me now. Faded parchment with torn edges and ink smudged beneath spilled tea. Two more turns introduce me to my first dead end. An impenetrable barrier on three sides, and my stomach drops as though I missed a stair, stepping out over thin air.

I retrace my steps, walking a little faster on the other path to the right. My grip on the crossbow grows sweaty.

After darting around another right corner, then a pair of lefts, the lantern glare catches something pale ahead. Without hesitation, my finger squeezes the trigger. The bolt releases. It cracks off the stone collarbone of a woman dressed in a flowing marble gown.

Her empty eyes watch me set down the lantern and fumble to reset the crossbow. I curse when panic makes my fingers clumsy, the string twanging when it slips. The last two bolts tumble from my pocket. What I wouldn't give for my rifle right now. I'll never take it for granted again.

Another turn, another dead end. A fist seizes my heart as the thought at the back of my mind screams too loud to be ignored any longer.

I am lost. Completely and utterly *lost.*

Hot, shameful tears spill down my cheeks as I backtrack again. It feels so pointless. There are four exits, one to each cardinal direction, yet I haven't the faintest clue which way I face. The hedges are so tall I can't see Prauen's rooftops, the mountain peaks. Only cold, remote stars. My breaths are too fast, head swimming a little.

I don't care about finding the monster anymore. Not in here. I just want out.

I need to get out.

No sooner does this thought eclipse my panic than I hear it: a clatter I both sought and dreaded.

I freeze, listening. It sounds like it's coming from the other side of the wall to my right. Iron casts the length of my spine, and I throw back my shoulders. I creep toward the forked path before me. If I turn right, that may lead me to it, and I can just—

A sob clogs my throat as I meet another dead end.

This was the worst idea I've ever had. More foolhardy than entering a legendary Hunt that might leave me dead in a few days' time. A noble decision executed in the shock of the moment. I stand by my reasoning, but how could I have been so stupid? I ran headfirst into a maze I no longer know with no company but a monster that needs body parts I can easily supply.

I need out. *Now.*

Alma and I never got lost in this labyrinth. I close my eyes. We figured out every route, yes, but there's also a trick hidden in its history. Once, during a scorching summer, the previous Wagner baroness was left so turned around she eventually collapsed in the heat. After the groundskeeper rescued her from the ordeal, she ordered a secondary path be cut from the center to the northern entrance, so she always had a way out.

I set my jaw, grip tightening on my lantern. Find the heart of the maze, find my exit. A feat that suddenly feels so much more possible. I know a large fountain marks the center; the bronze horse sculpture atop it stands tall enough to be visible from the castle windows.

Left, right, dead end; retreat, left, right, right, left—there.

The cry still trapped in my throat squeaks out. Ahead, its creamy stone soaked in moonlight, water cascading from beneath a rearing stallion, waits my salvation. I push forward.

It appears before me as a towering shadow.

Another step and I would collide with it. As it is, I barely slow in time, gravel scraping beneath my feet. Firelight flares against the underside of the unnatural skeleton I have but a second to glimpse.

Small lungs once belonging to an eagle hide behind a wall of ribs, the vital strands of them stretched thin and reaching for gaping nostrils. The shifting dangle of a wolf's tongue and esophagus against the upper portion of a spine. A desiccated glimpse of Emil's brain tucked inside an animal skull. From it fine threads of nerves spread out, winding around each and every bone, lashing the ill-fitting pieces tightly together.

And eyes. Eyes held lidless inside black sockets.

Pale, bloodshot, and human.

Only a second, yet it feels like an entire lifetime bloomed and withered within it. An eternity passes in a blink before I remember my wits.

It stole eyes I can't recognize in the glaze of the firelight. Are they Stefan's brown ones or someone else's? My hope of permanently stopping this monster may be gone, but I have to get out of here if I want any chance of an answer.

I jerk up the crossbow. The lantern tumbles and smashes at my feet.

The bolt slides between the Krauvel's bones with a metallic thunk. A wrinkled growl overhead is the only indication it found its mark. What I expected to happen doesn't. I wanted to split its spine, to remove a piece integral to its structure like a bridge collapsing without a keystone. My aim was true, yet none of the vertebrae separated. It remains infuriatingly upright.

A huff of fetid and impossibly hot air gusts through its nose, almost like a laugh. That small hint of intelligence sharpens my predicament into crystalline clarity. The useless crossbow falls limply at my side. A fragmented howl begins to climb, low enough at first to roll over my skin, then quickly raising the tiniest hairs.

I ram the final bolt into the Krauvel's eye and *run*.

After the hungry darkness between the hedges, the moonlight at the maze's heart is almost blinding. It sparkles in showers of water, a pool blanketed with lily pads. Even the leaves appear gilded. The bronze horse proudly kicks out its hooves atop a wet plinth, its nose pointing to freedom.

I don't notice the secondary path, narrow and left overgrown, until I speed past it. Evidently, my hazy memory of its existence did not extend to how well it blends in, especially in the gloom. My boots slip as I pivot. One leg slides out from under me, and I hear a loud splinter as the crossbow interrupts my fall.

The Krauvel trails close behind. Its bones click together, like Stefan's knee sometimes does when he climbs stairs. Except this is *all* the bones. Hundreds held together with macabre string and moving faster than they have any right to.

Click-click-click-click—

Terror roots in my chest. I scramble to my feet, digging furrows in the gravel, and hurl the broken crossbow. It slams into the Krauvel's braided ribs, glancing off. The bolt I plunged deep into its head protrudes harmlessly from the corner of its eye socket. Those perverted eyes—light in color, I see now—stay fixed on me.

Heart blocking my throat, I lunge into the overgrown path.

Branches grope for my shirt, snag my hair, scratch my boots. My imagination turns them into monster claws, and I wrench free with defiant shouts. I stumble onto a maintained gravel path and throw myself back between the hedges.

An avalanche of cracks and rustling crashes behind me. Amid the thrashing chaos, wheezing growls and clicking, clicking, *clicking*.

A few months ago, I stumbled upon a hare being chased by a fox. It was almost amusing to watch. How the hare practically ricocheted in and out of the trees, the fox snapping after its every bound.

I don't find it funny now.

Over and over, I spill from between hornbeam walls, drawing ever closer to the edge of the labyrinth. Ahead, through the last obscurity of golden leaves, the northern exit looms large and bright. Even the night air thins to cool my heated skin.

When something sharp curls around my upper arm, piercing through linen and flesh, there is no mistaking it for a branch.

"No!" I scream.

The Krauvel tries to pull me back into the hedge. Its claws scrape, searching for purchase. They hook into my shirt, tugging, tugging. I lash out. Liquid warmth spills down my arm, but a loud tearing sets me loose.

I burst out of the maze. My right sleeve stays behind, ripped at the seam and flapping like a bloodied flag. Frigid clean air sears my lungs. Behind me, the last snap of fragile branches falls silent.

Click-click-click—

I glance back, and the Krauvel, gold leaves tucked between the bones, appears as an eldritch god after my scent.

Never thinking more than a few breaths ahead, I forgot how little space I would have to run. Fewer than a dozen strides eats the distance between the walls of the maze and the balcony bordering a clifftop.

My scream echoes over the mountain valley as I come to a clumsy stop. Not fast enough, though, as my waist slams into the stone railing. Desperate hands push into the wide, flat rail, fighting against momentum to keep from flipping over the edge. One foot briefly leaves the ground.

I manage to hold on, but there's no time to savor that.

Instinct sinks into my muscles before my brain can direct. I throw myself back, away from the rail and to the ground. Gravel smacks into my chin, burns my skin.

By then, the Krauvel's paws have already left the ground.

Its growl roars as it leaps forward. Above me.

That hare I saw, for all the fox's efforts—it did escape in the end.

The Krauvel soars over the railing. With a tremulous howl and a clatter of flightless bones, it falls to the Forest far, far below.

Chapter Twenty-Two

The Krauvel's body hits the rocks at the base of the cliff. Too far away from me, there's no sound, but I imagine how it looks—nerves untied, bones scattered like broken glass with no hope of ever fitting back together again.

Stolen bones and organs, returned to Wielinde where they belong.

In uneven movements, I steady myself on hands and knees. My skin feels as though it was struck by lightning. Everything beneath the surface sparks and burns with frantic, pent-up energy. The gold of my binding scar, now exposed and smudged with blood, blazes against the night.

Once I'm able to trust my limbs, I struggle to my feet, using the balcony for support. I lean over, clutching the stone with a death grip. My small smile at the thought of seeing that monster in smithereens fades. The corners of my mouth soften, forming a small *O* of horror.

There is no spatter of bones, no painting made of crushed organs.

Far below, the Krauvel limps into the dark, leafless trees. Its bones are crooked, the misalignment of its body clear even from this distance. One leg rotated backward, an arm broken in the middle equivalent of its forearm, spine bent to the side.

But the *snap* of those bones correcting themselves—that I do hear.

As it slips beneath the branches, its spine jerks into place like a puppet wrenched upward by its strings. Another loud crunch accompanies the twist of its leg.

My eyes follow the Krauvel deeper into Wielinde. The crushing weight of helplessness settles atop my sternum.

I watch until it is little more than a few diamonds of ivory bone in the moonlight. Its color shifts to something darker, and then I lose sight of it entirely.

A sheepish Rudi waits for me at the mouth of the garden. When she spots me, the alpine pointer rises, head so low the tears I struggle to keep at bay burn. I fall to my knees and wrap my arms around her neck. Too late I remember the blood on my arm, but she burrows into my embrace with a sad sigh. Her warm, steady body mends something I didn't know was coming apart inside of me.

"I know," I whisper into her fur. "You're still my good girl."

One minute. I allow us one measly minute to be miserable together before the call of more pressing matters becomes deafening. A last inhalation of her fresh outdoor scent, held in my lungs to ground me. I need it for what's to come.

When we return to the castle, the scene is a busy one. A murmuring group gathers around the body at the foot of the stairs. The grand entrance doors to Prauen are flung wide. Golden light spills down the steps.

"Oh, thank heaven," Alma says in a shaky breath when she notices my approach. "What I'd have done if you—"

She shoves Hestia and Wilhelm aside to let me through, but not before snatching my abandoned coat from the older man's arms. I barely register the weight of it around my shoulders, but her hand is ice as she seizes mine. Clutches it like I'm all that will keep her standing.

No amount of time spent hiding in Rudi's fur was enough to prepare me for what she says in my ear next. "He's . . . he's all right."

I examine her profile, soft in the castle's glow yet so serious. "He's okay?"

"He's okay." She swallows before adding, "Mostly."

My steadiness falters. "What does that mean?"

"The monster didn't touch him. But . . . Come on, Magnus is with him."

Alma guides me between fretful faces, all belonging to castle staff. They offer sympathetic noises and consoling touches as we pass, and it makes my skin crawl. If any of them notice my binding scar beneath the flap of my coat, none say a word. My feet tangle with Rudi's as she sticks to me like moss on bark. Olga is last to step aside, and the familiar scent of sugar wafts from my cousin's curls as she pulls me close.

I can't bring myself to look at Stefan and instead observe the others around him.

Elena must have been ready for bed before she came running—the frilly edge of a nightgown peeks out from the bottom of her long coat. The groundskeeper holds a lantern aloft, the castle doctor working by its light. Magnus's hooked cane lies on the ground beside him. It must pain his bad leg to be on his knees, but that's never stopped him from tending to a patient before. Opposite him sits Aunt Carolina. Stefan's head rests in her lap. She strokes his hair back from his brow, and I have no way to put it off anymore.

My uncle seems . . . fine. Slack in his unconsciousness and looking far too old in the glare, but whole. Untouched. My shoulders slump, yet no relief warms my chest.

The Krauvel never took his eyes, but I think I already knew that. Stefan's eyes aren't blue like what I saw in the moonlight. But whose are . . . or were?

I grasp Alma's hand in both of mine. "Why is he still not awake?"

"Stefan sustained a head injury," Magnus says over her. His level voice is tepid, undisturbed by what worries the others. Nimble fingers unroll a clean white bandage from a medical bag that escaped my prior notice. I also didn't notice the red staining Carolina's hands, her apron. The blood on the stone where he lay before they rolled him over. My grip squeezes. "Looks like he fell down the stairs and gave himself quite the knock."

"Can't you use smelling salts or something? Wake him up."

The demand sounds as though given by a confused child, and Carolina answers me as such, gentle and soothing despite barely holding back tears. "It doesn't work that way, Katrin."

Magnus hums in agreement. Deftly wrapping Stefan's head, he adds, "Best thing we can do now is make him comfortable and wait for him to wake on his own."

"He's an idiot," Alma hisses, cross and wet. I glance at her in surprise. "Pa wasn't wearing his glasses *again*. He refuses to wear them while in denial that he can't see a thing in the dark without them. You watch, he'll wake up and that'll be the exact reason he fell."

"And I'll sew them to his ears right after that," Carolina says in a threatening tone, but her hands on his face are still so tender. "Stubborn, stubborn man."

As Magnus requests something they can use to carry Stefan inside, I pull Alma out of earshot, nearly tripping over Rudi. The dog remains fixed to my side as if to prove she isn't scared of the Krauvel after all. I never doubted her bravery, though.

"Why do you look so sour?" Wary joy lifts Alma's voice, and I so badly want it to infect me. "This is good! I mean, it's awful, obviously, and I already hate waiting for him to heal, but this means we stopped the monster. Pa has his eyes, even if they don't work right—"

"We didn't."

"—and I'm still—wait." Her brows lower. "Didn't what?"

"It already has its eyes."

"No. *No*," she says. Disbelief creeps into her tone, like one of her cakes falling flat in the oven. After a moment, she insists, "It's dark. The moonlight was just tricking you. And Pa is *fine*."

"Alma, I saw them with *mine*. Stefan was never its prey." As her head continues to shake, I hold both her arms and wait until she meets my gaze so there can be no mistaking the horrible truth I wish was a lie. "When we found them both, it already had what it wanted."

"But you don't know that. What if . . . what if it was after Pa for the next piece? The next body part?"

It's a thought that crossed my mind too. Accompanied by the gruesome image of my uncle strung up like a deer in the butchery, skin carefully peeled away by knife-like claws.

But the Krauvel never touched Stefan. He injured himself, and as much as it flies in the face of what I want to be true, I genuinely believe finding them together was a coincidence. The Krauvel does not seem to be in a rush to build its body. If it was, it could have stolen what it needed from not only any number of animals, but me. Alma and Elias too. It was only playing with me in that maze.

Reading all this as it passes over my face, she staggers back a step. Now she truly looks like I'm all that will keep her on her feet, but I resist reaching for her. "When is this going to end, Katrin?"

It hovers between us in the cold but punches me in the gut all the same. I don't know. I just don't know. My entire spirit feels drained by today.

Loud footsteps scratch through the gravel drive behind me. My body immediately shifts back into survival mode, but before I can react, Alma's eyes narrow on Elias.

"Where have you been?" Anger, hot and corrosive, coats her words.

Elias flinches beneath them. He takes the steps two at a time to reach us but stops beneath the combined force of both of our tempered glares.

"What happened?" he asks, out of breath. His cheeks flush red from exertion and the settling chill of the night. Rudi hurries over to him, and he absentmindedly pets her. "At the gate, they said something about Stefan."

I turn to face him fully, fists forming at my sides. "Where. Were. You?"

A hand cards through his hair, and he steps closer. He can't seem to decide which of us to address, whose attention will work out in his favor better. "I went down to Steigert. I—I had a letter to post."

"You could have left it with Klaus," Alma snaps. "You know he handles the mail for everyone."

"I needed a walk," he insists. The pipe smoke I smell on his clothes supports this. "A break. My hunting party was particularly annoying today," he adds with a knowing smile, since I should understand exactly what he means. But it's not funny tonight, and his grin melts to a contrite line as Alma's despair and worry find a target. I let her take the shot for us both.

"Out of all the nights you could have gone. Out of *all* the nights, when we *needed* you."

Another wince. "Alma, what happened?" He takes a step forward, but a rise of voices finally draws his attention to the handful of people coming out of the castle with a stretcher. Makes him notice Stefan still out cold on the ground. His face pales. "How—"

"Pa fell down the steps and hurt himself. The monster found him—"

"*The* monster?" His jaw drops. So aghast it makes me wonder if he's laying it on a little thick to survive her ire. "It was here? You saw it?"

"—and I suppose we should actually thank you for not being here. Because if we hadn't been looking all over for *you*, we'd never have found him in time."

She moves closer to him, looking up at him with such . . . well, I don't even know. It's not an expression my features have held before. Rage and disappointment and love all stitched together into a delicately intimate mask. His own holds that same affection beneath the remorse, and I look away for a moment.

"But Katrin had to chase that monster all by herself, and by the look of it, it chased *her*. She barely got away." She spares me a glance. "Did you? You're missing a sleeve and are bleeding, so I assumed."

"You assumed correct. It found eyes, Elias." I pull my coat tighter around my shoulders. "It has someone's eyes."

"Shit," he breathes.

"Yeah, shit," Alma agrees haughtily.

"I am so sorry. I know it doesn't change anything, but I'm sorry I wasn't here. Is Stefan . . . They weren't his eyes, were they?" And the pure fear in his face, like he just realized the worst-possible scenario might have come true, deflates my anger. I won't begrudge Alma hers, but there isn't room in my body. It just makes me tired.

"No. But we should tell someone." Who, I don't know. We've kept the Krauvel from everyone else, and August is probably too deep in his cups to do anything but laugh. "Someone else is hurt on the grounds and I don't—"

I withhold the rest of my sentence when I hear an odd shuffling. It comes from the nearby unlit passageway to the far right of the stairs and the commotion that stems from around Stefan. But the other two hear it as well. Bodies still facing each other, their heads turn toward the archway. The passage is short, leading to a small, octagonal outlook the expectant baroness likes to frequent.

The shape of a person—a man—comes slowly out of the darkness. A pale face first, his features blurred but streaked with red. A rumpled guard uniform. One hand clawing into the stone as he labors into the fire glow.

"Help me," Klaus says in a tiny voice. "Please."

The light never touches his eyes because there are none.

Alma screams.

I don't follow what happens next. Bewildered shouts from those carrying Stefan in, Elias shielding Alma, Rudi slipping into a barking frenzy. Klaus's fellow guards running to aid him, only to lurch back in horror or to throw up. Magnus pushing past us all and ordering us inside, that he would deal with it.

Elias, Alma, Rudi, and I walk down the main hall of the castle behind Stefan's escort, yet all I see are a pair of gaping, bloody holes. Two empty pits with impossibly clean edges. Where before rested bright blue eyes now sits *nothing*. I clap a hand over my mouth in a preventative measure. To vomit, scream—either is likely.

At the end of the hall, instead of moving straight into the Great Hall, the group steers the stretcher around the corner. Elena says something about taking Stefan to bed, but her voice sounds like it's underwater to me.

Through the open doors of the Hall, many of the nobles are distracted by food and their own terrible company, but most stand and watch. Ilse's interest is marred by her swatting her husband's comforting hand away; Rowena looks like a cat that caught a mouse; Lotte rolls her eyes and turns away to needle Schultz.

They don't know what happened outside in the last hour, how it could have been any one of them now blind forever. And I *hate* them. I hate them all for their lack of everything else. A lack of compassion, of concern; of kindness, decency, or hearts free of rot.

And the worst of them all stands separate from his guests.

August idles in the hallway before the door, twirling a horn of what I suspect is ale as he watches my uncle's form move past him. A tiny smirk plays at the corner of his mouth, but I resolve with aching, gritted teeth to ignore it. Stefan is my concern right now, not this ass. I already showed I wasn't to be trifled with by sending a bullet over his shoulder today. It's enough.

The moment my back is to him, my placid demeanor vanishes under the scour of his remark.

"Falling on the job. Tsk, tsk. He deserves to be an easy target for that beast."

Elias's hand at my arm can't stop me. He grabs my jacket, and I leave him holding only that. The anger—the *rage* that lives at a constant simmer beneath my skin—erupts. It boils, seethes, fills the world with clogging smoke. I transform into something feral and mean. My hands are my only weapons as I fly at August.

"You fucking miserable bastard!" I shriek. I can't decide fast enough what best to do with my hands, so claws of my own making reach for his face. His hiccupped yelp is *glorious*. The cup knocks from his grip, amber liquid and foam splashing down the front of his blue coat and white ruffles. "You pathetic, parasitic—I'll feed you to every goblin, barrow, and gaunt myself!"

But before my nails dig into his skin and tear it like the thin parchment I imagine it to be, an arm hooks around my middle. Elias pulls me back, lifts me up with Alma's harried encouragement as she strains to haul Rudi down the hall. My hands still scrabble for August's startled expression, and my thrashing feet join the fray.

"You tiny, insignificant man!" I bellow, spitting the words.

His wide eyes flicker to my sleeveless arm. If I ever wondered what a hare would look like after watching a bear grab a fox by the throat, the smile splitting August's face is the exact picture. A foul display of teeth that I know will haunt me to the end of my days.

"*There's* the little secret you've been keeping from me." He straightens his jacket and smooths his hair, his calm composure restored and confusion sluggish in my mind. His tongue clucks. "That wasn't so hard, was it?"

I don't understand this sudden shift. Not until I follow the line of his gaze, straight to the crook of my elbow. To my golden binding scar. Bloodstained from the Krauvel's scratches and no longer concealed by linen, wool, or otherwise.

A crack must split through the earth's foundation. It's the only explanation for why I feel like I'm falling and falling, heading for a bottom I cannot see.

Elias drags me down the hall, following Alma and my dog away from August. My efforts to free myself double. He staggers beneath my jostling weight, and my grip switches to his arm, trying to pry it up. Trying to unleash me. But he's too strong.

"Let me go, Elias," I snarl.

"No."

"Put me down!"

He doesn't relent until he carries me up the stairs and almost to the landing, where voices issue from my aunt and uncle's room. Only then does he set me on my feet, pushing me into the wall with a hand to my shoulder.

"When are you going to stop making stupid decisions?" he asks in a low and strangely threatening voice.

"When *he* stops being stupid."

"Katrin, be reasonable. You can't even harm him, yet you keep ending up in situations that test extremely dangerous limits."

He's right about one thing. Even if I had sunk my nails into him, it wouldn't have made a difference with us both under the Hunt's protection. But I don't see it like that right now. "It would have made me feel better. Why do you care?"

"I like you, Katrin. I think in time we're going to become very good friends." He leans in close, his breath smelling a touch stale. "But I need you alive to be my friend. You just showed August *all* your cards, and I'm not sure you're going to make it one day beyond the end of this Hunt."

I shove his hand off. "Even if I have to kill him in his sleep the morning after, I'm fucking done with this."

Without another word, I storm up the rest of the stairs and push into my uncle's crowded room.

Chapter Twenty-Three

ONE NIGHT UNTIL THE SCAVENGE MOON

That night, time stands still. The carriage clock on the mantel that Carolina winds before bed *tick-tick-ticks*. But seconds don't pass. Not really. Its sound is the same as being pinned beneath a steady drip of water. Over and over. Reliable, predictable, and dragging forth a slow madness.

My sanity teeters on the edge, but I can't leave my uncle's side.

Stefan has always been an immovable presence. As permanent in my life as the statues sequestered in the maze. The father I should have had from the start; the father I'm grateful to call mine anyway. Seeing him laid out like this, head swamped by the bandage—it's all wrong. The white linen turns his skin sallow, the heavy quilt pulled over his chest makes him small and vulnerable.

I stare greedily at his face yet can't reconcile it with memories of him in the Forest. Of teaching me tricks to shoot my target through greenery, to recognize a heart tree. How to leave teeth for the right Forest Folk and how to discern which of a herd, flock, or pack is the best to claim for the survival of the rest. This man is a hollow shell in comparison.

The awful, thick silence winces from each *tick-tick-tick*.

Carolina sits on her side of the bed, one hand stroking Rudi where she lays beside her, the other clutching Stefan's. Her locs shield her face from view, but the fragile set of her shoulders and her ragged inhales declare her as lost as I am. Alma perches in the armchair beside a stack of her mother's novels, glancing from her father to where Elias and I lean against the wall. I don't mind standing—from here I see every hopeful flicker of movement beneath Stefan's eyelids.

Magnus came in a while ago after seeing to Klaus's . . . loss, more shaken than I've ever seen him. The doctor checked Stefan over, then tended my arm on Carolina's insistence and despite my protest. Without a word, he used more bandage than needed to cover my golden scar. He left with the promise to return in the morning.

Eventually the ticking does stretch seconds into minutes, minutes into hours.

Soon after midnight, Alma falls asleep, curled in the chair like a cat. Elias excuses himself shortly after, but not before gently tucking a blanket around my cousin's frame. Carolina tells me to go to bed, too, but I only collapse in the chair someone brought earlier. Exhaustion weighs down my eyes, and somehow, I sleep.

At quarter past four in the morning, the ticking ceases. Carolina forgot to wind the clock.

I jerk my chin up from where it rests on my chest, braced for an attack. The sudden silence feels like it's hiding something, the dark its willing accomplice. It pokes and prods at my spine. Forces me out from under the haze of wretchedness and to remember that there is so much more at stake outside this room.

Rudi jumps softly off the bed as I grab one of my uncle's sweaters. The neckline hangs too low, the sleeves fall over my fingertips, but it's warm and smells of home. I step into the sparsely lit stairwell. Rudi's claws make more noise than the shutting door, and she runs ahead of me up to the next landing.

My uncle will be okay. He'll wake up—he has to. I need to yell at him, just the same as his wife and daughter need to. In the meantime, there are other matters to attend to.

Elias answers my knock the moment I finish rolling both sleeves up past my wrists. He sleeps bare-chested. Dark shadows lurk beneath his eyes, his light hair standing up every which way. His grogginess fades with his tightening grip on the edge of the door.

"Katrin?" he asks, voice hoarse. "Did something happen?"

I push inside and, by the light of the stairs, pick up a shirt and press it into his chest. "Let's go hunting."

We return as dusk settles onto its haunches. Cold, tired, hungry, led by all three dogs, and with nearly no teeth left in our pockets. No Krauvel, no Breimar Stag, and no signs of either. The lack of anything to show for such a long day leaves me with the ominous ticking of Carolina's clock in my head.

Hestia greets us at the gate, a rueful twist to her mouth. "Evening. August ordered us to tell him when you came back."

"And you're not going to," Elias barks, striding past her. Dirt streaks one cheek from where he slid down an embankment—an accident brought on by almost losing his nose to a vicious lichen nyx.

"Of course not," she exclaims. Disgust at the very suggestion digs a furrow between her dark brows. "What do you take me for? It's just a warning. He was furious there was no one to take them all hunting this morning."

"If he wants to go out so bad, he can fucking take himself," I say.

I'm not doing a single thing for that man anymore. For any of them. My job no longer matters. The secret August wanted was finally bared, raw and ugly. He's smart enough to look at every card I placed on the table, as Elias so put it, and understand *why* I entered. To think I would help anyone find *my* Stag now.

The Scavenge Moon rises tomorrow.

That leaves me with only a day and a night to find the Breimar Stag and kill August without dirtying my hands. One more day to save myself and my family. Once the protection of the Hunt lifts, I can't guarantee I *will* be able to slit August's throat the day after. Failure now means not only leaving Alma and my family vulnerable to August's proven cruelty, but also the terrible possibility of the Stag taking *me* back with him. As it is, returning empty-handed tonight feels the same as drafting an execution order—all that remains is to ink my name on the dotted line.

One day for the Stag. Two body parts for the Krauvel.

Tick. Tick. Tick.

Elias and I discard all our hunting gear before stopping in the kitchen. As much as I want to dash straight upstairs to see if there's been any changes with Stefan, Rudi and the foxhounds need to eat, and so do we. But entering the over-warm space and noticing both Carolina and Alma are still absent ruins my appetite.

My sour mood only grows mold from there.

A grim pall hovers in the kitchen like the steam from the boiling pots. We kept the Krauvel's existence to those who could seemingly do anything about it, but Klaus's eyeless appearance, coupled with Wesley seeing the monster themself, ignited a stick of dynamite in that barrier. Everyone knows now, and enough remember Greta's stories, even if they are broken pieces of a memory.

"But what came after the eyes?" they whisper over cuts of venison.

"Isn't it a stomach?" said over silverware polished.

"No, that's not even one of the parts it needs," spoken into the pot of soup stock. "It's bones next."

"You oaf," admonished above slices of freshly baked bread. "That was the start of it. Why do you think they brought back that strange bear?"

From all corners of the sweltering kitchen, conversation and speculation. They worry—and rightfully so—they might be next.

And they very well could be. The Krauvel has attacked on Prauen's grounds multiple times. A noble wasn't safe, nor was the captain of the guards. Predators don't stand a chance against it, let alone prey. But I'm wrung dry of comfort to give and decide to leave before I hear any more.

Although sitting in my aunt and uncle's room with the others isn't much better, it's at least quiet. Alma tries to talk, but none of us have the heart to pretend. We all resume our positions from the night before and settle in to wait. Even Petra and Milo, usually content to stay in Stefan's workshop, curl up at his side now.

Finally, after another hour keeping vigil, a shred of hope is offered.

"What's all this?" comes from the bed.

My head jerks back around from staring into the fire. Stefan blinks blearily at us all, and I nearly burst into tears. Alma does. She leans over to seize her father's hand while Carolina stretches out beside him and rests her head on his shoulder, a relieved smile softening her worries.

"You hit your head," Alma blubbers. So much for reaming him out. "*That's* what all this is."

"Who's that there?" He gestures with his chin to Elias and me, then winces from the gesture.

"Take a guess, old man," I say with a disbelieving laugh.

"Ooh, you infuriating man," Carolina practically growls. She sits up, snatches his dreaded spectacles, and threads them around his ears in a swift movement. "I don't ever want to see those off your face again."

Stefan blushes beneath the bandage, resembling a ripe tomato. A vivid red that makes him look alive and healthy. He grumbles a protest, but he's not winning this fight. This battle has Alma, Carolina, and me on one side, and we are highly formidable.

Elias steps out, returning moments later with Magnus. The doctor's examination is distant and efficient, but he flashes a radiant grin once finished. "Take a few days to rest up in bed, but you're in good shape, my friend. Lucky too." He collects his cane from where it's propped against the nightstand. "If you need anything, you'll find me with Klaus. But I don't think you will. Very lucky indeed."

I trail Magnus to the door. He must know what I want to ask, and his delight at my uncle's recovery dims as he beckons me onto the stairs.

"Klaus is not well, if that's what you want to know."

"Is there anything we can do for him?"

Magnus shakes his head. "Aside from the obvious"—he waves vaguely at his eyes—"he's fine physically. Mentally, well, he's in shock. He's gone somewhere else in his mind, and that may be for the best right now." His gaze flickers over my shoulder, and I sense that Alma and Elias followed me out. "Time is all we can give him."

He offers Rudi a perfunctory pat on the head and descends the steps. The other two take his place.

"We've been kicked out by Ma," Alma explains. She's her cheery self once again, and it's catching. "So we're going to eat and tell everyone the good news. I just want to change first."

She pulls at the collar of her blouse, as if it might stick to her skin. I realize then that, aside from my borrowed sweater, I'm still in the same clothes from yesterday too. And after a long, fruitless day spent in the Forest, a change of clothes and a quick wash sounds perfect.

Our joy over Stefan's health is temporary. A gentle breeze on a scorching summer's day, the brief reprieve before the uncomfortable heat glazes one's skin again.

I reach my and Alma's door first, and the others bump into me after I swing it open. Rudi growls low in her throat but sticks tight to my leg.

Frigid, storm-laced air curls over the threshold. The edges of the curtains flutter, the window latch broken and the iron hardware hanging by a single bolt. Bright moonlight pours inside, setting the dust sparkling like fresh snowflakes. Makes the exposed sinew on the floor shine.

Between the two beds, like a new rug, sprawls the body of a large, four-legged creature. I think it is—*was*, for mercifully it's already dead—a cougar.

"Oh, fuck." Elias turns away and claps a hand over his mouth, his shoulders heaving as he tries to pull Alma away too. She places a steadying hand to the wood paneling but says nothing.

Skinned and laid neatly in the center of the room, the cougar's snarling head faces the doorway. Like it was waiting to be found.

Like some perverted gift, just for us.

Tick. Tick. Tick.

Chapter Twenty-Four

The door to Brigitte's old room squeals on its hinges loud enough to disturb the dead. I grimace as it creaks even worse when I close it behind me. Mercifully, only Alma sleeps in this room, and nothing dead lies in wait.

Three stable hands were recruited to remove the poor, ravaged cougar. They lowered it out the window with a rope around each exposed paw, a far more charitable reversal of how it entered our room. Blood still stains the floor, and even with the window open, it smells like the butchery—copper and meat. There was no way either Alma or I would sleep there tonight, so this is to be our room. At least for one more night.

Tomorrow is the last day of the Hunt—who knows what will happen to me after that full moon sets.

Slightly smaller than ours and stripped of personality beyond the deep green wallpaper bearing sprigs of holly, the room walks the line between warm and stuffy. Rudi, brought upstairs by Alma earlier, thumps her tail twice in greeting from where she lies on her back before the hearth. A banked fire crackles there, but it's Alma's reliable candle that provides the most light.

Alma lies facing the wall in the bed on the right, every blanket pulled to her ears. She handled the cougar discovery with uncharacteristic stoicism, and that saddens and aggravates me in equal measure. The horrors of the last few weeks have hardened her. Chiseled some of the dreaminess out of her. What we witnessed are not things anyone should be okay with, let alone grow to tolerate. I for one feel violated by the Krauvel taunting us like that, making sure we know only its missing heart remains. It's probably as useful as bringing a toothpick to a duel, but I still jam a chair under the door handle and double-check that the window is firmly locked before changing into my nightgown.

I slip beneath the covers of the unclaimed bed and imitate Alma by sleeping on my side. A position I hold for no more than a minute before flipping onto my back. Then turn onto my other side, tucking one leg up to my chest. And back to lying flat.

My eyes snap open, watching the dance of firelight between the ceiling beams. It's close to midnight. In the past few days, I've seen multiple corpses, chased and been chased by monsters, feared for my uncle, and am now trying to ignore the real possibility of my own death tomorrow. I'm exhausted to the point of feeling sick to my stomach. I desperately need sleep yet doubt how I ever will.

Every time my eyes close, I see my bloody heart impaled on antlers, hear that awful clack of bone, coming closer and closer.

With a soft groan, I turn to face the wall again and order myself to sleep. To stay still. If I don't move, if I command my mind to focus on pleasant things, I can drift off. I have to.

After a few minutes of utter failure, a faint creak comes from the other bed. The soft shuffle of blankets and rustling nightclothes.

I freeze when my covers lift, a warm body sliding in behind me. Sweetness replaces the metallic scent still in my nose. Alma wraps her arm around my waist and snuggles her head in between my shoulder blades.

"What are you doing?" I whisper.

"Little hard to sleep with you flopping around like a dying fish."

"Sorry."

We lie in the near dark, quiet and content. I shift closer to the edge so she has more room on the narrow mattress. It's been a while since Alma and I shared a bed—she's taller than I remember. When the deep snows and hard ice finally settle over the valley, and the windows and fireplaces aren't enough, one of us will usually clamber into the other's space. But tonight, with the room nearly stifling, I know she's not cold. And I'm so grateful. Her presence soothes my fraying nerves and lets me sink into her embrace, limbs heavy and sluggish.

"You're doing this for me, aren't you?" she breathes into my nape.

I stiffen. My eyes drift along the wall, scrutinizing every unfamiliar dent and scratch made by someone else. If I hope to find words that will dissuade her within each flaw, only defeat stares back. Alma takes my silence as permission to proceed.

"Why you entered the Hunt, going after August—the reason you wouldn't tell me is because you're doing it for me."

Said so kindly and sweetly, like she never once doubted it.

"Does . . ." I swallow and lick my lips. "Does that bother you?"

She seems to mull it over for one long, gut-wrenching moment, her hold on my waist tightening and loosening as she readjusts to fit more comfortably on the bed. "A bit. I don't like that you did it without saying anything, or that you kept it from me."

"I didn't want to worry you." But it sounds downright pathetic now that it's finally out for her to hear.

She snorts, a huff of heat that ruffles my hair. "No, you just made me worry about fifteen other possibilities by keeping secrets, you twit."

My mouth puckers, the realization bitter. I hadn't thought of it that way. Seems so simple when put like that, black and white. To me, it's all felt like a maelstrom of grey. Smoke and storms I weathered alone for us. In the heat of the moments that stacked up to cement my decision to enter the Breimar Hunt, and then every snide remark from August after, it seemed too difficult to burden her. But I suppose that was never my choice to make.

"How did you figure it out?" I ask.

"Please. I'm not the one in our family who needs glasses to see what's been going on."

Anger bubbles anew. "Like? If he—"

Her fingers dig into my stomach. "He didn't do anything. I just mean I've noticed how . . . attentive August has been the last few weeks to me. You can't be around all the time to hiss at him, and he's come downstairs a lot lately. Plus, it struck me as odd this week when Ma stopped leaving me alone whenever he visited."

My hands fist in the blanket at my throat from the casual tone of her voice. Like she expected to experience this at some point, not that it's something she should ever. The fire gives a small pop, and I imagine it as my heart breaking. I entered the Hunt to shield her from what she's already being stalked by.

"He said some things, and I eventually connected the dots. Although, I don't think I really knew until I talked it all through with Elias."

"Aren't you two thick as thieves." I immediately swat away the thorny emotion that emerges. I don't mind that they confide in each other. It's what I want for her, another part of why I entered the damn Hunt. But a small piece of me still wishes to keep Alma to myself. She's my sister, and I've never really had to share her before.

"Don't worry," she says, assuring me with a deliberate squeeze. "You're still the love of my life. Which means I'm allowed to be worried and mad and everything else in between when you do these reckless things, like trying to claw August's nose off." Her words dissolve into a fit of giggles that make the bed shake.

"Not my finest moment," I admit, recalling with a pang what I lost to August's knowledge yesterday, but unable to smother my grin at Alma's mirth.

"His face, though. I only saw it for a second and I'll never forget. I think his eyebrows flew past his hairline."

Silence falls easily between us. The logs in the fire suddenly shift, and the light on the ceiling flares brighter. Rudi gets up with a big stretch and hops onto the bed, stepping heedlessly on our legs before curling up atop our feet.

"Alma?"

"Hmm?"

"Do you at least approve?"

"Of course I don't." Her voice comes out too loud. I flinch, and she quickly lowers it. "If I'm honest, I'm still furious that you entered the Hunt at all. You hate the whole thing, and so do I. For however noble a reason you think it is, it was still a dumb move. So you better win."

Molten warmth pools in my chest. I clutch her hand against my stomach. "I intend to."

"Good. I know you will, but I'll also never forgive you if you don't." She shoves my shoulder, and I lightly kick her shin. I feel her inhale deeply. "But, hypothetically, say you don't find the Stag, and he takes someone else back with him . . . What are you going to do?"

My eyes prickle, and even though she can't see my face, I quickly shut them. "I don't know. I honestly don't know." I'm not ready to think about it just yet. Not when there's still a chance for me to beat August once and for all. It's the only foolishness I pride myself in holding dear.

"Nothing will be the same, will it?"

"Probably not," I say, somehow being the one to soothe now. My thumb rubs back and forth over her hand. "August knows I'm in the Hunt now. I'm sure he figured out who for too. And with what I've done in the last few days . . ." Flashes of berating him in the woods, shooting over his shoulder, and trying to peel his face off with my nails—they crowd my mind as though to bury me. "He won't turn the other cheek. I just don't know what he might do to me. Or . . ." I can't say it.

Alma solves it on her own. "Or to me. To Pa and Ma."

I nod, feeling her curls against my ear. "I wouldn't be surprised if Felix is outside the door right now, Hunt's protection be damned."

"And Pa knows about . . . ?"

"He does, and Stefan will do what's best to keep everyone safe. I believe that with my whole heart." Unspoken is the fact that my uncle is still recovering in bed, but it doesn't change the truth. I entered the Breimar Hunt to protect my cousin, my family, and he'll protect however he must. Even if he has to drag himself down the stairs in a nightshirt.

A soft punch to my shoulder again, then a knee to the lower back. "I'm so mad at you. About all of this. I get it, I do, but I hate it all so much. I can't lose you, Katrin."

I turn over, looking at Alma. Her nose is only an inch from mine, her eyes dark and enormous this close up. "You do know that *you're* the love of my life, right?"

She laughs softly.

"I mean it," I insist. "There is no one else I would have entered this Hunt for. You're the only person I think I will ever truly give a whole damn about."

"A whole damn. Wow."

"Alma."

"I know," she replies. "You're my sister, and I know you think I shouldn't, but *I* won't let anything hurt you, no matter what happens after tomorrow. You have to get that Stag, Katrin. For me."

For her. Like there was ever any confusion on the matter. I press a kiss to her scalp, and we snuggle closer, just like we did when we were young children, a dog coiled at our feet.

Then, somehow, with Alma's heat softening my bones and her breath warm against my clavicle, I fall asleep.

Chapter Twenty-Five

THE SCAVENGE MOON

When I wake up, it takes a foggy moment to realize the room isn't collapsing around me. It's just someone at the door. A frantic barrage of knocks, without end.

"*Wassisit?*" Alma raises her head from the pillow—*my* pillow, that she shoved me off at some point in the night—and looks to me, bleary and confused. Over Alma's shoulder, Rudi trots back and forth between the door and the bed, nudging Alma with her nose and whining.

I shove hair out of my face, blinking hard against the bright light streaming through the uncovered window. My body is warm and languid, and it's quite rude of whoever's at the door to insist I move. I jerk the pillow back and reclaim a corner.

"Tell them to go away," I mutter.

"Katrin!" The muffled voice slips through the keyhole. Alma throws her legs over the side of the bed as the knob rattles, the wood protesting as it tries to open. But the chair I put in front works as intended—the door clicks back into place without moving so much as half an inch.

A splinter of alarm delves into my lethargy, cool as frost down my spine. I slowly push myself up to sit against the headboard, listening to the stairwell outside.

"Katrin, for fuck's sake. I know you're in there." More cold curls around my ribs as I recognize who is attempting to break through our door. "We need to go!"

"Elias," Alma whispers. Her bewilderment drains away the moment she also realizes. Unguarded curiosity creeps in as she stands, wrapping a blanket around her like an overlarge shawl. "What time is it? There's no clock in here."

I look around the room, still somewhat dazed. My insides turn murky as pleasant drowsiness clashes with the growing iciness. I feel like I'm missing something important. My eyes dart over the dead hearth, the furniture that doesn't belong to us, the empty shelves. Overcast radiance streams in through the closed window, but I still hear the jangle of tacked horses, the muted rise of voices in the courtyard below.

The sounds shock me to alertness.

"*Fuck!*" I shriek.

Alma releases a startled scream in response, the chair slipping from her grip before she can remove it. "What? What is it?" she asks.

"Alma." Elias's voice grows louder, as though his mouth is pressed to the very wood. "Alma, open the door, please. Get Katrin."

"We overslept," I say, panic usurping any calm I have left. Sleep sloughs off me like water from a reed hob's skin. "*I* overslept. Shit, fuck—*fuck!*"

I crawl over the bed, trying to free myself from the tangle of blankets. My body sinks into the imprint left behind by Alma. One foot finds the floor—and so does the rest of me, my other leg still caught in the bedding. My limbs won't move right. All I can manage is kicking and kicking until the blanket lets go.

This is bad. This is so bad. I scramble to my feet and rush to the window, press my nose and cheek to the glass to see what's going on down below. My breath fogs the view in an instant, but I make out enough for my heart to squeeze.

It's the last day of the Breimar Hunt. Elias and I planned to leave at dawn, abandoning everyone to their own devices a second time. I meant it when I said August could take himself hunting for all I care. The Scavenge Moon rises tonight, and while I've been sleeping away the morning, every noble staying in Prauen Castle has been preparing to leave on the Hunt. *Is* prepared, from the look of it.

There aren't enough curses I can hurl into this dusty room that will make me feel any better about my colossal mistake.

I tear off my nightgown, uncaring that Alma may be about to let Elias in. There's no time to lose. None. Literally and figuratively, the clock is counting down to the possible end of everything as I know it.

And I bloody well overslept.

"Shirt. Where is my shirt!" My bare feet stumble on the edge of the rug in my rush, but I don't know where I threw yesterday's clothes. They're filthy and smell like sweat and dirt and blood, but there isn't time to find anything else. Under the bed? In a corner? I find one lonely sock by my boots. Rudi paws at another.

"Clothes!" Alma points to the top of the flat dresser. "I grabbed them for you last night since I figured you would forget."

Unnoticed by myself earlier, there sits a neatly folded pile of my clothes, clean and unwrinkled. I pounce on them.

"Bless you," I breathe, shrugging on first the collared shirt and fir green sweater, then stepping into the brown trousers. There's a tear in the knee I still haven't bothered to sew up.

Another loud thump against wood, followed by Elias's next stifled plea. Alma removes the chair at last. The door flies open as I sit on the floor and jam on my boots.

Elias stands on the threshold, one hand holding him up on the frame, out of breath and cheeks flushed. "I have been waiting for you—for an *hour*."

My frantic fingers can't tie a damn knot. "I know, I know, I'm sorry!"

"August must have talked to the nobles because they're all up early."

"I'm aware!" I snarl in frustration as I fumble the laces again.

"Here." Alma bats me away and kneels to do it instead. She finishes tying both boots in a swift, unruffled fashion. I plant my hands on the floor, ready to leap up, but she grasps my calf. My cousin stares at me, fathoms of significance glinting in her dark eyes. "You bring that Stag down. You hear me?"

I nod, and she helps me to my feet.

"For me, but for you too."

The reminder of our conversation last night, her faith in me, steadies my bones. I pull on my coat without shaking and wrench her in close for a hug. I breathe in deep the sweet smell of her hair, reveling in how much it feels like home. "For us," I whisper.

When I let her go, I expect Elias to be ready to drag me from the room. Instead, he stands in the doorway, biting his lip, considering something. One glance at Alma seems to decide him. A piece slotted into the right place.

He takes two quick strides inside, cups both hands around her jaw, and *kisses* her. Kisses her, holds her, like he won't ever have the chance again.

Right away, I feel as though I'm interrupting something. They forget I'm even here.

Startled to stillness at first, Alma soon fists his collar and melts against him. Their height difference is most noticeable while in this . . . position. An arm drops to encircle her waist, lifting her onto her toes, but his head is still tipped down low to meet her mouth. It looks uncomfortable to me and yet they seem to fit perfectly.

I bet not one of the heroines in her novels has received a kiss like that.

Rudi barks once, shaking me from my own delighted shock. I move to the doorway and clear my throat pointedly. "We need to go, remember?"

Elias pulls back from Alma seconds later, just enough to stare at her, a little dazed. He examines her beaming face as though memorizing every facet before he snaps back to his senses and releases her. "Yes, let's go."

From the landing, Alma calls half dreamily, "Good luck," as we hurry down, Rudi in the lead. Then, sterner: "Come back in one piece!"

Following behind me and still somewhat breathless—albeit for a different reason now—Elias speaks over my shoulder. "I left all my stuff in the Bower. Everyone is waiting in the courtyard for us to guide their parties, so we can slip out the main entrance. But if we don't want to risk being seen by any of them, we should cut through the gardens."

Despite my fluster of emotions, I can't help smiling. A week ago he could barely find his way around without getting lost and now he's planning multiple escape routes. We'll have to go through the gardens, but I regret not being able to grab my gear. I feel so naked with nothing on me—

"My gun," I gasp. I halt in my tracks at the base of the stairs, and Elias crashes into me with a grunt. Rudi doubles back after realizing we're not behind her anymore. "I have to get my gun."

His eyes close a beat too long to be deemed a blink. "Where is it?"

"In Stefan's workshop. With *all* of my stuff."

"Katrin," he says with dawning horror. "Everyone we're trying to avoid is outside of that."

"I know, I *know*." I glance at the nearest suit of armor, but the spear propped in its empty gauntlet is not helpful.

"Can you borrow something from the guards at the gate?" His tone slides toward desperation, aligning with the panic returning to a high pitch in my body.

"The best Wesley had the other night was a useless crossbow. I can't risk that, not for the Breimar Stag." I dig fingers into my hair, using the slight pain at the roots to help me think clearly. Food or water I can handle not carrying; I'm capable of finding that in Wielinde. Venturing into the trees without teeth is not ideal, especially since they've not been of much use lately. But my gun—"I need my rifle."

Elias steps down to my side and looks to either end of the hallway. A shiver courses through him the moment we hear voices drawing near us. He swears before grabbing my wrist and stalking in the opposite direction toward the lower levels—and the courtyard filled with nobles eager to claim us for their own gain.

He doesn't slow until we pass the kitchen, bustling even without Carolina commanding their ranks. Doesn't stop until we lurk in the shadows of the entrance to the courtyard. The clamor of the nobles is too loud in this passage; it ricochets between the walls. I jump when Elias's whisper has the same effect on me.

"Some of them saw me earlier when I was looking for you," he explains. "It's how I figured out you were still upstairs. So I can distract them while you get your gear, pretend I'm still trying to find you. With August in your hunting party now, and Stefan still recovering, he won't let anyone go without him, and he *needs* you there."

I wince at this last remark. My mind absorbs each word of this haphazard plan while attempting not to dwell on how easily it could fall apart. I yank the hood of my coat over my head, trying to conceal my face, but it seems just as flimsy as this plan. "Meet in the Bower after?"

He nods. "Just be quick. I don't have to tell you about lost time."

"Okay."

"Wait until you hear me talking to them." Without another word, he steps into the light of the courtyard and disappears from view.

I press myself to the wall, taking long, deep breaths. I barely resist leaning over to see what's happening. The air is bitterly cold, and a glance at the few dense clouds I can see makes me wonder if the first snows are already upon us.

"Rudi," I whisper, watching the dog until she looks up at me, tongue lolling out of her mouth. "Stay here."

A few columns and some withering shrubs will be my only cover to reach Stefan's workshop. My hood is empty optimism to consider a disguise, but being tailed by the alpine pointer everyone now recognizes will be a dead giveaway. She'll obey, even if she won't like it.

Once I hear Elias's voice, questioning the gathered nobles about my whereabouts and receiving a rise of complaints in response, I move. Knees low, body bent almost double. My soles don't make a sound as I rush to the second door.

Stefan's workshop is still unlocked, just as I left it yesterday, and I open the door wide enough to slip through. It shuts with a click behind me. Only then do I straighten, leaning back against it for a full five seconds before surveying the room.

My pack sits on the bench at the far side. I send a small prayer of gratitude to the Katrin of yesterday, who thought to replenish the teeth, shells, food, and water in it last night. Its weight is solid relief. My rifle waits on its rack, and I snatch it down from the wall, pulling back the bolt to make sure it's loaded. Both sling over my shoulder and I turn to leave. Before I open the door, though, I pause to spy out the window.

Fog on the glass panes blurs the courtyard, the figures outside made indistinct with an almost ethereal quality. I try to count the number of bodies, but they're difficult to tell apart. Distinguishing between the vibrant colors of their outfits seems to be the only way to guess, and at least eight people shout at Elias in his dark coat. A few stable hands must mill about on the fringes, since three horses stand saddled and ready to go.

I don't notice a particular shadow move in close until it's too late.

The door explodes open, slamming into my shoulder, the side

of my head. Stars erupt in my vision. My rifle nearly falls, the strap catching in the crook of my elbow as I stumble into the corner of the table.

"There you are," comes August's accusing voice. "Thought you could pull the same shit you did yesterday and go out on your own, little bit—"

I don't hesitate. Trapped in this room by a threat, I act how any animal desperate to live would: I fight back.

Eyes streaming with tears, head still ringing, I swing my rifle into my grip and ram the butt of it into the baron's gut. He doubles over with a loud "*Oof!*" and trips backward. August catches himself on the doorframe but struggles to draw in a full breath. Before he recovers, I grab both shoulders and thrust my knee up between his legs. His strangled sound of pain is the most beautiful music I've ever heard.

Without waiting for him to collapse, I shove past, knocking him outside, and *run*.

"Elias!" I bellow. My hood falls back. "Go! Go!"

My boots strike the cobbles sharp as a slap, and he reacts as though I've hit him the same. Elias's eyes widen and his face drains of color as I race toward him. His stare flicks to August on the ground, banging his fist against the stone and moaning, and his jaw drops.

Every noble has turned to watch my approach with varying degrees of confusion, but I take vicious delight out of shoving my way between Lotte and Rowena. The former falls to the ground with a feigned shriek of hurt.

I reach Elias. Pass him. My hand snags his elbow and yanks him along behind me.

"This wasn't the plan," he yells.

"I had to improvise." It's a breathless snarl that holds zero regret. I've only stunned August—under the Hunt's protection, the pain is likely already gone—but the triumph coursing through my veins is addictive. Nothing is keeping me from Wielinde and the monsters it hides.

Together, we sprint for the passage that leads to the gate and out, our nearest and only exit now. I hazard a glance over my shoulder.

The nobles crowd together in states of dismay and anger. Gerwin attempts to run after us, brandishing one of his revolvers, but every bullet falls from the chamber. Schultz helps Lotte to stand while others only look back at August, staggering to his feet.

They all part, though, like hands through tall, quivering grass when Rudi lunges between them. Claws clack against stone, teeth snap with a fierce growl at Ilse before my dog runs after us.

A smile lifts my cheeks as I face forward. The three horses near the archway dance from side to side, the tumult in the courtyard making them nervous. One stable hand, a young man in his early twenties named Tobias, moves to soothe them. His gaze, however, fixes on me. As we near, his eyebrows raise in question, and an idea smacks me with such force I nearly trip.

"Yes!" I shout, waving a wild hand. "Tobias, yes!"

With two deft tugs, the leads tied to a rail come loose, and Tobias turns Sybil and August's gelding, Samuel, toward the archway for us.

"Elias, grab Sybil," I say as I veer to the outside of the horses.

"What? Oh no! Katrin—"

"Oh yes!"

The white gelding rears up as I thunder to a halt beside him.

Only Tobias's firm grasp on the reins keeps Samuel from bolting. "Here," he says, offering me his knee to use as a step.

"You are a saint." Hands shaking, I seize the saddle and swing myself up in one fluid motion. He's noticeably taller than Sybil, and not as broad in the chest. Before my other foot finds the stirrup, Rudi catches up and nips at Samuel's fetlock.

Hooves clatter as Samuel tears toward the gates. My boot slides into place almost by accident, and I lean low over the horse's withers. His white mane flies in my face as the wind blows against us. It's been weeks since I've had a chance to ride, the horses reserved for carrying supplies and tired nobles, and I feel impossibly light. My bag bounces against my thigh, my rifle clanks against the saddle, and I notice none of it. There's only Samuel's rolling gait beneath my legs and Rudi running free alongside us.

Elias is a little slower to join. I look back to see him seated atop Sybil, gathering up the reins. He looks very much at home in that saddle as he digs his heels into the horse's sides with a yell, and Sybil takes off after me.

I yank hard on the reins to turn toward the gates. Wesley and Friesen dodge to the side as we charge through, Elias close now. I laugh with complete abandon, relishing the shock on their faces, the chaos we left behind. I just stole August's horse, and I can't contain the elated cackle that possesses me.

"This way," Elias calls over the clap of hooves. He pulls Sybil back a bit to better take the turn off the road and into Atlin Bower.

I slow Samuel to a trot, straightening in the saddle. The bones that hang from the maple boughs overhead glance off my head, clacking together to create a macabre symphony. On the ancient binding stump in the center, marked in blood that includes my own, waits Elias's gear. Without stopping, he leans over and snatches his belongings.

I urge Samuel forward with a soft click of my tongue. As the first small snowflakes spiral from the sky, we ride into the deep of Wielinde to finish this Hunt, once and for all.

Chapter Twenty-Six

A branch whips my face as I urge Samuel on. "A little farther," I beg the white gelding. The horse doesn't have much left to give, but to flee stone nymphs, I only need a tiny bit more.

When the thin rivulet of blood from my cheek reaches the corner of my mouth, I pull back on the reins, bringing Samuel to a stop. Sweat lathers the horse's neck. With rising dismay, I know I can't ask him for more. Even Rudi is too tired. She trots past Samuel and collapses atop a broad, snow-covered fern, panting hard. Our breaths all steam between the drifting flakes.

All morning and afternoon, a modest yet steady flurry fell upon Wielinde, dusting it in a thin layer that fails to hide the green. It eased my anxiety about riding a white horse into the dark of the Forest. But the night is closing in now, and Elias and the black mare are regaining the advantage of concealment.

Sybil crashes through the undergrowth twenty paces away. Astride her back, Elias spots me and steers her in my direction. Although hardier than August's gelding, Sybil's hooves barely clear some of the fallen trees in her exhaustion. The knowledge frustrates me further, reinforcing that we have to let them rest.

"I thought stone nymphs never leave their caves," Elias says, his voice dangerously close to accusing.

"They're not supposed to," I snap back. That cave had been

empty a week ago. Finding it newly claimed as a nest was as much a surprise as the Forest Folk pair splitting the very bedrock beneath our horses as we galloped away—that kind of magic has always been contained by the mouths of their caves.

"Tell them that," he says, rolling his shoulder with a wince. "They've got wicked aim with those stones."

A soft thump, followed by a dull crack, drags my attention behind me.

"Did you hear that?" I say, barely more than a whisper.

After a beat, he responds, "Hear what?" and my heart sinks.

I can no longer convince myself Wielinde Forest isn't playing with us. Isn't mocking my burgeoning desperation by tugging on its fraying edges. I twist in the saddle, the leather creaking beneath my weight. My eyes narrow as I stare between the trunks on either side, peer through the white-marked boughs. Strain my ears with dread for that sound to repeat. Yet no matter how hard I try, I'm not certain if I heard that muffled crack or nothing at all.

"Never mind," I say faintly. I wipe the blood off my cheek with my sleeve before it freezes. Already it's scabbed over.

The shadows are growing longer. Dusk threatens to darken the thin cover of clouds above the treetops, and it makes my pulse quicken with the implications. Darkness adds shadow gaunts to the pot, mixing them with all the other Forest Folk that seem to be two steps away from feral. Unwed bough spirits, hungry moss mites, obsessive mushroom goblins—we've encountered them all. And I have no more teeth but the ones in my mouth.

"I think I see more gold markings, though." Elias points into the trees to my left. "On that stump there."

Hours ago, signs of the Breimar Stag had me leaping from the saddle and hurrying through the underbrush. Now I've lost the ability to muster any hope or excitement. It only kindles anxiety in my gut. For all the markings we've seen, gold dripped down trees and scarring rock, none have led us to the Stag. Or to anything, for that matter. Merely pulled us from one side of the Forest to the other. Two irritating flies drifting between the walls of the room, in search of a window long since shut.

Rudi jumps up at my whistle to investigate the new markings. Despite her weariness, she crunches ahead with a light tail, nose to the crust of snow. In the roots of the stump where luminous gold leaks between divots of bark, she takes her time sniffing before running back. There's no trail to follow.

"Let's keep going," I say, fighting to keep the despair from my tone.

I kick my feet out of the stirrups to dismount and almost crumple myself. My thighs ache from riding and my knees tremble from the constant ebb and flow of adrenaline. I clutch the saddle in a white-knuckled grip for a moment, trying to steady myself as Elias's boots hit the ground too. He offers me his canteen, and I greedily take it, the water near ice as it pours down my throat.

Everything I've pushed through in the last few days is tapping against my edges like knives from the inside. The fatigue, the hunger, the fear—the overwhelming dread of what may come after tonight. Soon, the pokes will become stabs, piercing through my belly and ribs, and I'm scared I won't be able to contain myself anymore.

We guide our horses into a small meadow. The tall grasses are limp, bowing beneath a finger's width of snow. Snow fay flit around the edges. Graceful moths of snow and ice, they turn whatever flesh they touch blue with frostbite, but are at least still easy to deter with a well-placed swat. A narrow creek severs the clearing in two—too small to hold a stream barrow, thankfully—and Samuel and Sybil both pull free of our grips to drink. Rudi as well, splashing directly into the water. I stare at the sky's wavering reflection as I refill my own canteen.

It was difficult to tell beneath the trees, but out in the open, it's clear the snow is slowing. Small patches of burnt rose peek through the clouds to the north. Within an hour, the Scavenge Moon will rise in full, and with it will begin the final countdown to the Hunt's end.

"Eat." Elias shoves a piece of jerky beneath my nose. "Don't make me force it down your throat. Your cousin will never forgive me if you collapse now."

I take the food and tear off a huge bite before throwing a chunk to Rudi. It's not very appetizing—the meat came from an old stag and wasn't good for much else—but I don't taste it. "Thank you."

"It's nothing," he says, already collecting the leads of both horses.

Except, it isn't nothing. Gratitude surges through my chest. He doesn't need to be here. For him, the Breimar Hunt is something he can let slip by. An animal he can decide not to shoot because the herd is stronger with it alive. Instead, he's by my side as night draws near, risking his own life and job to help me. It means more than I could ever express, but attempting to articulate it has to wait until this is all over.

We carry forward on foot in silence for another quarter of an hour before I spot more molten gold. These markings, though . . . They're different. Brighter, their drip thinner. My gloved fingers shake as I tether Samuel to an oak.

"What is it?" Elias asks. He hurries to tie Sybil too.

"Not sure," I say, partly lying. My true answer, I don't want it to rust in the air. Lost hope calls to me once more.

I gently push aside branches, knocking snow loose as I step cautiously through the brush to examine the golden markings on the moldering log. Rudi shows no such care. Her tail wags as she runs ahead of me without being told, nose snuffling, and that makes the hope ring louder in my head.

The scratches shine bright enough to imitate a lantern in the gloom. The scent of old coins lingers on the air now too. Hesitant, I remove my glove and swipe my finger through the longest gold mark. It's sticky, like sap from a fresh-cut tree, and *warm*. My breath catches. It's fresh.

My exhilarated cry for Elias dies as I notice Rudi standing stock-still. Her body frozen in a rigid line, one paw lifted, her nose pointing west.

A trail at last.

"Rudi, go," I whisper, giving her the whistle command to find the prey.

She takes off like a shot, flying over the log in pursuit of the Stag.

"Elias, come on!" Too loud in the dense quiet, but I don't care anymore. I pick up a sizable stick and drag it through the gold markings, coating the tip in its gleam. It's not much light to move by, but it's enough to see through the darkness. I dart after Rudi, rifle across my back. Elias's crunching steps follow behind.

Night has fallen in earnest now, and it reminds me why all of us gamekeepers prefer to be in the castle's proximity before sunset. This place I know and love in the light, it becomes warped and unsettling. Trees turn jagged. Their bare branches transform to dagger points and the visible green of needled boughs fades to blades of silver. Worse are the shadows. Thick and clotted, altering already dark spaces like wood knots and small burrows into ominous chasms that will devour your hand if given the chance.

As we race after Rudi's prints in the snow, the quiet is a disturbing thing. Because it's not quiet at all. As shadows pool over the ground, I hear the Forest Folk *everywhere.* The chitter of moss mites writhing beneath the greenery, the ghostly whoosh of a lichen nyx taking flight, an unnerving clacking like the chatter of teeth. My makeshift lantern shows them to me in faint flashes as we run. The weight of a dozen eyes causes me to stumble.

Suddenly, I lose sight of Rudi's tracks. My heart leaps against my ribs as I stop, slipping in the snow. I lower the gold-coated stick to the ground. Only the small prints of what is likely a fox cross in front of me. Where did she go? Did I miss her taking a turn, or did I lose her tracks in the bare ground beneath that last cedar?

The warning crackle of a bough spirit sliding free of her heart tree comes from deep in the trees to my right, and I breathe in deliberately through my nose.

We'll be fine. Elias and I just need to stay together. Even if Rudi gets too far, she always finds her way back to me. We've got the trail now, and we'll get the Stag and—

"Elias?" The glance over my shoulder shifts to my entire body turning back to him. My rifle rises in my grip, my voice dropping. "Elias, what's wrong?"

He stands only a few paces behind me. In the bare light of my stick, tucked in the cradle of my left hand with my gun, his pale brow glitters with sweat. He stares into the trees above, exposing his throat. His mouth hangs slightly ajar, but his hands are fists.

"Elias?" I ask again, and a tremor weakens my voice.

"I didn't want it to be true," he whispers, sounding so heartbroken, so *devastated*, it makes my blood run cold.

Then long, boned arms sleeved in brown fur reach down and yank Elias up into the treetops.

I stumble backward with a scream. I land on a stone buried in the snow, but the jarring pain up my spine is masked by my horror.

All this time looking for the Breimar Stag, and the Krauvel found us instead. And it has Elias. *It wants Elias's heart.*

This alone spurs me to motion. I leap up from the ground and tear after the deafening crashes through the trees above. It shouldn't surprise me that the Krauvel can climb trees, or that it's preternaturally agile at it. If anything, it nails hatred deeper into me. On foot, by wing, in the trees—this is the last time that monster takes from me.

I dropped the stick when I fell, but the Krauvel's path is easy to follow in the dark. Snow showers down with each motion of its enormous skeleton. Thick, obscuring clouds of white, serving as footprints to mark its progress. And the *noise*.

The cracks and snaps and breaks and *clack, clack, clack*.

It's getting away. I dig for more, but even my adrenaline has limits. I yell. For Elias, at the Krauvel, pleas and obscenities and everything in between. And still the dumps of snow stretch farther and farther ahead of me.

A pale shape, burly and tall, streaks out of the dark in the corner of my vision. I don't have time to wonder what it is. Something *slams* into my shoulder, knocking me off my feet. My head hits a tree, a rock—I don't know. It's hard and unbending and stars dance through the Forest.

Two faces, blurred by the tears in my eyes, loom over me. Both horrifying in a mortal way.

"Well done," the shorter of the pair says, his voice slurring in my ears. "Now she's mine."

Too many teeth arranged in a nightmarish smile lead me into the dark.

Chapter Twenty-Seven

When I come to, my eyes immediately shut tight. Vertigo spins the world hard enough to make nausea brew in my gut. I focus on keeping my breaths even, waiting for the sensation to pass. The edges of memories stick to my prying thoughts like cobwebs. The back of my head throbs. I raise a hand to touch it—

And find my wrist stuck. Both of them, tied tight behind my back.

"What the—?"

"Ah, finally awake," replies an all-too-familiar slippery voice. I freeze, the webs in my mind swept aside. That terrible snarl of a smile wasn't a dream.

The next time I open my eyes, I force them to focus.

My body is propped against a tree. Roots dig into my tailbone, rough bark scrapes my bound hands, and the ground is dry, a ring of trampled snow beginning beyond my outstretched leg. A lantern sits out of reach of my feet. The merry flame encased within casts its light surprisingly far in the dark, glazing the undersides of the hemlocks that surround me. Out of sight, a horse nickers. However long I was unconscious, it was enough time for the snow to stop falling. I push through the sharp ache and tip my head back to see a patch of starlight.

"I was starting to fear you would spoil all my fun and never wake up again."

Seated on the log opposite me, legs spread wide and expression complacent, his red velvet coat dark as blood, is one of the worst monsters I've encountered all night. No Rudi, no Elias. It's just me and the devil now.

August.

My mouth runs dry as my heart thrashes. I rub my wrists against the rope, testing the knot. The coarse restraints barely budge. A small, pitiful whimper breaks through my throat from the burn on my skin, my shoulders shifting painfully back.

"Oh, *shh. Shh,*" August says, tilting forward and raising a placating hand. His quiet tone only ratchets panic higher in my chest. The wavering light licks up his face and catches on the stubble, roughening his edges to something untamed. "It's almost over, Katrin."

"Why am I tied up?" I croak.

"Because it is necessary." He smiles, his teeth rotting pearls. "Thank you for all that noise you made earlier. Made finding you *so* much easier."

A long grating noise cuts through my alarm, and my gaze drops for the first time to his busy hands. To the knife he sharpens with slow precision. My boots dig against the ground, trying to press myself closer to the tree at my back. Needles and cones pepper the glass of the lantern.

"What the fuck is this?" I don't feel ashamed by the fear that strings my voice higher, louder. Pretending to be calm won't save me from this.

"Haven't you learned by now?" His attention stays fixed on the hunting knife. Its familiarity screams at me until I glance at my thigh and the empty sheath, and understanding rushes in. Tears glitter in my vision. "I always get what I want."

"And what is that?" I whisper.

"Same thing you want: to win."

His head lifts, and the gleam in his green eyes reduces them to a white sheen, rife with promise. Everything I risked these past few weeks, the choices I made—with one look he tells me it was all for nothing. The outcome I wished to avoid is inevitable to him. From how hollow I feel, the ground might have opened up and swallowed me whole.

"Although." He draws my knife across the stone once more, like caressing a cheek, and lifts it so its edge winks. "It seems we have very different strategies for that. And you appear to be at a severe disadvantage."

August rises with a soft grunt. To the space behind me, he says, "Get her up."

"Wait, no—"

I barely have the chance to struggle before thick, meaty hands seize beneath my arms and wrench me to my feet. Even less of a chance to use that to my benefit before Felix pins me to his massive frame, my bound hands trapped against his thighs. Straining against his hold is as useless as trying to loosen the ropes. I attempt to kick, and Felix hooks his leg around mine.

Fingers wrapping around my throat put a stop to all efforts.

My pulse thunders beneath his thumb, so delicate and fragile and easy to crush. Even protected by the Hunt, I don't want to know what that will feel like. He can strangle me, and I won't die. Not yet.

I'm only glad Rudi isn't here—they can't torment me by making me watch her die. And Elias. I don't have the fear to spare to think deeper about what is happening to him. If the Krauvel has already taken his heart, then it's too late for everything. The only monster that matters is the one before me.

"I confess, I'm still not sure if I should be furious or impressed by your choice to enter the Hunt." August moves nearer, each step a slight crunch over the compacted snow. His shadow pivots around him until he dodges the lantern and it looms over me. "It certainly was a bold one, from whichever angle I look at it. All that time with us in the Forest, searching for what we wanted, and all the while plotting to kill one of us."

"Just you," I murmur. If we're going to face this together, let there be no mistake about my intentions. He is still as much my target as the Stag is.

He sighs as though I've said something tedious. "Yes, I gathered."

"I hate you," I spit.

"Again, hardly news. I can't imagine why you would feel this way, but you have made a fool of me for the last time, my dear."

"How can you be so—"

Slowly, Felix's grip on my throat has tightened. Suddenly, I can't breathe. My ribs contract, I rise on my toes, but I can't *breathe*. Instinct jerks my hands to scrabble at the vise squeezing my windpipe, but they stay hopelessly stuck behind me. Terror makes it impossible to stay calm. My heart races louder and louder.

"Felix, please, I'm not ready for that yet."

The pressure around my throat lessens, but the brute doesn't remove his hand. Sweet, frigid air rushes back in through my mouth; I cough it all out in rasping wheezes. The chill stays with me, though, as August's words sink beneath my skin.

He means to kill me. The knife, the roughing up—none of it is for show. August is a viper waiting to strike and I am an idiot for not realizing it sooner. Not that I can do anything. He's the snake and I'm the mouse in his way.

"You can't touch me." The harried statement lands in the few inches separating us with a pathetic thump. It's an irrefutable fact due to the golden scar beneath my sleeve and at August's wrist, but with Felix holding me immobile, it feels like a contract already torn in half. "Either of you."

August leans down, his handsome face too close to mine. "What a lying little mouth you have. I've always known it. Delighted in it, even." His breath obscures my vision, smelling faintly of whatever liquor he must have drunk to warm himself. "But there's one thing I've always wondered."

He strikes. Without warning, he swoops forward and smashes his mouth against mine. I squeak in surprise. My hands are bound, my neck held in place, my body unable to move, to defend myself. I am entirely at August's mercy by force. The only way he would *ever* have me.

My lips press tight enough for my teeth to make an impression in their undersides. I would rather bite him, but I know it would only spur him on. Fire he so desperately craves in this cold. His eyes close, but mine stay wide. In horror, in hatred. My involuntary whimper makes August press nearer. I flinch as his tongue darts against the seam of my mouth, and Felix's grip constricts.

It's like having a dead fish shoved into my face. Wet, cold, unpleasant.

And a complete and utter violation.

I'll fix you. His words from months ago after overhearing how I have no interest in romance and all that comes with it. How I don't need it. Tonight, he broke something fundamental inside me instead.

When he finally pulls back, my breath is a muffled scream as I inhale again. It turns into a gag as I try not to vomit up the jerky from earlier.

He licks his upper lip, glistening from his intrusive efforts. Softly, he murmurs, "And how sweet those lies taste. Too bad we won't explore more tonight. I have no use for you anymore."

"I fucking *hate* you."

August ignores this. He straightens, takes a step back, and gestures with my knife to the crook of my elbow where my binding scar hides before examining it anew.

"You are right, Katrin, that we can't touch you, so to speak. Not yet. But the Scavenge Moon has risen. It will be gone in hours, and with it, the Breimar Stag. Maybe it will take one of us, maybe it won't, but the Hunt will be over. There will be no protections anymore. And unlike you," he says, eyes flickering past the knife to meet mine, "I don't need a Stag to kill."

A sob builds in my throat.

August presses a finger to the tip of the knife. The skin instantly parts, but like Ilse after his bullet careered into her temple, no wound appears, no blood. It seals right away without a mark. But watching him like a hawk, I spot the small wince as he feels the pain of the prick all the same.

The release of my cry sends splinters through my bones. Felix's iron grip becomes all that holds me upright.

This is it. This is how it all ends.

August is right. After everything I did to protect my family, he only has to wait until dawn to hurt me however he wishes. He doesn't even have to wait that long to torture me. While the Hunt is still on, I'll feel every cut he makes without a drop of blood spilled. As he said, retaliation for all the times I made a fool of him. Revenge for every instance he tried and failed to claim me as a prize. I made my threat of death to him plain and now no one will hear me scream.

All scraps of reason flee. My body thrashes before a full, useful thought can form. Bound hands try to find that vulnerable spot between Felix's legs. I pull with my hooked leg, hoping I can sweep his out instead. My pounding head is thrown back. Anything to give myself a fighting chance.

Felix only has to squeeze, complicit as ever in his employer's sins.

August laughs, low and pernicious. "All I need to figure out is where to start. Your face? Or should we peel back your clothes and see how soft you really are?" He pokes the knife at my belly. Like I'm a roast pig to be carved for a feast. "I already have the perfect tree in mind to hang your pretty little bones from. Right where your precious uncle will see them every time he leaves Prauen."

"Please don't do this," I moan through Felix's grip on my throat.

"I won't even tell him they're yours. All I have to do is say the Stag took you." His voice takes on a false, whiny tone. "I—I saw it happen with my own t-two eyes."

"You don't need to do this. I'll leave," I beg. "Please, I'll leave. Just let me do that. You'll never see me again." I hate this. I hate every word out of my mouth and how it feels like letting him win, but I can't do anything if I'm dead. I can't protect my family if I'm gone.

August dismisses my embarrassing pleas. "I want you to know, Katrin, that I won't stop with you." He points the knife at me, wrist limp as though he has all the time in the world. "That little cousin of yours? I think I'll keep her, just because I can. And then I'll—"

A clatter and a deafening growl is the only warning before something massive *flies* into the small clearing and seizes the baron.

Chapter Twenty-Eight

The scream that escapes my mouth, I don't recognize it as mine. It rings out, sharp and keening, as much a part of the Forest as the ghost that just tore through this space. Made of bear bones and human eyes and a wolf's final howl. Close enough that tendrils of hair still cling to my face from the passing wind.

Felix staggers back, and I slide from his grip to my knees.

"Sir?" Felix so rarely speaks, but I know shock is an uncharacteristic tone for him. His footsteps crunch to where August vanished, a pistol emerging from inside his coat. It resembles a toy in his large grip as he points it at the broken hole in the foliage. At the tremendous crash of noise through the trees.

Then he yells. "*Sir! Sir, call out!*"

I swallow down heaving gasps. My watery gaze drops to the empty footprints that once held August. Confusion bleeds into my frantic thoughts, but a telltale glint of silver distracts me. Ties my unwinding emotions tight for a little longer. I release a shaky laugh—my knife lies on the ground before me.

Quickly, I pivot on my knees and lean backward. My stomach muscles strain from the effort. I bite back a curse after my first awkward attempt pushes the knife farther away. Staring into the shadows of the hemlock, I find the cool hilt again and tip it into my grip. August honed it to a wicked sharpness—I nick myself twice before finding a sawing rhythm, keeping one eye on Felix as he works through his own bewilderment.

A frightened whinny whips my head around. The two horses August and Felix rode through Wielinde, both Sybil's kin, kick out and toss their heads. The roan Elias favored rears up, and the branch tethering them both snaps. They flee into the dark, tails streaming behind them.

Once the last strand of rope unravels, I fall forward with a tattered gasp, my hands barely catching my weight. My shoulders scream from the release of tension. I don't notice the cold with how fast my heart beats and beats and beats. It's a reminder that I'm not dead; I still have dangers to survive.

In the distance, far from where Felix's gun still aims, a tree falls with a prolonged splintering. I feel its rumble through the ground, and something crumpled inside of me straightens.

Then silence.

"What was that?" Felix demands. He turns on me. Still holding the knife, I clasp my hands behind my back before he notices. His hulking shadow prowls along the tree trunks as he approaches, leveling his gun at me. "Where is he?"

I squint up at him, ignoring the pistol for all the harm it will do me. "How should I know?" I spit at his feet for good measure.

He presses the muzzle of the gun to my forehead, cocks the hammer back. A sound that once sang through my head with fear now makes me laugh.

His brow wrinkles, but he holds firm. "August was there one second and *gone* the next. What. Happened?"

"A monster for a monster," I hiss.

An achingly familiar bark twines through the trees. Felix startles, aim skewing to the greenery behind him. The glass of the lantern sears my hand as I snatch it. I stand and smash it against the side of Felix's head.

Much like the knife to August's fingertip, the shattered glass leaves no lasting mark on Felix's face. But the flame has other ideas.

Fire eats into his fur-trimmed coat, starting at his shoulder and nibbling down his sleeve. I don't think he even notices, still too stunned by my blow. The scent of burnt paper floods my nose as I step back. Ahead, the foliage crackles.

"Shit!" Felix drops the pistol in the snow, scrambling to remove his coat. Sweat drips at his forehead from the heat. The flames, low and yellow, reach his elbow. Before he can pull an arm free, Rudi bursts into view.

With a vicious snarl, my beloved alpine pointer leaps at Felix. Her teeth sink into his arm. He releases a warbling yell, trying to shake her off, but she holds on tight. He spins on the spot, a blur of gold on one side, brown-and-white fur on the other.

"Rudi, drop!" I shout.

She releases his arm and runs to my side. Felix stumbles to a halt facing me, but before his attention can return to his coat, I plunge my knife into his chest.

Or try to. The blade sinks an inch beneath the skin before the magic—that left Ilse with no more than a momentary dent in her skull—resists. Fights to expel it and seal the wound. The second I let go, I know his body will spit it out. Mildly, the understanding that intent matters crosses my mind. August shot the countess for show, but I mean every ounce of strength behind my knife.

And slowly, I win.

It feels no different than gutting an animal. A terrible gagging noise clings to the inside of Felix's throat. He looks down at me with eyes that grow wider as I gradually twist the blade deeper. No blood, only what I hope is white-hot pain. The heat of the flames kisses my skin, like standing before a hearth after a long day.

I plant both hands on his chest and shove him to the ground.

Rudi leads the way into the newly carved path of destruction between the dark trees, racing over unnatural tracks pressed deep into the snow. The sharp scent of fresh sap melds with the charring. I beat back the rising guilt, despite its existence making no sense. Felix must only roll over to extinguish the flames in the snow. And once the knife withdraws, he'll be fine. He certainly didn't care about me.

The snow underfoot is slippery, and after several close calls, I finally wipe out, narrowly missing a thicket of brambles. Rudi hurries to my side and sets upon my face with wet, welcome kisses. Relief that we're both all right picks at the emotional knot my need to survive tied earlier and I, at last, come undone.

I bury my face in her warm shoulder and sob. I wail into her fur until I feel like a bloom pressed flat between the pages of a book, and still I cry more.

More times than I can count I have found danger in Wielinde—stumbled onto a mother bear, crossed a prowling wolf pack, nearly lost a foot to a moss mite—but *never* have I feared for my life as I did back there. To be that vulnerable before someone with my weapon in their hand—I don't think I'll survive feeling that way again. So exposed and hollow and *weak*.

My tears only stop when a bone-chilling scream spears through the quiet. The trees around me seem to amplify the horrible sound, bouncing it between each bough.

There's no time left. Wiping my nose on my sleeve, I release

Rudi. It's hard not to shake the sense that I've aged a decade as I stumble up to my feet.

Habit reaches my hand back for my rifle, and I sag when I realize I don't know where it is. I didn't see it after I woke up. One of the horses was probably saddled with it. Regret creeps in, tipping my gaze back the way we came. I should have stolen Felix's pistol or risked taking back my knife, but another shattering scream forces me to keep walking.

At its core, following the trail of a monster that treats full-grown men as rag dolls without a weapon is the height of foolishness. If Stefan were here, he'd tell me the situation I just escaped clearly taught me nothing. With every step, his soft admonishments fill my head. I find them oddly comforting. If my mind means to shame me into turning back, it's losing.

I can't come this far and not see. The confusion that teased my thoughts before digs its claws back in. The Krauvel took Elias. Hours ago. If it wanted his heart, that was the last piece. My friend was the final twisted puzzle piece the Krauvel needed to doom this Forest. So why take August too?

The next scream to cut through the Forest is louder. I slow, taking care to step in the compacted snow of the Krauvel's tracks. So near I hear a snuffling whimper before it lurches into another full-throated cry. Stuffed with enough terror to choke on—and made by a voice I wish nothing but suffering on.

As I lay my hand against the trunk of a maple, and a rising clacking sound keeps time for my heart, the clouds become gossamer. They part to let the Scavenge Moon douse a nightmarish scene in silver light.

At the northernmost point of the valley that cradles Wielinde

Forest, before the trees thin and the ground turns to treacherous, sloping rock, there dwells the oldest living creature of its depths: a colossal, withered oak. Its broad crown is still heavy with acorns, and gnarled roots—worn so bare they shine in the moonlight—push every other tree away by twenty paces. This is the heart tree of the first bough spirit. She is of no concern, though—she claimed her wife long ago. Her trapped face grew with the oak, swelling and stretching within the bark to become a grotesque figure that now gazes upon the monster at her feet.

The Krauvel stalks back and forth on its warped legs. Skeletal paws drag through the snow; crunch over scalloped, dead leaves and fallen acorns. It wears the cougar pelt like I would a too-small jacket. The fur clings to the bones of its back, sheathes its arms, wrinkles around its legs. Its head tosses with a distinct clicking noise, an animal in distress.

Clutched between its claws, howling his own chorus of beastly sounds, is August. Bear talons sink into his waist. Each time the monster crosses through dappled moonlight, I see the blood that darkens his red coat.

Rudi growls at my side, but she hasn't run yet. She's already proven her mettle against one villain tonight, so I stroke her head while I watch the Krauvel with bated breath. It doesn't seem to notice us. Maybe it doesn't care. As it turns to resume its pacing, I don't see a heart through the gaps in its ribs.

August is its final prey, one last organ beating in his chest.

Relief and bafflement blaze within me. I don't know what to do. This means Elias is okay. He had to have gotten away, but how? And where is he?

All of a sudden, Rudi's growls stop. My hand renews petting, only to fall through empty air. I freeze. Without her snarls masking it, I hear *everything*.

When I turn, it's to the sight of a dozen Forest Folk emerging from the shadows. From beneath the roots, fluttering from branches, crawling down the trunks headfirst, and stepping from between the trees.

Wild and primal—and holding my dog.

A pine bough spirit wraps around her middle, a stone nymph holds her mouth shut, and moss mites seal each paw to the ground. Rudi's brown eyes are wide, the whites showing as she tries to free herself from her captors. For one mad moment, I consider baring my teeth, like that will sate them. My arms are free, no brute holds me back, and for the second time tonight I am rendered perilously helpless.

"It's okay, Rudi," I murmur, almost nothing more than a breath. "You're okay, girl."

What they plan to do with her, I don't know. They've never shown interest in her before. My mind tears through countless scenarios and none end well. Especially when they drag her away, tucking her into the thick shadows with them.

"Wait, give her back!" Before I can move to follow, more Folk appear. They converge on me. Force me back, back, back, until I enter the oak clearing.

The rustle of movement, of leaves and branches and stone, begs my mind to focus. They lunge at me, flap their wings, but none pass beyond the tree line. Flickers of movement along the edge of the clearing reveal the arrival of impossibly more Folk. It's as though all who are able are congregating here. Like a willing audience for this final act.

But whose side are they on?

None of this behavior makes sense. And nor does the Krauvel's.

It took Elias but didn't use him. Now it has August, claws slipping deeper into his side, and still it doesn't attack. And I don't understand why. This is the final move in its long-fought game to victory. It's never had any qualms with mutilating to get what it needs to survive, so why is it hesitating?

"Finally. We've been waiting for you, Katrin."

The last person I expect to see, and yet the only one I should, rises from where he has been sitting unseen among the largest roots of the oak.

Elias.

Chapter Twenty-Nine

The Krauvel stops. With a grinding click of its head, that skull turns to look at me. Klaus's pale blue eyes are rotting to a blind grey, bulging to fit the larger, foreign sockets.

"Elias?" I softly ask, unsure how to react. His presence sends my unease into a tailspin. I study him as he steps over a thick, uplifted root. Aside from bedraggled hair and a few rips in his coat, he appears fine. Unharmed. "I don't understand. How are you . . . ?" My feet carry me forward without permission, and I stop myself, looking fearfully to the Krauvel.

"It's all right," Elias says with a tight, crooked smile. "He won't touch you. He has what he needs."

At first, I think he means August, held nearly upside down in the Krauvel's grip. Another claw slides deeper into his side, eliciting a howl. Then I realize Elias is referring to the Krauvel.

I step into the uncut moonlight, leaving the shelter of the trees and the wild audience it hosts behind.

August notices me. His eyes grow round, and his sobs shift to pleading. "Katrin," he gasps. "Katrin, please. Help me. You can stop it—use your gun."

But I don't have that anymore, thanks to him.

"Wh-what are you doing?" he demands in a strangled voice as I ignore him. I hold up my hands to show they're empty, wanting to reach Elias without provoking the Krauvel. Twin plumes of heat snort from its wide nostrils.

"No. No, no, no. You have to kill it." August's words dissolve into fresh blubbering.

As Elias stands peacefully beside the Krauvel, the monster and I take the other's measure. This is worse than all our previous encounters. Before, the pair of us were locked into agreed-upon roles, predator and prey. Now I don't know what I am. My mouth feels stuffed with cobwebs, my body too warm. Its terrible claws flex and retract. They scrape August's form and dig into the ground. Its restless head sways, hollow grumbles blowing through its mouth—it's frustrated.

The Krauvel is the first to break.

I hurry to Elias's side as it turns toward the oak in a crisp clatter of limbs, August held in front of it like an overgrown infant. The bark shielding the tree groans before splitting apart below the wizened face. Inside, the wood resembles a bleeding wound, but that nauseating glimpse is blocked by the spindly branches that skitter out as arms. I stumble as a thunderous crackling fills the clearing. The Krauvel places August into their grip. When the baron continues to scream, one wooden finger grows into his mouth, silencing him.

The monster pivots back toward us. I snap to my senses and grab Elias's elbow, but his feet might as well have grown roots for all he resists. When the Krauvel reaches for him with its fierce, blood-stained paw, I open my mouth to yell, but Elias confounds me further. He raises a hand to the Krauvel, stopping it in its tracks mere paces from us.

"You said I could speak to her first."

"What is this?" I whisper. I let go and stagger back. Away from him, from the Krauvel. But an army of Forest Folk waits behind me and there is nowhere to go. "Elias, come on. Get away from that thing."

When he looks to me, tears stream down his cheeks. "I'm so sorry," he says, a slight tremor in his voice. Elias looks so small, standing there beneath the mighty oak, his clothes rumpled, blond hair mussed. Like a young boy unsure of how to move through the world.

"Wh-what for?"

"It was me." He sounds so dejected, so full of despair. I would lunge to hug him if I wasn't terrified of how the monster at his back would react. "I did this."

"Elias, I . . . I don't—"

"I called his name. *I* summoned him." Anger strengthens his voice now. "I didn't mean to, didn't even remember until a few days ago. I *still* barely remember, but I know I did it."

I hold out my hands to soothe him. He keeps referring to the monster as *he*, humanizing it in a way that rattles me. There is *nothing* human about it. "It's okay."

"No, it's not."

"No, it's not," I agree. A choked laugh bursts free. "You're standing beside a bag of bones in a cougar coat."

His watery chuckle is answered by the Forest Folk. A chorus of unsettling voices that makes Elias's pallor turn grey in the moonlight.

"Can you . . ." I move a half step closer, gesturing for him to come to me, painfully aware of how close the Krauvel stands. So still it doesn't even click. Just watches with pinpoint intensity.

"There's no point, Katrin." His teeth clack together. So sharp there's no doubting how deeply he means it. He drags a hand down his face, stretching his features into an ugly mask. "He has to finish this. He's so close."

I nod, unable to do anything else. "Will you explain what happened?"

The tears drip from his jawbone, tracks of starlight in the dark. "It was a mistake to call it. A stupid, stupid mistake. Do you remember the other day, when Stefan was hurt?"

How could I possibly forget? The fear of that night for my uncle, of *that* hideous monster chasing me—it's etched into my skull. "You weren't there."

"I did go down to Steigert that evening, but it wasn't to post a letter." He takes a deep, tremulous breath, bracing for something difficult. "I went to talk to my friend, the one I stayed with before I came to Prauen for the first time. Bits and pieces had come back to me and they didn't make sense and I didn't know what else to do."

"It's okay," I insist softly. His voice is rising, tension stringing his limbs tighter. I don't know what it will take for the Krauvel to move, but keeping Elias calm is all I can think to do.

"We got drunk. So fucking drunk, and reckless. We both grew up on the stories, you know that, and my friend dared me to say it. He dared me to, and I *did*. Krauvel, Krauvel, Krauvel." I flinch. "Like it was the funniest joke I could have told.

"And when nothing happened, it got even funnier. We both said it. Outside of the gates, drinks in hand and yelling at the bones like we were invincible. It didn't matter that he said it too. I was the first. And it claimed me then."

My body jolts. "Claimed?" I look him over anew with a harder eye, but I see no signs of injury. Only a dense sadness beneath the skin.

"After I talked to my friend—because he remembered everything, what we did, what we said." His expression darkens, and I almost demand a name so I can pummel the supposed friend myself. "And he still found it hilarious, how it was just a silly old superstition. After that, I went to see Greta."

A new chill scrapes my stomach. "What did she say?"

His laugh is without any levity. "She forgot to tell us something."

I remember his words from before, when he looked up at the Krauvel in the treetops, come to take him away. *I didn't want it to be true.*

"There's an eighth piece he needs, and it was always going to come from the person who summoned him to Wielinde."

My legs feel like stiff stalks of grass, ready to break in a strong wind. My voice is just as brittle. "What is it?"

"Seventh in heart," he responds in a poor mimic of Greta's storyteller voice. "Then, last in soul."

His soul. How is that stolen from a human? A terrible image of the Krauvel clamping those sharp teeth around Elias's mouth and slurping it out like soup from a spoon arises. "How does she know? Greta can't know—she can't."

"Because the Krauvel got this far once before."

"Stop saying its name," I snap, knowing it's a childish request. It's the least important facet of this entire conversation, but I just feel numb to it all. Its name is something small and easy to digest.

"Didn't you hear me?" His tears continue their descent, darkening his lapel. "There's no point. I'm the last piece, and once he takes that heart, nothing will protect me. Even if I summoned him while living elsewhere, I'd have been drawn here against my will. But I'm going to give him what he wants."

"No point—what's stopping me from taking August away? It can't have you if I banish it again." I step toward the baron and am startled when Elias moves in a perfect mirror to block me. "Elias, there's a way out of this!"

"I'm not taking it." He sounds distracted, yet confident.

"Elias, we can—"

The Krauvel makes an impatient, ragged noise. My hand tightens around some invisible weapon, but Elias only glances back. Confusion seeps into my hollowness. He nods at the monster before returning my questioning stare.

"He wants to talk to you."

Three separate syllables get stuck in my throat before I croak, "How?"

With a clatter, the Krauvel's paw lands heavy on Elias's shoulder. He sinks a little deeper into the snow. Winces beneath the weight of bone. But the voice that emerges from his mouth is not his own.

"This Forest is your home, is it not?"

Whatever I expected the monster to say, it's not that. The words are soft but authoritative, bearing an arrogance that sets me on edge. But there's no denying the Krauvel sounds old. Weather-beaten and fed up. Elias looks somewhat baffled by it, an expression so at odds with the voice spilling from him.

"*Is it not?*" it repeats.

"Yes," I say fiercely. "More so than it is yours."

"Spoken like a true warden of it. But you are wrong; Wielinde is my only home. I deeply wish to make it so once more, and you must let me."

"*Let* you?" I laugh, harsh and sour. "You've proven several times that I can't do anything *but* let you."

"If I had my way, I would already be whole, and we would not be speaking. But this boy"—Elias's eyes widen as the Krauvel's grip tightens—*"has made his soul conditional on you first hearing the full story."*

"Why would you let that stop you? All you need is a heart, and it's right there."

"Yes, I am aware." A hint of annoyance enters its patronizing tone. *"But of everything, I must have a willing soul."*

"None of your pieces match and *that's* what you're picky about?"

Elias's teeth gnash together, an animalistic snarl rising from his throat. I step back. *"It is not comparable. A heart beats the same no matter what it comes from, but a soul is unique, volatile. I do not have a choice in the soul I claim, but one given unwillingly is tainted. I do not wish to harbor that for all eternity, so the boy's wish to wait for* you *is granted."*

I widen my stance, recognizing what lies hidden between its words. However inconceivable it may be after every close call we've had, I hold some form of leverage here. "How am I supposed to *let you* take the heart you need, killing my friend in the process, when I can just as easily stop you?"

"Because it would be a mistake."

"Not to me."

"The return of Wielinde's king will restore the balance of the Forest. Permanently."

I splutter. "You're the reason the Forest has been so off-kilter. The Folk didn't start lashing out or behaving strangely until *you* showed up!"

"The teeth you carry, the bones you hang—I can make it stop."

"Liar!" My yell echoes beyond the oak and up the mountain slope. The fury that always simmers beneath the surface turns to a raging boil, scouring away the hollow sensation. I am sick of others with any amount of power trying to twist me into doing their bidding.

Elias grabs the Krauvel's bony paw. His brows raise, as if pleading with me. Something passes between the monster and the boy, unspoken yet significant. When it releases him, he staggers back a step, barely keeping upright.

"Katrin, he's right," he says, breathless but in his own deep tone.

"About what?" I demand, ready to throw all caution to the wind to save him from himself. Even if it means saving August too. "You cannot believe this . . . this fairy tale."

"He would stabilize Wielinde. No, listen," he insists, cutting me off. No amount of melancholy lurks in his voice now, only adamance. "The balance of the Forest and the Folk acting the way they have for centuries—it's all off *because* he was banished."

"And I assume it told you that?" I snipe, bitterness flooding my tone. "It's just telling you what you want to hear so it can return and control everything."

He grabs fistfuls of his hair, threatening to tear it out. "No, Katrin! The Folk didn't know what they'd done until it was too late, but the loss of the Krauvel threw the Forest into this precarious state of give-and-take. It's constantly been missing something. If he comes back, the Forest and the Folk will be at peace. We won't have to hang the bones anymore. Everyone—us, the Folk—will be safe."

The fervor of his words shakes my anger from its mooring, and I wrestle it back into place. It sounds too good to be true. Surely he can see through all this. "Elias, they banished it for a reason."

"And he's changed since."

"Oh, come off it—" He's lost his mind. The Krauvel clearly stripped part of his brain away too.

"He told me that, yes, but so did they."

I follow his encompassing gesture and look around, to the Forest Folk clinging to every word. The Krauvel is not yet returned, so it cannot have any power over them. It strikes me then, truly hits to the core, that they are here of their own volition.

Eyes of wood and stone and shadow watch the scene with undeniable anticipation. They alone know what will happen. If the Krauvel is allowed to take its heart—*if I let it*—it will return as their king. Except, they do not resemble a group of beings about to lose their freedom. For all the strange behavior they've exhibited in the past weeks, they do not act as though the Krauvel's near victory is something they need to stop, to fear. It . . .

It makes me falter.

"Do you trust me?" Elias asks.

"Yes, of course I do," I answer in a heartbeat, tearing my eyes away from the tree line. The piercing gaze that greets me is steady, imploring. Grief spreads like frost across my insides.

"I believe him. Everything he says, it's the truth. And I wanted you to hear that. To understand why I'm willing. Why I want to do this."

"But . . . but you would die."

He nods, sadness slipping back in to soften his edges. "Yes, but it's my choice. You entered a Hunt to protect those you love from danger, knowing you might die. In a way, I am too. I go into this willing, Katrin. For Alma."

Elias steps to the side, giving me an unobstructed view of August, still hanging and gagged by the tree. I almost forgot he was there. His eyes dart between the three of us in the clearing, no doubt comprehending everything with perfect clarity.

"Now do you understand?" Elias whispers.

I stare at August. Despite the cold, sweat drips down his clammy skin. Just as quietly, I ask, "So what now?"

"The Krauvel has promised to wait until I give him the word. If you wanted, you could stop the Krauvel and I wouldn't interfere, but consider what it means. For everyone."

"If I wanted . . ."

"What do you want to do, Katrin?"

Such a simple question. One I've asked myself so many times in the last few weeks that it inadvertently grew endless layers I must peel back. Herein lies the leverage I so tenuously hold.

Careful and slow, I lock eyes with the Krauvel so that it follows my every move. It pivots on the spot as I step around it, never showing its back to me. Every crunch of snow beneath my boots sends a ripple of tension through the Forest Folk. They wait and watch, silent as a breeze through leaves, to see what I'll do, what decision I will make for them.

The Krauvel or the baron. The Forest or my home. One monster or another. What will be best for everyone I love?

Because that's what it always came down to: the things I can live with. The choices made to keep those I love in the safest position I can place them. Finding the lesser of evils to carve out an ending that leaves me content.

What do you want to do?

A question I've mulled over on so many nights that the answer already springs to mind, fully formed.

My feet bring me in front of August. His shoulders slump in the tree's grip when he interprets my presence as his salvation. August tries to talk, but the oak still gags him. His feet dangle above the ground. Low enough for his toes to graze the worn roots, but not enough to gain any traction. Close enough for me to look directly into his face and know he'll hear every word I say.

"It's just like you said, August." My eyes rove over his handsome face, drinking it in like I've never done before. The anger that has carried me through these past weeks—and the months before—turns my words into a scorching hot poker I stab directly into his miserable soul. "I don't need a Stag to kill you."

His eyes widen and his muffled screams rise to a fever pitch as I turn away, striding directly past the Krauvel. "He's all yours."

The moment I reach him, I throw my arms around Elias's neck and clutch him tight enough to feel the slip of his bones beneath the skin. He doesn't hesitate to return the embrace.

"For Alma?" I murmur.

"For Alma," he agrees.

"I'll never forgive you."

"Yeah, you will."

I hum. "I can hold a grudge like no other."

His laughter is warm against my neck. When he pulls back, he nudges me toward the tree line, but adds, "Give Alma a kiss for me."

His sad smile breaks my heart in two.

I don't stop walking until I cross the trees and find the Forest Folk who hold my dog captive. I wave them away from Rudi, half expecting them to hiss and take me as a prisoner too. Instead, they retreat, surprising me further. Rudi immediately presses against my side; my poor girl's body shakes. I crouch and pull her in close.

In the end, I will always choose my family. I will always choose Alma. Stefan and Carolina. Every person in the castle who helped raise me into who I am today. August hurt them all in some way.

Wielinde will live on with the Krauvel, in whatever shape it will take beneath bones strung from trees and offerings of teeth. I don't know if I believe that it will set things right the way Elias does, but I know with certainty that my family won't survive under the baron.

And I won't be satisfied until I hang his bones from the tree of my choosing.

So I turn and watch the consequences of my actions unfold.

Chapter Thirty

The Krauvel breaks loose. If I thought I'd seen the breadth of its movement before, I was wrong. What I witnessed, what I feared—that was an animal after a worthwhile scent.

This is a monster that smells blood and weakness.

Every bone strains against its net of nerves as the beast rises to its fullest impossible height. Each bone releases a gunshot *crack*, as though breaking and remaking itself in a single ripple. They resettle as the chilling burst of a wolf's thready howl slices the cold air. The Krauvel rounds on the baron in a series of sharp clacks that remind me of snapping teeth.

August thrashes in the oak's grip. A segment of branch breaks beneath the aggressive weight of his chest, but his cries pitch higher, shakier, as the remaining wooden fingers squeeze. Blood weeps from his sides to the scant snow below. Even from here, the whites of his eyes are visible, glistening in the moonlight. Tears paint silver streaks down a no-longer-handsome face.

The once-banished king of the Forest stalks directly up to the powerless baron, shrouding him in its shadow. With unnerving gentleness, it places one clawed paw on his heaving chest, over his heart, as if to first feel the blood pumping. August stills, holds his breath.

His body offers no resistance. He wails loud enough to shake the dead free from their trees, but beneath the Krauvel's claws, his skin is parchment. All five claws sink in deep. Through coat and waistcoat and shirt. Severing skin and muscle and prying ribs apart with no more effort than plucking an acorn from the branches overhead.

August screams while the Forest Folk hiss and chitter. Screech and grumble. Growl and burble and shriek.

While they all *laugh*.

Rudi stiffens at the cacophony that echoes throughout the Forest, pressing in on us from all sides. I hold her tighter, feeling her own rabbiting heart beneath her fur.

Mine is the steadiest it's been in weeks.

After making a perfectly shaped hole, the Krauvel slips its clawed hand inside August's chest. Slowly, it withdraws his heart.

No blood stains it. No gore or viscera. It's not even black and withered like I always joked it was.

And still it beats. Beneath the wild excitement of the Folk, I hear it.

Thump-thump. Thump-thump.

No longer connected to August, it beats as sure-footed as my own heart. Red and glistening.

August gasps for air. His chest rises and falls fast enough to hyperventilate, but the hole in his chest remains flawless, its edges clean and untouched. He remains inexplicably alive. He screams, but no one listens. No one cares.

The Krauvel turns away from August with the heart cradled in both bone paws. Its skull tips down to gaze at it, jaw clacking in anticipation, in victory. With the utmost care, it reaches up beneath its crossed ribs and secures the stolen heart in place.

I know the moment its body is complete. Not a single branch quivers, but the foundation of the Forest shifts all the same. I feel it deep in my bones and in the ground beneath my feet. Like the smallest pebble kicked loose to start an avalanche, something arcane surges forth from the monster in the clearing. An immeasurable severing, the ends tied into something lasting.

A lost king banished no more.

The Forest Folk perceive this too. Their calamitous voices quiet, and those who are able step forward and bow before the Krauvel. Leaf and bark, lichen and moss, subjugating themselves in whatever manner they can.

And Elias . . .

Elias collapses.

A puppet with its strings cut, he crumples. A soft, pained cry passes my lips. I move toward him without thinking and stop, remembering that he wanted this. My heart fissures as I look at my friend. His pale hair gleams like molten silver against the snow.

"I'm sorry," I whisper. But I could say it a hundred times and it would never be enough to appease this rotten hurt.

Although whole, the Krauvel is not yet finished. Lifting my gaze from Elias's empty frame, I watch the monster's appearance change. Its body shifts into something familiar yet profoundly new. The poorly fitting cougar pelt pulls taut, melding to its bones until it resembles poured oil. Through a patchwork of skin and bony gauntness, it conceals the lungs and heart, protects the throat and brain, and clothes its arms and crooked legs.

A roughshod creation made polished in all its eldritch glory.

Its altered gaze locks onto mine, and I inhale sharply. Its blue eyes sink deeper into the sockets to fit more snugly. But something distinctly human lingers in that piercing look, and it puts me strangely at ease with this creature.

August continues to scream, albeit weaker. Fainter. His thrashing wanes to twitches but still he shouts for help that is never coming.

The Krauvel jerks its head up with a snarl—the first movement made without an accompanying clack. As though flicking away a bothersome fly, it swipes at August with lightning speed. His eyes widen, but I don't see why. It never touched him.

Then a thin line of red opens along his throat, and the life remaining within August spills forth. I don't take my eyes off him. Not as his eyelids droop nor as his body slumps in the oak's grip.

I deserve that much at least.

The oak releases his body. Its fingers creak and groan as they spread, and he drops into the hollows of the largest roots.

And so lies August Ludwig Wagner III. Dead and already forgotten.

The Forest Folk rise from their deferent poses, and their woodland voices stir anew into a frenetic chorus that immediately sets my teeth on edge. When they begin converging on August's corpse, I grasp that as my cue to leave.

Slowly, I push to my feet and back out of the clearing, Rudi close on my heels. It doesn't feel right, fleeing when Elias lies there. But the Folk are the most capricious I've ever seen them. I don't trust them not to sweep me up into their madness and devour me too. Turning my back on them once was already terrifying, and I don't do it a second time until my vision contains more trees than the clearing.

Freedom feels like a cloak of wind. Each step over fallen logs and burrowing roots lifts me high. Alma was right: Nothing will be the same after tonight.

No more threatening presences waiting around corners. No more unwanted touches or encounters. No more arranging the time in my life around avoiding someone else for fear of what they might do. No more saying the word *no* and knowing it won't be heard.

I don't know what will happen next. What the Forest Folk will do now that the Krauvel has taken up its crown once more—I put my faith in Elias's beliefs, not the Krauvel's assurances. Its promises aren't worth much to me yet. No matter how badly I want to believe we won't need them any longer, I can't give up the old ways. I will continue to respect the Forest for what it gives, and I'll continue to hang the bones to honor it.

My steadying inhale of the night air shakes. I took a great gamble with the choice I made, but I will never regret it. Of the monster born and the monster made, I knew which I could live with. I only hope the others at home will agree with what I did.

Grief lingers at the edges of my triumph as I walk away. Not for August, never. But for Elias. My friend, who I came to know and trust and consider as another person to love, is gone. The pain of it is a termite in my heart, gnawing through the reliable muscle to weaken it ever so slightly. I have to come back for his body eventually. He deserves a proper funeral. No matter what I chose in that clearing, he knew what he wanted. The loss of him saved countless others, including Alma.

Alma—I don't know if she'll forgive me. She wanted August gone as much as I did, but Elias was never part of the equation to worry about losing. We saved her from one monster, only for another to take away her first love. This time, I'll tell her everything. No detail will be spared, but it won't change what happened. What was lost before it could fully spread its wings.

I haven't the slightest guess as to what time it is, but it must be nearing dawn. It's difficult to tell, sliced as it is by the dark trees, but I make out a faint lightness in the sky to the east. A shift in the impervious black of night to an inky blue.

I should backtrack to where Elias and I last saw the markings of the Stag. At least to hunt for my rifle, and maybe find one of the horses along the way. Again, no matter what the Krauvel said, I would feel safer traveling through Wielinde with a reliable weapon, so I angle my path toward the west.

My eyes weren't mistaken—dawn is close. A mist plays between the roots of the trees, but the sky above turns from black to indigo, violet bleeding to lilac, soft pink blooming. The Scavenge Moon still hangs above the mountaintops, but I know it's not long for this world. The Breimar Hunt is nearly at its end.

A strange mix of emotions washes over me. I never got my shot. I was so recklessly desperate for it, and now it's a bullet I have no need of. My binding scar prickles. It's been growing itchy since I left the oak clearing, and it sets nerves churning in my gut. This Forest still has one more life to take before the night is through.

Once I stumble on a clumsy furrow made by two sets of feet in the snow, it's only a matter of time before I find the imprint where I was knocked unconscious. I struggle to breathe properly. The air suddenly feels both too thin and too heavy.

Half buried in a drift a little farther away, my rifle gleams coldly in the feeble morning light. Rudi sits as I pick it up. A moss mite comes with, nibbling at the stock in a slow, measured pace. Just how it used to.

"Balanced again," I whisper, almost unable to believe it. I brush it off with a stick and a tender smile.

My expression hardens when a deafening crack sounds behind me. My gasp catches in my throat. Carefully placing my feet in the marks already made in the snow, I turn, raising my gun before me.

The Breimar Stag stares back with those burning ember eyes. He stands on the other side of a bramble thicket twenty paces away, tall enough that his legs reach beyond the highest thorn. In the gloom beneath the trees, his ever-changing white coat holds tiny sparks that race over his body.

Through the alarm that seeps into my limbs, I almost laugh at the absurdity of it. All these weeks spent searching with budding desperation, and *now* he finds me.

And I can think of only one reason why he would seek me out now.

Is this really it? My rifle falls from my grip and lands with a soft thump. I can't bring myself to shoot the majestic beast—I already claimed the only death I wanted. Nor can I even summon the anger I should feel. The source of it is all tapped out, empty and drained. For all that I dreaded this happening, I didn't expect a sense of peace. I almost yell for the Krauvel to come reach inside me and steal the emotion for its own.

I don't want to die. Not after everything I just won back. There's still so much I want to do, things to say . . .

The magnificent creature paws at the ground, air steaming from his nose. I give Rudi a hurried kiss that doesn't satisfy the ache in my chest and gently nudge her aside. She'll find her way back to

Prauen without me; Alma will take care of her. Dimly, I register the crunch of snow at my back, but it doesn't matter. Nothing can help me now.

I don't want to die.

I close my eyes, turn my head, as the Stag leans into motion, shoving through the thicket without effort and lowering those wickedly sharp antlers. My binding scar *burns*.

I don't want to die.

Hooves thunder toward me. As though the snow turns to stone with every step of his gait. The air thickens, pinning me in place with the weight of an entire atmosphere. A horrible trumpeting sound erupts from the Stag as he nears and . . . passes me.

My eyes fly open as I hear again the crunching snow behind me, but now it's louder, and each press of it blends together in a rough, frenzied note.

"Get back! Get *back*! Make it stop!"

The firing of a pistol whips me around. Once, twice—then it falls from Felix's grip so he can sprint. It's no use. His last bellow for the Stag to leave him be is cut off.

His body lifts from the ground, bowing backward atop the Breimar Stag's antlers. The creature continues to run.

I never tear my eyes from him, not even to blink. But with each placement of the Stag's hooves, he grows a little fainter, his ethereal aura a bit dimmer. A ghost, slipping through the trees. The air loosens as it fades entirely. The Breimar Stag returns beyond the veil with its chosen life, the victor of his own Hunt once more.

Behind the mountains, the Scavenge Moon sets.

Chapter Thirty-One

AFTER THE SCAVENGE MOON

"I have never been treated so terribly in my *entire* life." Lotte flicks what I suspect is imaginary lint off her arm before a shiver racks her entire body. When Tobias, struggling beneath the weight of three trunks, drops one in the snow on the drive, she snaps, "Watch it, you lout! Or I'll make sure it comes out of your wages."

Head propped in my hand, I sit on the icy steps to watch with grim amusement as the nobles invited to Prauen for the Breimar Hunt prepare to depart. The stable hand and I share an exasperated look as he bends to pick up the smaller case that doesn't even belong to Lotte. Too lost in her whining to notice.

"This really has been the worst party," Gerwin grumbles. He sits atop his own enormous trunk, waiting for this carriage to leave and the next to pull forward. His ridiculous revolvers still glint from their holsters, even though the worst he'll encounter on the journey to the train station is a handful of sheep.

Lotte turns to him, delight sculpting her face for not standing alone in her misery. "Inattentive host, guests dying, workers bleeding out on the steps or being entirely *insolent*."

I snort.

"Miserable weather," he adds. "Haven't been properly warm in weeks."

"And the *distance* we had to travel just to get here—with not a single hunting trophy between us."

"Oh, spare us." Adjusting her fur-trimmed sleeves, Ilse sweeps past me from the castle to join the others. With a scoff, the countess smacks away her husband's helping hand, only to nearly slip. "All you wanted was Schultz's head to hang in your textile mill's lobby. You couldn't have cared less about some deer and its antlers."

The fluttering hem of her coat flicks me in the cheek. I silently glower at her back, but Rudi, lying on my other side with her front paws draped over the top step, growls. "Shh," I intone, stroking her head.

"If you'd won, you might have added antlers to *his* head, though." Gerwin chuckles. "Really made a sport of it."

"There's always the next Hunt," the count says mildly. He opens the carriage door for his young wife while Tobias loads their luggage. Her maid and a lumber mogul I recognize from Stefan's group—sleeping off a drunken stupor by the looks of it—are already inside.

Ilse's voice hardens. "You'll be going by yourself. Besides the food and drink, there was very little to entertain me." She shudders delicately, fingers grazing her temple before climbing into the carriage.

Good, I think viciously. When her husband sits beside her, Ilse swaps seats with her maid. The door to the carriage closes with a soft click and I wish I could slam it. *Tell all your friends what a terrible time you had, how it wasn't worth it. Tell them to never think about Prauen Castle or Wielinde Forest ever again.*

"Speaking of inattentive hosts," Ilse says, leaning out the window, "where *is* August?"

Lotte pats her hair, nose turning up. "I haven't yet decided if I should feel insulted or furious that he won't even deign to see us off."

Gerwin snorts, crossing his arms with indignation. "Well, I, for one, am insulted. The nerve of him, abandoning us to run off into the woods after those children. And then never bothering to show his face after."

"Whatever happened to those two kids, anyway?" Ilse asks. "I have half a mind to see to their punishment myself."

"That wretched girl would deserve it." Lotte's smile turns into fangs. "The things she said to me—"

"You mean what I said before or after you nearly shot me?" I interrupt, feigning politeness. All three of them jump, guilt pinching their haughty expressions as they take notice of me, but only for a moment. After all, I'm the one who should be beneath their shiny bootheels. "Because *you* certainly deserved every word I said."

The ship magnate recovers first. Pointing at me, Gerwin demands, "You, girl—fetch August."

With a devil-may-care grin, I show him my middle finger.

Lotte steps forward. "Why you little—"

Rudi moves smoothly to all fours. Her lips raise alongside her hackles, revealing bared teeth. She brushes against my shoulder, and her snarl thrums through my body. A duet to the disdain vibrating in my heart.

Tobias, with excellent timing yet again, secures the last trunk and slaps the side of the carriage, indicating for the driver to go. He waves up the next carriage—led by the roan horse that found its own way home last night—and opens the door for Gerwin and Lotte. "I think it's time you all left."

With a final nasty glare I can only laugh at, Lotte turns her back on me. As if it's some kind of insult. Rudi licks her chops once, then settles down with a disgruntled huff. I lean back on my hands with a sigh, letting the chilled stone soak into my gloves. My head tips back to bask in the morning sunlight with the hope it might warm me a little.

In truth, I'm not sure how I'll remove this awful cold from my chest.

I need to sleep so badly, but I can't bring myself to do it. Not when this sensation tugs at me. It's like a chain has been looped through my ribs and threatens to drag me to the ground with each inhalation.

A few hours ago, I stumbled through the very same gate the count and countess now drive through, and the relief of surviving the Krauvel, of living beyond the Breimar Stag's choice, has been steadily watered down.

After finding Sybil browsing beneath a willow—Samuel was simply gone—I spurred her in a risky gallop toward home. But when the first spire came into view, I pulled her back to a trot. To a walk when the white stone flashed through the trees. To a complete stop in the Bower. Even after dismounting, it took too much to even pass through the gate. With each step closer to the castle, what started as a cloak of freedom turned into something strangling.

Telling Alma was exactly as hard as I feared. When she found me—or rather, lunged at me—storing my rifle in Stefan's workshop, it was easiest to lead with the news of August's death. Every gory detail of how it was done by the monster we wrongfully dreaded. How the monster we grew up with would never harm us again.

But that just made it more difficult to answer her questions about Elias. Splitting my sides with a dull blade seemed more feasible than saying the three words that would blow a hole in her happiness.

Elias is gone.

She didn't understand at first. Her attention kept swerving back to the door, searching the courtyard as though he merely stepped inside to wash up first. That was my fault—I could barely say the words without breaking into tears. But out the words came, and when they finally landed, it was impossible to shake the impression that I had just plunged my claws into her heart.

As Tobias knocks for Lotte and Gerwin's carriage to leave, Rudi's head turns at a scuffing sound behind us. I know without looking who comes to sit on my other side.

Alma gathers her skirts and releases a soft groan as her knees bend, making her seem far older than her seventeen years. The flowers embroidered at her hem look wilted. A glance at her face reveals her to be as wearied as my bones feel. But despite her red-rimmed and puffy eyes, there is something serene to the set of her jaw, the tilt of her chin, and it lowers my guard. I find her hand and clutch it.

After the truth at last hit its mark, she had gone blank. Empty and hollow; unseeing. It frightened me to my core, how someone so full of life and hope could drain like that. Even her verbal response after I vomited everything Elias said in his last moments was sparse. A single utterance of *Oh* before she excused herself and vanished into the castle. I didn't follow. I don't think she needed me then, but it smooths the frayed edges of my nerves that she's here with me now.

The last carriage pulls up the drive, and we watch Rowena and her fluttering lashes fluster some middle-aged viscount whose name I never bothered to learn. She clearly has a type, judging by the wedding ring on his finger.

Alma breaks the silence between us. "So they're finally leaving us in peace?" Her voice is hoarse, even after she clears her throat.

I nod. The first batch of them, at least. There aren't enough carriages for them to all go at once. "And being as annoying about it as possible."

"Good riddance." Then she stuns me by spitting on the stairs below us. Or attempts to. I don't think she's ever tried it before and most of it dribbles down her chin.

"*Alma,*" I exclaim, a little impressed against my will.

She swipes her chin clean, a flush entering her cheeks. "Don't tell Ma. She hates when Pa does that."

"Well," I say, stretching out the word with a smile, "you've got some practicing to do before you can compare *that* to Stefan's spitting skills."

She shoves my shoulder, and I push her back.

"I'll teach you how to do it properly," I whisper playfully.

Her head leans on my shoulder, and a balmy stillness settles in my chest, loosening those chains around my ribs. I stare at the roof where gaps in the slate shingles still remain from the Krauvel's claws. Everything was for her, and her steady presence here is all I need to know it was worth it.

The last pair of nobles bicker with Rowena over who will sit where in the carriage. It's pointless and frivolous and I resist the urge to yell at them to walk down the mountain instead.

Alma stiffens suddenly, snagging my every sense.

"Why would you say Elias is gone?"

"Because . . . because he is." My shoulders slump with dread—I didn't expect to handle denial. The memory of him collapsing in the snow is still difficult to speak around. "The monster has him now."

Her mouth forms the words with care, like she's biting back something more. "Then why is he walking toward us?"

"What?"

My head jerks back to the drive, but too much beckons for my attention. The carriage door closes with a snap at the same time as Elena vanishes through the garden archway with an armful of burlap. A flock of geese above head south for the winter in a staggered formation, their honking drowned out by someone's laugh spilling through an open castle window.

When the flick of the reins sets the carriage trundling around the curve of the drive, a ghost emerges. Blond-haired, tall, and broad; limping through the gate with a distant look in his eye.

What had been tucked under Alma's tongue was incandescent disbelief.

I leap to my feet, but she's already taken off. Across the drive and through the untouched snow covering the garden in the middle. Before she reaches him, her foot slips. Alma dives at Elias, bringing them both tumbling to the ground and proving he's not a phantom. My steps slow.

His grunt of pain morphs into laughter. With a dozen apologies, Alma clumsily gets them both to their feet, but he doesn't let her retreat. His arms wrap around her middle and lift her against him. With a joyous smile, he holds her like she'll shatter if she falls again.

By the time Rudi and I reach them, they've finished their long kiss. Elias sets her down to greet me. Snow sticks to their clothes and hair, and they cling to each other.

"You're here," I say, incredulous. "Alive." I stop short of pinching his arm and satisfy myself with how his fingers press indents in Alma's coat, brush curls out of her glittering eyes.

He flashes a small grin. "Miss me?"

"But . . . how?" Alma cradles his face with both hands. Hard enough to assure herself too.

"You told me—" I cut off, trying to organize my racing thoughts into something useful. My emotional state cartwheels between shock and joy.

"She said you were dead," Alma says. She glares at me. "You said he was dead."

I fling an accusing finger at Elias. "Because that's what he said!"

"It was my first time summoning a monster; cut me some slack." He shifts Alma so that she's by his side and he can better address us both. The color in his cheeks makes him even more handsome. "The Krauvel only needed a piece of my soul to ground him. Greta assumed it was the whole thing, so I did too. And he never corrected me."

"Do you . . . do you feel any different?" Alma asks gently, as though he's on his deathbed.

"A little. I don't know how to explain it. It's like—" His gaze turns glassy, lost somewhere else. "Like I went deaf in one ear overnight. I'm completely fine otherwise, but everything is unbalanced. I know my fingers are there, snapping beside my head, but I can't hear it." He shrugs. "It'll take some getting used to."

I splutter, still not understanding. "But you said you would *die*!

You fucking *said that.* And you . . . you . . . you collapsed dead. I saw it!"

He throws out his arms, grandly gesturing to his whole if battered figure. "I guess not!"

"And we're both thrilled about it," Alma crows.

I lunge at him with a hug of my own. Alma pulls back, but I grab her hand and tug her in too. "Let that be your first *and* last time summoning a monster, please. For the sake of my stress levels."

Elias laughs, returning my embrace nearly as tight as he held Alma. Even Rudi joins in, jumping up and planting her paws on our arms. It's less funny when her tongue laps at my ear.

We're going to be all right. I still don't know how the next few weeks will unfold with the castle and the Forest, but of that much I'm certain. My cousin, my family, my friend—all safe with the death of a single rotten man.

As the clatter of the carriage fades from earshot, a bellow rises from the depths of Wielinde. Deep as the mountains' roots and older still—a monster's lament. A note that blends the roar of a bear with the howl of a wolf and laces it with a human's scream.

"Exiled no more," Elias whispers.

Nine Months Later

The stag raises his head, dark eye landing in the sight of my rifle. I inhale slowly as Rudi settles deeper into the moss at my side. Hot summer sun beats down on the stag's tawny back, and although sweat pools along my spine, he seems unbothered. He chews on his cud with mindless devotion. My breath leaves me in one smooth—

Alma's borrowed gun fires into the trees above the stag.

I lower mine with a laugh caught in my throat. The animal bolts, bounding gracefully through the pines and out of sight. A pair of angry jays take flight—looks like she narrowly missed their nest. Rudi grumbles and I pat her shoulders. The alpine pointer's body quivers with her desire to run after the deer.

"Did I hit it? Did I get it?"

Tucking my tongue up into my molars, I close my eyes for a full two beats before looking at Alma stretched out beside me. White knuckles clutch her rifle. Her finger still squeezes the trigger tight.

"You have to keep your eyes open if you want to hit anything," I say drily. I pinch her grip off the trigger and tap her hand until it relaxes. She does remember to pull back the bolt to discharge the used shell, though.

"Was I at least close?" The hope in her voice is as bright as the sun through the trees.

"Closer," I say hesitantly. It's a vast improvement over her shooting abilities from a couple of months ago when she first declared her intention to learn how to hunt. Then, I was mildly terrified to stand beside her. Now she at least aims in the right direction, even if she hasn't yet hit anything on purpose.

With a sigh, I roll up to a seated position and stretch my shoulders. "Come on, we should head back. *Safety*," I firmly add.

Alma stares at me blankly before understanding dawns. Her fingers fumble for the mechanism, clicking it into place. "Oh. Right. Yes. Important."

We walk back along the trapline, keeping to the shade wherever possible. I should enjoy the heat. It only graces Wielinde for a few months before the cold steals back in, but as I retie my hair away from my nape, I find it impossible to enjoy anything when I'm sticky all over. I roll the sleeves of my thin shirt up past my elbows. As I always do without realizing it, I scratch where my binding scar once was. The skin is smooth and unblemished now, the golden line vanishing along with the Breimar Stag all those months ago.

"Here's one!" Alma exclaims. She stands over a snare, pointing down at the dead hare caught while deliberately not looking at it.

I'm still not sure how she allowed Elias to convince her to join us in the Forest, let alone learn to hunt. Then again, if Elias is involved . . . I squat and remove the hare, tucking its soft body into my bag. She's still too squeamish for this part. Unless it lands before her as a nondescript piece of meat to season and sear, she's not equipped to handle what comes before that.

She does have a knack for resetting snares, though.

A loud crackle sounds in the underbrush. I freeze, gesturing for Alma to hush after she gasps. Something large is moving toward us. I raise my gun, resisting the urge to tell Alma not to mimic me. Rudi, strangely, only sits beside me, tongue lolling out the side of her mouth.

The greenery clinging to the cottonwood in front of me catches my eye when it shifts. Moss mites. I count three, all crawling around the trunk to face whatever heads this way. Bright red mushroom goblins pop up in sporadic patterns, coming closer and closer. A lichen nyx in the complete shape of a raven croaks as a herald.

I lower my rifle.

The Krauvel pushes through the shrubbery. Skeletal paws silently part the long grasses, trampling wildflowers as it ambles on all fours across our path. The dappled sunlight gleams over the patches of bone visible beneath the cougar pelt. August's heart beats strong in its chest, steady as a newly wound clock.

When its pale eyes throw us a lazy look, I incline my head. This is not the first time I've chanced upon the Krauvel as it roams Wielinde. Each encounter is uneventful, the monster uninterested. Rudi isn't scared of it anymore, but I still wrestle down the instinct that screams to protect myself. I may never smother that feeling.

After what occurred beneath the Scavenge Moon, none of us knew what to expect. It was difficult to take Elias's belief that the Krauvel had corrected the balance of the Forest at face value. The first few days saw us shoring up Prauen's perimeter by rearranging many of the hanging bones, taking from the trees farther along the road and burdening those closest to Prauen until their groaning branches nearly broke. Pouches stuffed full of teeth hung from every belt. The Forest Folk ignored me in that clearing after the Krauvel restored its full body, but they were distracted. And why risk it? Until we knew for sure what the king's return meant, all precautions would be taken.

But the version of the story Elias told that declared the Krauvel needed a complete body to return Wielinde and its inhabitants to a stable state was the right one. We still cling to the old ways, returning the bones and organs for our own peace of mind, but I agree that we don't need to anymore. Proof of the Forest's perfect balance hangs from my belt loop.

The pouch I filled on that first day still holds the exact same teeth.

The monster pays us no mind, but it still helps us. When a lone, starving wolf was mauling several of the sheep down in the village, it delivered the animal to our doorstep. Sometimes, when we hunt, I see it walking alongside us, deep in the trees, as if making sure we gamekeepers are doing our jobs well. It even chased off the reporter—no doubt sent by Rowena—who dared come up the mountain in the dead of night to investigate the rumors about August's death.

The Krauvel turns away from us. It breathes out a harsh snort and disappears silently back into the undergrowth. The moss mites stay put, but the mushroom goblins follow, popping in and out of the ground behind the monster.

Alma grabs my arm, sharing an almost comical relief with me that it's gone. Facing it never gets easier, and this was only the second time that she didn't scream upon seeing it. We haven't even been brave enough to say its name out loud yet. My knees feel a little weak as we walk away.

By the time we reach Stefan and Elias, they've already loaded the buck they shot onto the small cart hitched to Sybil. Petra and

Milo stand guard inside the cart with wagging tails. At first, only the foxhounds notice our arrival. Elias is too distracted by the four lichen nyxes that keep trying to use his shoulders as a perch. A barn owl on one, a wren and two sparrows on the other. Alma can't quite cover her giggle fast enough at the ridiculous sight.

The Forest Folk he was so enthralled by when he first came to Prauen now annoy Elias whenever he enters the Forest. It's one thing that's changed since the Krauvel claimed a piece of his soul. That, and his bones sometimes click a little too loud when he stands. My theory is that by sharing a soul, however small a trade they made, the boy and the monster smell the same. The Folk can't be fascinated by him for any other reason. He just hasn't figured out how to make them stop yet, short of Rudi scaring off certain ones. Petra and Milo couldn't care less.

Elias glances up at Alma's laugh, and ease enters his posture. As Rudi barks at the nyxes, chasing after their flight, Stefan beckons me over. A beam of sunlight catches on the glasses he no longer removes except for when he goes to bed, upon order—and threat—of Aunt Carolina.

"Katrin, come help me, please. Hold this steady."

Alma immediately hurries to Elias's side and seizes his arm. They duck behind a large tree, and I follow my uncle's example by pretending to ignore them. They are decadently happy, almost inseparable by this point, and that's all I wanted. But there's only so much kissing I wish to witness.

As he adjusts Sybil's harness, Stefan prattles on about all the things we still need to do this week. Tasks that we once needed permission from a higher power to accomplish, now done because we know it's the right thing to do.

Life without August has been an adjustment, but for the better. Every guest left Prauen not knowing that what remained of him lay half buried in snow at the far side of the valley. When he didn't come to the capital like he always did for the winter months, eyebrows began to rise. Countless letters arrived with invitations and inquiries. It was then the baroness announced the death of her husband. Fell from the tallest tower, we decided. Tripped out a window.

The baroness took her husband's death—the truth of it—surprisingly well. Whether by a monster or if he choked on too big a grape in his study, I don't think she cared either way. He'd been nothing but a marriage of convenience to her. The baby was born a few months after August's death; a pretty little girl with his hair, nose, and eyes. Until the girl comes of age, the baroness sits as her steward. The baroness can be as vapid as the other nobles, but she's quiet and open to our thoughts. It was no hardship for her to give us freedom to run Prauen and its lands how we see fit.

And with the little baroness growing up under the wing of so many aunts and uncles, all teaching her the ways of Wielinde, she'll be a worthy leader one day.

Stefan takes Sybil's lead and guides her down the game path toward home. He whistles for Alma and Elias to knock off whatever they're doing, but it summons a panting Rudi first. As the four of us make our way back, Greta appears ahead, followed by Brigitte.

"And here I was trying to do something nice and bring you all lunch," Greta grumbles, visibly perspiring, "and now you're telling me if I had waited ten minutes I could have stayed in that cool cellar."

Brigitte sidles around her mother and hands us each a wrapped sandwich. "I told you, you didn't have to come, Ma."

"Well, you should have insisted harder." But she throws me a wink anyway.

Greta did not enjoy changing the story of the Krauvel to match the truth. Alma thinks it's because a monster come to destroy us all is far more frightening than one who spends endless days roaming the Forest and nulling half her other stories.

In the wake of August's death, she was the first to return to Prauen. Didn't even ask for her old job back. Just strode into the kitchen one day and sat down by the fire with a basket of the baroness's stockings to mend. Her tales have a little more life to them now, even if she doesn't like how they end.

Brigitte came back a month ago, albeit with some lingering reluctance. The consequence of August's heinous actions was dealt with, but she had been hurt, violated. She needed time to feel like herself again. Nearly as long to trust people, to be all right with anyone touching her. She told me yesterday with a blush that she was seeing someone in Steigert. A lovely young woman who worked at the post office.

Our loud group walks through Atlin Bower. I have no intention of ever adding my blood to that alder stump again, but the Breimar Stag will still come back in a few years. Elias asked the Krauvel a couple of weeks after everything happened, and it admitted that the Stag was too powerful a beast to control. He will return, and he will need a life, for that is his very nature. When the time draws near, we'll send out invitations again with the baroness as host. Perhaps we can convince Lotte to return.

Alma bumps against my side and threads her arm through mine, laughing at Elias's joke. I don't think it's possible to feel more content than I do in this moment. This is what I wanted, why I risked so much to smear my blood on that stump. As though I spent my entire life on the run and now have finally found a place to settle.

My family is safe and Prauen is our home. Nothing lies before us now except hope for a brighter future.

The gate comes into view. I extract myself from Alma's clutch, slow my steps to let the others carry on. Elias and Alma don't let me lag, though, and double back to stand with me. All three of us peer up at the hemlock. When the winter snows stopped and the spring melted all traces, I removed every bone from this tree. I had something else in mind for it.

The baron's bones hang neatly from its boughs. Each hole made with precision, every knot tied tight. I hung them all myself, with perfect pride and care.

Acknowledgments

Well, here we are. We made it! They always say book two is an entirely different beast, and they were right. This book, from start to finish, from that first panicked pitch to the polished manuscript now held in your hands, has been a *wild* thing. Better and worse and still something I am so proud of. And I couldn't have done it without so many incredible people in my corner.

Stuti and Pete—I continue to be so humbled by the work you two do for me. I literally could not have asked for better people to represent me and my career. You take everything I throw at you in stride and have solutions for it all. You encourage me to try new and scary things and know just how to channel my writing fervor into the right projects. And I cannot forget about Danielle, who keeps everyone organized and does not get enough of my thanks for it!

Emily—I'm not kidding when I say there is literally no other editor I would have wanted this book to be in the hands of. It's weird and unhinged and ace enough now thanks to you. Your feedback was, as ever, exactly what this book needed, and I am so grateful to you for seeing the potential in those flaming dumpster fire chapters I first sent you. It reads a *lot* better now.

To the team at Feiwel—where do I even begin? On this book and on *What Wakes the Bells*, you have been a wonder and I cannot thank you enough for all your hard work in making my books shine. Meg Sayre, my designer, for creating everything I ever wanted to see sitting on my shelf. Coey Kuhn for the absolutely to-die-for cover art—you made the spooky autumn art of my dreams. Kat Kopit, my production editor, for your valuable insight. Chantal, Tatiana, and Gaby, for hyping me up left, right, and center. And many thanks to copyeditor Emily Stone and proofreaders Jaime Herbeck and Lydia Gompper.

In Canada, thank you so much to Raincoast Books, and especially Erika Medina, for all the wonderful work you do for me at home. You make me feel oh so fancy.

Crystal—uh, "thanks" is not enough to cover what you've been to me in the last year. Experiencing debut and then the strife of writing book two with you—it has meant so much to me. You've answered every spiraling text and celebrated every win with me, and I'm honored to be able to do that for you too. One day, *one day*, I will finally get to yell at you in person.

Team Trash—y'all continue to be there for me. It has been so exciting to watch us all grow in the last five years as writers and as people and I can't get over how talented you all are. No matter what happens in any of our lives, I know you're still a group-chat message away and I love you each to bits.

Creative Cottage—I still thank my lucky stars at least once a week that I said I would join this random new group chat. You all have become so special to me and it has been an absolute privilege to not only have you cheer me on at every turn, but to get to celebrate the many wins this group has had in the last year alone. The party is just getting started and the world is not ready for the talent about to be unleashed.

The internet—specifically the spaces that let me find friends to holler at *and* with. Alyssa, Amanda, Brittany, Callie, Chloe, Elle, Elora, Emma, Jaclyn, Jo, Kalyn, Kara, Lyndall, Mikayla, Meryn, Noelle, Norees, Roselyn, Sierra, and Sonia. You have all been so supportive, and whether it has been through sliding into my DMs or through writing spaces, I'm so glad to have found you all.

Ceilidh, Emma, Kayla—you three were the first readers of this book. Full stop. And your feedback, your support, your reactions while you read, were literally everything to me.

Kattia, Haylee, Riki, Kayla—ignoring the fact that three of you now live in a different province from me (which I hate, by the way), you are the in-person friends I have known the longest, who have been my biggest cheerleaders. Everyone else can buy a copy and make me happy, but seeing my book in your hands and hearing what you've done to tell others about it, how proud you are—it has honestly moved me to tears several times. I don't deserve any of you, but I'm so glad you're willing to ignore that.

To my family—I know you don't need to hear this, but I love you, I love you, I love you. Mom, Dad, Danae, you have seen every spiral and tear and yell for joy, and it makes me so happy that I get to run to you to share them all. Even if I get annoying (sorry). But knowing how proud you are of me has me all mushy just writing this. And to every cousin, aunt, uncle, and grandparent who let me ramble about my book and publishing, who bought a copy, who celebrated with me, you all are my favorites and I'm sorry I don't get to see you more often to say it in person.

To my work family—every time one of you tells me you bought my book, a little piece of me melts into grateful goo. None of you have to support me in this other career of mine, and the fact that you all so strongly do makes my heart grow three sizes.

To every bookseller, blogger, reviewer, and reader who read *Bells* and thought, Hey, I should tell everyone about this book—you are the literal best. You are the people who make me a success and let me have this insane career and I cannot thank you enough.

And to you, reading this book now. Whether this is your first time reading a book from me or you came back for a second helping, please know it is a delight to meet you this way, and I hope we get to continue meeting.

About the Author

ELLE TESCH has lived just east of Vancouver, British Columbia, her entire life. Surrounded by forests and mountains, it was inevitable that she would daydream about what might lurk in those trees. She twists places she loves and writes what she knows best: hungry monsters, casually cruel villains, and ace-spec girls in the stories they deserve. When not writing, Elle can be found reading whatever she can get her hands on, wrestling with her current cross-stitch project, or rewatching *Pride & Prejudice* (2005) for the seventy-second time. She is the author of *What Wakes the Bells* and *The Hanging Bones.*

ELLETESCH.COM

Thank you for reading this Feiwel & Friends book.
The friends who made

THE HANGING BONES

possible are:

Jean Feiwel, Publisher
Liz Szabla, VP, Associate Publisher
Rich Deas, Senior Creative Director
Anna Roberto, Executive Editor
Holly West, Executive Editor
Kat Brzozowski, Senior Editor
Emily Settle, Senior Editor
Dawn Ryan, Executive Managing Editor
Kim Waymer, Senior Production Manager
Rachel Diebel, Editor
Foyinsi Adegbonmire, Editor
Brittany Groves, Assistant Editor
Meg Sayre, Associate Designer
Kat Kopit, Associate Director, Production Editorial

Follow us on Facebook or
visit us online at fiercereads.com.
Our books are friends for life.

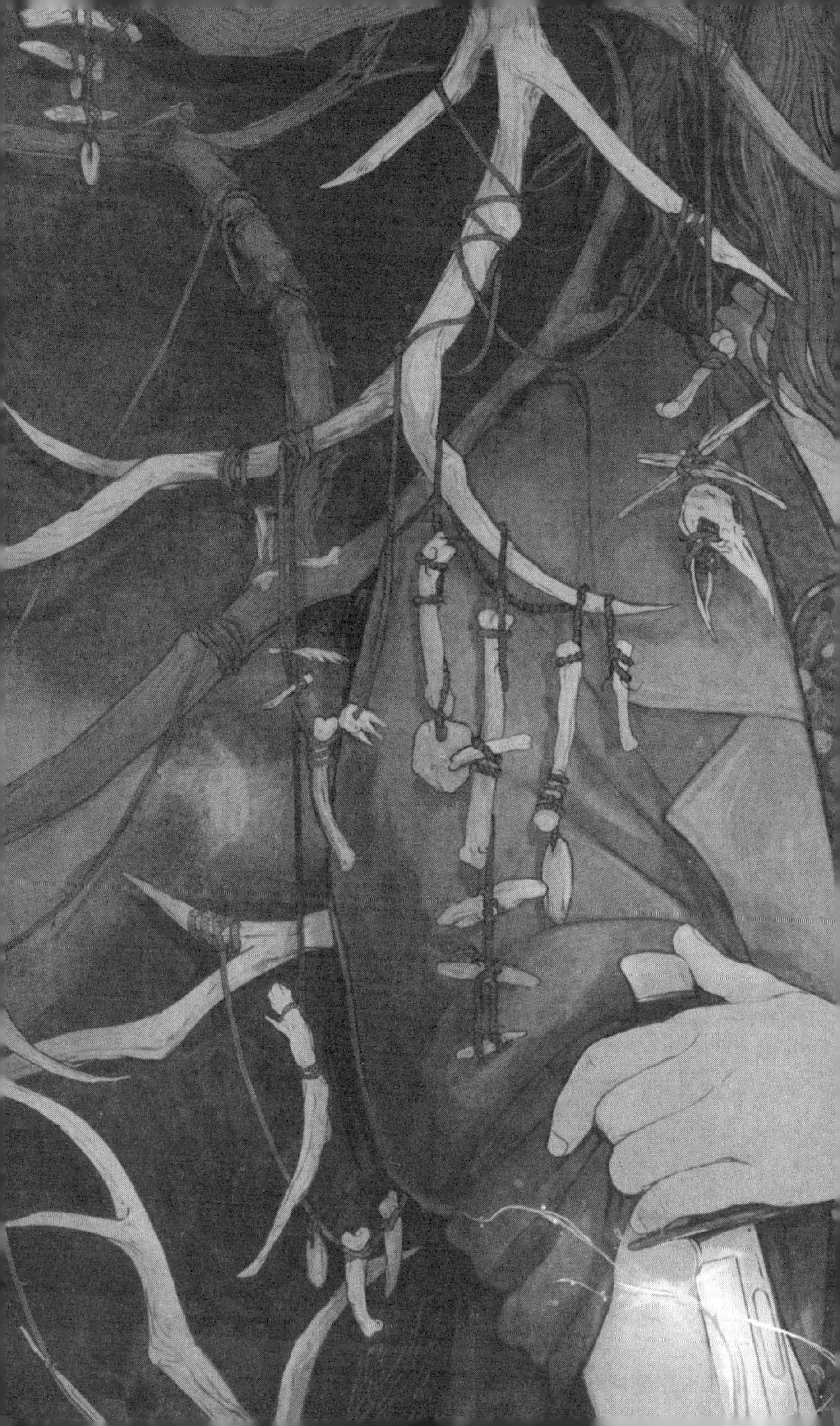